Coming Soon

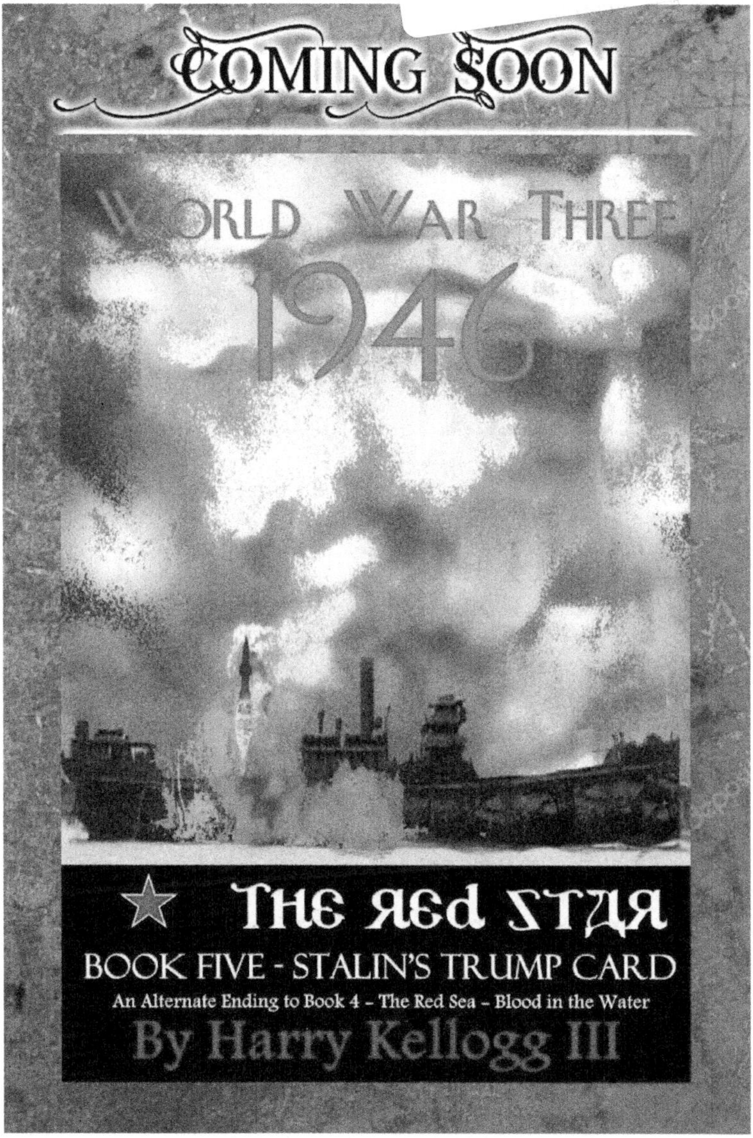
COMING SOON
WORLD WAR THREE
1946
THE RED STAR
BOOK FIVE - STALIN'S TRUMP CARD
An Alternate Ending to Book 4 - The Red Sea - Blood in the Water
By Harry Kellogg III

World War Three

1946

BOOK FOUR

The Red Sea –

Blood in the Water

First Edition

By

Harry Kellogg III

Co-authored by Mary Margret Jotz

Copyright © 2017 Harry Kellogg III

All rights reserved.

ISBN-13: 9781521139639

Be Forewarned

This novel presents one ending.

Soon to be published
Book Five –
The Red Star –
Stalin's Ace in the Hole,
presents an alternative ending.

Disclaimer

This is a work of fiction. Many characters in the novel are based on historical individuals.

The characters' imagined thoughts, and actions are purely fictional.

Forward

World War Three 1946 Series

Synopsis – Book One - The Red Tide - Stalin Strikes First

The Red Tide starts with the birth of Sergo Peshkova and ends with the Soviet Red Army in control of the majority of Western Europe. The Red Army is making slow but steady progress in breaking the NATO lines in the Pyrenees Mountains.

Our real departure from history is when Sergo is born in 1896. This is when the ribbons of time start to unravel; slowly at first and then faster and faster until the fateful day in 1943 when Sergo is bullied by Stalin at one of his infamous parties. It seems that Sergo has made himself an expert on all things' aerospace from gliders to rockets.

Starting early in 1946 the Soviets had delayed the US production of atomic bombs by assassination. Stalin decides to fulfil his deepest ambition and once and for all rid the world of Capitalism. He attacks Western Europe in May, 1946.

In a lightning and classic Soviet Deep Battle, the Soviet Armed forces quickly break through the weak and untrained US, British and French occupying forces.

The Red Army juggernaut continues its march to the Mediterranean Sea, the forces of NATO desperately gather behind the imposing peaks of the Pyrenees Mountains on the border of France and Spain and dig in.

Meanwhile, the US is apparently having difficulties convincing its citizens and corporations to make the sacrifices necessary to once again fight to liberate their European cousins. From Finland to Toulouse in France, the iron curtain of Communism has fallen on all of Western Europe as the NATO allies desperately try to counter the military might of the USSR.

Figure 1- Territory of the USSR September, 1946

Synopsis - Book 2 - Red Sky - The Second Battle of Britain

The Soviets are making progress in their quest for world domination. The Second Battle of Britain is unlike the first. With almost real-time intelligence-gathering abilities, the VVS has overcome all the constraints that plagued the German Luftwaffe in the initial battle. Within weeks, the RAF is virtually destroyed by a combination of an attack on their "bone yards", the Soviet use of captured US jammers and sheer overwhelming numbers on the order of five to one.

Only an attack by the US SAC using atomic bombs saves the RAF. The attack on the oil fields of the USSR diverts the Stavka's attention from the British Isles and the conquest of Iberia.

At the end of Book 2, Stalin is poised to invade Turkey, the Levant and Iraq with two objectives in mind. First and foremost, was to prevent NATO from attacking his oil production facilities ever again and to enjoy the immunity the United States has from this calamity of modern war. Second is to deny NATO the oil in Iraq and to close the Suez Canal to all shipping and eventually make the Mediterranean a Soviet lake by wrestling Gibraltar from the British.

Figure 2 - Location of Atomic Bomb Attacks

Synopsis – Book 3 – The Red White & Blue – A Giant Re-Awakes

The invasion of Turkey has begun. The air war over the Baku oil fields rages on. Loses are staggering on both sides.

Using the equipment mothballed after the aborted invasion of Japan, NATO traps millions of Soviet troops in a series of amphibious invasion.

Dr. B.F. Skinner and his team are playing a cat and mouse game with the mastermind behind the Wasserfal/Stalin's Fire anti-ship missile. To lose this battle of wits would be to lose the war.

Contents

Synopsis – Book One - The Red Tide - Stalin Strikes First 5
Synopsis - Book 2 - Red Sky - The Second Battle of Britain 6
Synopsis – Book 3 – The Red White & Blue – A Giant Re-Awakes 8
Different Strokes 12
Following a Force of Nature 17
Operation Kydoimos D-day +3 17
Combat Savants 19
Dislike and Respect 22
Gentle Giant 25
Reporter – Reporting 26
Waving the Flag 29
Eye Witness Report - 31
Sergo Loses Control 33
Secrets in Jeopardy 34
The Reds React 35
Interdiction 38
Chapter Two: Of Mice and Men 40
One Time Pad and Fate 42
Commanding a Corps 43
Zhukov at the Ready 45
Beria's Rage 48
Pattern Recognition 51
Stalin Calls 53
Chapter Three: The Levant 59
Utterly Ignored 60
Zhukov Gambles 61
The Barrage 62
NATO Dodges a Bullet 64
Konev Commits 66
Pain and Vindication 68
Beria's Endgame 69

World War Three 1946 – Book Four– The Red Sea

Operation Cutoff	70
Premeditation	74
Chapter Four: Inland	76
Tanks for the Memories	77
The Mechanic	80
Baghdad	84
The Beggar They Are	85
Sergo Underground	86
The Alley	88
Zhukov's Second Life	91
Konev's Forces Surrender	93
Shepherd's Watch	96
Bear Hug	102
To the Last	105
The Transplant	107
Missiles Miss	109
Big Brother	111
Chapter Six: Looking Up	115
Spy in the Sky	116
"Vertical Insertion"	117
"The Next Level"	118
Desmans Too	120
103 WPM	122
Rotor Wash	126
Brainstorming	128
Spoofing	131
Old Friends, New Enemies	135
Dead Corner in a Dead Sea	136
Maniacal Machinations	138
Doppelganger	141
Zhukov's Caucasus	143
Something is Afoot	145
Preparations on the Pyrenees	147
Cosmo is Late	150
Copenhagen	153
Task Force 125 Redux	156
Feet Dry	161
Explosive Carpet	164
And Died	166
Sergo Waits	169
Backdoor Man	170
How to Lose a War	174
Down by Her Head	176
A Matter of National Pride	181
Life, Revenge and Liberty	183
One Less Nikita	187
One More Nikita	189
A Fleet's Demise	190

468	195
Insurgent Army	196
The Toad	198
The Beach Chair	198
When Spoons Attack	201
Stavka's Plans	204
By Fiat	205
Power and Compulsion	207
Deadly Dose	210
That Bodes Well	213
Acceptance and Action	215
Fire, Flames and Cremation	217
Bleeding	218
Debating Unconditional Surrender	223
Armies Meet	225
New Tanks, New Tactics	227
What's New is Old	230
Resurrectio - Dux	232
Ursus Arctos Beringianus	233
Someday, Neither Them nor Us	235
The Offer	237
Three Stories	238
Winning and Influence	240
A Pain in the Ass	243
Just Dropping In, D-7 and Counting	244
Cousins	246
The Battle of The Sosna	247
Outside Man	249
Deaf, Smart and Blind	251
The Battle for Moscow 1947	253
Andrei Who?	256
Another Time Another Place	258
Trained to Kill	259
Viktor Nikolayevich Leonov	261
Regrets and Retaliation	263
Credit Where Credit is Due	267
101 WPM	269
Break Time	270
Mary	271
No Words	273
Sergo Arises	274
Beating the Odds Yet Again	275
Wham! and Double Wham!	276
A New Day a New Life	278
Epilogue	280
The Future	283
Coming Soon	285
Timeline for World War Three 1946	287

Book One - The Red Tide - Stalin Strikes First 287
Timeline for Book Two..289
Synopsis – Book 3 – The Red White & Blue – A Giant Re-Awakes.......................290

Chapter One: People

Figure 3- Unemployment in the US starts to hit home

Different Strokes

Private Phil Post knew nothing of the grand plan. He was just trying to survive this hell hole of a ship. His group had not even transferred to the smaller assault barges yet. If he was deathly ill on this larger transport, how would he survive a bobbing cork in the ocean? He missed his mom and dad, brothers, and even his sister. His big brother, Richard, was somewhere in this convoy as well. Because of his brother's great physical size and strength, Phil was worried about Richard. He hoped they recognized how gentle he was. Richard was not a killer. Luckily, they had all received excellent training that he was sure he would initially forget.

Phil was a very smart man and was something of a savant when it came to human nature. He knew instinctively who the killers were going to be, that meant he knew exactly who to follow into combat. You picked the natural born killer and stayed on his tail for the first couple of hours of mayhem. He instinctively knew that Private Warren Johnson was going to survive and even thrive in the coming days.

Warren Johnson and Phil Post

Johnson was a natural born killer and was chomping at the bit to fulfil his destiny. Phil just wanted to remain close to Johnson. Phil would be able to concentrate on staying alive and not on keeping someone else alive. Johnson was one of those people with eyes at the back of their heads. He would have made corporal or even sergeant by now if he were not illiterate.

Phil had helped Johnson hide this fact, putting Johnson in Phil's debt. You wanted a guy like Johnson to be in your debt when you were going into combat. Combat was Warren Johnson's gift. Without organized combat and the legitimate permission to kill a fellow human, Phil was convinced that Warren would be in jail for murder. A man like Johnson just could not survive in peace time. He guessed that after the last war, Johnson had killed someone and had gotten away with it.

Phil Post and Warren Johnson were the men for this job. Whether Phil or Warren knew it or not, the combination of their skills, talents, and training made them uniquely equipped to play a major role in the coming attack. This unlikely pair were currently in the hold of the troop transport ship experiencing sea sickness and vomiting into their helmets.

The next morning they were still on the ship which puzzled Phil. From what he had heard and from the map he had seen they should have been on the coast of Sicily and offloading by now. Then, came the announcement over the ship's intercom, piped in from the flagship. Some General named Walker was speaking. Whispers of "Johnny" and a few laughs were heard. The others quickly shushed the offenders up because they wanted to hear what Bull Dog Walker had to say. It was worth listening to.

They were not going to Sicily but to a port called Trieste. The trip would take 6 more days and at the end they would embark onto the continent of Europe. "This is the first step to the liberation of the European nations." Boomed Walker's disembodied voice. "Your hearts, guns, and boots will be the first to assault the godless communists. You will wade ashore and march into history. The day we hit the beaches will surpass D-Day in the annals of history. Stalin is a greater threat to freedom than Hitler ever was. Your attack will be the first in a series of blows that will bring him to his knees"…It went on like that for quite a while.

It was a good speech Phil had to admit and Warren was transfixed. Weak minds and all that, Phil thought. This General Walker had a good speech writer and he read it well. He remembered that Walton Walker was the commander of the whole First Army and they were part of the VIII Corps led by General Middleton and so on down the line. All that mattered to him was Sergeant Sims and Corporal Beesly. These two men controlled his life and destiny as far as he could see. He spotted both of them and they were listening just as intently as Johnson. That's good, Phil thought, at least someone believes this shit.

Six days later he was staring at Johnson's butt, as he led the way down the landing nets to the landing craft below. You didn't look down until you were almost ready to jump into the smaller boats. They lucked out. It was a DUKW. Maybe they would be able to ride to Moscow. At least, it would be a relatively dry ride to possible death. It was early May and still cool even here in the Adriatic Sea. That's right, yesterday was May Day. Wasn't that a special day for the Reds? Maybe May 2nd, 1947 will be a special day for freedom. Jees, now he was thinking like Bull Dog Walker.

***

Private Warren Johnson was transfixed by the images being woven by the voice of General Bull Dog Walker over the intercom. He could just see himself single handedly killing Stalin after a long hard fight that allowed him to brutally kill hordes of Reds. He envisioned himself kicking faces in, crushing skulls, gouging eyes, and shooting Reds in the guts to just watch them die. God how he loved being a soldier. He was about to join the French Foreign Legion when the Reds attacked. It had come just in time for him. He was planning on killing his pretty neighbor within weeks of the war starting.

He had killed before. It was a man in a bar fight that he started and ended with a knife to the throat. He had loved every minute of killing that guy and wanted more. For some reason he liked his new best friend Phil. He had never had a friend before. Phil had kept his deepest, darkest secret from the army. He was basically illiterate. He could sign his name pretty well and read a few important words like stop, go and men's, but that was about it. Even the Army did not take illiterate men. He wondered why all those who were so scared just didn't pretend not to read.

The speech had really made it hard for him to contain his urge to kill…someone. He would talk to Phil. Phil always seemed to know what to say that would calm him down. He wished he had known Phil before the Army. Maybe his life would have been different, or maybe he would have killed Phil.

On April 1947 at 0423 hrs. Warren could barely contain himself when he went over the side of the ship and got into the landing craft. He looked around and everyone was scared. He was so excited he thought he would piss in his pants. He couldn't imagine killing someone and actually getting away with it. Not only that, the more you killed the better your chances of getting a medal or a promotion and higher pay. This just couldn't get any better for Warren Johnson. And, then it did.

They rode the DUKW all the way to the first row of buildings. So far very few shots had been fired. Phil looked at Warren and they both just grinned and shrugged. This was way too easy. The DUKW stopped and they scrambled out. Warren led the way and Phil guarded his back just like they had agreed.

Figure 4 – DUKW

Following a Force of Nature

They were ordered to fan out and start clearing the buildings that were near the docks. The first building was empty. The second was as well. The third building was some kind of factory. Phil indicated to Warren that he had heard something inside. Warren looked under the door where there was a wide gap and saw a barricade at about 50 feet from the main entrance. He signaled the rest of the squad to wait and then spotted a window high up. Warren had been a very good pitcher in high school. That is probably why he actually graduated despite his illiteracy.

He pulled the pins on two grenades and held the handles to make sure the other squad members were well clear. The corporal finally showed up and let Warren continue with his plan. Warren threw the first grenade perfectly through the window, then switch hands with the second and did the same. The explosions were muted by the thick walls of the factory but the screams coming from inside were plainly audible through the window high up.

Without missing a beat, and almost before the second explosion, Warren smashed through the main door and screamed like a banshee as he ran into the factory. Everyone else but Phil was stunned and took a good ten seconds to follow. Phil was right on Warren's heels and true to his word he was making sure no one shot Warren in the back. Warren was taking care of everything in the front with amazing ease.

The stunned defenders were no match for Warren's ferocity. He was a killing machine who slaughtered anything that moved. When the smoke had cleared there were a dozen bodies, Warren was standing over the bodies grinning from ear to ear, and breathing hard. Phil had just finished shooting the last enemy soldier as she came out from behind a pillar to Warren's right side. The rest of the squad just stood their staring at the carnage having not fired a shot. Sergeant Sims threw up when he accidently tripped over a severed head.

Operation Kydoimos D-day +3
1 June 1947

The military term D-day stands for departure day. Every amphibious operation had its own D-day. The most famous was 6 June 1944. In reality it was just one of many.

On day three of Operation Kydoimos, General Hallett D. Edson 15th

Division had once again crossed the Mur River and entered the city of Leibnitz, Yugoslavia. The division had been driving hard and had had a dozen minor engagements with Yugoslavian forces. The 15th traveled 143 miles in three days and was due to be leap frogged by the "Lucky Seventh" Armored Division.

One of the last contingents of the Yugoslav Air Force, a squadron of captured German Ju-87 Stukas covered by another squadron of British-made Spitfires, came in under the radar coverage. The Yugoslavs bombed and strafed the command and lead elements of the 15th Division. This was the last action of the Yugoslav Air Force. On their return flight the ancient planes were intercepted by six F6F Hellcats. The better technology and training of the US Navy pilots proved the deciding factor. All the Spitfires and Stukas were destroyed either in the air or on the ground.

The Navy handed over the CAP (combat air patrol) duties to the USAAF at the end of this engagement for the lead elements of this D-day operation. The first airfields captured by the 15th Division were extensively upgraded to accommodate the F-80 Shooting Star jet fighter. The F-80 fighters gave the US a decided advantage in the air over even the best the Soviet VVS had to offer.

The attack on the 15th Division was the last air combat over ground troops until the VIII Corps reached Vienna. The decimation of Tito's air force was another indication that the Soviets were caught totally unprepared. At this juncture, only Yugoslavian ground and air forces had been encountered.

Tito's troops were being forced to fight in a conventional manner and could not use their tried and true guerrilla tactics as they had against the Germans. In World War Two, Yugoslavian fighters had effectively used insurgency warfare, melting away to the mountains and harassing the Nazis on an opportunistic basis. In this newest fighting, Tito had actively tried to prevent the US units from advancing through his country. The Yugoslavs were paying a very heavy price for no measurable effect.

It was reported to General Walker that the USAAF was keeping apace of the advance. The American air force was providing constant air cover, and interdicting the enemy's movements and supply lines.

Both General Walker of the US First Army and General Troy Middleton, the commander of the VIII Corps, went to bed thinking that the operation was going exceedingly well and that disconcerted them both.

Combat Savants

Phil did not sleep well for the last three nights. He kept having nightmares and flashbacks to the day in the factory. He killed his first human. He had to think "human" because it had been a woman. He couldn't think man because he hadn't killed a man. Phil was thankful that the rest of the squad gave him credit for a job well done, but he has still killed another human being. True she was trying to kill them. That didn't seem to help his nightmares. Mrs. Mable Post did not raise her sons Richard, Burt, and Phil to be killers. She did not raise them to hate.

The woman Phil had killed had been in uniform, and two of the others that Warren had killed with his bayonet had been female as well. It didn't seem to bother Warren. Phil tried to picture the woman he killed as just an enemy soldier. It would have helped if she had been ugly he supposed, but she wasn't. She looked like his 3rd grade teacher who he had a crush on. It was a pretty face, which in his mind, would be forever trapped in the surprise of death.

The squad stayed in the lead of the division and of the whole corps. They had gotten a new sergeant when their old one went crazy after their initial action. The first night after the action at the factory Sergeant Sims had repeatedly woken up screaming about the severed head he had tripped over. When the Corporal tried to calm him down the Sergeant had stuck him with his bayonet. Luckily for Corporal Beesly, Sims was so deranged that he missed anything vital. The Corporal was patched up and back with the squad after only a day.

The new Sergeant was a vet from WWII who really knew the art of command. More and more vets were signing up, and then showing up in the ranks of US units. They were extremely accomplished and very welcomed. However, they all had chips on their shoulders, and never let you forget what they already did for God and Country.

The new Sargent's name was Crystal. He hadn't seen much combat. He was always training for the invasion that never came. He has spent three months training for a special mission for the invasion of Japan. Luckily for all involved, including the Japanese, that mission was not needed.

Warren continued to impress the others in the squad with his combat prowess. The company commander took notice as well. The brigade commander was keeping an eye on the squad and that is why they were still leading the VIII Corps on the road to Vienna.

Besides watching Warren's back, Phil seemed to have a knack for spotting ambushes. Possibly it was because of his artistic abilities and propensity to think outside of the box. He had been the one who had smelled out the factory ambush and since then he had kept the squad from harm on three separate occasions. He really had an eye for dangerous situations and seemed able to read the mind of any enemy commander.

Quite frankly, Phil was very lucky as well. The last ambush he circumvented had involved booby traps, using sewers to hide in, and then sneaking up behind the Americans. Phil was taking a leak when he spotted that something was making ripples on the water from a drainage pipe.

He threw in a smoke grenade and that caused all hell to break loose. Fortunately for the Americans, they were ready for it thanks to Phil. It worked this way… Phil told Warren where the enemy was and then Warren killed them. In the meantime, Phil covered Warren's back and it all seemed to be working.

Today was 6 May, 1947 and the squad was on the outskirts of Graz. The Corps was only 12 hours behind schedule. Phil's squad had been given jeeps and had an escort of armored cars. So far, only obsolete T-34 tanks wielded by the Yugoslavian Army showed up to the party. Soon, there were more and more of them. It seemed that Tito had finally figured out where they were heading. From all Intel reports, Tito was having a hard time convincing Stalin that the US forces were, in fact, focused on Vienna. Beria had been fed some disinformation and Stalin listened to Beria. Besides, attacking Vienna just didn't make military sense.

Phil and Warren heard the tank coming long before anyone else did and told the Sargent, who told the Lieutenant who told the…and so on. Five T-34s without infantry support blundered into a perfect trap that was basically set up by Warren. He made suggestions and everyone just listened and did what he advocated. The team of Warren and Phil had not been wrong and had saved many US lives.

Three of the T-34s were destroyed in short order by the 17lbrs on the US Wolfhound armored car. A fourth and fifth T-34 tried to extricate themselves from the ambush, but were caught on the road by two US jets who hit them with rockets.

That made 12 tanks that Phil spotted with Warren orchestrated their demise. Pilots became aces after 5 kills as did tank crews. Phil wondered if there was any recognition for the grunts?

There was still no sign of the Soviets. The USAAF slaughtered a few supply columns but no massive reaction from the Stavka as yet. The theory was that Stalin and Beria were still confused and were paralyzed, but would snap out of it soon. The NATO strategists were counting on a Soviet reaction.

The newly captured airbases were being repaired and lengthened to accommodate the US jet fighters. Furthermore, brand new fields were being developed at a rapid pace. It was as if the US had been a coiled spring, and now it was being let loose. Almost all the equipment for this first invasion had been in mothballs after the invasion of Japan was canceled. This massive hoard of equipment was just waiting to be used. It seems the US could make a hell of a lot of stuff quickly, but they just couldn't seem to turn the whole operation off just as rapidly. The supply pipeline had continued to ship out stuff long after the war was over.

Phil and Warren were some of the many recipients of this cornucopia of death. They had the latest anti-tank weapons, the latest anti-air weapons and the latest artillery keeping them safe, and it was all on call in a matter of hours. Warren was very good at figuring out the coordinates for an artillery barrage and then passing them along to the Sergeant, who told the Lieutenant who dutifully called them in. The top brass thought the Lieutenant was a genius, when it was actually Warren. Warren's capability was even more amazing considering his inability to read. While he was illiterate, Warren excelled at math and was very competent with maps. Now, he was using these skills to the extreme.

In this unique pairing, each man continued to excel in his role. Phil kept Warren alive by covering his back and the company alive with his preternatural ability to detect traps. Warren kept Phil alive by killing anything that moved and kept the company with his instantaneous tactical decisions. Everyone else in the company just kind of let Phil and Warren work their magic.

The top brass was not aware that a couple of Privates were responsible for the unprecedented progress, the VIII Corps and the First Army were making. Phil and Warren were taking the lead, and the whole Army was following these two Privates; the VIII Corps combat savants.

***

The military invasion of Trieste was named Operation Kydoimos, after the Greek god of the din of battle and confusion.

***

Dislike and Respect

General Walker was walking the bridge. He was on the opposite side of where Nimitz was walking the same bridge. That bridge was located aboard the new aircraft carrier the USS Franklin D. Roosevelt (CVB/CVA/CV-42 also known as the "Swanky Franky," "Foo-De-Roo," or "Rosie," with the last nickname probably the most popular. The Rosie was the Flagship of the Sixth Fleet and for Taskforce 66.

Walker didn't like Nimitz and the feeling was mutual. Then again, Bulldog Walker didn't like very many people. They did respect each other and worked together in a very professional manner. They understood you don't have to like someone to work efficiently with them and to get the job done.

Figure 5 - Clear the decks as the USS Franklin sustains a near miss.

Walker's job had just begun. Nimitz job was half done. The Sixth fleet and auxiliary fleets had landed over 25,000 troops and supplies in 36 hours, A feat that surpassed D-Day in Normandy. The air, for 200 miles in any direction, belonged to the US Navy. That included the water in the Adriatic Sea from the surface to bottom. That was Admiral Chester Nimitz mandate and he had fulfilled it on a massive scale.

Walker's units were moving at a blistering pace. His Ghost army was fanning out all throughout the areas surrounding Trieste. Scout columns led by the new M38A3 Wolfhound armored car fitted with 17 pounders were probing every route leading out of the port area. If they encountered opposition, they engaged until it was apparent that more force was needed and the Navy was called in. The sixteen -inch guns of the battleships USS Wisconsin, Washington, Iowa, Indiana, New Jersey and Massachusetts cleared the way pretty effectively.

The majority of these scouting attacks were pure subterfuge. The only vital axis of attack was north-northeast to Vienna. General Troy Middleton's VII Corps was leading this column and things were going remarkably well. The Corps was only a few hours behind schedule. A particularly determined Yugoslavian unit and a timid US commander combined to halt the column for a vital 3 hours. The Yugoslavian unit was destroyed and the US Division commander replaced. The VII Corps was on pace to enter Vienna on 9 May, 1946. Twelve hours behind the planned schedule.

The actual landings went pretty much according to plan. They surprised a column of Soviet Naval Babushka Mini-subs preparing to enter the waters of the Adriatic. It took five minutes of 5 -inch shells from the close in destroyers to put an end to the Red's plans. If those ten mini-subs had been in the water, it could have been ugly but war is all about timing and luck.

The Mulberries were in place and working well. The southernmost artificial harbor was only at half capacity due to an unexpected mine field slowing up operations. The northern Mulberry was easily taking up the slack and Walker's troops and supplies were rolling out from Trieste like a colony of army ants.

On day two, the USAAF landed on airfields captured in Kranj, Yugoslavia, which is just outside of Ljubljan. By the end of the day, a squadron of F4U fighter bombers flew two sorties in support of the VII Corps drive on Vienna.

The supplies were flowing like water from the endless parade of cargo ships with only a few mishaps. Three Soviet Navy Babushka mini-subs had somehow gotten through the bottom to top defenses of the US Navy and had scored four torpedo strikes on three cargo ships. Two of the cargo ships were sunk and the other crippled. Two of the mini-subs were destroyed when they had to surface and the third was never found.

The air opposition was non-existent as expected this far from the Soviet lines. It appeared for all intents and purposes that the invasion had caught the Soviet Stavka by total surprise and the lack of any coordinated action supported that conclusion. No mention in Pravda or any other official communications of the landing in Trieste was apparent. It was as if the Reds were ignoring the situation hoping it would go away.

The Western press was in full throat. From banner headlines to radio coverage from Trieste itself, the free press was being willingly manipulated by the Pentagon. NATO wanted the Soviets to be focused on the bright shinny object placed on their southern border. The plan would not work if the Stavka did not react to the incursion in major fashion. The Red Army had to move and move decisively to crush the invasion or all bets were off.

A mere containment of the First US Army by the Soviets would be the smartest thing they could do. It was hoped that the inclusion of the US Army Air Force reaching out from its newly captured air bases would force the Reds to attack and expend resources they no longer had.

Nimitz was doing his job and so was Walker. They communicated whenever necessary, which was often. They were short and to the point. They never argued or even discussed any particular point. Walker told Nimitz what the Army was going to do and Nimitz told Walker what the Navy would do to assist.

Walker hated the US Navy and Nimitz was the epitome of the Navy. Nimitz hated the US Army and Walker was its leading combat general. Their official public relations duties were a fiasco. Walker just stood there looking tough and Nimitz looked efficient but somehow that was enough at this stage of the war. The press was satisfied that something was finally being done to defeat Stalin.

Mutual dislike is not relevant if you have mutual respect. You did your job and the other commander did his and that was how you won.

Stalin and the Soviet system, however, usually had a different outcome.

If you could destroy the people you disliked, you did so. Certain Soviet leaders had this ability and used it on the order of twenty million times.

Gentle Giant

Richard Gardner Post was a large man. He stood 6'4" and weighed 225 lbs. He was a competitive swimmer in high school and held many records in state meets. He was very, very strong. He looked like the perfect soldier. His corporal and then his sergeant soon found out that he lacked something, something that was essential in a soldier. That something was hate.

The brothers Richard and Phil Post were raised not to hate. Richard, in particular, could not be coerced into hating the enemy enough to kill. He saw all people for what they were. They were neither good nor bad because of the way they dressed or the color of their skin or shape of their eyes. He was not some kind of imbecile and knew when he was being taken advantage of. In fact, he was a very good businessman with a thriving construction business that he had to leave when he was drafted. He built homes, businesses and schools. He did the work of three normal men. He was quick and sure in his movements and choices. He hated no one.

Sometimes things just work out and for Richard, all of his stars seemed to be in alignment for once. The corporal talked to the sergeant who talked to the lieutenant, who talked to the captain who got Richard transferred to an all colored unit that was assisting the Seabees or Construction Battalions. The Seabees were specialized units the Navy created. The Navy expressly sought highly skilled recruits from the construction and building trades. Many times the units were made up of more experienced men. The average age of a Seabee unit was 37, far older than other units.

Richard had never seen a Negro until he was drafted into the army. He came from northern Wisconsin, which did not have many opportunities for interracial interaction. His new squad mates knew right off how special Richard was and Richard knew how lucky he was to be in their company. It was mutual admiration and a real kind of conjoint regard from the very first. Richard was one happy man.

Richard's unit was assigned to follow the naval Seabee unit that was right behind the lead combat units of the VIII Corps. The colored unit's mission was to assist the Seabees in building airfields in as short a time as possible.

The Seabees had extensive experience in the Pacific theater during the Second World War in setting up air fields quickly while under fire. In the landings in Leyte, Philippines they had an airfield ready within hours of landing. America's Ace of Aces, Richard Bong almost beat General McArthur in his return to the Philippines; the field was built so quickly. At Guadalcanal, the Seabees helped defend the air field from attack. At Wake Island the Seabees were captured and forced to complete the construction project. In the end, the Japanese summarily executed the Seabees.

The Seabee's first assignment was an airfield in Postjona. The Yugoslavian military spent a day trying to destroy their own airbase. The Seabees and Richard's battalion had it up and running in five hours. USAAF P-80 Shooting Stars were landing on hour six and taking off for missions on hour eight. The whole First Army's success depended upon air superiority in a 600-mile-wide corridor running from Trieste to Vienna and the Seabees were on track to meet that objective.

Richard's unit was commanded by a white officer. Experience had shown that officers from the south were not the proper choice for this job. Walter Wingate was from Vermont, and was indeed the correct choice for commanding this unusual unit.

The first time a group of soldiers from another company had tried to get Richard's goat for eating and sleeping with "niggers," they had been severely disciplined by Captain Wingate. Richard did not respond to their taunts and racial name-calling. His demeanor impressed Wingate.

Richard's extraordinary construction skills and strength were great assets to the company. However, one of his most valuable traits was his genial manner. People just naturally gravitated to Richard. In this time of unimaginable horror, it was comforting to know that such a gentle giant still existed and that all men were not natural-born killers controlled by hatred alone.

Reporter – Reporting

Marvin Cranston had a ringside seat to Operation Kydoimos. This was a bribe for being held prisoner without charges by the US Army when he stumbled upon a dress rehearsal in Maine for this very operation and the invasion of Trieste.

When he was released, he was offered a berth on an assault ship and unfettered access. He was allowed on the bridge of the flag ship and had observed the unusually reserved interactions between the very famous Nimitz and the new guy Walker. Both seemed, distant and cold towards each other, yet when they had to communicate, they did so very effectively. He was pretty sure that the censors would cut that part out of his story, but he had to try anyway.

From Marvin's limited knowledge of amphibious operations, things seemed to be going well and was remarkably similar to the exercise he observed in Maine before being "captured" by General McNarney. It had indeed been payback by the General, but maybe his Pulitzer was still waiting after this exclusive access to the first NATO counter attack of the war. He may ultimately get his revenge on McNarney

It's not like he was locked up during his month-long hiatus with the Army paratroopers. He actually had some good stories to tell about their training and such. They were an interesting group of men who jump out of planes for a living. He was confined to a base in the middle of nowhere without access to a phone.

Eventually, he was allowed one phone call and chose his editor who then informed anyone who cared. There were not many he assumed. He was allowed day -old newspapers and his disappearance never made it into print. Kind of disconcerting to be a prominent reporter for the New York Times, go missing and no one seemed to care. Clearly, he needed to work on his interpersonal skills.

He agreed not to mention where he had been, what he had seen, and the circumstances he was being held. In return, he gained freedom and exclusive access to this first US operation.

After walking the bridge and taking notes, Marvin was allowed to go ashore on the third wave. The resistance was minimal, with not a Soviet to be found, only Tito's Yugoslav minions. The Yugoslavian fighter's reputation, but not when it came to conventional warfare. They were easily defeated by the American combination of superior arms and combat knowledge. The Yugoslavs were brave but lacked modern command, control and weapons. He was surprised by the number of women fighters.

He was just pulling into the city of Gratz. He was trying to track down two Privates whose actions have caused the rumor mill to kick into overdrive. According to the rumors, the Privates have done some amazing things that make Audi Murphy look like a piker, and that was saying a lot.

Command did not provide him with a driver and vehicle. He guessed the Army's guilt or fear of charges did not extend that far. He had just got off hitching a ride on a DUKW when he heard firing ahead. It turned out not to be the Privates and was another fire fight with some locals.

He noticed that there were a number of locals that were flying the American flag from their windows. He put that in his mental "to -do list." do list". Are the local citizens of Yugoslavia ready to throw off the Tito regime? Nice angle he thought.

He asked around and got a line on the Privates. They were in the lead of the whole army and doing their magic in a town called Guntrans. This town was not on any maps he had. Based on the description he was given, the likely location seemed be by a major river crossing. As he looked at a very detailed topo map, he was impressed by all the possible defensive positions that faced both east and west. Someone did an excellent job of planning this operation.

He still didn't understand what NATO was going to accomplish here. He had learned that the First Army was going to take Vienna and then defend it and a 100-mile-wide corridor back to Trieste, but why? Either no one really knew or this was one of the tightest lipped group of troops he had ever encountered.

The next day he got to Guntrans, but the Privates had long gone. It seems they were given a bunch of jeeps and those new armored cars. Most importantly, their company had been given the freedom to do whatever it took to move as rapidly as possible towards Vienna. He had to catch up to these two mythical Privates and fast.

He did run into one of the Private's brothers. He was a big man working with an all colored unit on the construction site of an airfield in Wiener Neustadt, Austria. His name was Richard Post and his brother Phil was one of the mythical Privates. Richard was a nice guy, but was of no real help. He loved his brother and was worried about him, but had no knowledge of his brother's combat deeds. In fact, Richard was kind of mystified by the whole thing.

It seems that Phil was an artist and was going to become an art teacher. Their mother had raised them to be pacifists. That is why Richard was in this construction unit. He didn't want to kill anyone and couldn't imagine his brother doing so either.

This story was getting juicier by the minute. Headline" Pacifist Artist Becomes Killer." He had to catch up with these guys.

Curiously, he couldn't get anyone to talk about the other Private, Warren Johnson. Everyone that knew Warren was kind of nervous about talking about him. He must be some intimidating guy; Marvin thought. I mean these combat hardened veterans seemed to be afraid of this guy. Headline" Killer Terrifies All." He just had to catch up to these two. Shit, he hadn't filed a story in three days since he started following the Privates.

A reporter who doesn't report loses his job. A very crude American flag caught his attention and he had an idea for a quick bullshit story that would shut his editor up. He'd have to write some story about American flags flying from the windows of captured buildings and how the locals were embracing the NATO forces as liberators. His thought train was interrupted by a bullet striking near his foot.

He jumped or more accurately fell, into a ditch full of water. He was not a combat reporter and all this shooting and blowing up of things was new to him. He was not used to people literally trying to kill him. He wasn't afraid, just surprised that someone would want to shoot him personally.

Someone threw a grenade into a building and that was the end of the sniping. He noticed that the crude American flag was missing from the window and started to write.

Waving the Flag

Binasa Litvin had made the Yankee flag hours before the Americans appeared in town. She had no idea what the Yankees were doing so far into the Yugoslavian countryside. The flag had stayed in her window until that idiot Gafur shot at the Yankee soldier long after the first set of troops had left town. What was Gafur thinking? Was he trying to impress the local communist leaders? No good could come of it, that was for sure. So, she took down her Yankee flag just to be safe and not draw attention to herself.

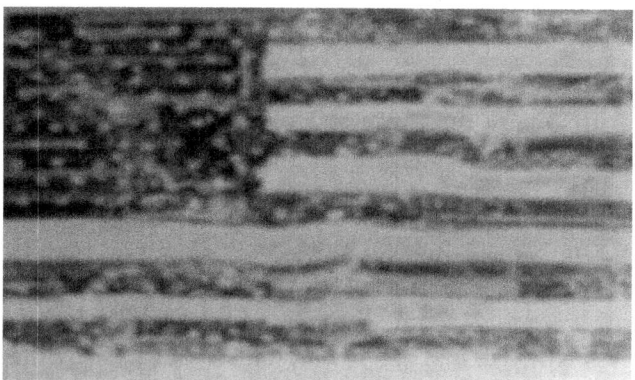

What did she care whether it was the Yankees, Soviets, Germans or Tito who took her pride? Men were men, and she was a widower who had had sex with many men since "he" died. She could not bring herself to say his name. "He" was short of stature but long on wisdom and love. Oh how she loved "Him."

It did no good to dwell in the past. After Gafur's shot, the Yankees would be going door to door so she had to prepare. She wanted to appear demur and reluctant, yet available to the right baby faced virgin she spotted. They were always the best and were easy to make them fall in love with you.

She looked in the mirror and liked what she saw, Full bodied, yet attractive. She always had a pretty face and that had saved her life a number of times. Unfairly, like so many, she was forced to use her body to survive.

She reflected on life under the Tito regime. It was hard to get food, but no one was starving. Everyone got along in their mutual misery, Muslims, Croats, etc. You had certain freedoms, yet everyone but a few were very poor with no hope of a better life.

Perhaps these Yankees would bring prosperity. She had heard that they had lots of pretty things to give to willing women. That was probably the biggest difference she expected. The Yankees felt the need to give you things in return for sex. They needed to feel it was a business deal and nothing more. From what she had heard few rapes could be expected from the Americans. There might be unwanted attention, sex and degradation, but not the extreme violence of the Russians or the cursed Germans.

She took a quick sponge bath, put on her best dress, pinched her cheeks and walked through the doorway to seek out a baby-faced soldier that would protect her for a few days or perhaps a week or two.

Perhaps, she could seek out the soldier who had been shot at and clean him up after he had fallen into the ditch. It would be a way to gain his confidence and get him aroused. Having a woman take care of you always seemed to work. She hoped he was not a virgin. She hated virgins, too much fumbling and needing assistance.

Perhaps she should put the Yankee flag out again. She found the soldier. He was not far from where he had fallen and of all the odd things… he was writing, furiously writing like his life depended on it. She put her hand on his shoulder and the age -old dance began.

***

Melvin Cranston returned to Yugoslavia, married Binasa Litvin and had three children, two of which were his own.

***

Eye Witness Report -
USAAF vs VVS – Ganz, Austria

7 May 1946

By Captain Morgan Ferguson

```
1. At about 0655, numerous enemy planes were picked up by
our instruments as coming towards the Ganz Area from the
East, distance about 255 miles. Four Squadrons of
fighters were ordered to intercept.

2. At about 0657, the entire Combat Air Patrol was
ordered out in different formations to intercept and
engage the enemy planes closing in on us.

3. This was the first major air combat to take place in
Operation Kydoimos between the Soviet Air force and NATO
forces. Approximately 40 aircraft took part in the
action.
```

      15   USAAF P-80 Shooting Stars

      12   VVS TU-2 Bats

12   Mig-9 Fargos

4. The two squadrons of P-80's were vectored in by USAAF radar air controllers and we were able to attack the enemy flight while coming out of the sun.

5. In the initial pass I claim one Tu-2 Bat shot down.

6. observed three more severely damaged enemy aircraft of the Tu-2 Bat type and one of the Mig-9 Fargo. I also observed a collision of a Shooting Star and a Fargo (later identified as Lieutenant Cummings) with both planes being destroyed in mid-air.

7. The tempo of the engagement and the maneuver of the two forces turned into a dogfight with both forces scoring hits.

8. Observation: The Tu-2 Bat medium bomber did not stay in formation and fought and maneuvered similarly to a fighter squadron. They were very nimble for a bomber and avoided most high speed attacks rather easily by out turning our planes.

The Mig-9 Fargo was slower than the P-80 Shooting Star but more maneuverable. Suggest using energy tactics and using high speed passes. Do not get into a turning fight with either aircraft.

9. Using energy maneuvers and keeping high speed we were able to down three more Bats and four more Fargos.

10. We lost five aircraft:
One to a flameout
Two to enemy gunfire from the Bat's tail gunners.
One from Fargo gunfire..
One from a collision with an enemy Fargo.

11. Strategic observations of the mission:
- The enemy aircraft were forced to turn back.
- The enemy seemed prepared and trained for high speed jet combat.
- New tactics must be developed to accomplish an air superiority mission.

- Rookie USAAF personnel were up to the task of jet combat due to our superior training programs.
- The 50 cal machine guns of the Shooting Star proved to be an effective weapon against the Fargo and Bat.
- Radar air control is vital to a successful mission outcome.

Sergo Loses Control

Sergo learned that a decision had been made without his counsel regarding the future of the Stalin's Fire Missile. Admiral of the Red Fleet, Nikolay Kuznetsov, had convinced the Stavka and then Stalin that they needed to employ the guided missiles for their original purpose, which was to sink ships.

Kuznetsov had argued that the Amerikosi had one great advantage over the forces of the USSR and that was their control of the seas. The Babushka mini-sub had only a marginal effect on the western power's navies. Turn the Stalin's Fire Missile into an anti-ship weapon and you have a very powerful threat to the enemy's control of the world's oceans.

The Admiral had secretly developed a long-range, anti-ship missile that traded altitude and speed for greater reach. The redesigned missiles now had a range that far out distanced even the largest naval guns and rivaled the range of carrier -based airplanes.

The Red Navy's engineers had added larger control surfaces that significantly reduced the missiles' speed. Extreme speed was unnecessary in this application, as ships were essentially stationary targets to a rocket. The engine was made more efficient and the rocket was longer due to an added fuel container. The final version was slower and larger with a range of 200 miles and a speed of 725 mph.

The redesigned missile was still faster than the speed of sound, and any jet fighter by over 100 mph. The operational plan was to fire the rocket in the direction of an enemy fleet. The avian pilots were prevented from guiding the rocket by retractable shutters over the viewing window and contact plate. Until the shutters open the missile would be guided by a system similar to the V2 rocket.

This initial guidance system consisted of two free gyroscopes (horizontal and vertical) for stabilization. At timed intervals, both shutters would open then three Columba Livia or pigeons, would take control of the rocket. The course and possible target would be chosen by two of the three operators.

If the settings were correct for distance and bearing the organic guidance system would begin searching for a target within their visual range. Then, they would do what they were taught. In this case, it was to collide with the ship.

The particular ship picked out, by the majority, would be somewhat at random. The Soviet trainers were able to teach the birds to rank certain shapes and sizes of ships. For example, they could easily tell a freighter from an aircraft carrier.

The sequence of targets, taught the birds, was aircraft carrier, freighter, battleship, cruiser, destroyer, etc. Aircraft carriers were a priority, playing on American's emotions. The US Navy loved its carriers and Kuznetsov knew that any loss would be psychologically devastating to the American navy.

The freighters were next on the list because they were carrying the men and materials to wage war. A shortage of freighters meant the Amerikosi could not continue the war. Generally, freighters were more valuable than aircraft carriers. More importantly, the sinking aircraft carriers would break the Amerikosi's spirit.

Sergo's priorities were at odds with the Soviet Navy. All the Navy's logical arguments were not lost on Sergo. He just did not agree with priorities. His greatest concern was losing an intact missile in enemy territory, thus giving away one of the best kept secrets his country owned.

Secrets in Jeopardy

Sergo Peshkova could imagine many scenarios for defeating a visually guided rocket. He was sure there were scientists working for the capitalists who could devise countermeasures as well. At this time, the Soviets key advantage was the Amerikosi had no knowledge of the mechanism guiding the Stalin's Fire Missile.

The whole notion stemmed from an American doctor's novel concept. Fortunately, the Americans summarily rejected the idea of a bird guiding a missile. Sergo had seen the reports of the scheme and knew it had been rejected based upon the concerns raised by a single reviewer out of a group of five. The reviewer did not believe the data presented by Skinner's group. The data seemed too good to be true and he accused Skinner of faking the results. The reviewer was present during a demonstration where the pigeons perform perfectly, but he still lacked the imagination to understand the potential of the project.[1]

This denial came in the face of overwhelming evidence that Dr. Skinner and his team had adhered strictly to the scientific method. Furthermore, they were meticulous in the handling of data collection and analyst.

The whole Project Pigeon concept was so foreign to the military that they used the one reviewer's errant challenge as an excuse to reject the project.

Sergo came upon the original data and studies. He knew that this Skinner fellow had done an outstanding job of designing and running experiments, interpreting data, and conducting demonstrations. From the very first, Sergo had no doubt that the idea presented by Dr. Skinner could easily become a practical weapons system.

Like the American military, the Soviet military skeptical of the idea. However, Sergo had the ultimate trump card in the form of Staling. Sergo convinced Stalin that the idea was valid and easily workable. Production began using the German Wasserfal missile as the base weapon.

Amazingly, it only took three months to train thousands of pigeons. Unbeknownst to the Americans, a Soviet agent purchased large numbers of birds from pigeon farms throughout the United States and shipped them back to the Soviet Union. The stock was augmented with the indigenous populations of European and Asian pigeons.

A breeding and training program had been designed by Sergo. Full-fledged production commenced, both Wasserfal missiles and its avian pilots.

With the advent of the Red Fleet deploying the missile over enemy controlled territory, all his work and the future of the Soviet system was in jeopardy if the secret was revealed.

The Reds React

Eisenhower was intently studying a list of recommendations for the replacement of combat units from the frontlines. All the other major powers rotated entire units. While the US waited until individual soldiers were killed or seriously wounded before they were replaced.

---

[1] - Engineering Behavior: Project Pigeon, World War II, and the Conditioning of B. F. Skinner by James H. Capshew

Towards the end of the war, American troops started to desert in alarming numbers. This was partly due to the replacement system of the US Army or more accurately the lack of a replacement system. The dysfunctional replacement system was a critical problem that and he was more than pissed off when his aide barged into the room.

"Sorry General, but you told me to come in anytime, anywhere when we received reports of Soviet troop movements."

Ike took a deep breath and indicated that his aide should continue.

"Recon flights over the Pyrenees Line show large troop movements. In particular, armored units are being loaded onto trains. Radio chatter has picked up all along the front as well. Furthermore, artillery pieces are being readied for transport according to a Basque partisan fighter."

"Thank you Glen. Get Marshall on the horn."

"Yes Sir."

Ike lights up one of his continuous cigarettes and starts to read again when his aide informs him that George Marshall is on the line.

Ike thought to himself…I wonder how George will try and influence me this time. Will it be "I'm sure that you've considered so and so, and so, and so." He won't say, "Don't forget to do this." He would just say, "I'm sure you've considered it. And I'm sure you will consider these things before you make your decision." The one thing he knew for sure is that whatever his decision was Marshall would back it.' Thank God, he could take that to the bank.

"George, you there?"

"Yes Ike, I'm not awake, but I'm here"

"Sorry George, but it looks like the Soviets have made their first move and it's a beauty. They appear to be stripping the Pyrenees Line of their armor and giving up on the offensive. They are digging in and going on the defensive just like we planned."

"Good news Ike. Now I'm sure you've considered…"

Here it comes, thought Eisenhower.

After the conversation, Ike reflected that Marshall made some good points as usual. Most thought of George as a master at bringing out the best in his subordinates, but he also had a keen military mind, which many did not know about him. His suggestions were sage and worth considering every time.

Both men agreed that the Soviets would take the easiest solution to the invasion of Trieste and the march on Vienna. The Red Armies closest and most battle-hardened troops were in Spain. Their tanks were of not much use in the Pyrenees Mountain range. Pulling the armored units was expected and planned for. Hence the use of the 7th Armored Division and its large compliment of Patton tanks.

The American strategists predicted that the first attempt at reaching the Trieste – Vienna Line from Spain would be through Northern Italy via Marseille and Milan. It was up to the newly formed 6th Fleet under William "Bull" Halsey to counter that move. Bull's job would be to destroy as much armor and fuel as he could. In addition, he was to close off the transportation lines out of Marseille. The Stavka would have to take a more northern route, dramatically increasing their transportation requirements and using up their precious oil reserves.

Next, it was thought that the Reds would try and skirt the Alps, or maybe even try to force their way through neutral Switzerland. All these routes would be well within the effective range of the 6th Fleet and Halsey, who would be hammering them all the way.

The conventional wisdom was that eventually the Reds would go through Munich. They would have to attack Vienna from the north and be forced to cross the Danube. All along this circuitous route they would be exposed to attack by the Navy and the United States Army Air Force fighter bombers. The US pilots had no fear of the Stalin's Fire SAM or the X-4 AA missile. Both missiles were relatively easy to out maneuver in a fighter plane.

Probably the Reds would try to force the Danube and be repulsed by the VIII Corps. Stalin's next choice would be crucial and determine where the ensuing hammer blow by NATO would land.

One if by land, two if by sea and in this case, it was all by sea. Sea power was NATO's greatest strength. Our supremacy would be seriously threatened if the USSR were to survive and allowed to build an effect fleet. Eisenhower and NATO's goal would be eliminating Soviet Empire. That was his and NATO's goal. He had no idea what may take its place but Stalin and the current leadership along with communism had to be eradicated.

He had even been approached to run for the Presidency. He had said "no" in no uncertain terms. Yet, in the back of his mind there may be a time in the future where he might consider it but not now! He had a war to win.

He called in the aide.

"Get Admiral King." God I hate talking to that prick; Eisenhower thought, What an arrogant SOB, Not sometimes. but always.

"Good morning Admiral. I have news of Soviet movements that will require the assistance of the Navy."

The phone makes noises in Ike's hand but is otherwise unintelligible.

"Yes that is right Admiral. They are pulling out a number of their armored units and we assume that they are going to try the most direct route to Trieste and then Vienna. As you will recall the 6th Fleet is to interdict such a move and to cause as many losses as possible to their fuel storage and transports.

Now is the time to call in our markers and get the most accurate information on troop movements, supply convoys, trains and fuel depots. We need Naval Intelligence to fire up all its agents and contacts. We need to know what route those Red troops are taking and we need to know when they will be where.

I further suggest that you fire up Halsey. We want a maximum effort by the Navy on this Admiral. Do I have your agreement on this point?"

An unintelligible answer came back through the phone's earpiece and seemed to satisfy Ike.

"Good, Admiral, I'm glad we are in agreement (for once) thought Eisenhower. I'm looking forward to reports of burning Soviet fuel and tanks, Admiral."

Ike ends the conversation and hangs up the phone.

His attention is once again drawn to the problem of replacements and its effects on desertion.

Interdiction

Billy Porter heard someone grunting and having trouble breathing. Was Billy the one grunting and panting? Was he having sex and passed out? Holy shit he was controlling some kind of machine! Wake up, snap out of it and figure out what you are doing.

The fog of near unconsciousness cleared and Billy remembered what had just happened. He was flying. Flying a jet fighter bomber and had just dropped some bombs on a train. The bombs made a very satisfying explosion and fireball, and he had waited too long to pull up while admiring his handiwork. The G-Forces had begun to suck the blood from his brain and sent it to his feet and legs. His brain had almost shut down.

He had to get him one of those G-Suits. Jenkins had one and could run circles and pull up on a dime compared to the others in the squadron. Rumors were that everyone would get one soon. The only real use was in ground attack. You couldn't get into a turning fight with either current Soviet jet fighter, the Fargo or the Feather. You had to be faster than they were in order to win. Boom and zoom, not turn and burn.

With a ground attack you had to pull big Gs most of the time. The Reds missiles were easy to avoid although they were quite unnerving in the way they turned and twisted as they tried to hit you. Imagine a bullet that turned corners to find you. If you knew they were coming and got eyes on them, you just had to time your turn. The missiles couldn't follow because they were so fast and had the turning radius of an ocean liner.

When his vision cleared a little more he found his flight and joined up. They passed over their handiwork. The train was a flaming mess. He could see the armored vehicles that were on the train all strewn about and many were on fire as well. Damn he hated napalm. He didn't like to use it himself after seeing what it did to a column of refugees that were in the wrong place at the wrong time.

Nobody used poisoned gas anymore. He wondered why they didn't do the same with napalm. It was horrible stuff and an awful way to die or even get wounded. The major powers had banned the dum dum bullet in the 1800s, yet had not outlawed napalm or the atomic bomb. Billy, knew he was just a pilot and knew he had no control over such matters. Maybe someday, he would make Admiral, but for now he just dropped bombs and shot at other aircraft.

Command had used his squadron because they had expected the VVS to send up some jets to defend the train. It appears they were right. His flight leader had come over the radio telling them that air control picked up bogies vectoring in on their flight. Too late Ivans, thought Billy. We, are, out of here.

The squadron running top cover would get to dogfight the Feathers coming in. It should be a good fight and he looked forward to hearing about it back on ship.

The P-80 was not the ideal plane to use on an aircraft carrier and the Navy was furiously developing its own jet fighter but in the meantime the modified Shooting Star was being used effectively. Once it got in the air the P-80 was a good plane. It just was not good at landing on an aircraft carrier. He had to admit he did not like the landing part, one bit.

Back on the ship, the reports were good on their airstrike. They had wiped out a company of T-54 tanks. Those were the newest in the Soviet inventory. The fact that Soviets were shifting the tanks towards Vienna was a good sign according to the Naval Intelligence Officer giving the briefing. Interdiction attacks like this were already making the Reds divert their trains to longer routes to avoid the US Navy and its carrier based planes. Billy thought, Handy things these floating airbases.

Soft Point Bullets

Also called soft-nosed, dum-dum or mushroom. This type of bullet has a Lubaloy jacket filled with a lead or lead alloy core, closed at the base, leaving an open point in the jacket at the nose exposing the lead core. The amount of lead exposed at the point depends upon the velocity at which the bullet is to be driven, and the purpose for which the bullet is intended.

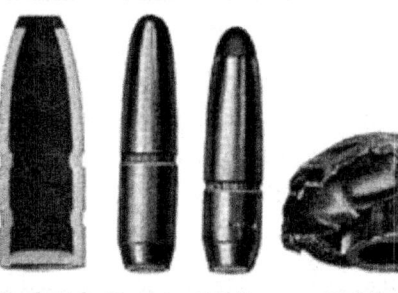

Section of Soft Point bullet. Pin Point lead exposed. Medium point lead exposed. Mushroomed 348-200-Grain Soft Point Bullet.

World War Three 1946 – Book Four– The Red Sea   Page 41

Chapter Two: Of Mice and Men

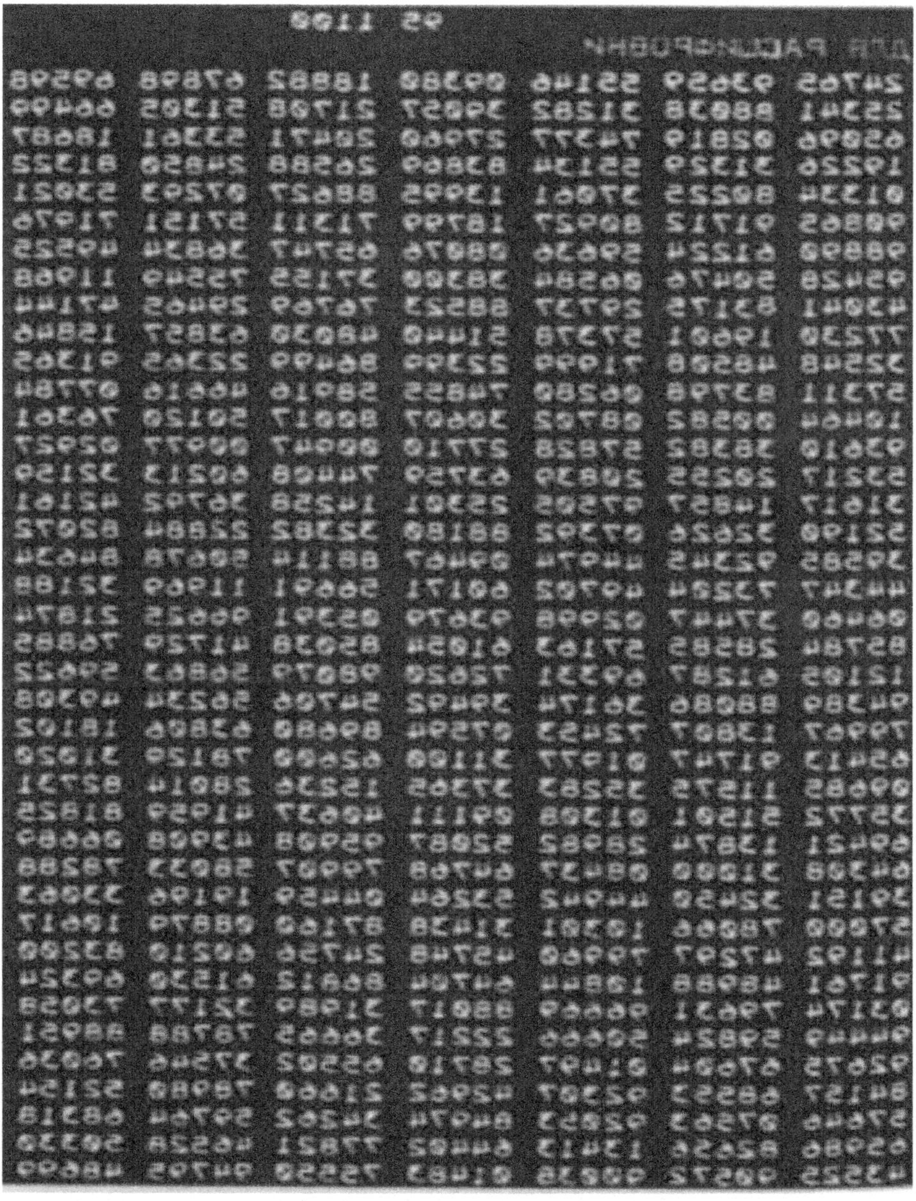

Figure 6 - Soviet One Time Pad

One Time Pad and Fate

Colonel Ralph Broussard III was under the gun, both literally and figuratively. His temporary office was under the aft turret of the USS Wisconsin with three of her massive 16 inch guns looming over his head. One Admiral Spruance and the Pentagon held another gun.

The report Broussard read and edited was based on a number of intercepted communications from the Stavka to Marshall Zhukov. If the report's assumption was accurate, the Soviets were assigning most of their mobile forces for a drive on the Suez.

NATO was intercepting, and more importantly, decoding greater numbers of Soviet communications each day. It was essentially real time information. However, it did take about a week to decode, translate and then disseminate the reports. The Soviets were using an unbreakable code based on the "one-time pad" of random numbers.

The one-time pad code was, and still is unbreakable. During their greatest national crisis of 1942 to 1943 the Soviets reprinted existing one-time pads to save time. They had done the worst possible thing they could do. These duplicated pads were the only way the US could break the Soviet codes and were used up by 1944. US code breakers did not discover this treasure trove of information until 1946.

The decoded messages were two and three years old by 1947 and of use only to American counter intelligence. The messages contained code names and other clues that identified many current Soviet spies. This decoding project was named the Venona Papers. [2]

A number of Soviet spies were caught but many disappeared when warned that their covers were blown. The Venona program was revealed to the Soviet Union by Bill Weisband, a NKVD agent who was also a United States Army SIGINT analyst and cryptologist. When the use of the duplicate pads ended in 1944, the US lost access to information about Soviets operations.

Now, miraculously the use of the duplicate pads resurfaced in early 1947 and the US was exploiting their use to the upmost. For some unknown reason the old supply of the re-printed pads were sent to Marshall Ivan Bagramyan who dutifully used them. This current release came from inside the Kremlin and might have been the work of an insider whose

---

[2] - Venona: Decoding Soviet Espionage in America By John Earl Haynes, Harvey Klehr

identity remains a mystery.

These were the messages that Broussard was reading. The critical information was a window into the Soviet military's thoughts. Soon, this portal would most likely be slammed shut.

The end result is that US Intelligence now had almost real-time access to the plans of the Soviet Stavka. These decoded messages revealed that the Soviets were actually in the process of executing a very brilliant strategic move. Unfortunately for the future spread of the communist cause, their plans were an open book to the Pentagon and a new trap was set.

The stars seemed to be aligned for NATO and the West once again in this newest of world wars. A number of instances of sheer luck had often aided the Allied victory in World War Two. This string of good fortune seemed to follow the cause of freedom just when we are at our lowest ebb.

One has to question why fate or God had allowed the enemies of freedom to win the initial battles in both world wars, but that is a debate for another time. What is not in debate is that NATO's fate took a turn for the good when the first duplicate one-time-pad of World War Three showed up on the desk of Colonel Ralph Broussard III.

Commanding a Corps

The airplane lurched violently to the right. The metal groaned as the plane twisted in the air. The pilot fought with the flight yoke to keep the plane from yawing to the left. The violent motion woke up the General.

General Oscar Griswold was dreaming about his life. He was back in his hometown of Ruby Valley, NV. Smelling the old smells of home and his mother's cooking. She was a great cook and loved to make his favorites. He was a plain man with simple tastes.

He was then transported, as dreams are wont to do, to his school, the University of Nevada, Reno. He was back in the dorms walking the halls and reliving the discussions he had about life with his classmates. Once again smells permeated his dreams. He recalled the stench, from his roommate's drinking binges.

Suddenly in his dream, he was back to his first taste of combat in World War One. He was commanding the eighth division as the Lieutenant Colonel leading the charge of his battalion in the Meuse Argon offensive. Again smells permeated his dreams. The smell of death, of smoke and fear.

The smells of World War Two were different. He was in a command position far from the front and smells of combat. The only time he relived the smells of World War Two, was when he passed through combat zones yet to be cleared. His dreams passed through many battlefields on his way to wakefulness. In his dreams he relived killing fields from New Georgia, Bougainville and the Philippines, where he saw atrocities a man should never see. The carnage was committed by Japanese soldiers retreating after their defeat. The enemy bastards were eventually annihilated, far from their homes and families. Their bodies were left rotting in the jungle.

Wakefulness brought Griswold back to the present where he was in command of the US Seventh Army. His Army was about to invade the city of Beirut via the Mediterranean Sea. Leonard Gerow was in command of the Seventh Army's vanguard corp. The Corp's mission was to lead the charge on Baghdad. If the operation was successful they would trap 250,000 Soviet troops between Montgomery on the Suez Canal and a NATO defensive line running from Beirut to Baghdad.

Griswold looked over at General Gerow and it gave him a tremendous sense of confidence. Gerow was one of the finest Corps Commanders of World War Two. He had performed admirably in the Western European Theater and he was now using those same skills in the Mediterranean. Normally he would have been elevated to command an army but, he was so valuable as a Corps Commander Ike decided to keep him in that capacity.

Being a corps commander was actually a tougher job than being a general leading an army. As Corps Commander you control generals who are leading divisions. Division Commanders are typically newly minted generals. These rookies are usually untested and out to prove they are the best, hardest driving and bravest assholes in the US Army. Trying control these guys is equivalent to herding cats.

Corps Commanders have proven their abilities, been under the microscope, and are not so anxious to get killed. They are truly committed to a career in the army and generally take orders well. There are very few rogue Corps Commanders whereas up to 25% of Division Commanders tend to burn out during a campaign.

In the early stage of the last war, Ike and Marshall had no idea of their true combat abilities of their Division Commanders. A number of peace time officers proved ineffective during their initial combat experience. But after three years of continuous combat in World War Two, most Corps Commanders have been vetted and had proven their worth.

A Corps Commander was, as one general describes him, "the last man toward the rear who directs tactical fire on the enemy. He is the commander who conducts the battle."

General Matthew B. Ridgeway, who successfully commanded at division and corps levels during World War Two, describes in his memoirs certain characteristics of U.S. Army Corps Commander:

"He is responsible for a large sector of a battle area, and all he must worry about in that zone is fighting. He must be a man of great flexibility of mind, for he may be fighting six divisions one day and one division the next as the higher commanders transfer divisions to and from his corps. He must be a man of tremendous physical stamina, too, for his battle zone may cover a front of one hundred miles or more, with a depth of fifty to sixty miles, and by plane and jeep he must cover this area, day and night, anticipating where the hardest fighting is to come, and being there in person, ready to help his division commanders in any way he can."

General Gerow exemplified an archetypical Corps Commander. He embraced his duty. He was not upset that he did not command an army. He was confident in his abilities and knew where his key strengths lay. Gerow was a true team player and understood that his reward would be the liberation of Europe.

Zhukov at the Ready

Marshall of the Soviet Union Georgi Zhukov was at his best. Like the Battle of Berlin his preparations for the final assault on the British and NATO lines were proceeding apace. Again, he would do whatever it takes to crush the enemy, even if it meant absorbing tremendous casualties.

The reinforcements from Spain of two Tank Armies greatly enhanced his offensive capabilities. His supplies and air cover had finally caught up with his fast-moving tank armies. The additional squadrons of ground attack aircraft were just what he needed to decisively rid the Middle East of the British Empire. Their historical meddling in the region caused massive suffering of the local populace. Soon the world would be purged of the British lion and all it stood for.

He was already blessed with large formations of his favorite weapon, the Queen of the Battlefield, artillery. He had cannon and rocket battalions in abundance but lately there had been a shortage of ammunition and fuel to transport them. The biggest guns and most devastating rocket launchers are useless if you can't move them or provide the shells and rockets to fire.

Figure 7- Scores of Incoming Katyusha Rockets

The Stavka rightfully chose to isolate the American incursion to Trieste and Vienna. Having to divert around the NATO troops added significantly to the travel time from Spain but it was manageable.

An assault on the Americans in Vienna would have been disastrous. The Stavka and Stalin had made the correct decision by not playing into the Amerikosi's game. Let NATO waste all their naval resources on Trieste and Vienna while he closed the Suez Canal once and for all.

Zhukov was informed the Bagramyan was getting bloodied in Kuwait. The British colonial troops were putting up a stiff resistance. The oil fields of Kuwait were seen by the Stavka as a bonus. Capturing the fields was not a necessity because much of the supplies and reinforcements had gone to his forces instead of Bagramyan. The added combat units came with new threats and serious consequences if he did not perform. It reminded him of the race to finish the Nazis in Berlin. He was able to win that battle. Now he was determined to break the British lines and march on Cairo.

He was proceeding with unusual haste on this final phase of his offensive. He was assured by Intelligence Services that the Amerikosi had used up the majority of their amphibious forces invading Trieste and Vienna. Zhukov decided it was of the essence to take advantage of NATOs current lack of resources.

If he thought the American Navy could launch an invasion similar to Anzio in his rear, he would strengthen the defenses of his supply lines. The use of paratroopers and fast moving amphibious had dramatically changed the Art of War. Oh, how he would love the resources to suddenly appear in the enemy's rear as Americans and Brits had done time after time.

His second in command, Vassiliev, came in and disrupted his thoughts.

"Excuse me for interrupting you sir, there is unusual naval activity off the Egyptian coast. We have multiple reports of nine NATO aircraft carriers observed steaming east."

"Were there any amphibious forces spotted as well"?

"Nothing had been reported, Marshall."

"How many aircraft can nine American carriers support Vassiliev?"

"Each can carry up to 100 I believe sir."

"That would mean an additional 900 planes maximum would be added to the British defenses. Is my thinking logical Vassiliev?"

"As always Marshall."

"We have received how many additional aircraft in the last two weeks?"

"I believe close to 1200, Marshall."

"So our advantage in the air might be marginalized. The estimate of the British planes was 800 while we now have over 3400. With the additional American planes we still have a decided advantage, but the report is disturbing none the less. The Amerikosi do not put their carriers in harm's way on a whim. My instincts tell me to be cautious.

Contact Beria on my personal orders, and ascertain if there is any possibility of Yankee amphibious forces appearing in my rear. If he is not 100% certain that the American navy is incapable of supporting another invasion, then I must take measures to guard my supply lines. We will then have to postpone the assault on the Suez. Is your assignment clear Vassiliev?"

"Yes Marshall, of course."

"Go!"

"Yes Marshall."

Beria's Rage

Lavrenti Pavlovich Beria had just finished terrorizing a 12-year-old girl named Soya Slavski. He decided not to rape her but still wanted the thrill of hearing her scream. He loved the high-pitched screams of little girls. Even as a child he enjoyed scaring and hurting his sisters and cousins.

In any other society, he would have been executed or killed by an outraged father or brother long ago, perhaps as early as 14. His first assault was a gypsy girl. Luckily for him the gypsies treated their women almost as badly as he had treated that child. His father was able to pay for the experience with cash instead of Beria's blood.

Beria's behavior as a young boy was a precursor of the heinous creature he would become. He was always seeking out and planning more and more gruesome and, for him, exciting ways to terrorize women. The more beautiful the victim, the more pleasure he experienced. Woe the pretty girl who caught his eye. His only regret about why he used women and increasingly girls, was that he could only rape and kill them once. Beria would have liked to have kept a "collection" of his victims but he always got carried away and ended up killing them. He had a need to experience that final thrill of taking another's life and watching their eyes turn from terror to dead.

Now, Beria was the second most powerful man in the world. If he wanted a woman, he just took her. If her father or husband started to cause trouble, he had them killed. Only Nazi Germany or the USSR, both home to the greatest mass murderers of all time, had the capacity to so easily overlook such diabolical behavior in their leaders.

Beria's aide brought him another report on an invasion by the Amerikosi near the border of Yugoslavia and Italy in the oft-contested city of Trieste. Why there, he thought. There is nothing there or even near there of military or even political value. This Tito character must be seeing bies under his bed.[3] The little shit probably sleeps with a loaded gun. Beria never liked the people now called Yugoslavians. He been taught that they were all subhuman and impossible to tame. However, they are good allies always willing to do your dirty work. Let's see how they do with this little "invasion" they claim is happening. Who and why would anyone invade Trieste? I'd better find out the details just in case.

Beria motions to his aide to come closer.

"Dispose of the body in the quiet room and then get me Zhukov on the line…No wait, he thought, Zhukov is busy in the Levant.

"Get me Marshall Konev instead."

He can handle the situation in Trieste with some troops from the Pyrenees and Tito's goons. The fighting should kill a lot of Yugoslavs…less mouths to feed.

The program to exterminate great swathes of useless proletariats was under way. There was actually plenty of food to sustain life in the Soviet warehouses. It was better to have the most productive workers healthy while letting trouble makers starve.

Citizens who lived in the city and could possibly organize and riot had to be fed. Most revolutions involved large numbers of idle young men

---

[3] - A form of demon. The Early Slavs: Culture and Society in Early Medieval Eastern Europe by Paul M. Barford -Page 192.

gathering together. The fear of revolt is one of the reasons why Beria had urged Stalin to attack. What better use for idle soldiers than to die for their country. Now it was time for disloyal peasants to assist the communist struggle in the best way they could…by dying.

Beria's mind came back to Tito's whining, Beria thought he had better work on a contingency plan that involved Konev. His first thought was to just contain the invading Amerikosi forces already on the ground and let them sit there in Trieste. Who cared? He would advise Stalin and the Stavka that they should only move enough forces to contain any adventurism and wait to see what the Capitalist Pigs did next. It seemed that the whole NATO operation was a very costly enterprise.

He needed more information. His spy network had been gradually shrinking and he was utterly blind to the intentions and objectives of this operation. He would have to call forth some of his most deeply hidden moles and sleeper agents. Trieste had to be the American trash's last gambit. All the indications were that the Amerikosi could not have enough resources for additional invasions.

His aide returned too quickly to have contacted Konev.

"What is it you fool? Do you have Konev on the phone or not?"

"Sorry Marshall."

"I told you not to call me that."

"I…what…Sorry Marshall…err sir…."

"SILENCE! Now tell me what it is that you have risked your life for."

"But sir…I…yes sir. Marshall Zhukov's second in command Vassiliev is on the phone and demanded to talk to you in person…Sir."

Beria was beside himself with rage. How dare that buffoon and bully Zhukov command me! And to use Vassiliev is beyond an insult. Demanded did he! I will get him in my chair soon, along with Vassiliev, for this insult.

The aide is standing there in stunned silence watching with terror as Lavrenti Beria visibly tries to control his rage. He almost faints as Beria's eyes finally focus again looking straight at him.

"Sir…What should I do?"

Once again Beria is lost in just what he is going to do to his aide once he deals with Vassiliev and Zhukov. You will beg me to kill you. That's what you are going to do, keeps racing through his mind.

Finally Beria speaks to the visibly trembling aide.

"Leave the room and transfer the call to me. Don't say another word. Just go."

The aide almost says "Yes Sir" but catches himself in time and runs out of Beria's office.

The conversation between Vassiliev and Beria and then with Zhukov himself is not recorded. Later Beria relieved his rage by strapping his aide to his favorite chair. The aide died rather quickly. However, he did last long enough to calm Beria down, and that prevented Lavrenti from doing something stupid involving Zhukov.

Zhukov remained confident that the Americans still had the capacity to invade despite Beria's rabid insistence to the contrary. He was unable to allay Zhukov's concerns of a possible strike against his supply line. Zhukov stated that he was going to postpone the attack against the British on the Suez Canal and strengthen his defenses.

Beria would have traveled through the phone lines and attacked the fool if at all possible. Instead he used his aide's life as a tool to remain in control. He was so infuriated and enraged that Zhukov would question his sources and statements regarding the Amerikosi. Who was he to doubt the powers of Lavrenti Beria?

After his session with his aide, he was sufficiently in control of his anger towards Zhukov to appear sane. He called for his car and went directly to Stalin's dacha. He was very pleased with the results of his visit.

Pattern Recognition

Sergo was in his office when his thoughts suddenly turned to a report he just received from England. It was from Cairncross via Beria regarding a man named Alan Turing. Sergo was very anxious to meet the great man. He understood from Beria that a plan was in place to bring Turing to Moscow. Hopefully, it would not involve violence. He really hated physical confrontation and did not wish it on anyone.

Sergo had been watching Turing through the eyes of Cairncross for years. Cairncross had become as close a friend to Turing as there will ever be.

Sergo had plans to merge the Lalleri gypsies with their unusual skills and Turing's unlimited imagination. With these gypsies as his minions, Alan Turing could create a whole new way of interacting with machines. There would be no stopping the cause of Communism if you combined the resources that Sergo offered with the mind of Turing and the gypsies' abilities.

The irony was that the gypsies had skills that were almost totally useless in today's society. They weren't strong, talented, or more intelligent than your average person. In fact this group ranked well below average in every measurable test administered by Sergo.

He read about a man named Charles Babbage who used cards with holes punched in them to control a machine.[4] Some years later, Ada Lovelace showed how to use this language to compute symbols as well as numbers. Ada had written a "program" to calculate a sequence of Bernoulli numbers using Babbage's Analytical Machine.[5]

Sergo foresaw a future where analytical machines, or computers, would alter the way humans interacted with each other, with the world and eventually the universe.

Just yesterday he had seen cameras that sent remote images to an electronic screen miles away. The engineers achieved this feat by creating a unique language based on numbers.[6]

His tests revealed that the whole tribe excelled in a type of pattern recognition. Sergo was convinced that their singular skill would lead to turning a mathematics-based language that could control a machine or even store information.

A month ago Sergo had arranged a meeting with the defectors Joel Barr and Alfred Sarant. The pair had clandestinely shipped millions of crystal diodes, resistors, capacitors and vacuum tubes from the US to the Soviet Union before they defected. All three were in agreement that the electronic parts they had acquired could be combined to make a super calculating machine. Alan Turing was exactly the man to make their dream a reality.

Only Sergo knew about the gypsies and their specific talents. It would

---

[4] - Charles Babbage: Pioneer of the Computer by Anthony Hyman
[5] - A Female Genius: How Ada Lovelace Lord Byron's Daughter, Started the Computer Age by James Essinger
[6] - The History of Television, 1942 to 2000 by Albert Abramson

be his secret until Turing was in hand.

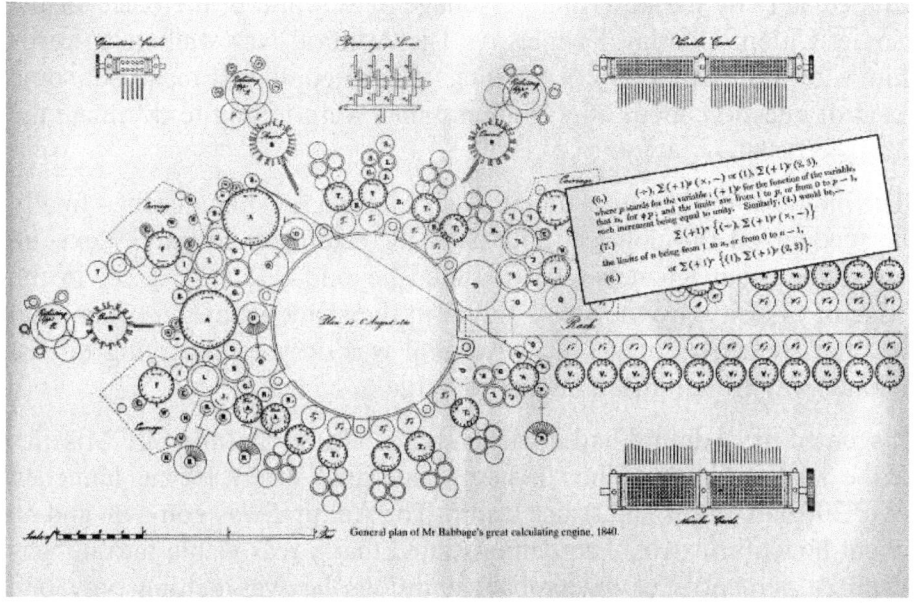

Figure 8 - Babbage's Machine and Ada's math

Stalin Calls

Any normal human being would have been scared out of his mind. Sergo was far from ordinary. He had trouble feeling emotion. He was not in the least bit concerned by his summons to appear before Stalin. His mind did register irritation at being interrupted and forced to leave his office and go to Stalin's dacha. During the half hour ride the grim NKVD agents said nothing, which was just fine with Sergo. He kept his mind busy with the usual puzzles and conundrums that occupied most of his waking hours. It was irrelevant to Sergo that his challenges involved running a huge military and industrial empire. The endless puzzles and their solutions kept him engaged, and as a result, the Red Army supplied.

It was apparent to most in the Soviet ruling elite that Stalin's irrational behavior was continuing to escalate as the Third World War progressed. His senseless actions never concerned Sergo as his brain was not wired to consider such issues.

Now, it might be his time to face the ultimate fate that millions had suffered under Stalinism. Only the increasingly damaged synapses of the brain of one Joseph Stalin would decide his fate. Sergo could be one mini stroke away from torture and death.

He was finally escorted into Stalin's inner sanctum and was confronted immediately by the imposing personage of Admiral of the Fleet for the Soviet Union, Nikolay Kuznetsov. The Admiral was walking towards him screaming at the top of his lungs. Sergo could just make out some kind of question about why "his" missiles were failing to decimate the Yankee fleets.

The illogic of the situation took him aback for a few minutes then finally he recognized the political and survival techniques at play. Next, he understood that Kuznetsov was scared beyond reason. Scared, to the edge of insanity, by the small figure in the shadows of the office who had not spoken as of yet. The Admiral was desperately trying to cast blame away from himself and on to Sergo.

It seemed the Admiral had launched his modified Stalin's Fire Missiles at the Yankee navy and they had only a marginal effect. He had launched over 200 and only 2 had struck a ship. The Admiral was going on and on about how all his tests had demonstrated that a reasonable hit rate was over 20 percent. Yet in combat conditions he was getting only one percent.

Kuznetsov alleged that the dismal hit rate had to be the fault of Sergo's guidance system. Sergo thought, Logically the Admiral was probably correct. I have to quiet him down enough to collect the data needed to make the proper adjustments. The man was clearly scared into irrationality and this was just unacceptable. I have to do something to halt this harangue and make some actual progress in solving the puzzle.

Sergo finally spoke and address Stalin, not the Admiral.

"Your Excellency, please make this man stop shouting. I suggest that you assure him that if he cooperates and gives me the facts that I need, he will not be harmed."

The little figure finally stirred and started to move out of the shadows. A calm, yet very menacing voice, addressed the nearly comatose Admiral.

"Kuznetsov, call in your aide. He has the facts and observations that Sergo requires."

Kuznetsov starts to stammer.

"Comrade Stalin I assure you that I have all the knowledge needed to…."

The now visible personage of Stalin leans just a little closer to the Admiral. In that instant the Admiral understands what he must do and rushes out to find his second in command. No one else moves or says a word. The world's most powerful lunatic and the chief architect of his success, stand in silence.

The Admiral hurries into the room practically dragging a junior officer and starts to stammer again. Just a glance from Stalin shuts down the beginnings of the tirade that was sure to follow. Sergo does not wait for permission and begins to question the Admiral's aide. He covers all manner of subjects. He is particularly interested in the anecdotal evidence collected to date on the missiles' performance.

The junior officer is surprisingly collected and lays out a rather clear picture of what has been reported. A daring pilot had gone over one of the American convoys in a MiG 9 Soviet jet fighter. The pilot did not encounter US jets and easily outran the propeller driven Corsairs sent to intercept him.

He observed a volley of missiles flying over the convoy. They appeared to ignore the Amerikosi ships below. They flew directly above a number of large transports and continued on. The MiG pilot did observe two hits. A smaller vessel was struck amid ships and sank in a manner of minutes. A second missile slammed into a freighter passing right through the whole ship without exploding. The device detonated only after it exited the other side of the ship.

The Admiral started to accuse Sergo of all sorts of various incompetence's and errors in designing the Stalin's Fire Missile. Sergo weathered the repeated attacks until Stalin cleared his throat and Kuznetsov realized that his accusations bordered on absurdity. Sergo ignored the Admiral and continued to question the junior officer.

After about five minutes of seemingly random questions, Sergo's calm manner and queries stopped when the aid mentioned that a number of Soviet pilots had reported very odd paint schemes on most Amerikosi ships. They were painted in very peculiar geometric patterns that were very easy to see from a distance. Sergo asked if any of the Babushka mini-subs or ground forces had mentioned this odd paint scheme. The Admiral appeared to jump out of his skin answering in the affirmative. He was attempting to show Stalin about how knowledgeable he was on the subject.

Sergo ignored the outburst and asked if either of the naval officers had seen a photo or drawing that he could recount or even recreate for the group. The junior officer asked Stalin's aide to bring him a piece of paper. He began to sketch a recollection of several photos taken by a mini-sub.

Sergo studied the drawing intently. He seemed lost in thought. Finally the Admiral could not contain himself and started to bluster once again.

Sergo raised his hand and to the surprise of even the Admiral, Kuznetsov stopped talking.

Sergo immediately began to explain his theory and seemed excited to have an audience as he worked on this latest mystery.

"This pattern could have an effect on the pigeon's ability to discern the targets properly. I believe I've seen an image like this before. If my memory is correct a British artist devised this paint scheme to fool the German submarines in World War One. The designed made it extremely hard for submarine commanders to judge the distance to target and accurately aim their torpedoes.

In addition the camouflage made it difficult for naval gunners to target enemy ships with the proper range. The advent of radar made the paint scheme irrelevant for the most part. It is just possible that it has been resurrected for the purpose of fooling our guidance system.

I am led to the conclusion that the Amerikosi have discovered our secret. This is a very disturbing development."

Stalin moves closer and speaks.

"Surely you have thought of this eventuality, Sergo Peshkova, and have developed a number of alternate solutions? Within 24 hours you will present the Stavka with an effective strategy that will be implemented immediately. Have I made my self-clear Sergo Peshkova?"

###

At this point, dear reader, the spaced time continuum will once again split. One path will lead to a possible dire end for Sergo Peshkova and all that it entails for the future of the Soviet Union. Another path will once again save his life. This book follows the former path. The next in the series of World War Three 1946 - Book Five – The Red Star – Stalin's Ace In the Hole) will be another look into and alternate history and what might have been.

What if for the second time, the Navy rejects Dr. B.F. Skinners theories? Can you imagine a world where Stalin has the ultimate naval weapons system? What could that system do to the convoys that are Britain's lifeline and providing America with the raw materials it needs to wage modern war?
***

Chapter Three: The Levant

Figure 9 - Beirut, Lebanon, 1946

Utterly Ignored
Soviet Occupied Jordan

15 May 1947

He finally woke up. A man had kicked him in the head. He immediately crawled over to the person he loved and needed most in this world. He was shouting and crying. He was so upset he almost passed out from yelling so hard. Nothing he did seemed to make the slightest difference. In his haste to make himself understood, he forgot how to walk and continued crawling over to the familiar form on the floor. She was usually standing and watching him as he performed and tried to tell her what was wrong. Today she had been lying there since he last ate. He was very hungry.

He had tried his usual tricks and techniques to get her to respond but nothing worked. No one else in the house seemed to be paying attention to him as well. They were all lying about except for Poppa. He was apparently sleeping in his favorite chair but once again nothing he could do would wake him up.

His butt felt terrible and burned. That was one of the reasons he usually tried to get Momma's attention along with being hungry, in pain or just plain bored. Now he needed all three and nobody seemed to care. He tried a new word or two but even that brought no response.

Earlier, he crawled right up to Momma and said "I'm hungry" but she said nothing. She didn't even move a muscle. It was as if she hadn't heard him uttering his first sentence. He would have thought that this would have brought a huge response from someone…but again nothing from anyone.

He had started to climb the forbidden stairs, which usually brought everyone running to stop him. He shouted to let people know he was doing a no-no. Not one person came rushing over to grab him. The fact that the small gate was open at the bottom of the stairs bothered him. Most changes in the household routine flustered him.

Now everything had changed and he was very upset. To make matters worse he could not stand any more. He had fallen down the stairs after climbing them and could only drag his legs behind him. They didn't seem to work anymore. He felt no pain…they just didn't work.

The bad men had come and made loud noises scaring Momma and

pointing their sticks that shot flame. Then the man kicked him. When he woke up everyone was very quiet and he was hungry. He kept throwing up anything he found to eat for the longest time. Finally that had gone away and he could even see straight again. Everything was kind of fuzzy before that.

After all this trauma he felt tired and weak. He barely had the energy to moan or whimper anymore. He dragged himself over to Momma and put his head on her arm and tried to sleep.

Everyone smelled and there were big mice eating something off of Poppa. Everyone had pooped and peed themselves and there were flies everywhere.

He got excited when Momma seemed to move but it was something under her skin wiggling around. He played with it for a while but it escaped further into her body. He thought it was one of those white worms he had been seeing.

The only reason he was still alive was a broken pipe leaking water in the kitchen and a tin of crackers that had been ripped apart and spread around the floor.

He was too weak to cry anymore. He had no idea what was wrong. What troubled him the most was that Momma seemed not to care even when he screamed, cried and pulled on her hair.

He did not comprehend war or violence. Before today his life had been the bliss of his mother's arms. World War Three changed all that.

Eventually he fell asleep. He slept like a baby, the sleep of innocence. He never woke up.

Zhukov Gambles

The Marshal had just started to issue orders calling off the attack on the Suez Canal when his second in command, Vasily, placed him under arrest. He had just gotten off the phone explaining his reasoning to the Stavka about a possible attack on his supply lines by the Amerikosi. They had not expressly forbidden him from taking defensive actions. However they insisted that he attack as planned. He had chosen to ignore that last order.

Vasily Sokolovsky must have been listening in on the conversation and reported to the Stavka the minute he started to call off the attack. Vasily had tears in his eyes as he ordered his arrest. Zhukov immediately and publicly forgave his friend. Unlike Zhukov, Sokolovsky was just doing as ordered.

The Marshal was stoic as he was led in handcuffs out of his headquarters and driven to the airfield to be placed on a transport. Protests would not alleviate his current predicament. The plane had just landed and Konev was just getting off. They exchanged looks and he thought he saw a hint of compassion and even admiration in Alexander's steady gaze.

A forbidden bit of text from Shakespeare kept running through his thoughts "My pride fell with my fortunes." He could be denounced for reading Shakespeare as well as disobeying orders.

He remained convinced that he made the correct assessment of the situation. He could see in Konev's gaze that Alexander also understood the danger lurking off shore. He had never thought before of using Konev's first name. Yet here he was seeing him for possibly the last time and thinking of him in the familiar.

Ironically only the Amerikosi could exonerate him by attacking as he predicted. If he were strapped to Beria's chair, he would both dread and welcome an American invasion. Such an attack would mean a massive defeat for his former command. Yet, if his precautions proved correct he might be saved.

Before he was escorted out of the headquarters he had overheard Vasily countermanding his last set of orders. If the Amerikosi attacked, nothing could help Alexander Konev and the Soviet Levant Front. An immense defeat was sure to follow.

The Barrage
The ferocity of the barrage came as no surprise to the NATO units on the banks of the Suez Canal. However, it was the duration that shook then to their core. The terrain in the Pyrenees Mountains had made massive concentrations of guns extremely hard for the Soviets to engineer. Consequently, even veterans of the Pyrenees Line had never seen such a show of pure, raw power.

Here on the flat, hard sands of the Sinai the Soviets were able to do what they do best. And, that is gathering heavy artillery and rocket batteries and aiming them at their enemies.

Not since World War One had the British and Americans experienced the devastation that hours of shelling from thousands of heavy artillery guns can create. The Germans experienced this type of concentrated fire power many times on the Eastern Front in World War Two. The current generation of NATO soldiers were experiencing it for the first time.

Within 12 hours of the attack commencing, a bridgehead had been established over the Suez Canal by a Soviet regimental sized unit. The Reds were withstanding all counter attacks by the British 8th Army. The British forces were fighting as if their country's future depended upon the outcome. As far as the Tommies knew this would be the deciding battle of World War Three. They were desperate in their attempts to throw the Reds back across the canal.

The Soviet forces in the bridgehead felt the same. In their minds, this was going to be the battle that would end the war. Once they reached Cairo they would be victorious and could finally go home. But first the Suez Canal had to be crossed and then held.

Many a soldier had been unable to aim or shoot his gun with any effectiveness due to sheer enervation and trauma. The fighting was reduced to hand to hand combat on the Western shores of the canal. The Soviet troops were exhausted by crossing the 300 -meter -wide canal. They were met by British soldiers shell shocked from 152 mm projectiles detonating in near proximity to their bodies.

Konev was true to his word and threw his forces into the battle in ever increasing numbers. He was behaving a crazed loader blindly feeding bullets into a wrecked machine gun. Bullets were hitting dirt and air while the men were being wasted. Eventually the sheer mass of Soviet attackers began to overwhelm the severely stretched British lines.

The hours long Soviet barrage had torn gaps in the British communications network. An isolated sector was unable to communicate its dire predicament. For the first time in his long military career Montgomery was totally unaware of the danger his forces were facing.

The much -needed reinforcements were not sent and units of the 2nd Guards Tamanskaya Motor Rifle Division poured across the Suez Canal stepping on the dead bodies of the overwhelmed reconstituted British 7th Motor Brigade. The Second Battalion also known as the Sherwood Foresters took the brunt of the casualties. The Sherwood Foresters took three times their number of Soviets to their graves, but in the end, it was not enough.

After the Soviet forces crossed the canal they quickly organize their defenses before Montgomery knew the true situation. By the time he was able to send the proper reinforcements it was too late and the Soviets had secured the bridgehead.

Monty was preparing to pull back to a second line of defense when word reached him of the landings in Lebanon. He was relieved to hear that the enemy supply lines were cut but upset that he had not been informed of the operation planned by the Americans.

The backbones of the British troops significantly stiffened once they learned of the American invasion of Beirut. Almost immediately the psychological warfare units of Montgomery's command started broadcasting propaganda to the Soviet troops designed to inform them of their dire situation. For the first few days the broadcasts seem to be ignored and the Reds continued to advance. The reality of the situation started to sink in when the fuel and bullets ran out. Finally, the Soviet troops resolve started to erode.

If the Americans had not invaded Lebanon the Soviets would have been in Cairo in a matter of weeks. Zhukov's prediction was ultimately realized. The fortunes of war had decided on another ending for Konev's Levant Front. It would not be his destiny to march triumphantly into Cairo.

NATO Dodges a Bullet

Communications Room

Mediterranean Theater Command

18 May 1947

"Jones, get over here quick. Take this message to Headquarters and insist that it can only be delivered to Ike or George Marshall himself. I heard that Marshall is visiting the front."

Private Jones answers "Yes sir." and leaves the room.

Major Craig Yost leans over and pokes the other communications officer in the room, Lieutenant Bill Henderson.

Yost comments, "I like that Jones never asks questions."

The Lieutenant answers then remarks that "He doesn't have to. He knows everything that comes out of the teletype just by listening to the sounds of the keys."

"No shit."

"No shit. It's amazing to watch. He demonstrated for me. He can recognize the vowels and a few of the major consonants when the keys hit the paper and our Model 15 teletype is not very fast."

"Well I'll be damned. That may be a breach of security. Still an impressive skill and demonstration of initiative. I'll need you to write up a report just in case.

"Ah, Craig, he told me what the last one said before you sent him on his way. Am I in trouble?"

The senior officer's demeanor changed immediately as he looked at his friend and colleague and spoke after a long pause.

"I don't know Bill, I really don't know. What did he say exactly?"

"Listen, Craig it was just harmless gossip. We didn't mean anything by it."

"Let's not get ahead of ourselves Lieutenant! Now tell me exactly what he said! Is that understood?"

"Sure it is Craig, err Major Yost. I completely understand.

He said that NATO had just dodged a bullet when some Soviet Marshal named Konev replaced another guy named Zhukov. Apparently this Zhukov guy had guessed right about our impending attack. He was sending out orders to fortify Beirut and the surrounding area, and was starting to pull back from the Suez Canal. He smelled a rat and had sniffed out our plan to land behind him.

We were lucky Zhukov was replaced by this Konev guy. Otherwise our troops landing in a reinforced Lebanon might have faced a blood bath. It looks like our plan will work. That was just about the gist of the message."

"How exactly did we know of this development?"

"According to Jones, we have broken the Red's code."

"Is that what he told you?"

"Yes."

"Listen very carefully Lieutenant. I am not going to deny or confirm

Jones'…version of that highly classified message and what you just told me. I want you to transfer Jones as far away from that teletype as you can and I mean within the next 10 minutes. Then you will wait for me back at our barracks. You will speak to no one. If anyone asks you will say that you are sick and are not to be disturbed on my orders. Is that perfectly clear Lieutenant Henderson?"

"Yes, Sir."

"Off the record Bill, I really don't know what I'm going to do about this. I know both of you are loyal Americans and would do nothing to betray your country or this unit. But I have to cover my ass as well. I'm going to pose a hypothetical question to Major Quincy of G2. Depending on his answer I will decide what to do next.

You are dismissed and will go to your room in the barracks after transferring Jones. You will be under house arrest. I will try and keep this off your record Bill, but I can't promise anything.

Now do you understand your orders, Lieutenant Henderson?"

"Yes, Sir, Major Yost, Sir."

Konev Commits

Alexander Konev was on his way to the Headquarters of the Red Army Levant Front. He had been ordered to relieve his arch rival Ivan Zhukov. He relished the task. From what he understood Zhukov had done the unimaginable, he defied Stalin. He did not know the details but would find them out soon enough. Zhukov had thrown away all of the victories, all the metals and all the glory in one stupid decision that will probably cost him his life.

Konev was not going to make the same mistake. He was going to follow orders and attack with all his resources. His opponents were the NATO forces arrayed on the Suez Canal. This action was Zhukov's mandate and he had chosen not to follow orders from the Stavka.

He was exceedingly jealous when Zhukov was given the majority of heavy artillery and armor along with squadrons of heavy ground attack planes. These weapons had been denied him and he was relegated to containing the Amerikosi in Trieste and Vienna. Now he could use all of Zhukov's modern weaponry to drive the enemy forces from the Middle East.

His plan was simple, attack, attack, attack. In his race with Zhukov to capture Berlin, both Marshalls used men's lives like a machine gun uses bullets, 90 in every 100 is wasted. This fight would be similar and would be won by sheer numbers of Soviet soldiers. Chief Marshal of Aviation Alexander Novikov had personally assured him that the addition of the American carrier planes would have no effect on the Red Air Force's ability to rule the skies over the battlefield.

The rumor was Zhukov believed that the appearance of these aircraft carriers was a telltale sign that the Americans were planning something in his rear. Konev secretly thought that Zhukov might be correct, but the threat of Beria's chair was enough to ignore that possibility.

Konev's personal assessment suggested there was a 50/50 chance that the Amerikosi could mount another amphibious assault to cut off his supply lines. However, there was a 100% chance that he would end up arrested like Zhukov if he did not attack within days of his assuming command.

His plane landed and Zhukov was unceremoniously escorted on before he could exit. They didn't say a word. Both men knew that their fates could change within hours depending upon the Stavka and Stalin. They did make eye contact and Zhukov was defiant which Konev admired. Ivan had to know what was in store for him at the end of his long journey. He was sure the journey would not be long enough for Zhukov. If he were Ivan he would wish the trip would be endless.

He was driven to the headquarters facility. It was a modest apartment building in Bir El Malhi, Egypt. It was far enough inland that they did not have to worry about the American battleships shelling them. Good choice of locations, he thought. Zhukov was not his equal but very close to it.

The first thing he did was to send Zhukov's second in command to a frontline unit. He was sure that Vasily Sokolovsky was the one who had informed on Zhukov. He had heard that they were good friends but in the empire of Stalin there was no such thing as friendship. Friends got you killed.

Next he set about reversing many of Zhukov's orders Ivan had given before his arrest. He discovered that Vasily had already negated most of them and was impressed, but not enough to trust the man. He looked around and saw many officers watching him with distaste. The same sentiment would have been true if Zhukov had replaced him. As long as they followed orders and did not think about contacting the Stavka he was comfortable with their hate.

He gave a rousing and threatening speech about the need to attack in 48 hours before the enemy could strengthen its defenses further. He warned exactly what would happen to anyone who dared disobey orders or contact higher command. All communications were to go through the proper channels or he would personally shoot any transgressors.

When he asked if they completely understood every officer had nodded in the affirmative. He then ordered all units forward and prepare to attack in what was now 47 hours at 0400 17 May 1947.

Pain and Vindication

Lavrenti Beria's favorite room was inside Lubyanka Prison, there he was about to start his second assault on Georgy Zhukov's body. The first had been rather mild by Beria's standards and Zhukov was missing all of his fingernails on his left hand before he passed out. Beria was disappointed. He thought that the tough talking Marshal would have been able to stand more pain considering how much he inflicted upon his enemies and the men he led.

No matter he was a patient man.

Suddenly the door to the room banged open and a contingent of Stalin's own body guards seized Beria before he could offer protest. He was bound and gagged before Zhukov's now open eyes. The Marshal was having trouble believing what he was seeing and thought he was still unconscious.

One of the same guards undid Zhukov's handcuffs and told him to go home. As he stumbled outside there was a car waiting and somehow, he made it into the back seat with the help of the driver. As he was being driven away he saw the inert form of Lavrenti Beria being put into another car.

Just as Zhukov was about to turn away, there was an explosion. His driver accelerated from the area with an alarming disregard for life and limb.

Zhukov found his voice and demanded to be taken back to find out the fate of Beria but the driver didn't acknowledge the Marshall's outburst. Without hesitation or comment he drove directly to Zhukov's Moscow home. His wife was home and Georgy Zhukov's body could not function further. He was carried to his room. His wife Alexandra put him in bed.

Beria's Endgame

There had not been an explosion at Lubyanka prison since the Bolshevik Revolution. Two of Stalin's men were incapacitated immediately the other two were stunned. Beria's second in command calmly walked up and firing a pistol shot all four guards in the head.

He then got in the car with Beria in the back seat, and drove off to location unknown. Beria had known that this day would come and had an elaborate endgame to save his life and those who assisted him. His place of hiding had been well chosen. If need be a plastic surgeon was waiting to alter his features. As planned, a well-choreographed propaganda machine started spreading the word that Stalin was gravely ill.

Nine months ago, Beria had a very secret and special prison built. It was for the sons and daughters of highly placed NKVD leaders. Within 24 hours his loyal followers had abducted 29 young progenies of these officials.

A whole new dimension in blackmail and manipulation was created once he began using his hostages to extort the parents. In the resulting chaos the manhunt for Lavrenti Beria was poorly executed.

After 48 hours, what was said to be his badly burned body was pulled out of a house about three hours' drive from Lubyanka prison. The shootout had been elaborately staged. A man who bore a striking resemblance to Beria was inside tied to a post. The sacrificial man died of smoke inhalation and third -degree burns.

Two doctors, three senior ranking NKVD officials and a member of the Politburo, all certified that the body was indeed Lavrenti Beria. The body's fingers and toes were burned off in the fire thus eliminating any possible finger print identification.

Unbeknownst to Beria, Stalin was truly in grave health. In Stalin's stead Nikita Khrushchev, Molotov and Malenkov ordered Beria's arrest.

The opportunity presented itself after Zhukov was proved correct and the 350,000 troops of the Levan Front were trapped along with Marshall of the Soviet Union Ivan Konev. Exactly as predicted by Zhukov, the Amerikosi landed a force in Lebanon cutting off Konev's supply lines and means of escape.

Konev bravely fought to the end. You can't bring a knife to a gunfight and expect to win. In his arrogance, Beria had uncharacteristically failed to see the threat to Konev's forces.

After he woke and cleared his head, Beria was shocked when informed that Zhukov was vindicated and that the Amerikosi had attacked Lebanon. He knew almost immediately that NATO had broken the Soviet code. It was the only explanation he deemed possible for his failure.

At once he set about smearing Konev and Zhukov.

Step two was to gruesomely and very publicly assassinate Khrushchev, Molotov and Malenkov.

Step three was to poison Stalin.

Step four was to rise from the dead.

Operation Cutoff
Off the Coast of Beirut, Lebanon

18 May 1947

The NATO attack on Beirut began as dozens of other American led invasions had. Instant mayhem was generated with a devastating naval barrage and fighter bomber attacks. The intelligence gathered on the region was excellent. They correctly determined that the Soviets had not fortified their rear areas. The first Marine Division waded ashore against very light opposition. Within hours they started to spread out and occupy defensive positions facing south in the area around the initial beachhead.

The Soviet units in the area were third tier. They were basically administrative troops, supply units and soldiers recovering from wounds suffered in combat. The Red troops in the vicinity of the invasion sites were overrun in a matter of hours. Beirut fell in less than 6 hours. The surviving Soviet soldiers that escaped retreated to the northeast.

General Leonard Gerow, leading the V Corps, was on shore within 4 hours of the commencement of the invasion. He was a man of firsts. He was the first Corps Commander ashore on 6 June 1944 and was the first American Major General to enter Paris after its liberation.

Included in Gerow's corps were a number of units that had been languishing in Trieste and Vienna. Combat there was minimal. He requested that the now underused veteran forces be added to his command. He specifically wanted their expertise leading his initial assault force.

The two soldiers known as "The Combat Savants" and their company were among the added troops. Phil Post and Warren Johnston were in the first boat of the V Corps. Phil was now the Sergeant of the 3rd Platoon and Warren was a corporal with Lieutenant William Grupe commanding.

Within two days, 10 full American divisions had landed and were pushing towards Baghdad. The defensive line had been formed facing south assuming a response from Marshall Konev. The Soviet forces had been cutoff in the Levant and were now rushing north in an attempt to break out of the trap.

The Soviets were moving with astonishing speed. They made their first attempt at breaking the NATO lines on 20 May 1947. It was a surprise attack minus the usual massive barrage of shells and rockets. It almost caught the defending American forces unprepared.

Defending at the point of the enemy attack was General Charles H. Gerhardt directing the US 29th Division. He was an experienced combat commander. Also he was one of the most controversial figures in the European Theater during World War Two. His division in that war, had the highest casualty rate. It was said that he commanded three divisions, "one on the field of battle, one in the hospital and one in the cemetery."[7]

Gerhardt did a masterful job of using his reserves and plugging holes in his lines as they appeared. Although the first attempt failed it was a closer fight than anyone anticipated. The Red Army units were desperate to escape and they knew that time was not on their side.

The next breakout attempt was even more ferocious and costly to both sides. Konev's fighters were within a kilometer of freedom when three battleships of the Royal Navy appeared over the horizon and shelled the advancing Soviet units. The British had always been known for their accurate gunnery. At the behest of General Gerhardt they poured it on and caught many a Red in the open.

The shells came from an unexpected direction, the seemingly empty sea to the West. The V Corps was shelling the enemy from the North and the Royal Navy from the West. Both were using the VT fuse to deadly effect.

---

[7] - Beyond the Beachhead: The 29th Infantry Division in Normandy By Joseph Balkoski

The timed fuses exploded over the heads of the Soviet soldiers spraying them with lethal shrapnel shredding any hope of escape.

Ivan Stepanovich Konev, winner of the Order of Lenin, Order of the Bath, Legion of Merit and Hero of the Soviet Union was seen leading the final charge. A 15-inch shell from the HMS Queen Elizabeth exploded within 2 meters of his last known position, leaving only a red mist where the Marshal had been seconds before.

Figure 10 - Ivan Stepanovich Konev

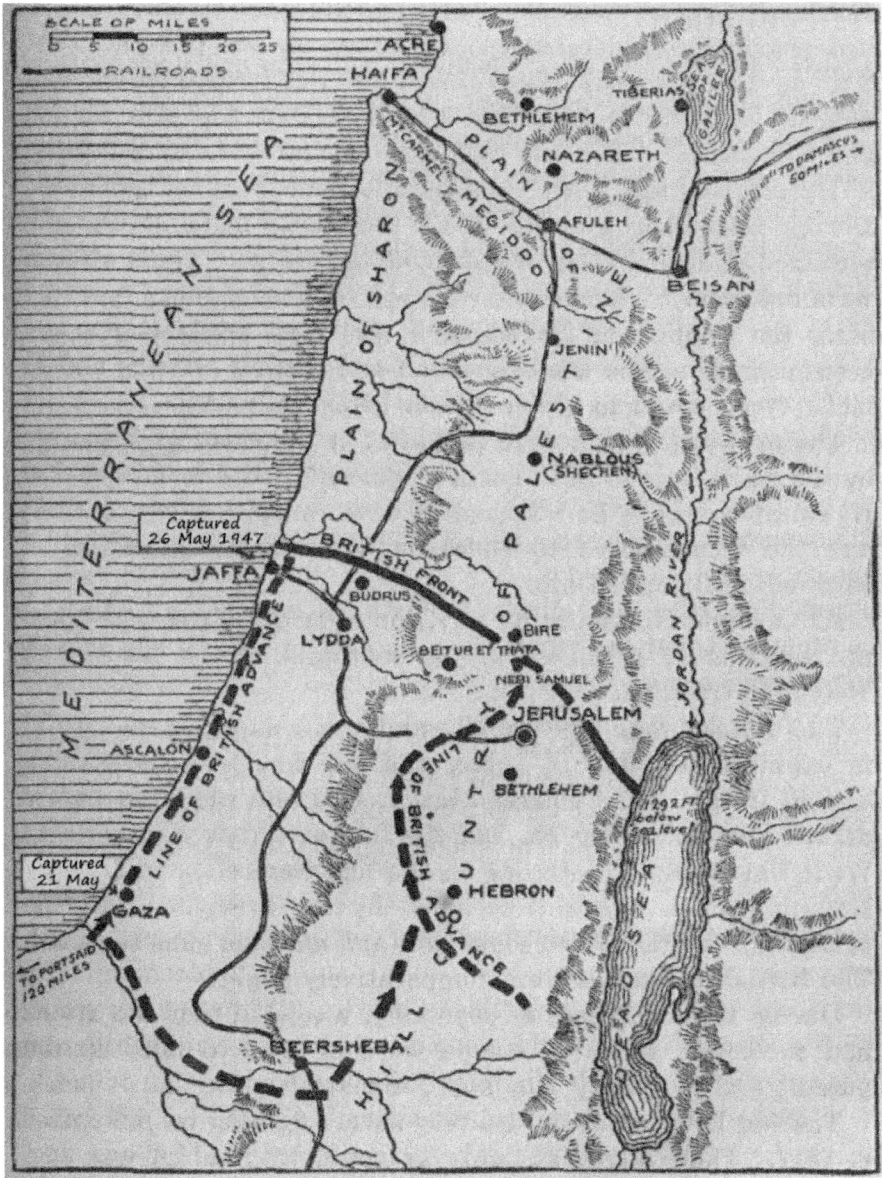

Figure 11- British Breakout May 1947

Premeditation

Neither Phil nor Warren was enamored with their new leadership roles. Both missed the days when they were independent wholesalers of death. Phil was still bothered by his only personal kill. He made himself indispensable by crafting his own ambushes and circumventing ones devised by the Reds. He had a gift for thinking like the enemy and was a master at what he called "double jeopardy."

His initial explosive devices were simple. He would setup a fairly easily discovered booby trap or obvious ruse. After disarming the first mechanism the enemy would usually let their guard down, that's when Phil's evil genius and creativity really kicked into high gear. Sometimes double and even triple acts of havoc occurred shortly after the initial contact.

Phil would setup Rube Goldberg type contraptions that would roll grenades down drain pipes a few minutes after the first trip wire was disarmed. At the same time he might have Claymore Mines arm themselves behind the group when another grenade rolled into their trigger mechanism.

He used Limpet mines, TNT, C4 and Bouncing Bettys. He incorporated various forms of pencil detonators such as the Lead Delay, Percussion Ignitor and his particular favorite the Number Ten Delay Switch in his bombs. His creativity knew no bounds and the Soviets soon recognized his work and put a bounty on his head.

Warren was on the edge of being out of control. Phil had used up all his options to prevent Warren from killing at least three of his fellow Americans in the last 30 days. One of the targets of his murderous anger was the current Captain of the company. Phil had confronted Warren as he lay in wait armed with a garrote. Post had talked him out of attacking the Captain but he was not confident that he could continue to stop Warren from carrying out one of his planned "revenge" killings.

It seems that Warren's fame had gone to his head. He violently resented anyone who dared to limit his actions. In his mind he was winning the war all by himself. How could anyone dare question one of the publicly named Savants of Combat was beyond his comprehension?

He only listened to Phil because he was an equal partner in their success and his only friend. In Warren's way of thinking, the captain was a 90 Day Wonder and not worthy of command and especially of commanding him. Phil's intervention the previous night, had only postpone the inevitable. The Captain would die and soon.

In the meantime, he and Phil did their jobs as only they could. He was exceedingly grateful for Phil's friendship. Where he used brute force and the instincts of a killer, Phil was smart and sneaky. They eliminated the enemy in numbers that were astounding to anyone reading the reports.

Phil's methods were the only thing that scared Warren more than the nightmares of his father's beatings. He was awestruck by Phil's evil genius and Phil was staggered by Warren's capacity for violence.

For his part, Phil knew the day was coming when he could no longer control Warren. It would come down to who would kill whom first. To Phil, the most troubling part was if he used his usual methods his plan would be premeditated. Premeditation is one of the prerequisites for first degree murder.

In contrast, Warren would almost assuredly act out of instant rage. He would be guilty of an act of passion and one could argue that he was insane. Phil on the other hand would have to be totally sane to succeed.

On 21 May 1947, Phil Post provoked a fight with Warren Johnson. He shot his friend in the heart with his service weapon when Warren attacked. He then cradled him in his arms until the Corporal died. Later a story was concocted about the heroic death of Corporal Warren Johnson while leading a counter-attack against overwhelming odds.

No charges were brought against Sergeant Phil Post.

Post disappeared from his unit on 29 May 1947.

He was said to have joined a Turkish unit and continued to kill Soviets. The last reported sighting was in Albania in late 1947. His body was never recovered and there was no report of him being seen alive again.

Chapter Four: Inland

Figure 12- The waters of the Tigris provide both an obstacle and opportunity. Reed boats and floating bridges make crossing possible and a source of revenue.

Tanks for the Memories

Fortunately for infantry, you can hear a main battle tank from up to half a kilometer away. As a foot soldier upon hearing a tank's engine you immediately run for cover and call for help.

Both sides are now using the latest armored vehicles in their respective arsenals. The engine noise is deafening inside the hull and the crew's visibility was minimal.

The Soviets were mass producing the T54A in astounding numbers. These armored vehicles were mechanically straight forward and extremely robust. The level of education needed by the crew members to operate the tank was minimal. It had simple controls with a few easily understood gauges.

For a main battle tank they were small and very mobile thanks to their relatively light weight. Because of their size they could easily be transported by rail or flatbed truck. The tank's wide tracks gave it lower ground pressure that allowed it to cross soft ground. All were equipped with a snorkel for fast river crossings.

The T54As size presented a smaller target for its opponents to hit. Its gun was a very lethal 100 mm D-10T that could take out any NATO tank with one hit.

The tank's compact size presented a number of drawbacks that NATO was well aware of. The cramped interior and lack of a turret basket resulted in major difficulties in loading the gun quickly. Crew members were required to be under a certain height in order to mitigate the problems caused by the T54's confined space.

An undersized turret prevented the main gun from being depressed by more than 5°. This limitation prevented one of the most useful tactics available to a tank crew. The particular tactic is called the "hull down" position on a reverse slope.

Figure 13- NATO Armor Assuming the Hull Down Position

In the hull down position the only target visible was the tank's turret that was hard to hit and very well armored. A hull down tank could still visually locate and fire on any available opponent.

The T54A was easy to produce and Sergo had further sped up the process with his innovations. These tanks were reaching the battlefield in ever increasing numbers and were a force to be reckoned with.

Figure 14- Soviet Column of T-54 Tanks

The Americans and most of her NATO allies had adopted the M-50 Patton Main Battle Tank.[8] The new tank's design was based partly on the British Centurion tank that just missed action in World War Two.

Design features included a cast armored turret that easily accommodated a four-man crew. The relatively spacious interior further improved crew mobility for a faster rate of fire compared to Soviet tanks. The turret's unusually narrow forward profile dramatically reduced the penetrating ability of enemy armor piercing shells.

When assuming the hull down position a M-50 was very hard to damage or destroy. Even in the hull down position the M-50's larger turret could easily depress its gun to cover all fields of fire. Presenting a turret to the enemy was a very decided advantage.

The Patton's main armament is the 90-mm M3 gun, fitted with a muzzle break and a bore evacuator. The secondary armament is a coaxially mounted .30-caliber Browning machine gun, with a .50-caliber Browning machine gun mounted before the tank commander's hatch for use as an anti-aircraft weapon.

The engine is a Ford V-12 GAC engine, from the aborted T-29 heavy tank project. The engine is rated at about 770 horsepower. With the more powerful engine they get from 100 to 110 miles before refueling. The fuel consumption per mile is very good for such a large tank.

The Soviet T-44 Medium tank and IS-3 Super heavy tank were almost invulnerable to all but the gun of the American M-26 Pershing. The ill-fated Pershing was underpowered and had a delicate transmission that failed regularly. It could hold its own in a standup fight from a hull down position. The nearly insurmountable challenge was getting it to the battlefield in working order.

The marriage of the British Horstmann suspension, the American turret and 90-mm M3 gun in the Patton was a vast improvement over the M-26 Pershing. The M-50 heavy main battle tank could now get to the dance and mix it up with the heaviest of Soviet armor.

Being able to fully engage the enemy was a very welcome and novel situation for the American tankers. Whenever a German Tiger tank was spotted during the last war, US armor usually withdrew and called in air support. In the initial meeting engagements at the beginning of World

---

[8] - World War Three 1946 - Book One – Stalin Strikes First by Harry Kellogg III pg. 173

War Three the same tactic was repeated.

With the introduction of the M-50 Patton, the advantage now lay with the American tanker for the first time in modern warfare. Who prevailed came down to who fired accurately first. The Americans were about to make full use of the element of surprise and their increased maneuverability.

The soviets were in for a rude awakening. Both sides now could kill each other at long range. It came down who was the firstest with the mostest in a tank knife fight.

Figure 15- US M-50 Patton Main Battle Tank

The Mechanic

Bill Philips was the engineer of a LCVP or Higgins boat.[9] The LCVP was military speak for Landing Craft, Vehicle, Personnel. The boat could ferry a platoon of 36 men, or a jeep and a dozen men.

Before the war Bill's main activity was the same as the Higgins boat, both worked for bootleggers. The repeal of prohibition ended their involvement in the moonshine business for both man and boat.

---

[9] - Andrew Jackson Higgins and the Boats that Won World War II by Jerry E. Strahan

World War Two and Three had given Philips a new career. As the engineer, Philips was now part of a crew of four that was landing troops and supplies ashore off the coast of Lebanon. The other three members of the crew included a coxswain, bowman and sternman. Bill's job was to keep the engine running.

The 225 horsepower Hall-Scott gasoline engine was life and death to all in the boat. The engine had let him down only once. It was off the coast of Okinawa and a small Japanese cannon took potshots at them for over two hours as they drifted helplessly out of control.

During the last war as part of his duties he was preparing the boat for the landings on Okinawa. Eventually the long hours and loss of sleep had made him accident prone. He had overlooked a very minor fuel filter that was in a very hard to reach spot in the engine compartment. The fuel filter's failure should not have been enough to shut the engine down completely but it had.

As they were under fire, the other members of the crew and the platoon on board threatened to throw him overboard a number of times as he frantically tried to figure out the problem. By the time he got the engine running again the passengers on the boat were preparing to swim ashore.

The whole incident had left a lasting mark on Bill's psyche. He vowed that the engine would never fail again. He was obsessed with keeping the mechanics of the boat in 100% working order. This quest basically consumed all of his waking hours. Bill constantly cleaned, adjusted, replaced and tweaked every single nut, bolt, filter, gasket and screw on the boat.

When you talked to Bill, you talked about the engine. Bill always steered the conversation towards how the motor was functioning and where he could get spare parts. At the same time the rest of the crew was thinking about women and food, all Bill was thinking about was his engine.

In today's operation near Beirut, the Higgins boat had made six round-trips between the Landing Craft Infantry ship and the shore. They carried 150 Marines and three jeeps to the beach without incident.

During the seventh trip a riptide caught the coxswain off-guard and pushed the little boat 25 feet to the south of their intended course. As the coxswain tried to bring the boat back in line the motor suddenly quit.

The now helpless Higgins boat was carried into a minefield by the current. No one on board knew the kind of mines now surrounding them or how they worked.

In their ignorance the passengers and crew spent close to an hour keeping the boat from coming in contact with the mines. In fact the mines in this area only exploded when they detected a magnetic field caused by a large metal hull of a ship.

The Higgins boat was made of plywood and only had two metal parts, the front ramp and the engine. Unbeknownst to the crew of the boat the magnetic signature of the Higgins was too small to set off the mines.

Everyone had looked to Bill in panic. His story was legendary. Bill started to work on the engine. With the motor off they realized that shots were coming from the shore.

A Soviet sniper had spotted the small boat and started shooting at it. His first shot had missed everything but the engine. That lucky shot had hit a vital area and the motor just stopped. Although the bullet did not penetrate anything it did enough damage to bring the engine to a halt.

The sniper continued firing. Bill Philips was the third person hit as his fourth shot passed through the wooden sides of the Higgins boat, through the pant leg of the lieutenant commanding the platoon and finally into Bill's brain via his left eye.

Ironically Bill's engine never did fail again. The sniper was eventually hunted down and killed by a marine on shore. The boat and its passengers were rescued. The damage to the engine was discovered and repaired. A new engineer was assigned and the boat completed another two dozen trips before it was abandoned as scrap.

An enterprising, local fisherman claimed the boat and used it for another 30 years before the engine finally gave out. Bill was buried in Beirut along with thousands of others. His last thoughts were how he had failed once more.

World War Three 1946 – Book Four – The Red Sea

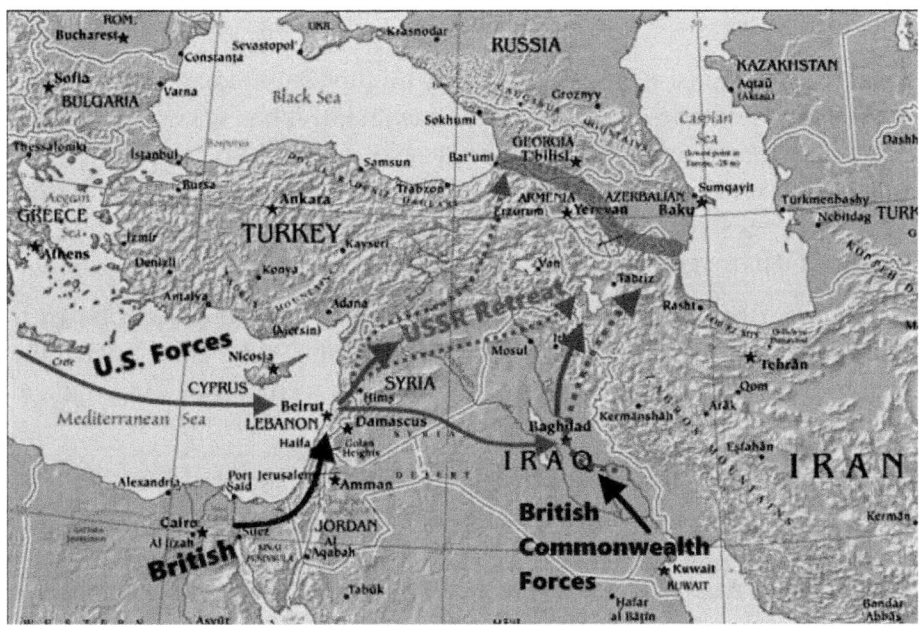

Figure 16- The Middle East May-June 1947

Baghdad

Baghdad was once again the focus of mighty empires as in ages past. The city existed primarily because of one factor. It had water. It had been established in the eighth century because of this life-giving element and quickly became a major population center. Eventually the region grew into the largest city in the world and a center of learning, until the Mongols destroyed it in 1258.

The city suffered periodic visitations of the plague and cholera for over two hundred years. The area languished until the 20th century when the cause and prevention of both diseases was discovered. By 1938 Baghdad was once again a major metropolitan area.

The Soviet forces had looted the city when they occupied it on the way to the Suez Canal. Anything that was shiny or clearly valuable was taken. Stone sculptures and pottery were ignored left behind or smashed. As in the centuries past all roads in the area still led to Baghdad and the water still flowed.

The city had become the supply hub for all Red Army forces south of the Caucasus Mountains. Baghdad's capture would spell doom for the Soviets in the Middle East. On a particularly fine day in June, the US Army was closing in from the east and the British Commonwealth Forces from the South.

On 14 June 1947, the first NATO forces entered what looked like an empty city. Some booby traps and mines where scattered about but very few Soviet fighters were observed. The Reds did leave behind a hospital full of wounded. It was a mix of civilians and gravely wounded Soviet soldiers who could not be moved.

In the last war with the Germans, the Soviets would probably have killed these men. Memories of once being allies with the Americans must have been a factor in letting the wounded men live.

At the end of that war returned Soviet POWs were very often killed as traitors and their families disparaged by the authorities. Allowing these wounded soldiers to live was a possible sign that the convictions of the Red Army Commanders had deviated from the party line. One wonders if Stalin and the STAVKA were aware that the local commanders were acting on their own initiative in this matter.

The Beggar They Are

Akram was a beggar in Baghdad. He had been a beggar all his life. When he was very little his father would send him out alone. He was very cute and fearless. He came back with a fair amount of food for his efforts that his father and older brother ate. His father said that if Akram got fat he would not look like he was starving, as a result he did not get much of the food he worked so hard for.

When he became older his looks matured and he could no longer bring in as much food. In time his father acquired a new little boy. Akram was left to fend for himself. On his own he actually did quite well since he got to keep all his proceeds. For the first time in his life he got the nutrition he had been lacking.

He became a very good looking teenager, albeit slight in stature, and started to trade sex for food. Food was the only medium of commerce in Baghdad during his first 14 years of life. When the Russians came food was the only commodity exchange for beggars. While ammunition was abundant, bullets had no value when it came to trading for nourishment.

Then the Americans came. They had other things besides food, wonderful things. The first item he got in payment was American cigarettes. These cigarettes were made from incredibly smooth and good tasting tobacco. For the first time he found he enjoyed smoking instead of just smoking to alleviate his habit. Soon American cigarettes were all over the streets and you could use them to buy food.

Cigarette lighters were the next article of trade to appear. These lighters were wonderfully intricate pieces of metal that with the flick of a finger would create a flame. These flames could be used to light cigarettes and to trade for more cigarettes and food.

There were many other wonderful things that the Americans brought as well.

Akram took immediately took delight in these exciting new developments and the opportunities they offered. He was never so well fed, smoked so many cigarettes, or felt so good. Life was better than he ever imagined.

Overtly the Americans were not interested in sex with boys. However, he easily found some that were. Secrecy was paramount to the soldiers and they paid handsomely. Apparently it was taboo for men to have sex with boys in America. No matter, there are always ways to get what you want.

Akram was talking to other beggars about the Americans when Kasim mentioned that his American was paying him not to tell others about their having sex. Akram thought about this idea for a long time and decided to try it out.

He was having regular relations with an American captain, Captain Richmond. Captain Richmond was on the fast track to becoming a major. He had distinguished himself quite well in combat. His men liked him and he was a good leader. If word got out that he liked boys his career was over. Akram did not know all the implications of his relationship with the Captain, he was just experimenting with a new way of making a living. The term or meaning of "blackmail" was totally unknown to him.

When Akram brought the subject of payment for silence to the Captain's attention, the captain paid him an extra pack of cigarettes. He was very pleased with this new way of getting paid more for doing the same thing.

Later that day he tried the same approach with Sergeant Patterson and he got two extra packs of cigarettes. Akram was beside himself with joy. He thought to himself, What an easy way to become rich.

After he and Lieutenant Biscoe had pleasured each other later that evening, he asked the Lieutenant for a whole extra carton of cigarettes for his silence and received just that. He then asked the Lieutenant for his lighter as well. The Lieutenant looked at him for a couple of seconds, walked over to his clothes, drew his gun from the holster and shot Akram in the head.

Akram was not missed. Life in Baghdad continued on without losing a beat. The only one who even asked about Akram's whereabouts was Captain Richmond. Soon the Captain was rotated back to Beirut. Within a week Sergeant Patterson was killed by a land mine. Lieutenant Biscoe shot himself two days after the murder he committed. Within 30 days there was no one left in Baghdad who remembered Akram.

Sergo Underground

Sergo's latest encounter with Stalin had not gone well. He had presented a number of practical solutions to the challenges brought on by the American naval paint scheme. Stalin had listened instead to the advice of Admiral Kuznetsov, who pronounced all of the solutions temporary and impractical. The increasingly erratic dictator then ordered that Sergo provide him a permanent solution to the problem immediately.

Sergo convinced Stalin that he had to gather some information from his office located in the manufacturing facilities outside of Moscow. Stalin became distracted and waved a dismissal to Sergo. He then told a pair of guards to accompany Sergo to the office. It was understood that they were not to let him out of their sight.

Like Beria before him, Sergo always knew that his days as an advisor to Stalin would not last forever. Also he had planned ahead for his eventual fall from grace.

Sergo had read about an American named Dr. Henry Howard Holmes.[10] His real name was Henry Webster Mudgett and he was the most prolific murderer in America's short history. It was not his 200 victims that fascinated Sergo. What captured his attention was how Holmes was able to construct and then hide a complex chamber of horrors in plain sight of a daily stream of passersby.

He had constructed a very large building as a hotel in downtown Chicago. The structure was massive even by the standards of 1886 Chicago. The locals dubbed it "The Castle."

Homes employed a unique method to disguise the Castle's true function. He would constantly hire new workers and fire them for incompetent work after they had constructed part of his building. By hiring and firing dozens of workers Mr. Holmes made sure that no one had a complete understanding of the Hotel's unique features and configuration. The Castle was filled with secret rooms, torture chambers, trap doors and a furnace room to dispose of the bodies.

Sergo used the same technique to build a very special room beneath his office. By using one craftsman after another to work on various parts of his refuge he kept secret its purpose. The only entrance was through the safe in his office. Once the small safe was closed, it was impossible to detect the door leading to his hiding place.

The only way to discover his safe shelter was to tear down the area surrounding his office. Trying to locate his highly-concealed space would involve shutting down this massive facility on what could only be a hunch. There was no paper trail or physical evidence that the chamber

---

[10] - Devil in the White City by Erik Larson

existed.

Over the years he had acquired enough water and supplies, etc., to last for over a year and a half. With the guards following close behind he entered the factory where his office was located. He caught sight of his henchman Georgie. He signaled to him that the time to instigate their escape plan was at hand. Georgie quickly dispatched the guards, said goodbye to his friend, and left to enter his own hiding place to wait out the storm.

Sergo entered his office, initiated the complicated procedure needed to enter and then secure the entrance to his haven. He was prepared for the end of the Soviet Union. He remained convinced that all was lost when Stalin rejected his ideas and would listen only to Admiral Kuznetsov.

He knew Dr. B.F. Skinner would continue to develop countermeasures that would negate Soviet guided missiles. As far as Sergo was concerned this weapon system had been the main reason for the Red Army's success and now all was lost.

The Soviets were at least six months behind the Amerikosi in radar development. In those intervening six months, the Soviet Union would be at the mercy to all manner of new weapons being developed by the countries of NATO. His rejected solutions would have given the Red Army the breathing space they needed to catch up and possibly surpass the West in electronic warfare.

Admiral Kuznetsov was going to squander the millions of electronic components acquired by the former Americans Joel Barr and Alfred Sarant. In his errant quest to develop an alternate guidance system for the Stalin's Fire SAM, the Admiral would doom the Motherland.[11]

Sergo had every confidence, that in time, the Soviet system could outperform the capitalist pigs. That time was now lost due to the vagaries of an insane megalomaniac.

The Alley
Mario Fiat had once again slipped into the role of an itinerant Kurdish worker. This persona made the American spy almost invisible. He had successfully used this disguise during a previous visit to the area. He was able to move up and down the Turkish Straights almost at will. It was

---

[11] - The Red Sky – Book Two – Second Battle of Britain by Harry Kellogg III page 152

not a fast migration as he could only travel on foot. A poor worker could never afford a taxi or ferry ride. Even a stint on a donkey going to market would be out of character.

After his last trip to the Bosporus, Fiat had made his way north intending to walk all the way to the entrance of the Black Sea. He was ordered back to perform one final reconnaissance mission of the region. Being on foot was actually an advantage. He could take his time inspecting the state of the Russian defensive works along the Straights.

He was particularly interested in any possible naval minefields. It appeared that the Soviets had not placed many mines to date. There was a large amount of traffic up and down the Straights between Istanbul and Gallipoli. Much of the supplies being transported were military in nature. The materials were probably destined for units in the Levant.

He suspected that the Stavka would now turn its attention towards the Caucasus Mountain range. He imagined they would setup a defensive line to cover their remaining large oil fields and production facilities. The Reds would be hanging on for dear life.

They had no real choice in a matter. Building the line was the only logical strategic move open to the Soviet army at this juncture of the war. Even the Lesser Caucasus Mountain range was a formidable barrier. A defended barrier here would protect Baku by thwarting any NATO attempt to reach further into Soviet territory.

Such a defensive line here would shorten the Soviet supply lines dramatically and could easily be connected to the Trans-Siberian railway. Reducing the amount of time to receive provisions would provide a huge advantage to the Stavka over NATO. Armies always tended to falter if their supply lines became too long. This fact had proven true for the Germans in their Operation Barbarossa as well as Napoleon, the Japanese and the United States in the Pacific.

Fiat was a scholar of Sun Tzu and had virtually memorized an untranslated version of The Art of War. The current NATO strategy brought to mind the quote "You can be sure of succeeding in your attacks if you only attack places which are undefended." [12]

First Mario had to make sure the coast was clear…literally. He was just outside Sariyer late on the night of 29 May 1947. He was looking for a

---

[12] - Sun Tzu: The Art of War (Illustrated) - By Sun Tzu

spot to bed down for the evening. He needed to find an out-of-the way corner that no other beggar or refugee had already claimed. Suddenly he heard a voice he recognized speaking in Russian. His mind reeled at the possibility that he had been discovered. It took every bit of his self-control not to turn around and confront this past tormentor. [13]

It was the Russian officer who had bullied him at several checkpoints during his previous mission. The man was drunk and larger than Fiat remembered. He could tell he was not a good drunk and in fact, he would bet his life that he was a violent one as well.

The big man walked towards him smacking his right fist into his left hand and muttering threats in Russian. He kept going on and on about how some Turk had stolen his camera. Unfortunately for Mario, he was in the wrong place at the wrong time. The drunk Russian was going to make him pay for someone else's transgression.

Under normal circumstances Captain Fiat would simply throw the guy using one of his many jujitsu moves. Since the man was drunk he should be easy to disable and then Mario would be on his way. But, because it was their third encounter, it was likely that the Russian was going to remember the scrawny, helpless workman who kicked his ass. Any altercation would probably mean a general round up and undue attention aimed squarely at him just as he was about to finalize his mission.

This final piece of surveillance was probably the trickiest and of course the most critical. All of his other work would be compromised if this last bit of spy craft was unsuccessful. He could not accomplish what he needed to do with a Soviet Officer trying to hunt him down.

All of these thoughts took a few seconds and in those seconds the goon was about to get within arm's reach. With such proximity would come the first clumsy, yet very powerful, attempt to hit Fiat in the head.

Mario pretended to stumble at just the right second and ducked the swing. It still caught him a glancing blow and almost stunned him. He had to end this quickly. He rolled past his attacker and shot a glance back at the street to make sure the coast was clear and got a kick in the ribs that knocked the wind out of him and probably cracked one.

Shit, this guy is faster than he should be for his size, thought Mario as he

---

[13] - World War Three 1946 – Book Three – The Red, White & Blue by Kellogg and Jotz pg. 131

just missed getting kicked again. Even when he was seeing stars he could anticipate the Red's next move...and there it was. The oaf raised his foot in an attempt to stomp on Fiat's head. The Captain spun on his left hip as he was lying there and landed a straight on blow to his tormentor's knee. Both heard something break.

He knew a scream was about to erupt from the Russian and his next strike was to the man's throat, as the now helpless giant, was falling towards him. The end result of that blow was the Red could no longer breathe, much less scream. Mario finished him off with the man's own knife and made his way into the street to blend in with the crowd.

In his quest for a secluded spot to rest he had gone down a blind alley. In this case it turned out to be a dead end as well.

Zhukov's Second Life

He was staring at his left hand. The fingernails were just beginning to grow back. He looked around the large room as memories of the last time he saw Beria flooded his thoughts. He had one of Beria's chairs brought to his home and it would follow him to his new command post in Sheki at the foot of the Caucasus Mountain range.

The Stavka had reinstated him with full command authorities. He was to stem the capitalist pig ground invasion coming from the South. It was essential to prevent them from capturing the Baku region and its oil production facilities. The best defensive terrain before the oil fields at Baku were the Lesser Caucasus Range. The mountains offered a number of 8000-foot peaks and numerous smaller mountains as well as the Kura River, and several large lakes and marshes. Also, The Lesser Caucasus Mountain Range was anchored by the Black Sea on the West end and the Caspian Sea on the East end.

Further impeding attacking army, the Amerikosi atomic bombs had created a no-man's land around Tbilisi and Baku. No sane NATO commander would place his troops in the nuclear hellhole that had now existed. The Americans would be well aware of the extreme hazards in the area and would avoid exposing their men.

Political prisoners from all over Eurasia were being shipped into Tbilisi and Baku to repair and expand the oil production facilities. They were dying in large numbers due to radiation poisoning. When they became too weak to work they were shot and dumped in mass graves.

These detainees all had relatives that were being held hostage in their homelands. Fear for the wellbeing of their families quelled any thought of rebellion. The captives literally worked themselves to death.

Zhukov was no stranger to using slaves and prisoners for building defensive works. His former German prisoners of war had done an excellent job of erecting the defenses of Leningrad. Ultimately these very fortifications led to the death of many of their own countrymen who attacked the city. It is amazing what humans will do to survive.

Zhukov was engaged in just such an exercise at the moment. He was working 18-hour days for a man who had ordered his torture and death just weeks before. Zhukov could have easily made his way to the front and surrendered to the Amerikosi. He cared little for his wife, and for his two married daughters who had abandoned him when he was first arrested. He barely knew his youngest child, 10-year old Ella. Instead he remained loyal and stayed to do his duty.

His defensive line on the Lesser Caucasus Mountains would be strong and deep if the Stavka supported him. If not, he knew that eventually the American Air Force would wear down his air units. He knew that losing air defenses would result in his land troops being attacked relentlessly from the air. His only defense against the American fighter bombers was his own fighter force that was becoming alarmingly slimmer by the day. So far, the Stavka were holding back numerous squadrons for the defense of Moscow. They were fools.

The supply of oil, the lifeblood of modern warfare, would soon cease to be available. No oil would ground fighter squadrons and Zhukov would be unable to stop the capitalist forces. As a consequence of limited fuel, the planes sitting around Moscow would be useless. The Soviets would be in the same situation as the Germans and Japanese found themselves at the end of the last war. They had enough planes to defend their airspace but no trained pilots and fuel to fly them. The two Axis powers were completely at the mercy of the American bombers.

Novikov was in concurrence with Zhukov's assessment of the state of the air war. So far the air battle was a draw and the only way to lose was to run out of fuel. He knew that the US air forces were losing men and planes like he was. The deciding factor would be NATO's ability to overcome their 10,000-kilometer-long supply line.

Zhukov was cognizant of the fact that at the end of World War Two, the

West was dangerously close to running out of resources, including fuel, when the Soviets captured Berlin and ended the war.

Between his defensive line and NATO's long supply line America was facing an almost impossible task. In Zhukov's estimation shipping enough fuel needed to fight all the way to Moscow and on to the industrial centers beyond the Urals was prohibitive. If the Red Army could save the oil production centers in Baku and reactivate the ones in Tbilisi and Rostov-on-don, the Soviet Union would survive and prosper. If not, it would die.

Konev's Forces Surrender

The word had spread quickly of Konev's death. For a week, it had been used to inspire the flagging Soviet troops into fighting with even more disregard for life and limb. As the supplies started to disappear, casualties where mounting, and with no possibility of escape, individuals started to surrender in ones and twos and then as whole squads.

The Red officers and newly minted commissars shot the first deserters when they caught them. This practice soon stopped and only the most ardent and diehard of Konev's once formidable force remained. They were slowly being crushed between the British and their coalition of forces retaking Palestine and finally the Golan Heights. The newly landed Americans were giving no ground on a line running from Beirut to Baghdad.

After 8 days of relentless assault the NATO onslaught ceased. An intense psychological warfare program was deployed. For days the remaining trapped and seemingly suicidal Red soldiers were subjected to every method of psychological warfare. The British had honed these techniques through centuries of ruling their worldwide colonial empire. Each diabolical procedure was carefully designed to completely undermine the resolve of their enemies.

Hundreds of loud speakers were placed along the Southern Front by the British and on the lines outside of Beirut by the Americans. At 0254 all the speakers simultaneously started blaring distorted jazz and forbidden Soviet compositions at the Reds trapped between the two armies. Six hours later dozens of planes dropped 12-page pamphlets containing a cartoon version of George Orwell's anti-Stalinism book Animal Farm.[14]

---

[14] - Animal Farm a Fairy Story by George Orwell

Every fifteen minutes the sound system would announce a reward of

water, food and a warm bed for surrendering Soviet soldiers who possessed one of the pamphlets. All the defectors had to do was walk towards any NATO soldier with the pamphlet and both hands raised above their heads.

Soon the psychological warfare started to take effect. The first few Soviets attempting to surrender were shot by their officers. As if on cue, the officers were disarmed or prevented from harming the next group who went forward carrying the pamphlets. The numbers were not large by any means. The vast majority of Konev's former command stayed in place and endured the constant attempts of coercion meted out by the surrounding NATO forces.

After another week, it was estimated that 5% of the trapped troops were surrendering each day. Their former comrades were put on the loud speakers imploring the remaining troops to surrender as well. The deserters extolled the treatment they were receiving and tried to assure the hardliners that it was not like giving up to the Germans.

During World War Two Soviet soldiers that surrendered suffered a 60% mortality rate. A "weeding-out" program allowed the best and strongest to live. These prisoners were used for slave labor and literally worked to death. 3.3 million out of 5.7 million never returned home.

After 21 days, the floodgates seemed to open and thousands of troops a day were surrendering. The last unit surrendering on day 28. These brave souls had endured over a month without food and were on their fourth day without water. Most were carried out by their comrades and were sent directly to hospitals in the area.

The newspapers and newsreels were churning out copy and film on an hourly basis describing how well the Soviet prisoners were being treated. Reporters and various government officials went out of their way to emphasis that these were our former allies against Hitler and who had been led astray by the equally heinous Stalin.

The

"Animal Farm" book and comic book version shot to the bestseller list. The novel was considered mandatory reading throughout the nations that comprised NATO. An animated cartoon version was within months of completion by the Disney Studios.

There was a complete news blackout in the territories controlled by the USSR, yet word did reach much of the occupied territories of a major Soviet defeat. The news of this defeat inspired an increase in partisan activities. In turn the newly installed Communist governments began to crack down even harder on dissidents within France, Germany, Scandinavia and the Low countries. Atrocities kept pace with the increase in partisan attacks and the age-old cycle of action and retaliation continued.

Shepherd's Watch

Mihalis was a shepherd on the island of Crete. Most days he just watched his sheep and goats. He was a very successful shepherd and had a large flock. Today he was watching his sheep and, what he was told, were Americans. The Americans were extremely entertaining. They rode in large trucks most of which were towing cannons with some towing trailers. Almost all of the trucks were filled with soldiers. Every so often a long line of tanks would pass by as well.

He and his flock were high up in the foothills. He could barely hear the noise the convoy was making yet he could see it clearly for he had excellent eyesight. The sheep were startled at first but quickly got use to the noise.

Mihalis had only seen one tank in his life. It was a wreck from World War One that was in the town square where he grew up. Compared to the old tank these new ones were not very impressive. The tank left over from World War One was much bigger and had much larger guns. In fact, it had multiple guns sticking out from both sides.

Figure 17 – World War One Italian Fiat 2000 Heavy Tank

He had no idea what tanks were used for but he guessed that these new ones did the job better than the old one, whatever job that was. He supposed that their task was to scare enemy soldiers into running away. Mihalis knew he would certainly run away if he were to see one of those machines coming at him.

What really impressed him was the large number of Americans soldiers that were passing by. They were all traveling neatly one after another along the road that led from Heraklion to his village. He thought that the port in the capital city must be full of Americans. Possibly the capital's port was too busy and they needed his town's port as well. He could see them loading men, equipment and supplies into smaller boats for transfer to larger boats off shore. It was all very amusing to watch.

He guessed that all these American soldiers were going somewhere and they would once again get off their big ship. Then they would get back onto the smaller boats and land on some other foreign shore. It was probably some place he had never heard of. He was certain there were many places he did not know.

The columns of trucks and vehicles were more interesting than watching the large numbers of American airplanes take off and land in the various airports that were within sight of his meadow. There seem to be less and less of these planes every day. Compared to a few months ago he guessed there was about half as many. Either the Americans had moved to other places or they were somehow losing their planes.

Mihalis was a smart man but he lacked any education or knowledge of what exactly the American planes and ships were doing here in Crete. He had heard rumors of another war in Europe. From what he knew Europe was very far away. Of course, to him the capital Heraklion was very far away as well. He had no frame of reference from which to compare distances.

He had never been in a moving vehicle other than a horse drawn cart. Mihalis knew that it was a two-day trip just to get to Heraklion from his mountaintop. However, he had never visited the city and had no reason to. The city contained nothing he needed or wanted. He wondered where all these Americans were going, and what they needed, and wanted.

He had seen a number of the American planes crash. He had no idea what kept the planes up in the air in the first place as their wings did not flap like birds. They created very loud explosions as they hit the ground and upset the herd. The first time a plane came down he was frightened as well. He had heard stories of guns and war. He had never seen a gun until the Americans started using the port at the foot of his mountain.

They had setup, what he was told, was a shooting range. One of the villagers had advised him never to go near it. Mihalis was informed that occasionally the Americans missed what they were shooting at. He understood that the bullets could travel very far and it was possible that they could kill one of his sheep or goats. Mihalis could not afford to lose any of his animals so he had avoided getting anywhere near the Americans and their guns. Luckily, they did not shoot any of their big cannons.

***
A second shepherd 1300 miles away watches the Soviet Army begin to deploy
***

Saba was a shepherd in Kusapat, Georgia at the foot of the Lesser Caucasus Mountains. Most days he spent his time spying on his wife and watching his goats. He spent an equal amount of time doing both.

His wife was exceptionally beautiful. If he had known that she was going to grow up to become so attractive he would have married the older sister. His wife was very ugly when they were married. She was eleven years old when they married with missing teeth, and was very skinny with bad skin. Saba found it difficult to consummate their marriage on their wedding night because she was so homely. He should have known better, for her eyes were stunning. It was the only part of her that was attractive at 11.

Within three years she had grown beautiful around those eyes. It was driving him crazy with jealousy and the constant need to defend his honor. As the proverb says, "A pretty face is the key to locked doors." He had to break down some locked doors in the last few years.

He was hoping that another proverb would soon come to fruition "A handsome shape sags out quickly." So far after two children and at age 20 she was still desired by every man that set his eyes on her.

His goats on the other hand were easy to care for. He had a good dog and his pastures were covered with sweet grass year after year, until this year. His problem this year came from the Ruskies who had come from the north and taken over a number of his best meadows.

This group of Muscovites seemed to be well led and for the most part under control. So far no one had tried to steal his goats or his wife. The Non-commission officers seemed to be very professional. He shuddered to think of what might happen if they lost that control. Everyone had heard the stories from the north of what second line troops had done to the German women.

Instead of worrying, he wondered if maybe he should use his wife's beauty for his own gain. She was going to get raped anyway. Why not make it as pleasant as possible for her and profitable for him. The Ruskie officers were very rich. Some even had watches.

He could exhibit her in the market the next day. He would not have to spend money on new clothes. Her charms were so obvious to any man who liked women. He would watch and see which fine, and of course, wealthy officers watched her

There would be no shame in her being used by a Russian if he profited from it. The other men in the village would see the wisdom of bowing to fate and making a profit at the same time. It would also be kinder to have her "loved" by a nice, rich man rather than raped by a smelly, violent Cossack who probably had some horrible disease.

He could send their children off to his sister's home. His wife could then be free to live with the officer and steal things for the family. As long as he kept the children she would always come back and he would be wealthy from all the things she would appropriate or accept as gifts. Most men are fools when it comes to a pretty face and body. The officer would defend her from others as well. This seemed to be a much better situation than him having to do it himself and risked getting killed. It was a good solution for all concerned.

Now, how was he going to protect his goats from the Cossacks? They were sure to appear soon once the Russians left. He had heard that they always followed the Muscovites.

The Ruskies were burying metal things all over some of his meadows. He was told that if he touched them they would explode. He would not touch them. He was no fool. You didn't have a flock of 300 goats by being a fool.

Over on the next mountain the Ruskies had hauled up a huge cannon and were in the process of putting it in a cave he had used many a time during early winter storms. He hoped they would step in his shit and piss in the back.

Between the mines and entrenchments, he had lost the use of more than half his fields. He only hoped that his wife could make up for the losses by acquiring some good treasures from a soldier.

He had noticed that there were only a few of those metal monsters they called tanks. He supposed they would have a hard time getting them up the mountains and so would any enemy.

He wondered not for the first time, "who was the enemy in this war?" The Nazis had been defeated, had they not? Everyone in town said it was the Amerikosi but he didn't believe it. They were our allies against the Germans, why would they now be our enemy.

He guessed he would find out soon enough.

Figure 18- Children and a Cretan soldier watch the NATO invasion preparations.

Chapter Five: Changes

Figure 19 – Russian terrorist Ignaty Grinevitsky First Suicide bomber kills himself and Czar Alexander II

Bear Hug

Leonid Ilyich Brezhnev was visited in the night by the ghost of Lavrenti Beria. Brezhnev suspected that Beria was still alive when his son Yuri disappeared from school. He was contacted within hours by one of Beria's former henchman. The subject matter was the kidnapping of Brezhnev's 13-year old son.

At the end of World War Two, Brezhnev is a Major General and winner of the Order of Lenin. He was previously second in command to Nikita Khrushchev as the Ukrainian Front's Political Commissar. He was beyond reproach as Khrushchev's understudy. As a decorated hero and high-ranking member of the military he had full access to most facilities and attended many of the political meetings in the Kremlin.

Vyacheslav Mikhailovich Molotov was the Soviet Minister of Foreign Affairs. Since the war started he had not been traveling internationally. He was assigned by Stalin to oversee the newly formed communist governments in Germany, France, Greece, Italy, Sweden, Norway, Finland, the Netherlands, Denmark and other former western countries now under the control of the Red Army.

Molotov was spending a lot of time in Moscow and required that the new heads of state travel to meet him. The meeting today involved the newly installed head of the Greek communist government. Nikos Beloyannis had risen to power in the usual manner of dictators. He was given the title General Secretary of the Greek communist party and was ensconced in office shortly after the Soviet invasion.

The meeting between Molotov and Beloyannis was to symbolize his taking the reins of power in cementing relations with the USSR. It was to be mainly a ceremonial meeting and Leonid Brezhnev had attended many such gatherings. Usually his wife Viktoria attended as well. The finest foods and spirits were served in great quantities and Viktoria was loath to miss such fare.

It was rumored that their son was sick as he had not been seen in weeks. When questioned, Brezhnev reinforced this belief. A number of his comrades wished for a sound and speedy recovery. His son's illness also explained his wife's absence.

Brezhnev was in his prime. He was 6 foot two and in great physical shape due to his military service. The imposing Major General appeared to be nervous however, and was sweating profusely. He was wearing a rather

World War Three 1946 – Book Four – The Red Sea

bulky and unflattering suit jacket. Several people suggested that he should take his jacket off since he appeared to be so uncomfortable wearing it. He declined and slowly made his way towards Molotov and his guest. At exactly 2115 he was standing next to Molotov and suddenly gave the leader a bear hug and shouted for all the others to exit the room immediately.

Molotov struggled to escape but was no match for Brezhnev's strength. As Leonid became more and more adamant that people should leave the room, most of the crowd complied.

Just as the security guard was about to seize Brezhnev from behind, Leonid shouted at the top of his lungs, "FORGIVE ME!" A deafening explosion rocked the room. As the smoke cleared, there was a smoldering crater where Brezhnev, Molotov and the security guard had been last seen.

Killing an enemy by throwing or placing a bomb near them was almost as old as gunpowder itself. Deliberately killing yourself in the process was not. The act of strapping an explosive vest to your body and purposely getting close to your intended victim was a novel method of assassination in 1947.

At the same time that Brezhnev was obliterating himself and Molotov another was doing the same to Georgy Malenkov near building outside of Lenin's Tomb in Red Square.

This assassin's name was Alexey Alexandrovich Kuznetsov. His motives for killing himself remain mysterious. Rumors that he had a daughter named Alla that Beria was holding hostage, yet no record of her was ever found. Perhaps she was illegitimate or the records of her birth were lost in the war.[15]

The results of both explosions were essentially the same. In this second bombing, pieces of Malenkov and Kuznetsov, along with 12 others were buried together as the building collapsed.

A third assassin targeting Khrushchev never made it close enough to strike. He was late and by that time word had spread of the nearby attack.

Everyone around Nikita was required to take off his or her outer garments and any article of clothing that could hide an explosive vest. The would-be killer's name is lost to history as he quietly agreed to leave

---

[15] - Stepan Anastasovich Mikoyan: An Autobiography pg. 141

the area and then blew himself up without harm to others.

He was believed to be Khrushchev's (for lack of a better term) pimp. It was alleged that he provided Nikita with a steady stream of willing female partners for over a decade. He was not missed as others stepped in to fulfill this function.

At first most believed that Stalin was behind the attacks, but then reason prevailed. If Stalin wanted you dead, you were arrested and killed. He had no need for suicide vests and bear hugs. You were just killed. Then Beria's name was whispered.

Someone who knew both Brezhnev and Kuznetsov commented that both had children who had not been seen for weeks. This observation was verified and set off a nationwide round-up of all the high-ranking parents with small children. All these parents were required to produce their offspring and those that could not were sent to a holding facility. Under questioning several admitted that their children had been taken and they were being blackmailed into committing crimes against the state.

Several were implicated in Beria's newly discovered resurrection. All the admitted and suspected parents and their families were sent to various gulags throughout the USSR. For over a year the bear hug-like greeting, so prevalent in the Soviet Union since time immemorial, was banned.

Figure 20- Leonid Ilyich Brezhnev

To the Last

Ivan Vetrov was the last Soviet soldier of Konev's Mideast Front to surrender. He lasted for two weeks without water by drinking his own piss. None of the Americans wanted to die assaulting his well dug in position. A few tried to throw grenades into his hole at first but after about ten attempts they decided to just wait him out.

Meanwhile they bombarded him with constant dissonant music and propaganda broadcasts. The American intelligence officer found one of Vetrov's old comrades. The fellow was sent to talk him into surrendering. Ivan shot the man in the leg.

The 1321st Engineer General Service Regiment transferred from duties in Trieste and landed in Beirut on 30 May 1947. They were assigned to watch Ivan until he surrendered. The unit was primarily Negro with the exception of its commander Lt. Colonel Arthur Ramsey who replaced Colonel Aldo H. Bagnulo. The remaining white officers the recently promoted Sergeant Richard Post stayed with the unit.

Richard had been partially responsible for the 1321 being assigned to the assault on the Levant. He had put the bug in his Lieutenant's ear who passed it up the chain. Richard had gotten a reputation for getting things done that should not be possible.

The Regiment took turns, 12 at a time, surrounding Ivan's lair. The duty was very tedious, but someone had to do it. When not watching Ivan the troops, performed their usual engineering duties of constructing roads, bridges and airfields.

In truth Richard was here to find his brother Phil. Word had reached him of Phil's desertion and he was going to find Mrs. Post's youngest son and bring him home. First, he had to wait for Ivan to die or become incapacitated.

Richard knew that Phil was still alive and somewhere near the Turkish border with Syria. The Turks fighting alongside the Americans would talk to the Negros in his unit and tell them things that they would not tell their white comrades. Phil was rumored to have joined a group of mercenaries killing Russians who were guarding or transporting Syria's and Turkey's treasures to Moscow. Gold coins, statues and even diamonds fueled the stories of riches being righteously taken from the godless commies.

Richard had reason to believe the stories for they contained details that corresponded with Phil's newly found skills at ambush and creatively using explosives. Phil and his traps had become the stuff of legend. The Army maintained that he was dead but Richard knew better.

However, his first priority was Ivan. With Ivan captured his unit would likely move further north and closer to Phil's location. On his own initiative, he had interviewed Ivan's former friend, the one who Ivan shot when he tried to talk to him about surrendering.

After a long conversation, Evgeny mentioned that Ivan was addicted to a special version of Borsch, the Soviet beet soup. His particular style of the beet concoction originated in his hometown Pskov. Pskov was located on a huge lake 100 miles south of the Gulf of Finland and 150 miles SSW of Leningrad.

The Borsch soup that Ivan grew up eating used dried fish instead of pork or beef. A smelt is just thrown in the boiling liquid giving the soup its unique flavor. The taste for this stew needed to be…developed. Ivan had acquired his craving over a 20-year period.

Richard went back to his company cook dragging Ivan's former friend with him. The three of them experimented and over the course of 2 days came up with a reasonable facsimile of Ivan's boyhood soup.

The Levant version of Pskov Borsch was re-heated downwind from Ivan's lair. After a few hours Ivan crawled out of his nest and surrendered.

The power of youthful memories triggered by the sense of smell proved to be an irresistible combination. Ivan was finally driven to sanity by memories of childhood.

The Transplant

For the last couple of weeks, the Soviet Union had been proceeding along on automatic pilot. Two of its Ruling Circle had been assassinated. Stalin had not been seen in public for over 21 days. The remaining members of the Politburo were in seclusion due to the assassinations.

To some, a miracle then occurred. To others, it was a curse.

In 1933 Soviet surgeon Yuri Voronoy transplanted the first kidney from one human to another. [16] The patient died 2 days later. At the time the reasons for the failure were unknown. Later it became apparent that the donor and the recipient had different blood types and the kidney had been naturally rejected.

---

[16] - A History of Organ Transplantation: Ancient Legends to Modern Practice By David Hamilton

By WWII blood transfusions had become fairly common. The different blood types were known as well as the consequences of crossing them. Incremental progress had been made over the intervening years in human-to-human transplants but no major breakthroughs.

Stalin's kidneys were failing. He had only weeks to live when a long-lost half-brother was located.

Stalin's father was a violent drunk who smashed the windows of the local tavern and assaulted the town's police chief when the future dictator was ten years old. His father was told to leave town and went to the city of Tiflis. He cut all ties with his wife and family. Besarion Jughashvili had a number of affairs in the following years.[17] As far as Stalin knew until 1939, his father did not sire more children. He was wrong.

A roaming prostitute became impregnated by Besarion. When she discovered that she was with child she was 300 miles away in Lagan and destitute. Somehow, she survived the pregnancy and gave birth to a son. She immediately placed him in an orphanage and disappeared.

The boy was 12 years younger than Stalin and grew up in Lagan until the age of 16. He chose his own name, Lazar Lissitzky.

Another Lazar Lissitzky [18] came to the attention of the NKVD as an instructor at a school that taught abstract art. In 1922 the Soviet government turned against such decadent art forms and the artist Lissitzky fled to Germany, only to return in 1925. His behavior and trip to Germany put him in the spotlight of the authorities in 1939. This coincidence of events is the reason Stalin's only living sibling, and the second Lissitzky, was under investigation.

Both Lissitzkys were eventually caught up in the same inquiry and eventually the brother and his origins were traced back to Besarion Jughashvili, Stalin's father. Besides Stalin, only a handful of officials knew of Lazar's.

Dr. Yuri Voronoy was consulted on the possibility of once again attempting a human kidney transplant on an unknown patient in June of 1947. Since 1933 it was known that the best possible match for an organ

---

[17] - Stalin: Volume I: Paradoxes of Power, 1878-1928 By Stephen Kotkin
[18] - El Lissitzky: Beyond the Abstract Cabinet : Photography, Design, Collaboration By Margarita Tupitsyn, Matthew Drutt, El Lissitzky, Ulrich Pohlmann, Sprengel Museum Hannover, Museu d'Art Contemporani (Barcelona, Spain), Museu Serralves

transplant was a close relative of the patient.

Stalin's half-brother was detained in January of 1946 and place in a luxurious prison cell. As Stalin's condition worsened, Dr. Voronoy was notified that he should prepare for another human-to-human kidney transplant. Despite his objections, he was told he had no choice in the matter. The Doctor was not informed of the patient's name.

He was allowed to choose his transplant team and location for the operation. He also received the latest equipment and supplies for the upcoming operation.

Lazar Lissitzky's kidneys were harvested by another surgeon shortly before he was killed by asphyxiation. By this time all of the tests possible had been done and it was determined that the blood types matched. The now comatose Stalin was prepared for the surgery. His identity was concealed from the surgical team and the operation commenced.

The kidneys were brought in from the adjoining operating room and one was immediately implanted in Stalin's leg similarly to the operation that Dr. Voronoy had performed 14 years earlier.

After two days it was determined that the transplanted kidney was functioning properly. At this point, both of Stalin's disease kidneys were removed and his brother's second organ was implanted. Another 12 hours later the first kidney was relocated.

By some unknown quirk of nature both kidneys started to function properly with no sign of rejection. No one on the surgical team or the following group of attending nurses and doctors understood why the operation had succeeded. All that mattered to them was the care and health of their patient.

The end result was a rapidly recovering Joseph Stalin who was gaining strength by the hour and demanding answers.

Missiles Miss

The unusual phenomenons inherent in an object traveling faster than the speed of sound were becoming known to science. The effects of an explosion followed by the projectile's sound waves were not common knowledge to most Americans. The Brits of London had experiences random explosions followed by the unnatural noise of missile engines hundreds of times. Hitler wanted to especially subject the British to the combination of unexpected explosions followed by the disturbing din of a rocket engine. These features were unique to the V2 Rocket. He had spent a large percentage of his military budget on a weapon of dubious effect trying to terrorize his implacable enemy.

The Soviet missiles aimed at the convoys off the coast of Italy were based on the same V2 Rocket weapons system. If you were lucky you heard the missile's engine a few seconds after it passed overhead. If not your ship exploded, you either died or were wounded. To have a ship hit before there was any indication of danger was especially unnerving. The anticipation of a possible missile hit was highly stressful and surreal.

With large caliber naval guns you had the same effects of a direct missile hit before you heard the shell ripping through the air. The difference being that it was very rare for the first rounds of canon fire to actually hit anything of consequence. Great geysers would appear in the ocean or ground around the intended target. The initial close calls warned all that the enemy was near. Lookouts would then search for flashes on the horizon indicating that more shells were on their way. You could even count the seconds until they detonated to estimate the enemy's distance.

Missiles, on the other hand would come in one at a time from far over the horizon with sudden and devastating results. There were no near misses.

Thank God, Billy thought, most of the sons of bitches are just going overhead. There would be hell to pay if a majority of those warheads hit the ships in our convoy. Billy must have seen 30 missiles fly by, or more correctly seen the contrails from their journey.

The word was that the weird paint job they were ordered to apply to their ships was the reason for the misses. If this observation was true, a combination of scientist and artist had saved thousands of American lives.[19] One out of 20 missiles still hit home. This hit rate was a far cry from the slaughter that would have occurred had the missiles been more accurate.

Each of the troop transports were carrying a larger than normal load of over 3200 men. Billy could just imagine the carnage if one of those guided bullets slammed into the side of his troop ship.

His ship was named the USS General A.W. Greely AP-141 and made an

---

[19] - World War Three - The Red, White & Blue - Book Three – Subchapter – Razzel Dazzel by Kellogg and Jotz

18,000-ton dent in the water when fully loaded. Greely was a famous Civil War commander who had led an expedition in 1881 to study the area near the North Pole.

Billy had done some research and Greely was the first of only two to receive the Congressional Medal of Honor for noncombat service, the second being Charles A. Lindbergh. He had also discovered there was possible evidence of cannibalism on Greeley's expedition when they were stranded for two years. Not a very comforting fact to find out about your ship's namesake.

His convoy was rumored to be on the way to Crete. The total absence of information on their next port of call was the subject of much scuttlebutt amongst the crew and combat troops in the ship's holds. Idle men always make-up theories and tall tales, and there was some whoppers floating around.

One theory even suggested that their true destination was Istanbul and eventually the Black Sea. Everyone in "The Know" said that was very unlikely. What the hell would they accomplish by taking Istanbul and at what cost? This very strategy had been tried 20 years ago. The results being the British and French had been almost slaughtered to a man by an inferior Turkish enemy.

The battle had occurred during World War One when The Allies attempted to invade Gallipoli at the southern mouth of the Turkish Straights. All the "experts" pontificated on the difficulties and dubious rewards of the effort. In the end, this idea was dismissed out of hand. Bets were placed and Beirut was the odds-on favorite.

Big Brother
The US 2nd Armored Division was pressing the enemy hard. Richard Post and his unit the 1321st Engineer General Service Regiment, were hours behind the lead combat battalions. The front-line detachments increasingly needed the assistance of the engineers to clear minefields and other obstacles placed by the retreating Reds. Booby traps and other lethal devices designed to slow an enemy were being employed in ever increasing numbers by Zhukov's forces.

Richard was looking for his opportunity to go on a "temporary" absence to locate and bring his brother Phil to safety. Whether the trip was authorized or not didn't matter to Richard. He was going and going soon.

A corporal in his unit had relayed some information gathered from local sources. Phil had been sighted 45 miles away from their current position in Batman, Turkey. It was an ironic name for a town since The Batman, of comic fame, was Phil's boyhood hero. Richard would not be surprised if his brother had changed his name to Bruce Wayne.

Richard had connected with the International Red Cross and corresponded with a Dr. Marcel Junod. The good Doctor had promised to assist Richard in enabling his brother's immigration to Switzerland where he could wait out the war.

The Doctor himself would accompany Phil. He had heard about the younger Post and his exploits of both taking and saving lives. Phil had been responsible for saving over a hundred Soviet soldiers who were about to be slaughtered by tribesmen from Turkey's Anatolia Hill Region. Phil was able to negotiate their internment with the Turkish military and had been seriously wounded for his efforts.

It seems that at the final negotiations a tribal leader became very angry at the turn of events and had plunged his dagger into Phil's side. Luckily the thrust had missed anything vital.

The attacker was suddenly dispatched by his fellow clan members. They were mortified that a guest in their home had been assaulted. As a result, custom dictated that they grant their wounded guest's request. Consequently, they agreed to let the Soviets live.

Phil's wound had become infected and he was in serious trouble without antibiotics. Junod received many letters of appeal daily requesting his help. He had heard about a wounded American named Phil Post. He recalled, a letter from a Richard Post in time he connected the tales of the brothers and decided to assist. It would hopefully be his last action in Turkey before he made his way home to Zurich.

Bringing this hero, who had fallen from grace to asylum, would be a fitting end to his time in Turkey. He sent a messenger to Richard Post and proposed a meeting in a conflict-free zone. Despite the power of both the Red Army and NATO forces, there were still areas where neither had gained control or possibly even wanted to. They were isolated areas where most feared to enter ruled by fiercely independent tribal leaders and their followers.

Junod was given access to some these safe havens. His reputation preceded him. He was an honorary and revered member of a number of tribes in these ethnic regions.

The messenger on his way to Richard was carrying a special talisman that gave the bearer privileges of both passage and hospitality in the most secretive areas of Turkey. When Richard received the amulet he was instructed in its use when he became free to travel. A member of the clans would lead him safely to Junod. Post was told that he would have 7 days to engineer his departure from military service.

One day after receiving the invitation to rescue his brother, Richard was given medical leave. He disappeared to the north with the assistance of the hospital staff. He was heading for Batman, Turkey. He avoided a number of incidents by showing the talisman and using his new skill at speaking Turkish.

He had discovered that he was surprisingly adept at learning the local dialect. He supposed he had always possessed this trait. But, until now there had been no opportunity for its use. He began to wonder what other skills he might have and vowed to explore them in the future.

After a day and half's walk he was blindfolded and led to a cave at the base of a mountain. He later estimated that mountain was over 9,000 feet. Inside the cave was his brother Phil attended by a highly trained local woman. The wounded warrior was very weak and was totally astonished at seeing his older brother. He broke down and cried in his brother's arms confessing all the things he had done in tearful sobs.

Richard listened knowing that Phil needed to complete the litany in order to heal his soul. Richard was taken aback upon hearing of the murder of Phil's former squad mate, Warren. He listen further and decided that it was a case of kill or be killed. He completely understood having been put in a somewhat similar situation himself.

After the tearful reunion, Phil seemed to come out of a fog. Soon he was close to being his former self the gentle artist instead of the killer the US Army and Warren had created. After a series of long, into the night, heart-felt conversations both decided that Junod's offer of a new life in Switzerland was the best choice for Phil Post.

Three days later Junod himself was escorted into the cave. Discussions on Phil's new identity and exit strategies ensued. True to Richard's prediction Phil chose Bruce Wayne as his new name without the older brother even suggesting as much. It turned out that Phil's' nurse was trained by the Red Cross, and was a big fan of Batman as well. Another couple of hours were spent discussing DC Comics and superheroes.

With his brother on the mend and Dr. Junod on the scene Richard felt it was time to get back to his unit. Phil tried to talk his older brother into going to Switzerland with him. However, Richard was adept at explaining to his younger brother the realities of life. Not for the first, time he felt guilty for not being there for Phil.

Their final argument had been all about Mom and Dad. How could they endure losing two sons? Richard had to return to Wisconsin to give them the happy news of Phil's resurrection as well as see to the wellbeing of brother Burt and sister Eloise. After all, that is what Mable and Harry Post had taught them both. In the end it was agreed, taking care of siblings is what big brothers do.

Figure 21- Marcel Junod : the Red Cross Dr. who personified "the spirit of the thing"

Chapter Six: Looking Up

Figure 22 - Anti-Aircraft crew watches the action as they wait their turn

Spy in the Sky

It was the first flight for USAF pilot Major Jessie Roth in the FP-80A Reconnaissance model of the Shooting Star. This stripped-down version of America's first jet fighter was streaking over the narrowest parts of the Danish Straits. He was assigned to do aerial photo reconnaissance on the Oresund portion.

This three-mile-wide stretch of water was presumed to be heavily mined. Yet indications were that the Soviets had yet to take seriously any kind of incursion into the Baltic Sea from the Atlantic. The British MI6 had reported that the Soviets were in the process of clearing the shipping channels of mines. This action was in anticipation of using the Danish Straits and Kattegat for their own shipping and naval purposes. The Soviets removing their own mines was welcome news to the planning teams of the NATO allies.

Major Roth was to take high resolution pictures that would assist in refuting or confirming the reports on the ground. Not that a plane flying at a height of 45,000 feet could gather much intelligence but every little bit helped.

The flight was at the maximum range of the airplane. The mission would be extremely long but headquarters thought the risk was worth the effort. So here he was approaching the area from the west at over 450 mph.

Submarines, divers, land-based spies and intercepted Soviet messages were also being used to determine just what defenses lay between the Atlantic and the Baltic Sea. If the Soviets were strengthening their defenses then the planned operation would have to be called off. If not, then all lights were green and NATO would attack.

Any mine fields of consequence were to be dealt with in a unique manner but first they had to be identified. Luckily all of the Soviet ships capable of laying large minefields were well documented. His images would hopefully show whether any of these ships were in the area.

The British had once again found a break of good weather or the Major to fly through. Without the clouds, he had a clear view for the cameras and radar in his plane's nose. From Roth's lofty perch he could not see anything with the mark one eyeball.

Head Quarters was counting on their Spy in the Sky to deliver photos that revealed all Soviet activities and land and sea.

"Vertical Insertion"
0600

Training Field

Pope Army Airfield

Outside Fayetteville, North Carolina

General Maxwell Taylor was particularly impressed with all the hard work that he and his planners had done in advocating for and utilizing this new and novel method of warfare: the new term coined for it by the powers that be was heliborne vertical troop insertion. General Taylor used a far simpler and more appropriate term: air assault.

Over the past couple of months, General Taylor and his counterparts in the USAAF on this project were working feverishly to convert the newly-reconstituted 13th Airborne Division to Air Assault status, adding the Sikorsky H-19B and Piasecki H-25C helicopters as integral air assets of the division. This move was unprecedented as all air units, regardless of size and mission, were controlled by the USAAF command structure in support of U.S. Army missions. The helicopter aviation regiments would be modeled after the cavalry in that their mobile units would be broken down by squadron, and each squadron was paired with an airborne battalion.

Over the past three weeks, General Taylor has rigorously drilled the soldiers and airmen of the 13th Airborne Division (Provisional Air Assault) until they worked as a finely-oiled machine. Today would be their final exam and their exhibition to a very select group of generals admirals, and congressmen, who approved the project, along with the Secretary of War, Robert Patterson. They would not fail.

With the launch of a star flare, the soldiers ran from their staging areas to the waiting, warmed-up, helicopters. As each helicopter was filled with soldiers and their equipment, they received clearance to take off, assuming a moderately dense formation while in flight to their target landing zone. The helicopters made staggered landings, with H-19's carrying troops and H-25's carrying Jeeps and other light equipment, all off-loaded in an astonishing small amount of time into the landing zone.

In a matter of less than an hour, the division was assembled in the landing zone and had begun to establish their defensive perimeter, as they would have under actual combat conditions. General Taylor was rather impressed himself with the performance of the division, as was the Secretary of War, who congratulated the General on his hard work and proposed that he draw up plans to convert two more divisions to "Air Assault" status. With a salute and a handshake, the future of warfare had been changed yet again.[20]

Figure 23 - HUP1 H25 Mule

"The Next Level"
0630

Dry-dock Slips 43 & 44

Newport News Naval Shipyard

Newport News, Virginia

The three experienced men stood amid the loud din of ship construction, and marveled at the two hulking hulls being refitted, at break-neck speed,

---

[20] - Reprinted from World War Three 1946 Addendum One - Far East Theatre, Weapons Development, Intelligence By Thomas Figueroa

from their original purpose: Iowa-class battleships. They looked in wondrous awe at the transformation as both ships had been razed to the deck-line, the former BB-65 Illinois and former BB-66 Kentucky were being converted into something resembling aircraft carriers, but different.

There was a test flight of the Army's new helicopters, H-19 and H-25, borrowed by the Navy, on behalf of the Marine Corps. The results were phenomenal. The most amazing part was that the tests were conducted off of three Essex-class aircraft carriers, off the coast of Newport News, Virginia. The irony could not have been lost on the Powers That Be. Three squadrons of 15 helicopters (10 H-19's and 5 H-25's) each were flown from ship to ship, then from ship to shore, in a coordinated operation. All of the helicopters were piloted by freshly-trained Naval Aviators, who passed the Army's rotary-wing training program at Camp Rucker, Alabama, and in the last exercise, carried full complements of Marines with full combat loads, to disgorge them onto a target zone. To the admirals and Marine generals in attendance, this test was a resoundingly amazing success.

As a result, the two hulls that were destined to be built as modern floating long-range artillery batteries, were now slated to be built as combat assault ships. In other words, these ships were to be helicopter-carrying super-troopships, purpose-built to take the U.S. Marines' fight directly to the heart of the enemy. They would be known as the Peleliu-class Combat Landing Ship (Helicopter). The first two ships of this class would be LPD-1 Peleliu and LPD-2 Iwo Jima. All the while, their crews will be training aboard the three original aircraft carriers the tests were conducted on: CV-13 Franklin, CV-17 Bunker Hill and CV-20 Bennington. [21]

---

[21] - Reprinted from World War Three 1946 Addendum One - Far East Theatre, Weapons Development, Intelligence

By Thomas Figueroa

LPD-1 USS Peleliu Receives First Flight of H-25 Helicopters

Desmans Too

Yeorgi had somehow made it back to the Caucasus Mountains near his grandparent's home. He had spent many a summer here when he was younger. He was now 21 years old but felt more like 61. The toll of battle had weighed heavily on his body, mind and especially spirit.

He had personally killed over 47 men. He had seen his bullets rip through their bodies through a Mosin Nagant model 91/31 PU sniper scope. You get a pretty good view of the results of your shots through 3.5 magnification. These images will forever be etched in his mind.

He had purposefully only missed a target once. He still did not know why he did not kill the young Spaniard who was clearly in his sights. Perhaps it was because his commanding officer was not present and looking through the spotting scope or maybe he was just tired of the killing that particular day.

Or it may have been the call of the Desman [22] he had heard just minutes before the opportunity arose to take the shot. For whatever reason, he had missed and missed on purpose.

The Spaniard would have been his 38th kill but that dubious honor was given to another. The fighting in the Pyrenees had slowed down considerably after his miss. Personally, he was glad for the change.

A few months later he was ordered to get on a truck and to make his way towards Vienna. He was one of only a handful of his squad ordered to

---

[22] - Hutterer, R. (2005). Wilson, D. E.; Reeder, D. M, eds. Mammal Species of the World (3rd ed). p. 303

the east. He was almost killed twice by marauding Amerikosi planes in his three-week trek to Austria. Once there he was placed across the river from the Amerikosi and did not have many chances to increase his score. Which was just fine with him.

It was a curious assignment to just sit there and watch the Yankees. No major attempt was made to attack them and he considered the Red Army units facing the Americans to be of inferior quality to the ones he served with in Spain. It almost seemed like they were here just to keep the enemy from advancing further and there was no thought of actually launching an offensive to dislodge them from Vienna. Who was he to second guess the Stavka? Better to not think of such things.

He was on the river for only a couple of weeks when he and his new unit were ordered to board trucks once again and told they were headed for the Black Sea area. The rumor was that a large Soviet force had been trapped in the Levant by the Amerikosi and they were now on their way to the oil fields of Baku.

His heart almost leaped out of his chest when he heard this news. Could it actually be that he was going home? That he would be assigned to be near his grandparent's village?

On the one hand, it would be wonderful to hear the Desman's shrill cry once more but on the other his grandparents would be in danger. He thought about asking his commander for a leave of absence if he was assigned close to Stavropol. His grandparent's village was close by. After all he was a decorated hero.

The area they were going to was pretty quiet so why not give the troops some leave? He began a rumor that they were all going to be sent home for a rest before the Amerikosi arrived. It wasn't true but he wanted to see if he could generate the idea. Maybe they would be allowed to visit Novorossiysk. It was a beautiful city with a white sand beach and one of the best harbors on the Black Sea.

His grandparents had visited there once the Great Patriotic War was over and they mentioned in a letter that the port facilities were devastated. The facilities were attacked by both Soviet and German forces at various times during the last war.

He had heard of the legend of Malaya Zemlya or Small Land. A disastrous and rare Soviet amphibious assault on 3 February 1943 that was almost completely destroyed. A small party of naval infantry succeeded and establishing a bridge-head and held off all Nazi attacks for 225 days. [23]

The Soviet strong point near the harbor denied the German's use of the port during those 225 days. Novorossiysk was liberated on 16 September 1943. The story was a source of great pride for any true Soviet who heard it. It was an amazing feat for any group of men.

Oh how he would love to wet his feet in the warm waters and feel the white sand between his toes. Even if the port facilities were destroyed he doubted that all that beach could have been ruined. There must still be some clean sand remaining and the waters had probably washed away the stains of war.

103 WPM
5 July 1947

William White had become an even faster typist. He could now type 103 words a minute with 98% accuracy. Whatever security concerns the CIA previously had about him suddenly disappeared. Currently he was typing the most Top Secret documents the government had.

Today's was a whopper. The report was over fifty pages long and he was to type it by himself. In his mind, it was quite an honor. In reality, it was probably a matter of practicality for his boss.

The communique was a very comprehensive wrap up of where matters stood in the war to date. As usual his mind wandered and he was able to cut through the standard bureaucratic mumbo jumbo and get to the true meaning. As he typed what was on the handwritten original he mentally paraphrased, for his own amusement, what he was reading without missing a beat.

Over 250,000 Reds were trapped when we invaded Beirut. Even an amateur like him could see it was a brilliant move by the Joint Chiefs to invade behind the commies who were attacking the British positions on the Suez.

The operation was very similar to the landings at Anzio, Italy during World War Two…executed to a tee by US 7th Army Commander General Griswold and his lead combat commander of the V Corps General Gerow…. Gerow would lead his Corps from as close to the front

---

[23] - Memories and musings by Kumara Padmanabha Sivasankara Menon

as he was allowed.

New subject: The bombers were still taking it on the chin despite the Soviet's loss of oil production…LeMay might have to be relieved for psychological reasons…just doesn't seem to understand that 14% losses are unacceptable and unwarranted. He just keeps sending his men into the fire.

Atomic bomb program officially on hold but CIA backed super-secret effort still underway.

Red losses estimated to be on par with ours in the air but their supply lines shorter…Ruskie oil production still increasing and will be up to full capacity in four months.

Shit, that's disappointing…. There appears to be a slight decrease in Soviet pilot training but ours is declining as well. Air war a drain on both sides.

New subject: Navy is doing very well…Commie mini-subs being beaten back and shipping increasing to Trieste and Beirut invasion sites…camouflage (damn mistake…hate that word).

William stops for a brief moment and snatches his round pink typewriter eraser and eraser shield to make a quick correction. Using the brush on the eraser he sweeps away the crumbs. Luckily the CIA's use of heavyweight, high-rag-content bond paper hides errors.

Figure 24 - Typewriter Eraser

Stupid shit, he thought, where was I?...Oh yeah.

The Skinner paint jobs are continuing to be effective. So far the Soviets have not trained their bird pilots to improve accuracy. Upwards of 50 missiles a day are launched at convoys plying the Mediterranean and the English Channel. On average, three missiles a day strike ships for a 6% hit rate. Still devastating, but manageable.

As I recall over 20 ships a day were being sunk by the German submarines during their "Happy Time" in World War Two. There are indications that the missiles are becoming more accurate with ten hits already this month, and it's only the fifth.

The defensive line from Trieste to Vienna had tied up 25 NATO divisions against approximately 60 of the Soviets. Weeks ago, the Reds had stopped attacking Vienna and were digging in. It was estimated that the commies had used up a month's worth of fuel getting their units in place, including a good portion of their air force. Many of the Ruskie casualties were reportedly caused by US Naval and Air Force attacks. The NATO forces were able to take advantage as the enemy transferred up to 40 divisions from the Pyrenees and Western Europe to the Vienna and Trieste areas.

The US Navy was keeping the Reds from effectively attacking Trieste and any part of the Trieste/Vienna Line 200 miles north of the bridgehead. VIII Corps Commander General Middleton was receiving high praise for his use of defensive positions and tactical movement of combat units. First Army Commander General Walker was his usual irascible self but was incredibly skilled at getting Middleton what he needed.

Admiral Nimitz and Walker had developed a good working relationship (that's a surprise). Walker was chomping at the bit to expand his area of control. Also Walker, was expressing irritation at all the resources General Griswold was receiving in his drive from Beirut to the Caucasus. Eisenhower assured Bulldog in a personal letter that his day was coming as soon as the Baltic Sea operations commenced.

The helicopter maneuvers are proceeding. Humm…it appears that there are a number of screw-ups but enough men are being transported to accomplish the mission.

I wonder what the hell that means? What in tarnation is a helicopter?

"The aircraft can hold up to 7 soldiers and drop them in a clearing with great accuracy up to 100 miles from a Combat Landing Ship (Helicopter)."

There's that helicopter word again. Must be some kind of parachute transport that can land on ships. Sure beats me what it is. The terms used are Vertical Envelopment and Heliborne Operations.[24]

Let's see…"Vertical Envelopment will occur in critical points along the attack route and Heliborne Operations will precede the naval taskforces eliminating Soviet defensive placements along the proposed path." Hummm…"see Attachment 14". Didn't give me that one. Sounds like a complex plan.

"The 8th and 15th Air Force will conduct Carpet Bombing in selected areas along the proposed route." Wow, haven't typed the term "Carpet Bombing" in a long time. I thought those tactics were over due to those Soviet SAM missiles. "Concentrated bomber formations can be used

---

[24] - "a tactical maneuver in which troops, either air-dropped or air-landed, attack the rear and flanks of a force, in effect cutting off or encircling the force"

over lightly defended areas such as the scheduled Operations Triple Cross and Backyard. Ground, air and naval intelligence operatives and overflights have confirmed the lack of air defenses in both areas of operation. Large caliber guns and naval barriers have been marked and located. The invasion routes will be nominally free of major obstructions and mine fields due to the efforts of the Freedom Partisans in critical zones of ingress.

The fortifications and minefields that remain will be attacked by air units and Vertical Envelopment." The Turkish are to be commended for their willingness to sabotage their own strongpoints leading along the route chosen for Operation Triple Cross…Swedish and Dane partisans are finishing up the identification of all newly placed obstructions etc.

Hours later William is reaching the end of the report.

Finally, the wrap up… The scheduled Operations should induce the Soviets into consuming about 4 months' worth of fuel. This projected amount of oil would be necessary to move the minimum required units into blocking positions opposing a NATO advance. Such a counter move should drain the remaining fuel and, as a result ground the VVS and halt all Soviet air to ground attacks.

NATO forces should be able to drive back the Soviet defenders who would be lacking ground attack support for the first time in this conflict. In contrast, the US Air Force would be able to gain overall air superiority, negating one of the Red Army's most effective capabilities.

If Ruskies screw-up and don't use the fuel to transport troops into defensive positions, millions of Red soldiers will be trapped throughout Europe.

William thought, Holy shit, that's really something. The Reds are sure in a dire predicament. Damned if they do and damned if they don't.

Rotor Wash

"Jeeeesus those things are loud."

"What!"

"Very funny!"

"What!"

The din of one HUP-1 25 helicopters landing close by is deafening. The racket of a dozen is almost overwhelming. Over 72 individual rotors tearing through the air with no regard for noise abeyance is harmful to the ears at 120 decibels.

General J. Lawton Collins and General Lucian Truscott are witnessing one of the final run throughs off the coast of Greenland. The terrain chosen was similar to what they would encounter later.

General Collins speaks first.

"They're going to hear those things miles away Lucian. At least parachutes are quiet. Those things are slow as well. What's the max speed anyway?"

"Matt we've been over this before. The sound of the helicopters is so unusual that the Reds will never know what hit then. We've done all the tests using both British and Canadian troops in dummy runs on facilities in the UK and no one reacted until it was too late.

It will be just fine and a stellar operation and you know it."

"Well your wrong…I don't know it. Give me my boys hanging from some fine proven silk any day over those noisy eggbeaters. Shit we had 2 crash just last week."

"That was last week Lawton and you know we found the problem. Come-on, this is not like you. You have been embracing change your whole career! Are you going to crap out on us now?"

"You know I got your back Lucian. Just pre-game jitters is all."

"I suggest that we keep toeing the company line and not let anyone else know of your concerns. It's a little too late to change the game plan, don't you agree?"

"Of course, I do and I appreciate your candor.

And another thing Lucian, we've never really worked together before and I want to thank you for the opportunity."

"You know as well as I do Lawton that commanding a corps is three times harder than running an army. It's where the rubber hits the road.

"I jumped at the chance to work with the 82nd and 101st Divisions in such an important operation."

"They've made the transition well thanks to your leadership Lawton. Think of it this way using the helicopter we can land or move troops with unheard of accuracy. No more drifting with the wind and having to spend days forming up while fighting through the enemy. In this operation you will only have to take the objective and hold on for a matter of hours instead of days or weeks like you did in Normandy and Arnhem.

Your own helicopters will re-supply you if need be. All indications are that the surprise will be complete and we'll be landing your support and relief before you have to dig a slit trench."

"We will give it our all Lucian, you know that. The 82nd and 101st don't back down from a fight. We showed that at Bastogne. Even with all the new recruits we are still the best we got."

"I agree Lawton and we are going to need you to prove it once again. What changes have you made since I was last here?"

"We increased the loadout from 6 GIs to 7 by boosting the engine power. It also helped that the pilots have gotten more training time and can deal with the extra weight better now. Before it was a little too much to ask."

"So, same amount of ammo and supplies for each man?"

"Yes."

"That is great news Lawton, just outstanding. How are Gavin and Taylor adjusting?"

"Just fine Lucian. Both are real innovators and have each added their own spin to the SOP developed before we had any real experience on how this was going to work. Once the units are united on the drop zone they function pretty much as they have since the inception of the airborne concept."

"Outstanding!"

Brainstorming
The room was beyond spartan. Irritatingly bright lights filled all the space with the point of being blinding. There were no windows and the air ducts were barely working. For such a new and costly building the Pentagon was surprisingly devoid of modern conveniences.

Figure 25 - Skinner's Office Pentagon

Skinner was settled in his new office inside the huge five-sided building. He was working 16-hour days ever since he was informed that the Stalin's Fire Missile strike percentage on ships had increased. The spike started on the first of July. The increase in hits was approaching an alarming number rapidly.

The Doctor and Jim had been brainstorming all morning with a group of artists and experts in camouflage. The goal was to anticipate the Soviet's next moves and develop counter measures. With the Razzle Dazzle paint job they had guessed correctly. But they felt that the odds were not in their favor, given the surge in missile strikes.

In the afternoon another meeting was scheduled that would include their artists and engineers pulled from all disciplines to create new ways of hiding in plain sight.

While Skinner and his teams understood that their solutions were fixes and were only temporary, they recognized that it was the function of The Joint Chiefs of Staff to determine the long-term solution. Everyone was aware that the situation was similar to the Allies of World War II capturing the launching sites of the V2. Now, NATO needed to capture or destroy the Red's:

1. Means of production
2. Launch sites within range of NATO's shipping lanes.

Skinner and Jim had learned how to work well together. Between them, they developed their own brainstorming exercise based on the original work of Alex Osborn and Skinner's experience. Their new method had been responsible for most of the ideas being currently under consideration.

Jim Crenshaw learned the "brainstorming" technique, from of all people, his father. His hated parent was in one of the first groups of sales people trained by Alex Osborn.

Later, his father had held training sessions at their home after a company vice president deemed the exercises a waste of time and banned them from company property. The sales force knew better and decided to run their own sessions.

Voices coming up through the heating system from Jim's living room had put him to sleep for years. The only time sounds of excitement and enthusiasm filled the house were when his father was leading the class. Between the monthly training sessions Jim's house was filled with drunken rage.

Sixteen-year old James Alexander Crenshaw had been unwittingly trained by a master of the brainstorming method…his father. Who would have imagined that voices heard through the heating duct would create an idea producing prodigy?

The combination of Jim's developing skills and Dr. Skinner's Behavioral Psychology expertise assured that no idea was dismissed out of hand and all suggestions were given a fair review.

Osborn's rules were simple:

1. Go for quantity
2. Withhold criticism
3. Welcome wild ideas
4. Combine and improve ideas with the slogan 1+1=3 emphasized

Figure 26 - Brainstorming Session 1947

Spoofing

Skinner and his team were developing ways to spoof the pigeons that were guiding the missiles fired at the NATO ships. Following the Razzle Dazzle paint jobs success the next innovation was inspired by the observation that missile hits seemed limited to specific kinds of ships.

It was Jim who first pointed out that certain ships had similar superstructures. Luckily Skinner's team had developed a possible solution. The group quickly contacted a manufacture who was able to provide lightweight, folding, tent-like covers that could be placed quickly over a ship's antenna array.

The Navy complained mightily about the coverings affecting their radar abilities. Skinner pointed out that the Soviets had very few ships left and none of them were on the open seas. The Soviet Babushka Min-subs could not be seen on radar at any rate and posed a much smaller threat than the missiles. In addition, the missiles were too small to be seen by the naked eye as they traveled toward their target at 900 kph.

The first ships to receive the antenna covers were almost immune to the Red's new targeting scheme. The Navy brass shut up and issued new orders to ship captains. Crewmen aboard the vessels were soon fabricating covers and soon the missile strikes became rare once more.

The next project on the drawing board was an instant smoke screen generation system using rockets launched from the targeted ships.

For this concept to be successful, two coordinated components had to be in place. The first element was an infrared device mounted aboard planes to detect the missiles.[25] The second element was a smoke generating system to obscure the target. The spotting device would alert the Navy that missiles were in flight and the release of smoke would blind the organic pilots.

The time from missile launch to impact was estimated to be 7 to 13 minutes. This time frame would be the window of opportunity or releasing the smoke screen. The screens only lasted a few minutes. Timing and coordination remain paramount to confusing the pigeons and preventing missile strikes.

Skinner and his team theorized that the next innovation by the Reds would be to enhance their own infrared scopes and incorporate them into anti-ship missiles. Ships make very large heat signatures when surrounded by cooler water. Even a very primitive scope could create an image good enough for a keen-eyed Columba to peck effectively and keep its missile on target. The combination of the Soviet's version of Skinner's pigeon guidance system and their own advanced heat detecting scope would assure that the missile hit the ship.

Assuming they were correct in anticipating the Red's next move Skinner's team began work on ways to thwart an infrared guided missile system. Concepts under discussion with Naval Ordinance include:

1. Exploding clouds of gas designed to blind or attract the infrared guidance system
2. Barrage balloons suspended above a convoy with heat signature similar in size and shape to the ships below

---

[25] - AGARD-AG-20 - History of German Guided Missiles Development – author and editors BENECKE, T., QUICK, A. W. , SCHULZ, W. Pg. 201 – 217

3. Heated chaff dropped from planes or rockets

At a previous meeting a number of team members mentioned that Soviet technical advances were not arriving as often as expected. Intelligence operatives had been hearing rumors of a major change in the leadership of Soviet research and development.

Intel proposed that a single genius might be responsible for many of the Soviet breakthroughs. Further, they suggested that this person had gone missing. Also, they presumed that Stalin had once again purged his ranks and was feeding his paranoia.

At the conclusion of the meeting the group agreed to pursue the new spoofing ideas of gas, balloons and chaff. These countermeasures eventual implementation should buy the Navy another two months of freedom from the unerring missile strikes. It was just another day in the seemingly never-ending battle of spoof and counter spoof.

Figure 27- Early German Infrared Detection System Mounted in Me 110

Chapter Seven: Meanwhile Up North

This well-worn copy of the iconic freedom-fighting armband has belonged to none other than Captain Gunnar Frijsenvang, who was the head of the Resistance Movement in Aarhus on May 5, 1945.

Old Friends, New Enemies

Gunnar Dyrberg and others had resurrected the Danish resistance group Holger Danske. The group had been instrumental in actions against the Nazis in World War Two throughout occupied Denmark. Their missions included the assassination of Danish collaborators, and towards the end of the war particularly heinous Germans.

Holger Danske was founded by five men who initially fought on the Finnish side against the Soviets during the Winter War in 1939. These experienced fighters had the particular skills needed to gather the type of intelligence NATO required for the coming operation. They were being called upon to identify Soviet defenses along the Danish Straits.

Overtime Danish resistance fighters had adopted the "Ten Commandments" written by Arne Sejr during World War Two. He drafted his list in an effort to compel his fellow countrymen to resist the Nazi occupation.[26] A new version of the Commandments were revised to the following after the Soviet invasion in 1946:

1. You must not go to work in Soviet lands.
2. You shall do a bad job for the Soviets.
3. You shall work slowly for the Soviets.
4. You shall destroy important machines and tools.
5. You shall destroy everything that may be of benefit to the Soviets.
6. You shall delay all transport.
7. You shall boycott Soviet films and papers.
8. You must not shop at Communist stores.
9. You shall treat traitors for what they are worth.
10. You shall protect anyone chased by the Soviets.

Join the Struggle for the freedom of Denmark!

One group in this newest conflict, rejected the new Commandments and embraced the invading Soviets. They were members of the Borgerlige Partisaner or BOPA. BOPA had been formed by communist sympathizers. Since their inception in World War Two, they remained

---

[26] - Hitler's Savage Canary: A History of the Danish Resistance in World War II by David Lampe, Birger Riis-Jørgensen

true believers in their interpretation of Karl Marx's writings.

Holder Danske and BOPA had fought alongside each other against the hated Nazis for years. Each member of the two groups had probably saved the lives of individuals in the other group at one time or another. Now they were sworn enemies based on political ideology.

The Soviets tried to use BOPA in an attempt to eradicate other resistance groups. Curiously BOPA was unusually ineffective in operations against Holder Danske.

There appears to have been an unwritten understanding between these two groups. Each had looked the other way when unexpected confrontations occurred. In the life and death of war, experiences shared with fellow fighters can often be of paramount importance in future encounters.

Holder Danske's primary NATO task was mapping out all Soviet manned fortifications on the Danish shore from the Skagerrak through the Kattegat and into the Baltic Sea. In addition, information on minefields was requested. Special emphasis was to be placed on the Great Belt and Oresund passages.

The members of Holger Danske were almost finished with their assignment when they were confronted by a patrol of BOPA communist supporters. A few terse questions were asked and fists started flying. No one was seriously hurt but the incident was the first time the groups had come to blows.

The survey had taken three months and revealed that virtually no improvements had been added by the Soviets. The information was now in the hands of British Intelligence. Surprisingly, many of the strong points operating in the last war were not being manned. Minefields still remained in place but their locations were well known. NATO planners were eager to incorporate all of the gathered reconnaissance material into their plan of action.

Dead Corner in a Dead Sea

The plan was bold. It was almost as bold as forcing the Turkish Straits. Both operations would involve large clandestine operations and innovations on a scale never seen before. Included were massive amounts of firepower to be provided by the guns of the world's remaining battleships. In addition, squadrons of naval airpower would be launched from an unprecedented number of aircraft carriers assembled at the mouth of both the Danish and Turkish Straits.

The combat ships were tasked with giving up their very existence to protect the real strike force composed of troop transports and their logistics tail. The battleships were considered obsolete in the new world of aircraft carriers. However, current circumstances demanded that the pinpoint accuracy of their 16-inch guns once more. These old battlewagons were to put themselves time and time again between enemy forces and the fragile transports.

The surviving shore batteries could easily punch their way through the thin sides of a Liberty or Victory ship. The 12 inch armed steel belt of the USS Wisconsin was a different matter altogether. Her 16-inch guns easily outranged, with astounding accuracy, all enemy weapons likely to be encountered.

22 American battleships remained in service along with eight Royal Navy battlewagons. These 30 ships were ready to play a large role in the two largest, brazen and some would say most perilous military operations ever planned.

The minefields and anti-ship obstacles had been located and identified with procedures designed to clear them. The planners at NATO were very surprised at the lack of new minefields. It was thought that the Soviets would have committed their resources on mining the straits. Thankfully they had not.

Operation Triple Cross was scheduled for the third week in June. From all indications, everything was on schedule to meet the target date. The forcing of the Danish Straits had rarely been considered, attempted or much less accomplished.

The operation in the Danish Straits was so outrageous that even if the Soviets had been informed of exactly what was about to happen they would probably dismiss the evidence as a smoke screen for some other mission. The thought that NATO would put such a large force at risk for no obvious gain would have caused the Reds to look for the "real" target.

Other more likely locations for a planned invasion of Europe had been presented to a number of known Soviet agents. It was hoped that the informants would pass along the erroneous information to their Soviet handlers. The sham sites included The Bay of Biscay, Pas de Calais and once again Normandy.

The staging area for Operation Triple Cross was not England but Shetland, the islands north of Scotland by 200 miles. The distance from the Shetland Islands to the entrance of the Danish Straits was comparable to the distance from Okinawa to Japan.

Okinawa had been the base of the planned invasion of Japan, an operation twice the scope of Triple Cross. The Japanese invasion was ultimately aborted as a result of dropping the atomic bombs. The Shetland and the Okinawan bases of operation, support and logistics are comparable. These facts suggest a good outcome for Triple Cross.

The Baltic Sea was known as "a dead corner in a dead sea". The real questions were, what would NATO gain by putting vast amounts of valuable assets into such an endeavor? Why enter a blind alley? For what overarching purpose would anyone put thousands of lives in such peril?

Maniacal Machinations

He was hiding in plain sight, within minutes of the Kremlin. Lavrenti Beria was waiting like a snake for his chance to strike and kill.

His face and even his physique had been altered. He occasionally walked the streets in the very shadow of Stalin's former office. He had practiced disguising his gait during the hours he was recovering from surgery.

His network of operatives claimed that the only man Beria feared was close to death. Then it was reported that Stalin had recovered thanks to some kind of new surgery that could replace vital organs. The details were very murky. Beria dismissed them out of hand as a sophisticated ploy to make fools believe that Stalin would live forever by having his organs replaced one by one.

He was also aware of Sergo Peshkova's disappearance. In addition, Beria knew all about Sergo and his underground hiding place. He had elected to keep all this information to himself. He was planning to resurrect Peshkova when the time was right and use him for his own purposes. Lavrenti had a true gift for recognizing genius when he encountered it.

Sergo, the brilliant problem solver and organizer, would come in very useful in the new Soviet Union. Beria was convinced that if Stalin had listened to Sergo the US Navy would have been decimated. Instead the Dictator's usual demons had poisoned his mind to anyone who could truly defeat their enemies. He was again relying on idiots and toads.

Nikita Khrushchev had missed his appointed death by dismemberment.

The fact that Beria failed to kill his intended target obsessed him. Focusing on his failures was Beria's true Achilles Heel. He was spending many hours and using up far too many assets in his quest to finish off Nikita.

The irony was that he actually liked the man. However, he clearly recognized that Khrushchev was a roadblock to his path to power and that he had to die.

He had another ace up his sleeve in the form of an agent who was poisoning Stalin. She was still in place and carrying out her deadly task. By now, other organs should be starting to fail. If in fact Stalin had received new kidneys, they would likely be the first of many organs to be replaced.

The only catch to his plan was the Red Army might just lose the war before he could assume power. Beria was above all a pragmatist. He believed the current leadership was sure to fail and would be defeated. Consequently, he understood he would have to time his rebirth carefully.

If he was too late, and the war already lost, he would end up the leader of nothing. He would have to wait for a decisive Soviet battlefield victory to make his bid for control. In fact, a local victory, no matter how small, would put him in place to negotiate from a position of strength. The overall outcome seemed to be adhering to the old adage win the battle but lose the war.

Beria was sure Nikita would do exactly the opposite until all was lost. Khrushchev would assuredly open negotiations after a major Red Army defeat. As a result Nikita would be in the worst bargaining stance possible. He would be forced to negotiate from a position of inferiority and weakness.

Beria was willing to trade any territory conquered in World War Three for access to the vast financial resources that America could provide. In addition to Western Europe he would offer autonomy for Estonia, Latvia and Lithuania as the final incentive. The offer had to be perfectly timed and he was the only leader that could orchestrate such a feat.

His first attempt on Khrushchev's life had failed because the Pimp was late for his appointed "Bear Hug". The next try had to be perfectly implemented. Once Nikita was out of the way Lavrenti would be free to kill Stalin. If Stalin died first he was sure the army would support the supposed "hero Nikita" of Stalingrad and not him if it came down to a confrontation.

He was in the process of vetting a sniper he could blackmail. Assassination by sharp shooter was not the most common method in 1947. In fact Beria did not recall any political leaders who had been killed at long range. Most of the recent attempts and successes had been up close and personal.

He certainly had many exceptional shots from which to choose. The Red Army seemed to be especially adept at producing long-range shooters. There were a dozen former Soviet snipers with over 400 kills each. What he needed was a proven killer yet one that was virtually unknown in Moscow.

He had zeroed in on a female Czech sniper with 30 kills. Enough proven skill to ensure a kill but not ostentatious enough to warrant fame. Her name was Marie Ljalková-Lastovecká. [27] She was perfect for the part. His real challenge was how to force or coerce her into shooting his old friend Khrushchev.

He was confident no one would suspect a babushka. She would pose as an old woman just getting out of the cold in an apartment building. He was betting no one could imagine a female being a threat to Khrushchev. The sniper rifle would be placed ahead of time in the building chosen and would wait for Marie's skilled hands.

---

[27] - The History of World WAR II SNIPERS By Steve Markelo

Figure 28 - Marie Ljalková-Lastovecká

Doppelganger

Stalin was down to one man he could trust, the Little Bear Nikita. His gapped tooth smile and balding head were a comfort to the dictator. Even as a young man Khrushchev had been losing his hair. Stalin enjoyed mentioning Nikita's baldness constantly and then would comment on his own thick head of hair. The fact that they were of the same height was also reassuring. Both could walk around in each other's presence and not feel inferior.

The two men knew that Beria was still alive which meant their lives were endangered beyond the norm. Beria and his henchmen had to be found promptly and eliminated. The search was a great distraction and a huge drain on the few remaining trustworthy men they had.

Also, there was consternation over the disappearance of Sergo Peshkova. Sergo could be very dangerous to the Soviet cause if he were captured alive or defected. Sergo's second in command, the giant Georgie, had disappeared as well. So many people disappearing in such a short time was cause for concern unless Stalin himself was responsible.

Brezhnev, the man who had assassinated Molotov was on the verge of entering the inner circle when he had killed himself. Stalin could not understand someone who would give up his own life to save anyone else, much less a child. His children were certainly disposable if a situation demanded it.

Both men knew that Beria was going to strike again. Each had set about finding surrogate lookalikes to attend essential public gatherings. Nikita's doppelganger had gone so far as to visit the troops on the Caucasus Line to boost morale. The man was an excellent actor and could fool all but the most intimate of Khrushchev's comrades.

Stalin's doubles were not so talented but were well suited to the purpose of being a target. His best double was named "Rashid" and had spent two years studying with Alexei Dikiy who had portrayed Stalin in several propaganda films. Another political decoy was Felix Dadaev. These men and several others attended all number of gatherings in the hopes of drawing out an assassination attempt. The thought of being killed by mistake did not seem to hamper their performances. Perhaps there were other incentives more compelling than your very life.

All the actors were wined and dined and treated like they were one of the most powerful men in the world. In public people jumped when they spoke and did exactly whatever was requested. Their families were treated like royalty in their hometowns. Except for the constant threat of death, they led very good lives. Of course, the doubles had to be very careful what they said or asked for. The wrong request at the wrong time could get them tortured and their families massacred.

Stalin and Khrushchev use their surrogates quite freely. The two leaders enjoyed the freedom of missing the many mundane public appearances they usually were required to attend. Also, they found it was a great relief to not be a target.

A number of famous books used doppelgangers in their plots. Charles Dickens' Tale of Two Cities, Mark Twain's - The Prince and the Pauper, and the most famous of all, The Man in the Iron Mask by Alexandre Dumas comprised a short list of examples.

By 1947 the doppelganger was a familiar plot twist in novels and plays. The British had used a number of them to fool the Germans in World War Two. In 1944 an Australian actor, Clifton James, was sent to various locations posing as General Montgomery in attempts to confuse the Germans as to the location of the D-Day landings in Normandy. Reports of Monty's whereabouts in Gibraltar and North Africa reached German intelligence.

Only time would tell if these Soviet sacrificial lambs would give up their lives and potentially lead to Beria's whereabouts. At the very least an attempted assassination would squander one or more of Lavrenti's assets in this newest game of cross and double cross.

The loss of a few doppelgangers was of no consequence when taken in the larger context of world wars that had exterminated millions.

Zhukov's Caucasus

Marshall Georgy Zhukov was in his element. He was so busy he had forgotten about his missing fingernails and what had caused them. Wars often forced many who survive the chaos to live in the present. Throwing oneself into your work was a sure way to forget the past. Doing your job meant the life or death of your friends or in Zhukov's case the lives of hundreds of thousands of troops.

Although the NATO forces had move swiftly, his troops ran to the north and rear even faster. He had reached the Lessor Caucasus before the Amerikosi and was in an excellent position to repel all attacks launched by the Capitalist Pigs.

The few blocking forces he threw in the way of the enemy had given him enough time to setup a proper defense. His comrades were as ready as they would ever be. This was not tank country so the lack of said vehicles was of no concern to him. In any event the Stavka seemed to be hoarding them for their own purposes.

Right now Zhukov's main concern was a shortage of ground attack airplanes and fighter cover. The Sturmovik was his flying artillery and best source of information on enemy locations. Without fighter cover the "flying tanks" were easy pickings for the Amerikosi jets. Though still not present in large numbers these NATO jet fighters posed a major threat to his planes.

The Stavka was stockpiling away the Soviet's own versions of jet fighters. The new jet engine, the Klimov VK-1, was designed by Vladimir Yakovlevich Klimov. This innovative engine made the Mig 9 Fargo and Yak 15 Feather competitive with the American F-80 Shooting Star. Klimov had been greatly assisted by the defector William Perl using the components provided by Barr and Sarant.

Georgy was confident that he had the tools to hold the line against NATO. The VVS was the key. If the air force kept the skies reasonably clear of enemy planes he was sure he could hold long enough to outlast NATO.

He had been assured that the Amerikosi had no more atomic bombs in their arsenal. However all bets were off if they did deploy an atomic bomb. That got him wondering…what was NATO's end game? How did they expect this conflict to end? Once again, his instincts were telling him that the capitalist war mongers were up to something, but what?

An invasion of France or Germany from the sea would accomplish little but retake already decimated lands stripped clean by Stalin's armies. The forces in the Pyrenees would be hard to dislodge and could easily retreat giving up space for time.

Marshall Konstantin Rokossovsky was in charge of all the Red Army forces in Europe including the Pyrenees Line. Zhukov had every confidence that Konstantin could extradite the Soviet units in Western Europe if warranted. In retreat there would be many NATO casualties.

Rokossovsky was one of the best commanders at Stalingrad and the Battle of Kursk in World War Two. He had stood up to Stalin insisting at the beginning of Operation Bagration that two points of breakthrough would be required. His proposal was at odds with the Stalin's mandate of a single massive effort to breach the enemy's defense lines. He had convinced Stalin that his reasoning was valid. It had taken three tense meetings, any one of which could have meant his death.

Zhukov had challenged his staff to consider ways to defeat their own defenses. His goal was to find potential weaknesses in his plan. Georgy had one particularly talented colonel who identified several flaws that the enemy might exploit.

In addition the Colonel presented his idea of a possible enemy plan. His fictitious NATO plan involved investing Istanbul and using their fleet to land in the Crimea. Such and amphibious assault would circumvent Zhukov's forces in the Caucasus. He quickly gave the Colonel a reward in the form of a promotion and upgraded his family's living quarters back in Moscow.

Georgy then called Marshall Mikhailovich Budyonny, who was the commander of the Transcaucasian Front. Zhukov made it clear he wanted the Turkish Straits strengthened immediately. Budyonny advised him that the quickest way to bar passage to any invasion force was with mines.

Zhukov then called the other members of the Stavka and convinced each to sign off on diverting all stores of naval mines to Budyonny's Transcaucasian Front.

Leaving the details to his staff, Zhukov moved on to other issues like all good leaders.

Something is Afoot

General Lenard Gerow was too close to the fighting in the opinion of the General's Aide, Colonel Jerry Richardson. The fact that Jerry was in danger as well might have added to his thought process. Gerow had been warned by no less than Ike about putting his life in needless jeopardy but the General was not one to take advice from the sidelines.

The Colonel had narrowly missed being killed twice while sitting beside the General. Once a sniper's bullet had taken a chunk out of their driver's shoulder. The second time he himself had been hit by a piece of shrapnel at the beginning of a Russian rocket barrage. Luckily, the Katyusha rocket had landed just north of the hole they were crouched in near Van, Turkey. Minutes before they had been admiring the view of Lake Van.

The Soviets were no longer in a headlong retreat and were becoming increasingly aggressive. The advanced units of the V Corps included Combat Command B of The Big Red One or 1st Division. CCB had taken the lead from CCA who were sent to the rear for R&R after a brutal advance that had covered 330 miles in 10 days.

The Reds had started to fight back outside of Kasrik, Turkey. After the fighting died down in the area, the General had taken a side trip to Mount Judi. The mountain was the supposed "Place of Descent" where Noah's Ark came to rest after the great flood. The General had come away a believer. Jerry, on the other hand, was more interested in the sites location which did not impress him in the least.

Biblical scholars now put the site of the grounding as Mount Ararat that was 100 miles to the north. This site was much more impressive at 17,000 feet. According to the local Rabi, Mount Judi was the true site and Ararat was chosen later because it was higher.

In reality Jerry didn't care one way or the other. He was happy that the General was content with Mount Judi because the Reds were currently swarming all over Ararat and he wanted nothing to do with that scenario.

Figure 29 - Resting place of the Arc? Mount Judi in the background

According to the General their mission was to chase the Reds until they met heavy resistance and nothing more until further orders were received. The General suspected that something else was afoot (as he put it) in regard to strategic plans. He commented more than once that the Caucasus Mountains were no place to attack. To his thinking, there were probably plans to by-pass the Reds that were digging in along the Caucasus foothills.

Once again the General's thoughts on the subject were fine with Jerry. He had been involved in the assault on Monte Cassino 28 in World War Two and that battle was a piece of cake compared to what they would soon face. He had overheard a briefing by G2 claiming that the Commies were using the Lesser Caucasus as their mainline of resistance. A defensive setup in this location would save what was left of the oil fields in Baku and Tbilisi.

The Lessor Caucasus were approximately the same height as the Pyrenees at about 8,000 feet. By comparison the Caucasus themselves

---

[28] - Monte Cassino: The Hardest-Fought Battle of World War I By Matthew Parker

made the Pyrenees range look like a picket fence. The peaks in the Caucasus were on the order of 14,000 to 18,000 feet high and a good 30 miles wider than the Pyrenees. 30 miles was a long way when it meant climbing up and down an 18,000 -foot mountain.

These towering peaks were the fallback positions for the Reds so Jerry was glad there was something "afoot" to avoid fighting through them. No one wanted to assault a dug in enemy especially one that had the high ground. And the Caucasus were the highest ground around.

Neither he nor General Gerow knew what was up. Rumors were running rampant. Gossip ranged from paratroops to flying saucers. It never ceased to amaze Jerry how outlandish rumors could become. There was even one about taking the City of Istanbul and entering the Black Sea for Christ sake.

Some of Griswald's 15th Army's divisions had been recalled back to Beirut. For the life of him the colonel could not find out who's command they had been transferred to. It was like they disappeared. Jerry was warned not to dig any deeper and had to back off despite General Gerow's prodding to find out.

The fact that the 15th Army was getting smaller as they approached the Soviet defensive works in the Caucasus was another indication that something was "afoot".

Preparations on the Pyrenees

The fog was almost so thick you could walk on it. This would have been a good day to start the attack, thought General William Hood Simpson. A dense fog like todays would masked the racket made by our troops as they move up to a line of debarkation. Just no way around it. Without the fog, the Reds will hear us and know something is up. Hopefully they won't have anything left after the Baltic and Black Sea attacks.

"General Brooks come here for a minute please."

"Yes, Sir"

"We can cut out the Sir stuff when were not in public Ed."

"Thanks Bill."

"Interesting how Ike has paired officers together who have never served with each other on this little soiree he has planned. There must be some method to his thinking."

"Well maybe he knows us better than we know ourselves. So far it seems like you and I are reading from the same playbook and I hear Walker and Middleton have hit it off in Vienna and Griswold and Gerow are moving faster than expected to the Caucasus."

"Yeah it has been a pleasure serving with you. We expect that the other attacks will further drain the Reds away from our front. They will have to respond and when they do we will pounce. As you know the British, Spanish, French, etc., will take the lead to rid Western Europe of the Red Army.

On paper, we will be the backup and they will do the heavy lifting but you and I know that they are not up to the task and at some point we will have to leap frog past them and take over. I suspect it will be sooner than later"

"I concur Bill. Our European allies are fought out. Imagine being overrun twice in six years and then losing the air space above your head. It must have been hell in Britain until we showed up again."

"Alright then...Let's get to that meeting."

Fifteen minutes later, General Simpson's aide calls the assembled command staff to attention as the General enters.

"Sit down gentleman and smoke em if you got em. General Brooks could you please briefly go over our plan of attack into France."

"Thank you, Colonel Williams. Briefly the operation will commence with a broad demonstration on the enemy's front by the 84th, 102nd, 39th and 40th Divisions. These will be limited attacks designed to fix the Red units and to keep them from reinforcing their 18th and the 4th Guards Rifle Corps. The 18th and 4th will be assaulted by the British 7th Army and the Spanish 3rd Army.

If you will recall the 3rd is populated by former Spanish Republican Communist veterans and Basque fighters. These men are trying to win clemency for their participation in the Civil War that ended in 39. The unit is expected to suffer severe casualties. Opposing them will be some of their former pals in arms and communist comrades who the Soviets have drafted. It should get real ugly.

We are going to stay out of it for the first couple of days. We will provide support as required while the two old allies go at it.

Joe, you will be liaising with a Major...um...Grec of the Spanish 2nd

Corps and he will be suggesting fire orders. Feel free to double check if you have the time but don't put our allies in danger.

Mac, you will be working with Colonel Richardson of the British V Corps and you can pretty much trust their calls.

Richard your counterpart will nominally be the RAF's Wing Commander Roland Falk. I'm sure he will assign someone else in the short run.

You are to keep in close contact and to coordinate closely on all ground strikes. There will be no friendly fire incidents on this operation. That is our goal gentlemen…Am I understood!"

"YES Sir."

"Good, now…where is Jennings?"

The assembled officers look around and finally a Major speaks up.

"He took ill Sir and is in the …er… shitter."

"Who in god's name is filling in Major?"

"Colonel Wilkins Sir."

"And where might he be?"

"He also had to … run."

"Charles, you will take over the 102nd until things are sorted out. Major, get General Busbee up to speed in an hour. I know you can do this Charles. You've been asking to get out from behind those guns of yours so now's the chance."

"Yes, Sir."

Brooks continues the pre-mission briefing for another 14 minutes. Then General Simpson takes over. The General gives his usual rambling version of a motivational speech.

William Simpson is much beloved as a commander and as a combat leader. His men will follow him anywhere. But he is one of the worst speakers in the US Army, and that is saying a lot. His men practically have to pinch themselves to stay awake at this hour of the morning and without their coffee it would be impossible.

An unfortunate British officer was present to coordinate and could not find any tea. He dismissively declined coffee. Missing his caffeine intake he nearly fell out of his chair. He meekly wandered over and got a cup of Joe that he grudgingly swallowed as Simpson droned on.

One of the problems with General Simpson speaking techniques was his lack of inflection and monotonous delivery. Luckily for all involved he normally repeated what the earlier officers had outlined compounding his tedious delivery but doing no harm.

The basic plan was the British and Spanish divisions would hit the Soviets hard starting out at 0400 hours and push continuously. Their 2-day goals were within 30 miles of the debarkation line. The allies' main objective was to wear the Reds down while letting the artillery and fighter bombers work their magic.

The US divisions were to cover the flanks and repel the expected counter attacks.

According to G2 the Red Army units they were facing had been stripped of most of their assets. The Baltic and Black Sea operations should draw down even more of the enemy's strength. The end result would be ridding France of the Godless Commies.

Cosmo is Late

Master Sergeant Erin De Cosmos is late for the first time in his long Army career. His jeep was run off the road outside of the village of Quraf on the Shetland Islands. A truck full of hay pulled out of nowhere and his driver was badly injured when the jeep rolled over. Tracking down another vehicle to commandeer took 55 minutes that he could not afford to lose. He tried to sneak into the pre-mission briefing as General Truscott was well into the briefing.

"The reason I'm telling you ground pounders this is because these actions will allow the Navy to get our asses on shore and take the fight to the enemy.

This is one of the most audacious…that means "daring" to you Cosmo…"

Laughs erupt and Erin De Cosmos turns a bright red.

"No offense Cosmo. As you know gentleman this attack will initially be aimed at taking 100 miles on either side of the Skagerrak and Kattegat as well as Copenhagen proper. It involves a fleet equal to the D-day landings and our newest innovation, the helicopter.

If all goes well the Task force will pass through and into the Baltic Sea proper with a full 20 divisions. These divisions will land and invest Gdansk/Gdynia, Poland taking the newly repaired port facilities there.

The Navy will initially be covering our butts with 16- to 3-inch naval ordinance and 10 carriers full of fighter bombers.

The USAAF will follow up within days using the airfields we capture along the way. All in all we should have continuous air superiority on the order of 3 to 1. The word is that the Reds and their air force will be strung out from Spain to Turkey and Moscow to us in Poland.

Mind you they still have to extradite themselves from Western Europe or be cut off by us. Walker and the First Army in Austria are posed to step out as well. Also, the Commies will have to watch for 15th Army near the Black Sea. What this all means is that we should expect very light opposition for our initial operations. Then all hell should break lose somewhere along the line as we head south and link up with the boys in Vienna.

This is a classic pincher movement on a continental scale. The end result will be the isolation of the enemy far from home. He will have no fuel to move much less attack. Refined oil is the key to this war as it was in the last. Our advantage is that our oil sources are in Texas whereas the Reds' remains within our reach.

All you really need to know is how to get your boys ready and quickly moving to your first objective. Speed is of the essence.

That last bit was me showing off by the way and is of no concern to you mugs. "

Laughter erupts again.

We will be advancing until we link up with Walker and his First Army. This means 24 hour continuous action with 18 hour shifts and sleeping on the way to the next fight. Units will be moving by bounding overwatch on a brigade scale.

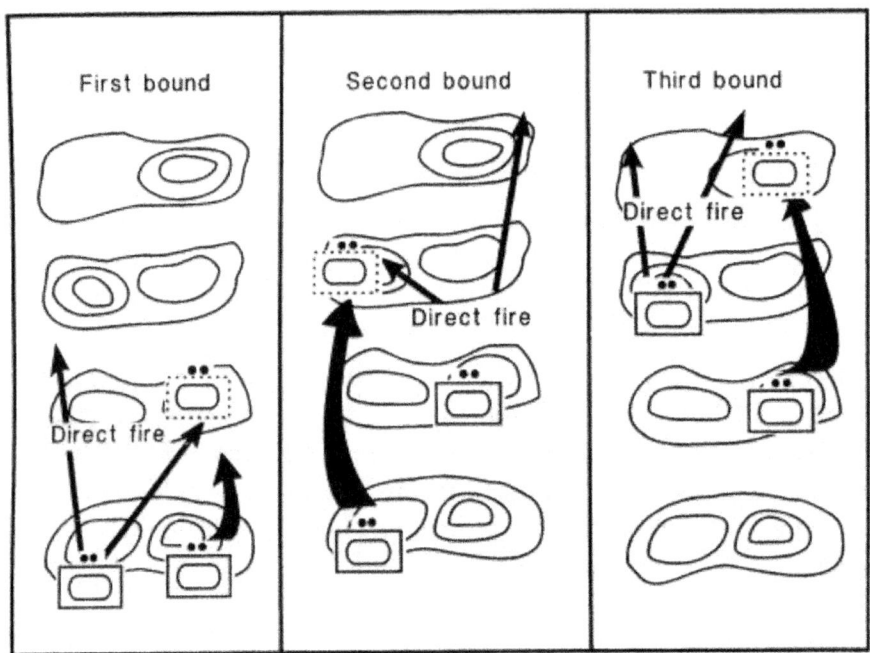

Figure 30 - Bounding Overwatch

The helicopters will be our eyes along the way. Our Patton tanks and Wolf Hound armored cars will be our artillery and heavy weapons. You will be the men who capture and then hold the ground until relieved. If we fail we will be trapped instead of the Reds...so we will not fail. IS THAT UNDERSTOOD!

A resounding "YES, SIR" bounces off the walls.

As mentioned before the Commies have graciously repaired the port facilities at Gdansk/Gdynia. I'm sure they did not foresee what we had in mind when they did so. We will thank them for their work as soon as we take it from them. While we are at it we can repay them for all the GIs that they have captured and killed.

There should be no need for landing craft on this whole operation. Thanks to the helos and the excellent off loading facilities in both Copenhagen and Gdansk/Gdynia we should be able to keep our feet dry and take the fight to the Reds.

Our first goal once we are rolling is Warsaw. That should get a reaction like an electric shock to a frog from Stalin and crew. Once they start shifting their forces around Walker, his First Army will attack to increase the pressure on their already stretched supply lines.

I think you've all heard rumors about our Coups de Grace that should end this thing quickly. The Joint Chiefs are counting on our little demonstration to set off a series of rebellions in the territories now under Soviet domination.

Let me read from this report…"

Truscott picks up a couple of pieces of paper that were sitting on the table near him. He begins to read.

"History has shown that when a subjugated people can see salvation and independence on their doorstep they will respond by rising up against their oppressor. We will be emboldening all resistance fighters and partisans with supplies and encouragement.

The war for the hearts and minds of the conquered western Europeans has begun in full earnest. Many have responded and are just waiting for our landfall to start their long road to liberty. The famous French Resistance movement increased dramatically in the lead up to D-day and continued to grow as we fought our way to shore.

Given the chance people will find the courage to join the fight for their freedom."

He puts the paper down and stares into the crowd as if collecting his thoughts. He begins again.

"Well … enough of that rah rah stuff. Be mentally prepared to witness the same kind of atrocities against innocent victims that we ran into in Germany. Reports are that Stalin is a bigger murderer than Hitler by far. We should see evidence of his crimes along the way to Warsaw. So be prepared and keep your troops under control.

We don't want any vigilantism or our own version of Malmedy.[29]

Copenhagen

The now familiar thump, thump, thump of helicopter rotor blades tore through the undisturbed air over the ancient and formidable star-fortress near the harbor in Copenhagen. You could just make out the distinctive shape of the earthworks from a helicopter traveling at a height of 30 feet.

---

[29] - Fatal Crossroads: The Untold Story of the Malmedy Massacre at the Battle of The Battle of the Bulge By Danny Parker

The five-point design had vexed invading armies for centuries with overlapping fields of fire. Eventually the wide spread use of powerful cannons was able to overwhelm the defenses. This particular fort was named Kastellet. It was built in the 1600s it had not been used as a fort since 1807.

Lieutenant Louis and his company were on their way to make sure Kastellet wasn't being used as a fort in this war. US Army G2 had confirmed the Reds were occupying the citadel as a headquarters. Capturing the senior staff was the main reason for taking the fort. The Lieutenant hoped that his 150 men were enough to secure the area as they neared the earthworks and rapidly began descending.

Figure 31- Kastellet

The lead helicopters gently settled down. Louis and the other two-dozen men with him started to jump off. They spread out and immediately prepared to provide cover fire for the next squadron of helicopters.

Luckily the Soviets were using the main building for both their barracks and headquarters. The second set of transports was just settling down when the first dazed Ruskies stumbled out of the building and stood there gaping at the strange machines making an unbelievable sound. Then they noticed the oddly dressed soldiers pointing extraordinary looking and very menacing, assault rifles at them. They were so stunned by the circumstances that the Ruskies complied like sheep to the broken phrases in Russian ordering them to surrender.

At the same time, all over Copenhagen additional helicopters were landing and disgorging hundreds of trained Special Forces. These men were responsible for taking out or capturing key points. Similar scenes of stunned compliance to orders of surrender were reported throughout the city.

The lead NATO Naval Task Force had seized or shelled into oblivion the Soviet manned defensive strong points. So far, the helicopter troops had not met any opposition primarily due to the novelty of their appearance. Some local enemy commanders had sent out frantic calls trying to describe what was happening to them. So far, their superiors had not responded to their wild tales of hovering aircraft with men jumping out of them.

NATO had added their own bogus radio traffic about men from outer space and other outlandish tales. Also, they continued to capture enemy radio equipment. The local commanders who managed to get through to higher headquarters units were marginalized by these tactics.

Land lines had already been cut all along the Danish Straits by the Danish resistance. The only way to communicate was through radio. The locations of the most powerful transmitters were well known. Some sites were visited by helicopter borne NATO soldiers and eliminated early in the assault. The remaining equipment was used to disseminate misinformation and further confuse the absentee headquarters staff back in Moscow.

The USS LPD-1 Peleliu looked like an angry nest of hornets with HUP1-H25 helicopters coming and going at a dizzying pace. Other ships were sending out landing craft full of seaborne troops who would secure the already captured sites and allow the airborne troops to move on to other targets.

The Red Army was spread so thin throughout Eurasia that there were very few Soviet units within 150 miles of the Danish Straits. The Stavka would have to expend millions of gallons of fuel to begin to contain the NATO incursion. Millions of gallons they did not have.

Copenhagen was secured with the help of the Danish citizenry within 48 hours. Many of the NATO units were greeted by cheers and jubilant crowds on both the Danish and Swedish sides. A few troops did encounter the hanging bodies of communist collaborators or Soviet soldiers. For the most part the isolated Red troops surrendered peacefully with the encouragement of locally made pitchforks and axes.

A small fire fight with a company of veteran Soviet artillerymen almost got out of hand when the local men decided to burn down the armory the Reds were holed up in. It seems that these Reds had shot the town's mayor in the heat of the moment and the crowd was bent on revenge. A squad of Swedish regular troops was all that was standing between this proposed barbeque and reason.

Luckily a company of French commandos was sent to take in the Soviet unit and arrived just in time to prevent any more violence. The Captain of the Ruskie unit had been wounded by a very well thrown brick as he left the building. The act seemed to calm the crowd down along with the timely arrival of the NATO soldiers.

Copenhagen had been liberated quickly and easily with minimal collateral damage.

Two divisions poured out of troop transports to secure both sides of the Great Belt and Oresund giving NATO control to the entrance of the Baltic Sea. NATO Task Force 125 was on its way to sweep clean the Baltic Sea of all Soviet naval craft and forces.

The first use of helicopters in combat had been an unqualified success largely due to their innovative use and the element of surprise.

Task Force 125 Redux

Gunner's Mate Napoleon Reid was one of the few colored sailors on the U.S.S. Tulagi (CVE-72) sailing with the Task Force 38 into the Baltic Sea. He had put up with a lot of abuse to his pride to be here. He had stood up to the taunts and insults because he hated Hitler more than he hated the men who tormented him. He knew his decision was correct once he saw what the Nazis had done in the concentration camps throughout Europe. He knew he was on the right side.

He now has a new enemy to channel his hate towards. Stalin was just as bad as Hitler from what he read and his soldiers just as white. Oh how the citizens of Copenhagen had pointed at him as the Tulagi slid past the narrows in the Big Belt. He just ignored them and did his job.

Being on board a ship had its advantages for a Negro in the military. Your fellow sailors were up close and personal. You all had to learn to get along. You were forced to get to know your comrades in arms as they were forced to get to know you. There was nowhere to hide for long on a ship at sea.

His contemporaries in the Army were, for the most part, placed in all-Negro units. A few Navy ships were manned by all-Negro sailors, but for the most part the crews were integrated in this war.

World War Three saw a dramatic increase in the number of non-white troops. Following World War Two 11 million veterans were looking for jobs and whites got most of the openings. Unemployment was so high in the inner cities and the rural south that the military was the only place to make ends meet for many non-whites.

Reid was assigned as one of the lookouts on duty on this fine day in June. The Task Force was still in the relatively narrow part of the Baltic where theoretically some Commie artillery unit could take a potshot at them.

An incident had happened a few days ago but the USS Wisconsin BB 64 had put a stop to that in short order. The Soviet gun crew probably never knew what hit them as they prepared for their 4th shot at a troop transport. The first three shots were wide of the mark by a good 100 yards. The USS Wisconsin was on target with her first salvo of 5-inchers. Needless to say the 16-inch gun crews were very disappointed at not being called on to join the fun.

Reid was vital to the safety of his ship and had just spotted a rogue naval mine floating in the middle of nowhere. The mine could have done serious damage to the smaller ships in the group. A couple of shots from the 20 mm crews on the starboard side had taken out the mine and a chicken near the shore. Napoleon was given a commendation for his excellent spotting skills.

Figure 32 - Gunner's Mate Napoleon Reid

NATO Task Force 125 had used the same force structure it had on D-Day, 6 June 1944. Minesweeper group 125.9 was leading the way. The minesweepers were followed closely by Bombardment Group 125.8 composed of three battleships, two heavy cruisers, ten destroyers and five destroyer escorts. Causeway Construction Unit 125.15 had been assigned to assist with offloading the Copenhagen occupying forces.

Task Force 125 had leapfrogged 124 and was now leading the way into the Baltic Sea. TF 124 had taken some damage and one catastrophic loss. The hard luck CV USS Franklin was once again on the end of a near crippling incident. Just before Copenhagen the destroyer escort USS Solar suddenly careened in front of the huge aircraft carrier. The DE was split in two and sunk within minutes. A deep underwater explosion followed seconds later damaging the Franklin. Only 13 crew were saved from the ill-fated smaller ship.

The Franklin herself had earlier survived an attack by a Japanese dive bomber late in the last war and had just completed repairs. Again, Big Ben was in trouble. A number of plates in her hull had been battered by the Solar's underwater explosion. She was taking water at an alarming rate.

Several of her crew remained on board from her first brush with death. They were very experienced at keeping her afloat. She somehow survived this latest catastrophe, leveling off enough for her 96 aircraft to launch. They transferred to newly captured land based airfields. They continued to provide air support throughout the campaign.

Big Ben would slowly make her way back to Britain where she would eventually be scrapped. The wreck of the Solar leaked bodies for the next three years from the cold depths of the Skagerrak.

It was never determined why the destroyer escort suddenly veered into the path of the much larger ship. The USS Solar was the only major loss of life in the initial phase of Operation Triple Cross.

Task Force 38 was following TF 125 and was chocked full of fast carriers. TF 38 was the mobile air arm of the invasion forces of Operation Triple Cross. Admiral Marc Andrew Mitscher was in charge operationally with Raymond Ames Spruance in overall command of the newly designated Baltic Fleet that included TF 124, 125 and 38.

Spruance was the victor of Midway, which many consider the turning point of the war in the Pacific. His career had been sidelined for years by, the now ailing, Congressman Carl Vinson who was a Halsey fan. With Vinson's stroke, Spruance was given his proper due and his long - delayed promotion.

TF 38 had a full complement of 8 Essex class carriers with over 90 planes on each ship, a full quota of support ships and a dozen smaller carriers. The combined hulls could put over a thousand planes in the air within an hour. On an operational level this naval air force could overwhelm any attempt by the VVS to attack either the convoy or the troops who would soon be landing.

It would take months for the Red Air Force to counter this invasion. The plan was to bleed them to death by a thousand cuts before they could cobble together an effective counter attack.

Besides playing defense, Spruance's first mission was to attack the home of the Babushka Seehund Midget submarine. He was to prevent any more of these underwater killers from entering the Baltic and threatening his troop transports.

Gdansk was the manufacturing hub of the Babushka. Hundreds of the midget subs in various states of assembly were waiting transport to the oceans of the world. At dawn Spruance's air arm would destroy as many midget subs, hulls and components as possible. Then the army would invade. Their first mission was to destroy any remaining traces of the Babushka facility.

The Soviet Baltic Fleet was expected to make an appearance at some point. The Red ships were not considered a major threat and their current locations were well documented. They would be dealt with in due time. For right now the midget subs were considered the greater threat.

As both massive task forces started to push their way through the ancient waters of the Baltic, there was optimism in the air. You could feel it and see it in the movements and cheerful tones in the orders being issued and their acknowledgements. It's pretty hard to communicate feelings through a voice-pipe, yet the ships' crews were managing to do it. [30]

---

[30] - Marine Engineer and Naval Architect, Volume 14 pg. 475

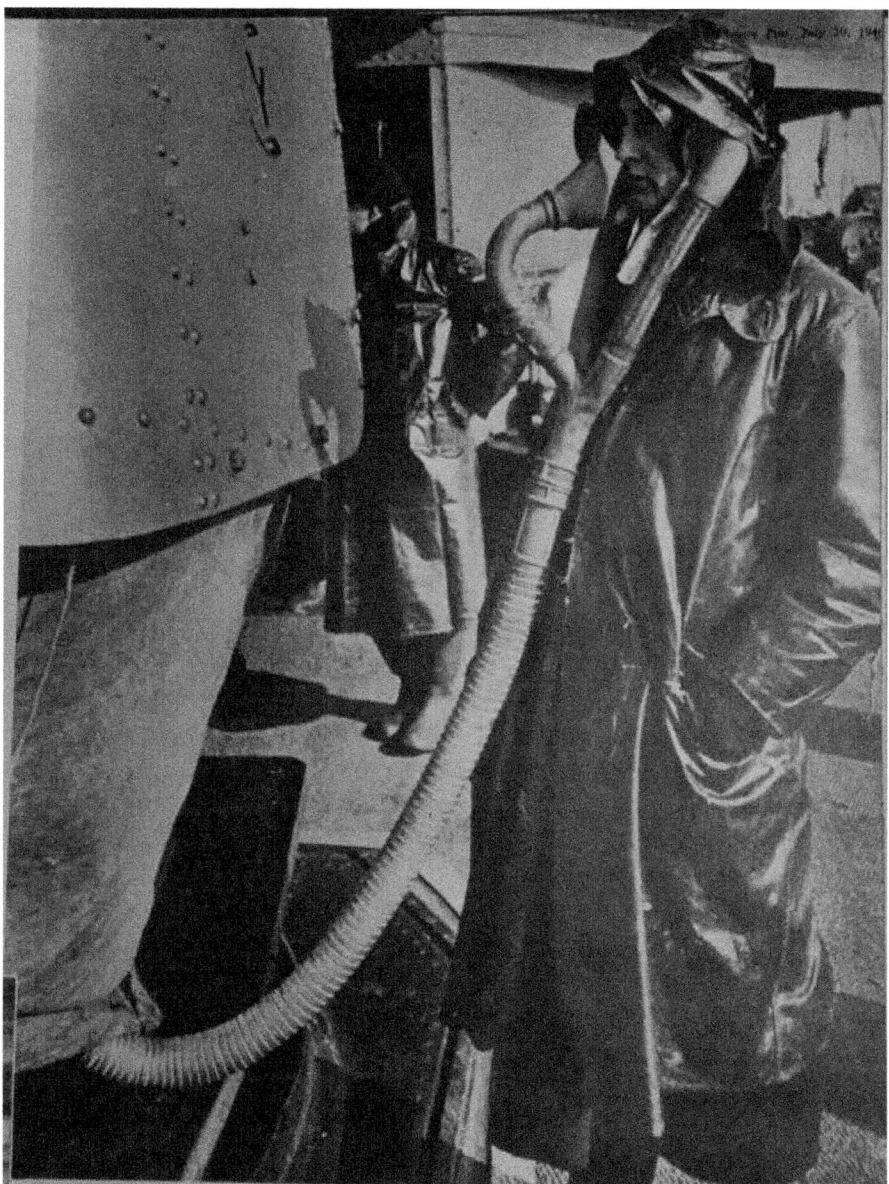

Figure 33 - Voice-Pipe Aboard a Destroyer

Feet Dry

Once again, the helicopters came as a complete surprise to the Reds. You would think that they might have caught on by now. This was the third major operation where the helicopters had been used. Once again, the airborne forces landed virtually unopposed as the Red Army soldiers seem mesmerized by the thumping of rotor blades.

James Osborne was on one of these helicopters. In fact he was on the second helicopter as the pilot call "feet dry." This bit of military lingo indicated that the helo had transitioned from flying over water to land. Their target was on a cliff and posed a threat to the beaches of Gdynia.

Protecting the beaches was essential to the coming invasion. Gdynia's sandy, slopping beaches were perfect for the type of landing craft that most of the invasion force rode on to shore.

The landing craft to be used in Operation Triple Cross had been transported all the way from the Pacific. They had been built, but never used, for the invasion of Japan. Now the Higgins boats would fulfill their destiny by debarking tens of thousands of men and tons of material onto the shores of Poland.

Jimmy was looking down at those beaches. They reminded him of Jaws Beach in Nassau except for one big difference. He was a thousand feet up and hanging on like his life depended upon it, as of course it did.

The novelty of standing in an open doorway of a helicopter had not worn off or become second nature. Being bounced around by thermals and catching glimpses of the helo blades traveling at incredible speed just above your head had not become mundane or normal. Combined with the adrenaline rush of combat, Osborne was beginning to feel like he was going to puke.

In World War Two Jimmy and his men had been stationed as liaisons to the British in Nassau, Bahamas for over a year. Most of their dads were no longer in a position to pull strings. Some of their dads were voted out of office and some had died in the fighting of the last war. For whatever reason the sons had lost their golden ticket and were now heading into harm's way.

Many vets and other rookies knew that the members of this unit had been dodging combat. The result was a lot of bad blood between the various groups. Jimmy's company had gotten all the shit jobs and now they were out front without a net.

As a newly minted Lieutenant, Jimmy had to hold it together. His men were watching him both out of curiosity and out of desperation. His whole squad was made up of Midwestern draftees who thought they were going to wait out this war. These guys had done exactly that during the last war by sitting on their keisters and letting some other poor schmucks fight and die. Their unit was full of rich boys and politician's sons who fully expected to be pulling duty in the Bahamas like the last war.

Suddenly the lead helicopter took a hit from a rare burst of flak and disintegrated before Jimmy's eyes. Ryan, Williams, Kasen and Biltmore were on that bird. Now they were no more. Holy shit this is getting serious, Jimmy thought. A former senator's son and a multi-millionaire's boy were just obliterated like any other Joe would have been. What the hell good was being rich if you couldn't even get out of this shit! What a waste. It should have been those goobers from C Company. Not a penny between the whole bunch, yet they're still alive.

Oh shit, Oh shit here we go! The helicopter banked to the right at an incredibly steep angle. Osborn almost lost his grip. He was caught off guard as he was looking to see if any of the pieces of the downed chopper were big enough to carry survivors.

His squad's mission was to invest a mansion that overlooked the beaches. In theory, they were to land in the front yard and storm through the veranda up the grand staircase and then play it by ear. It was suspected that some Red officers had ceased the place, and they were to be captured or killed.

Hopefully the Reds in question were as unprepared as he felt his men were. While his "Golden Boys" could relate to the mansion and its grand staircase, it was flying bullets that worried him.

The Lieutenant happened to be very familiar with grand staircases as well. His family had three of them in various locations throughout the US. Jimmy's father was the Assistant Secretary of War under Howard Peterson. Basically, his father, James Osborn II, bought his office by donating large amounts of money to the Democratic Party.

The Osborn family was wealthy and had been since the Civil War. It's funny how wars seem to make certain kinds of people rich in capitalistic societies.

Now linage and wealth were irrelevant. His men were looking at him for some leadership after what just happened to the other helicopter. Unfortunately, he was pretty much paralyzed by what he had just seen. James Osborn III made a show of locking and loading his M1 carbine and put on his best game face. Then he pointed at the mansion. It seemed to do the trick. Also, he had no idea what was going on in the other chopper and had no idea if any of his men would follow him as he leaped through the door when they landed on the manicured lawn.

He almost tripped over a large recessed pool and fountain just as he caught a glimpse of something moving to his right. He raised his weapon and shot the man cold dead right in the head. Then he noticed that he had wet himself.

So much for Feet Dry, he thought and deliberately ran through the water to disguise his wetness. He stopped behind a low wall and statue peaking around the side. By god, there was another guy in uniform shooting at something. Damned if Jimmy didn't raise his carbine and plug that guy as well. Shit maybe he was actually good at this.

He screamed something and started to run towards the open front door. He noticed that his boots were making a squishing sound as he ran.

His company overran the mansion and even defeated a counter attack by some local Polish communist militia. The rest of the brigade shut up about the "Golden Boys" after that action.

In total they lost a senator's son, three heirs to multi-million dollar fortunes and a sitting congressman's son along with two Yale alumni and one graduate of Harvard.

Explosive Carpet

Even its proponents realized that Carpet Bombing is a horrible way to wage war. Especially when it is used on innocent civilians who are the people you are trying to save. Tens of thousands of Frenchman were killed by bombs dropped by the USAAF and RAF during World War Two.

967 B-29s, B-17s and B-24s were once again flying in the classic formation that maximized the destruction below. This time they were bombing narrow areas of water in the Turkish straights.

Small bombs or bomblets had been designed to explode all manner of marine mines on the surface and under the water. Each bomblet had a prescribed depth at which it would explode or on contact with a mine or the bottom, which ever came first.

The theory had been tested out on an old mine field known as the Northern Barrage. The Barrage was a failed attempt to stop U-boats from passing between Iceland and the Faroes Islands and was halted in 1943 when other projects proved more useful.

World War Three 1946 – Book Four – The Red Sea

Three test runs by 200 bombers dropping the new bomblets had proved their effectiveness. The mines were cleared to 90% from a depth of the surface to 300 feet. No portion of the projected invasion routes through the Turkish or Danish Straits were deeper.

Each B-29 could carry 3600 bomblets and the B-24 and B-17 over 1400 each. That meant quite a large pattern could be cleared per bomber. The challenges were two-fold.

1. Keep the pattern tight enough to hit all the mines possible.
2. Fly at the right altitude that was safe enough for a big bomber yet low enough to maximize the area cleared of mines.

The optimal altitude is 1000 feet. This allows for the bomblets to be clustered enough to clear the mines yet is high enough for the big boys to fly.

This magic carpet of bombs had shown to be an effective and quick way to clear a narrow channel through a confined waterway. The key, as always, is execution. Over a million small bomblets will be raining down on a 5 mile by 1000-foot-wide area and that comes out to a lot of explosives landing in a small amount of time.

When they initially hit not much happened. A few did explode either by accident or because they struck a surface mine. The real show started when the bomblets started to hit mines floating under the surface or once they hit their prescribed depth. Fifteen percent were designed to only explode either on contact or after 5 minutes had passed.

After a few seconds the underwater explosions started to occur. Within two minutes all hell was starting to break lose and detonating mines and bombs were going off almost continuously for miles in a rolling barrage of churning water and surface eruptions.

A few thousand of the bomblets had landed in very shallow water or the shoreline on either side of the designated path. The bombs did not disperse with one hundred percent fluidity but poured out somewhat haphazardly.

The individual bomblets were not large weighing in at 2.5 kg each. The mines they were designed to set off were large. The explosions involving the mines were indeed impressive with up to 300 kg of explosives lighting off all at once. In addition, the naval mines were not armored and no special detonators were needed by the bomblets to penetrate their outer casings.

Two unfortunate small fishing boats were enjoying the isolated fishing grounds just off Hellebaek Denmark when the first bombers appeared. They must have thought the worst was over when only one of the small bombs hit one of their boats and did not explode. One of the sailors was seen by a bomber crew holding the little bomb up and laughing at his escape from death when the explosions started to erupt from deep down beneath. Both little boats were obliterated by the same 220 kg mine moored at a depth of 15 meters. They had probably thought themselves immune from the mines due to their small size and wood hulls.

The bombers followed the helicopters and proceeded Taskforce 124. A million small bomblets easily cleared the way through the hastily sewn mine field that had been reported just a week ago by the Danish Partisans. 200 mines exploded within 20 minutes from direct hits or secondary explosions. A few escaped or slipped their moorings and were on the surface and these were taken care of by the lead group of minesweepers in short order.

An explosive carpet had been laid down by the bombers of the 8th Air Force. A carpet that had swept away a hidden menace.

Task Force 124 passed through the still churning waters and the last barrier before Copenhagen followed by the remainder of the NATO Baltic Fleet and Assault Task Force 124.3 through .7. Nothing stood in their way and it was clear sailing ahead for the troops transports loaded with a force of 25 divisions.

And Died

Major Stanislav Honchar of the NKVD was sitting on the stairs that led up to Sergo's office. He was looking through the doorway at the now empty office. At the far corner of the room was a trapdoor. He knew that when the escape hatch was opened there was about a five foot drop down into a large crawl space.

His colleagues were comfortable with interpreting the scene before him as a straight forward getaway scheme. Yet to the Major, the whole setup just seemed too easy. How had both Sergo and Georgi evaded his repeated personal searches and simply escaped using such an opening when no one was looking.

His men had combed the entire factory complex at least a dozen times.

Finally the search had to be called off and the slave laborers allowed back in. The factory complex was simply too valuable and productive to the war effort to be closed any longer. Even Stalin was unwilling to give such an order.

Where were they hiding and how did their location escape his trained eye? Dogs had been used and came up with nothing except an initial trail leading away from their offices and the complex. The trail picked up across the street and continued onto the barracks. The Major had tortured every man who was in the barracks just for good measure. A number the men had finally admitted seeing two strangers moving through the barracks during the guard's shift change.

Next he tortured all the guards on the shift. In the end, two guards had made false confessions. Stanislav hated torture because he knew it didn't work. People just said what they think you wanted them to say to stop the pain.

Brutalization was the lazy man's way of taking revenge and working out his personal demons. Torture never led to the truth but it was expected, so he had done it.

The trap doors and scent trails to the street were intended to convince people that the two men had somehow evaded capture. The ruse had worked on everyone but the Major.

Conventional wisdom suggested that Sergo and Georgi had hidden themselves somewhere in their offices. Now it seems that after the search ended they had been able to sneak out past two squads of guards. Any reasonable person would accept these explanations once all the other possibilities were eliminated.

Stanislav was totally unable to believe the current scenarios. He was anything but reasonable and conventional at times like this and that is why he was so good at his job.

He had once caught two prisoners who supposedly escaped a gulag 1400 km from the nearest food or water in the middle of Siberia. Major Honchar was called in after a week and solved the case in less than 6 hours. His intuition told him they were still in the compound. He found their bodies in the latrine. They had weigh themselves down and were breathing through tubes that looked like feces. The unaccounted-for methane gas had killed them within a short time.

The level of shit never varied due to a system of spillways. He had noticed the two almost perfect turds while staring at the cesspool. The two turds in question didn't seem to move amongst the newly laid ones that were added by the thousands every day. The prisoner's breathing tubes were attached to these turds.

In this current situation regarding Sergo and Georgi's disappearance, it seemed to Honchar that the safes were the most logical place to hide an exit. He was fixated on the fact that the safes were built into the very structure of the factory complex.

He tried to order the excavation of the area. However, the engineers told them that digging more than a few meters deep would require closing the factory for months. Again no one would agree to disrupting the factory's operations.

Honchar was pouring over the facility's construction records last night when he noticed something strange. No worker or team of workers, who worked on the projects were still prisoners. Another unusual detail was no one worked on the offices for more than a few days. All had then been transferred and released or both.

Tomorrow he was going to track down all of the former slave workers. He had a hunch that every single one who worked on both offices had disappeared or were dead. He decided to have one last look at Sergo's office before morning and that is what brought him here sitting on the stairs.

He had brought an archeologist's brush and a small air bulb. He began to dust off and blow air around the area where the safe was installed. The wall was now hacked and gouged men trying to hammer their way through a solid rock.

He was about to give up when he saw it. Just a hint of a line on the wall where there shouldn't be a line. It ran diagonally and that was why no one noticed it before. He made a mental note to look up who had been the stone mason. The seam was barely visible only if you brushed away the dust in the right direction. He reached out and touched the seam with his fingers.

Suddenly the Major felt a deep pin prick on his ring finger and thumb. He pulled his hand away and sucked on the spots by placing them in his mouth. Almost immediately he felt light headed. He tried to get up from his crouch and fell backwards hitting his head. He crawled and rolled over to the door tumbling down the stairs and died.

Figure 34 - Bulb and Brush

Sergo Waits

Sergo heard the needles fire and retract. He had known this day would come. Which is why he designed this last failsafe. He had no way of knowing whether it had worked or not. All he knew was that something or someone found the last seam that would lead to his hiding place. The bedrock was firmly in place but whoever found that seam would know that something was behind it. Therefore, they had to die.

The needles were coated with snake venom of the Inland Taipan. Each was in a small vial of the venom and shot through the rubber top to a length of 4 inches and retracted in a matter of less than a second. One strike of this venom covered dart should be enough to kill any person. There were 20 of them in the final seam. The needles could fire 10 times. His mind raced as he tried to think of how someone had gotten this far. Luck he supposed. Wasn't that always the way. Luck had been his companion for the last couple of years, but maybe it was time she left.

He was ready for what, if anything, came next.

He had the proverbial hollow tooth implanted with a poison that would save him from Beria's torture. He suddenly remembered that Beria had disappeared. He was sure someone else would take his place in any event.

All he could do was wait. His tongue roamed around his mouth and felt his fake tooth for the 100th time that day. He was not going to be taken alive.

After a couple of hours, he relaxed. He guessed his little trap had worked and some poor investigator was dead. Better him than me, he thought. He wondered how many others would die before they finally broke through.

He kept himself busy trying to organize the copies of documents he had been hastily collecting and storing in his hiding place. These papers, films and recordings were the best way for him to protect his legacy and to see that the true story of World War Three survived.

So he sorted, filed and waited.

Backdoor Man

Mario Fiat couldn't believe he was back in Turkey and once again looking at the Turkish Straits. He thought he was done with field work after his last assignment. He had been looking forward to tracking down Betty Grupe and seeing if he could make her his wife. Instead for the third time he was impersonating an itinerate Kurdish worker.

Talk about rockets' red glare. Jesus, when one of the American battle ships fired off a salvo into Koybasi Battery, it was something to behold. He counted nine massive explosions with columns of debris being thrown a hundred feet high. He supposed some of those fragments and pieces contained Mikhail Orloff.

Mario had gotten to know the group of Red soldiers who manned the 100-mm battery in the old fort. His motives were sinister but the end result was something akin to a friendship. Mikhail and the others in the gun crew were not monsters at all. They were ordinary men caught up in extraordinary circumstances.

He had come to admire Mikhail in particular. This young man had been through so much it was amazing he was alive. His home had been on the border between the Reds and the Whites in the Russian Revolution for almost six months in Kronstadt. This small city is on Kontlin Island across from what is now Leningrad. Before the revolution in 1917 Leningrad was named Petrograd.

In 1917 Petrograd was the home of the new communist government and the center of much conflict. In addition, the port city of Kronstadt was part of that turmoil. The port was also the home of the Soviet Baltic Fleet. Other facilities in the area included a naval yard and numerous forts in various states of decay.

Imperial Russian Navy personnel were instrumental in the successful February Revolution of 1917. The revolution was isolated to Petrograd and lasted less than a week. The immediate result was the abdication of Czar Nicolas II.

The more famous October Revolution of 1917 eventually resulted in the formation of the Soviet Union led by Lenin. This larger conflict was between the Red Army of the communists and the "Whites" of the old Imperial Army and supporters.

The former Czar's allies involved foreign armies including the United States who landed in Arkhangelsk and Vladivostok. Additional troops comprised 15,000 Japanese soldiers that invaded the Eastern region, a British landing in Vladivostok and 23,351 Greek fighters who marched on the Crimea. The Multi-national troops were opposing communism and all it stood for.

In 1921 Kronstadt had an uprising of its own against Leninism. What was happening in Moscow was not their idea of what true communism should be. The work camps, total party control and lack of freedom of speech, corrupted the true meaning of the revolution and a group of naval officers in Konstadt took up arms against the Bolsheviks.

Leon Trotsky, (then in charge of the Red Army), responded by sending a large force against the rebels. A major battle ensued as Trotsky's troops crossed over the frozen waters from Petrograd. thousands of lives on both sides of the conflict were lost in the fighting.

Petrograd was renamed Leningrad after the death of Lenin in 1924. During World War Two the Germans surrounded Leningrad and the forts in Kronstadt. Both cities were under attack by the Nazis for 900 days. Constant bombing and shelling were Mikhail's life until 1945 when the horrific siege of Leningrad was finally lifted by a victorious Red Army.

A young Mikhail experienced starvation and witnessed cannibalism.

He was 17 by the time World War Two was over. He was drafted into the army in February 1946. He was still in training when World War Three broke out and he was thrown into the thick of the fighting in Turkey. His unit remained behind to guard the Turkish Straits.

This is where the spy Mario Fiat met and seemingly befriended Mikhail. Orloff had told him his life story one night as he watched the stars and Mario watched him and his comrades. It soon became apparent that the young soldier was not worth the spy's time yet Fiat hung around for a few more days despite the urgency of his mission.

He was fascinated by the simplicity of Mikhail's outlook on life and his complex story of survival. Now the young man was gone. He was gone in a flash when a 16-inch shell detonated next to him.

The USS Iowa and USS Mobile loosed one more salvo and the old fort was nothing but dust and stone. Fiat thought I might be the only one who remembers Mikhail. I guess I'll have to write a book. For now he had to forget about the demise of Mikhail and his squad and get on with the job at hand.

Figure 35 - One of many destroyed forts in the Turkish Straits

He watched in fascination as the awe-inspiring group of NATO naval vessels slid passed him on their way north towards the entrance to The Black Sea. Just about an hour before, a steady stream of bombers had dropped thousands of anti-mines ordinance on selected stretches of the Turkish Strait. The following explosions were truly impressive as mine after mine was detonated by bomblets.

He had heard of this new method for clearing minefields during a briefing before he was sent to Turkey. Now seeing it in action he understood the excitement of the Navy concerning its implementation. The shotgun approach was truly revolutionary and made minefields obsolete. Of course you needed 200 bombers or more to even contemplate using this method. Not many countries had the resources to put 200 bombers in the air simultaneously.

Mario followed the task force as closely as he could. Every few miles helicopters would leave and fly off to drop Special Forces along the route. Even he was surprised by the speed of the advance. The Airborne troops certainly made this kind of progress possible.

Fiat had heard that helicopters had been used quite successfully in gaining entrance to the Baltic Sea. One by one the Soviet defenses were falling and the NATO task force was blasting its way towards Istanbul and eventual entrance into the Black Sea.

His work had been fruitful. He had organized the Turks and convince them to make their own defenses that faced the Mediterranean inoperable. Luckily some Soviet had not put the pieces of the puzzle together regarding the sabotage. Mario was told if the Soviets had significantly strengthened their defenses leading into the Black Sea, the operation would have been canceled.

Facing minimal resistance from the Soviets, Operation Backdoor was launched. The NATO Task Force 38 was barreling down the Turkish Straits with the lead elements approaching the entrance to the Sea of Marmara.

The Sea of Marmara, during the Battle of Gallipoli, had been the goal of the British and French fleets during World War One. Mines placed in the straights by the Turks critically damaged the ships leading to their sinking or capsizing. The loss of three battleships in the span of a few hours halted the combined fleet from entering the sea.

The NATO force currently entering the sea consisted of three battleships, eight cruisers, 34 destroyers, 21 mine sweepers, 15 oil tankers and enough supply ships to carry 20,000 US Marines and Army personnel along with two months' worth of provisions and ammunition. Mario never did see the beginning and end of the Task Force that made-up Operation Backdoor.

He had a job to do and could not spend any more time sightseeing. His job was to find Soviet Marshall Georgy Konstantinovich Zhukov and to make him and offer he couldn't refuse.

How to Lose a War

Dr. Skinner was on to the next project. His group still had to run a few more trials using their newest method of masking a ship from a sharp-eyed pigeon. Pigeons are known for their remarkable eyesight. All the better to see hawks with before a hawk sees them, he guessed. Just one of Mother Nature's ways of keeping enough pigeons alive to procreate which provide more targets for hungry hawks, and so it goes.

Skinner had guessed right about the Soviets training their pigeons to ignore the wild paint schemes. The next tactic the Reds tried was zeroing in on the ship's antenna arrays. Skinner and his team had devised covers for all but the radio masts. The covers had worked for another couple of months.

Now it looks like the Reds were trying a new tactic. Recently they shot a few missiles at some convoys in the dead of the night. The fact that it was pitch black could only mean that they were starting to use infrared detection. He had been informed that earlier in the war over Britain they had deployed some form of heat seeking devices.

For reasons unknown, the Soviets had suddenly stopped the program. There had been no further activities along these lines for several months. Possibly they ran out of components or trained birds. Whatever the cause, Skinner was sure that they were now about ready to start using the detection system against NATO ships.

Lately he had begun to notice a lack of urgency and decisiveness in the Soviets choice's. He wondered if there had been a change in leadership. Perhaps he should mention his concern to someone in charge. It may be a significant change that could greatly affect the counter moves the Reds would try next. If someone less innovative or sophisticated was now making the decisions, then NATO would need to alter their thinking in response.

Skinner knew his enemy and so far, had anticipated his adversary's every move concerning the missiles. The doctors training and innate people skills had allowed him to see into the mind of his opponent. If he was no longer jousting with the same man he would have to get to know his new nemesis. He feared that he would guess wrong and lives would be lost because of his mistake, because he failed.

Of course, the answer was simple, don't fail. Don't fail and hope for a speedy end to this war. He had just heard about the invasion of Denmark and Copenhagen. Not being trained in the military arts he had no idea what Eisenhower hoped to gain from entering the Baltic Sea. At this time, considering the strategic implications of the war were beyond him. He had enough work simply trying to outwit a flock of pigeons and anticipating their trainer's next move.

Just then Jim stuck his head in the office and reminded him of their brainstorming meeting in ten minutes. Skinner wrote a note in the margins of the outline he was working on. He wanted to remind himself to mention that he suspected someone else was in control of the Soviet ORCON project.

He made a mental note to revisit the profile he created and maintained of his long-time, yet unknown enemy. He carefully considered the behavior of his "Mr. X." Skinner had grown quit confident in his ability to imagine and accurately anticipate the decisions of his faceless Soviet peer.

His ability to guess in advance his enemies next move was the reason his team was having such a string of good luck in designing counter measures. The recent subtle and dramatic shifts in the pace and follow through by the Soviets rendered his profile useless. He and his group would have to begin again from scratch.

Luckily there was physics. His invention could only do so much. His pigeons could only learn a finite amount of behaviors. The pigeons were totally dependent on the format the Soviets were able to present to the birds.

So far the first two methods had used pattern recognition, then an infrared device that was probably a scope of some kind. He knew from his own experiments that the birds could be trained to ignore very bright lights like a flare.

The next two solutions NATO had in the pipeline were heated barrage balloons and large exploding gas clouds. The challenge was to make these new decoys more attractive than the real thing. His group was confident that initially the birds would choose the brighter more shinny object.

It would likely take the Reds a good month or two to figure out what was happening. Then they would need another good three weeks to retrain the birds. Finally another week or so to relocate the birds to the various combat zones.

If his math was right that would mean they had two to three months' lead time to figure out the next way to spoof the birds. He was told in utmost secrecy that if their efforts kept the ORCON system at bay until September, the war would be over. And if the Reds started to score a significant number of hits on the Navy's ships before September, then the war was lost.

No pressure in that pronouncement from on high, Skinner thought sardonically.

Down by Her Head

Napoleon was doing his job aboard the jeep carrier USS Tulagi.[31] He was awake, aware and constantly scanning the horizon and starboard side of the ship.

There was movement in the water to the south. His eye was caught and his brain's attention turned to identifying whatever it was. He started looking with his naked eye and was confident that he saw something. He kept his eyes on the spot while he brought up his binoculars. As his eyes adjusted to new focal length, the object was just left of center. He zeroed in on it. Before his cerebrum comprehended what he was seeing, his amygdala caused him to reached out and immediately hit the alarm. He then grabbed and keyed his microphone and in a calm clear and forceful voice spoke the word, TORPEDO followed by... BRIDGE—STARBOARD LOOKOUT-TORPEDO WAKE BEARING WUN WUN ZE-RO-1000 YARDS—TARGET ANGLE ZE-RO TOO TREE—CLOSING RAPIDLY ON TROOP TRANSPORT—BEARING WUN SIX FIFE. His call to arms coincided with the first

---

[31] - The Little Giants: U.S. Escort Carriers Against Japan
By William T. Y'Blood

blast of the alarm Napoleon set off. [32]

The First Mate asked for confirmation just as another lookout screamed TORPEDO! The second lookout was admonished when he failed to give a bearing and speed. After Napoleon confirmed his sighting, the escort Tulagi took a sharp turn to the North towards Bornholm.

Jeep carriers are not as large as fleet carriers and only have 28 aircraft aboard. Yet these smaller ships were not particularly nimble. His ship lurched dramatically as it made its turn. The turn was an emergency maneuver done at high speed.

Napoleon had to brace himself as he continued to scan the horizon by eye followed by a sweep using his binoculars. Meanwhile, he was hoping that someone had warned the nearby troop transports that torpedoes were coming their way.

Suddenly he spotted another torpedo that was now heading for them. BRIDGE—STARBOARD LOOKOUT—SECOND TORPEDO WAKE BEARING WUN TOO TREE—AIT ZE-RO ZE-RO YARDS—TARGET ANGLE NINER SEV-EN—CLOSING RAPIDLY...

This time no confirmation was needed and the Tulagi turned to port as fast as her rudders could steer her stern and her hull could displace the water. The torpedo slid off the starboard side missing the Tulagi by 80 feet.

---

[32] - Naval Lookouts are taught to use the phonetic alphabet

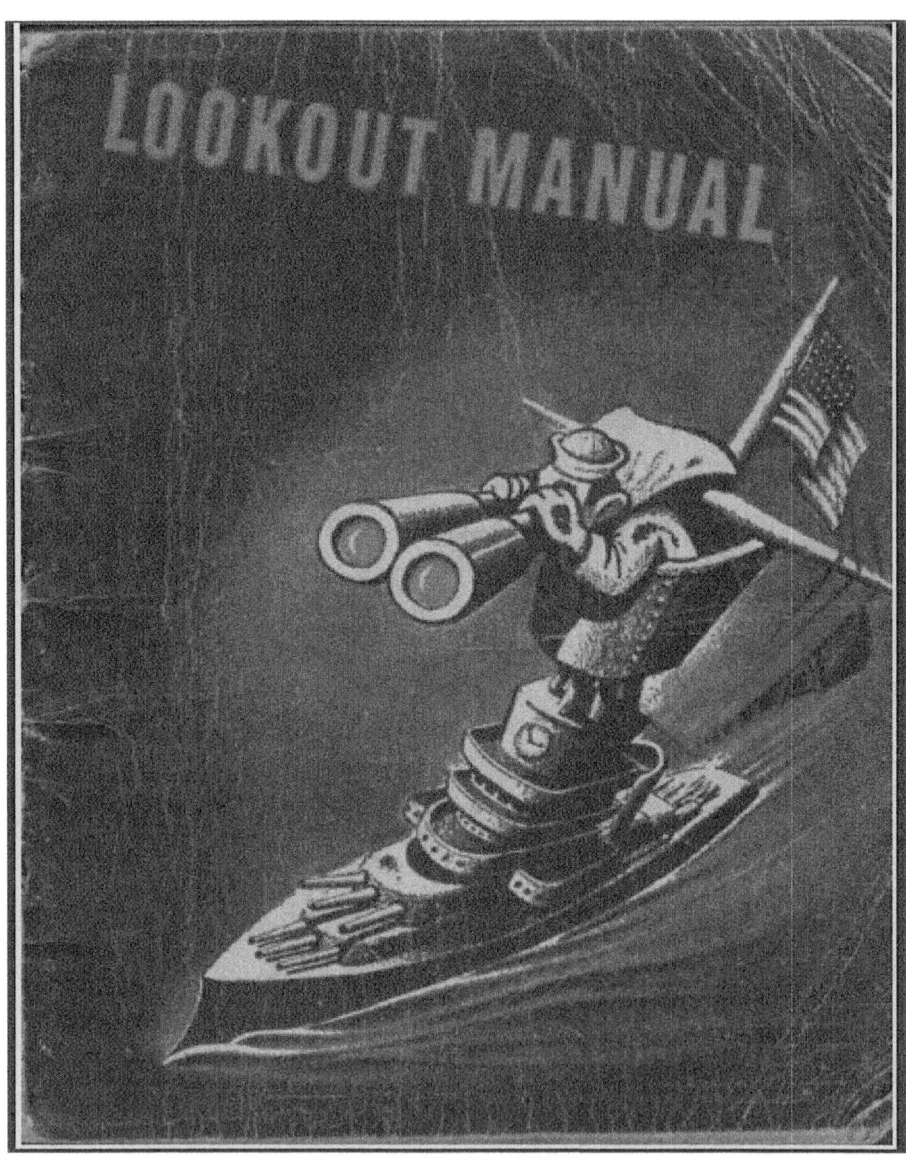

Figure 36 - NavPers 170069

Napoleon was the first and almost the last one to see the second torpedo. The Task Force had entered the Baltic Sea a day ago and was making good time towards Gdansk/Gdynia and its shipyards and docks.

Apparently the Tulagi had the best eyes of the task force. The single five-inch gun on the small carrier fired on what appeared to be open sea. As Napoleon followed a second shot he finally saw what some sharp-eyed gunner had seen.

It was a periscope about 5000 feet away. Napoleon made the appropriate report and then watched in fascination as the Tulagi's five-inch gun became only the third aircraft carrier to hit an enemy ship with its own guns. Aircraft carriers were supposed to stand off and send their planes to attack and not be put in harm's way.[33]

What turned out to be a Soviet midget submarine must have known it was being shot at yet it just kept coming and didn't dive. The Tulagi's third shot, it the periscope and possibly some other vital piece of the conning tower that was just under the water. The immediate result was the little sub made a rapid ascent and surfaced not more than 4500 feet from the little carrier and practically right next to a quickly approaching destroyer escort.

The destroyer escort skidded right past the now floundering sub. The captain came about so violently that the ship's guns could not bear on the enemy. In the ensuing interval, the Tulagi held its fire so as not to strike the careening destroyer escort.

In the meantime, the two crew members climbed out of the precariously rolling submarine. They were indicating their willingness to surrender. All the Americans that could see the drama were highly amused at the antics of the Red sailors who were trying not to get shot. Simultaneously the bystanders were attempting to watch the destroyer escort frantically get into position to capture the mini-sub and its crew.

Needless to say, the Captain of the destroyer escort would be attending remedial ship handling classes after his repeated failure quickly to close in on the floundering Red Navy Babushka Mini-sub.

The Tulagi and the remainder of the task force had a job to do that

---

[33] - The Battle Off Samar: Taffy III at Leyte Gulf by Robert Jon Cox. Escort carriers USS St. Lo and USS Kalinin Bay are the first carriers to hit an enemy with gunfire. USS Gambier Bay is the only US carrier to be sunk by enemy gunfire. Admiral Clifton Spruance was the Commander of Taffy Three TF 77.4.3

couldn't wait for the very entertaining farce to play itself out.

In a few minutes, the Tulagi and its sister ship the USS Petrof Bay would launch their routine combat air patrols. While there was no expectation of enemy air opposition it was always best to be prepared. The operation would also give the flyboys added practice. You could never get enough practice in landing on a Jeep Carrier. They looked noticeably smaller than fleet carriers at 2000 feet altitude and quite noticeably smaller at 100 feet when trying to land.

Napoleon once again started to scan the horizon as the little jeep carrier swung around to continue on its way. He saw the black cloud almost right away and focused in on what was underneath.

Someone had failed to warn the troop ship of an incoming torpedo or perhaps they just couldn't maneuver in time. Underneath the cloud of burning oil was the wreck of the USS Edmund P. Alexander.[34]

The torpedo had hit just aft of the bow. Her speed must have been a contributing factor with water rushing in and pushed by momentum until she was dead in the water.

€

---

[34] - Troop Ships of World War Two by Roland Charles pg. 20

Figure 37 - Edmund B. Alexander formerly German Passenger Ship Amerika

Napoleon could see that the ship was sinking slowly, which was a blessing, considering that it was carrying 4,000 men and their equipment. The men who needed rescuing were almost 15% of the troops in this invasion force.

Already at least a half a dozen ships were getting into position to receive the rescued personnel. Life boats were ready to launch. It looked to Napoleon like few lives would be lost.

The soldiers from the Edmund B. Alexander had been scheduled to debark onto landing craft in less than a day. Consequently, the men would spend little time exposed to the elements aboard the larger ships.

Napoleon mentally saluted the brave souls who manned the sinking troop transport. After decades of service to the US Army the Edmund B. Alexander was going down by her head.

A Matter of National Pride

General George C. Marshall was pacing back and forth, which was unusual for the man. Marshall was not given to second guessing or displays of nervousness. However, he did yield to second guessing in private and this was one of those moments.

The upcoming operations of Triple Cross and Backdoor were unusually daring for Eisenhower. True, Ike's strategies were based on proposals from Douglas MacArthur before he died. Ike had immediately embraced MacArthur's concepts wholeheartedly and without reservation. This seemingly blind acceptance worried Marshall. It was totally out of character for Eisenhower to be so bold. George's gut told him that Ike was one of those rare men who knew a good idea when he saw one. Moreover, Ike had the capacity to adapt, improve and implement the thoughts of others. His unique alibies were why George had chosen him for leadership. Even recognizing Ike's innate skills didn't alleviate his feeling of unease.

Marshall invariably listened to the facts, made a decision and then gave his opinion, whether it was asked for or not. More than once after challenging superiors and fellow officers he had been told that his Army career was over.

Yet, here he was worried that Ike was being too audacious. So far, everything was going like clockwork, which in itself was a reason to worry. War was chaotic and messy. Operation Backdoor and Triple Cross were not.

The Soviets were lured out of their comfort zone. They were far from home and about to lose their mobility. Triple Cross was designed to force the Stavka to choose the lessor of two evils. Depending upon the decision, there were a variety of NATO contingency plans ready to be launched.

In any event, the Soviets needed to mount a response to the loss of Copenhagen and the consequences of the landings in Gdynia and Gdansk. Further delay on their part could quickly lead to catastrophic outcomes from which there would be no recovery.

The current strategic situation was the equivalent of the British actions in the Great Lakes during the War of 1812.[35] The British were able to strike at will from the water. Now NATO had the ability to do the same along thousands of miles of Soviet shoreline.

---

[35] - 1812: The War of 1812 by Walter R. Borneman

It was intolerable to the Soviets to have enemy forces in what they considered their private lake. Controlling the Baltic Sea's waters was a critical national priority.

The largest enemy naval force ever to enter the Baltic was armed, dangerous and capable of taking extremely grave actions. Yet the Stavka seemed unable to organize a counter offensive. This state of affairs was much like the initial inaction of the United States in 1812. Eventually the American hero, Oliver Hazard Perry, led a ragtag flotilla and "Met the enemy and they are ours."[36]

Now it was wait and see time for NATO. If the Soviets moved to contain Truscott and the 5th Army in Gdansk using minimal forces then it was a go for Operation Backdoor to enter the Black Sea.

If the Reds pulled out all the stops and brought in massive reinforcements to drive Truscott into the sea, Walker and the 1st Army would breakout from Vienna to cut the Soviet's supply lines. Hell they might just do both Operation Backdoor and unleash Walker to really mess with the Stavka. Marshall really wished he could be in the Stavka headquarters room when the High Command are told about Backdoor.

Meanwhile, General Hailslip, his 10th Army and the bulk of the other NATO forces would be attacking Soviet army groups on the Pyrenees Line eventually moving on Paris.

Life, Revenge and Liberty

The Chief of Staff, General Marshall, glanced briefly at the map he was about to present to the Truman and select members of Congress. Hopefully, his proposal along with the map would be simple enough for the politicians to understand.

After the public meeting George was to have a one on one with the President. In this conference, he would be outlining the Joint Chiefs of Staff's final strategies and tactics to end World War Three. But first, Marshall had to go through with his dog and pony show for the public servants. He went over in his mind how he hoped the meeting would play out.

Truman himself was a very quick study and a former captain in the

---

[36] - Oliver Hazard Perry: Honor, Courage, and Patriotism in the Early U.S. Navy by David Skaggs

Army. He would easily grasp the audacity of the plan.

Somehow that idiot, the junior senator from Wisconsin, "Tail Gunner Joe" McCarthy had wangled his way into the meeting. If the past was any indication, Marshall expected most of the elementary questions to come from the Senator.

Then McCarthy would launch into his "communist around every corner monologue." At one time his claim may have been true. Many former members of the Communist Party of the United States of America had since seen the light. These idealists could not forgive the recently revealed atrocities ordered by Stalin. Most of the Reds had been cleared out of the Federal government by now. George was sure that few had escaped.

Also, he was just as sure that McCarthy would ignore all the evidence to the contrary and continue to shout "Commie" at anyone who stood in his way. It was essential that the military stayed out of this domestic controversy created by McCarthy. While the armed services could do nothing overt, they could and did clean their own ranks.

The various branches caught a number traitors including a few that held high offices. From all indications, the Brits were far behind in their efforts at cleaning house. They were spent after what they went through at the hands of the Nazis and then the cowardly attack by the Reds. To make matters worse the Soviets were our former allies. Somehow it's worse when erstwhile "friends" are the ones who stab you in the back.

After a few minutes, Marshall planned to shut McCarthy up and address the current situation. Using a prop like the map usually helped his audiences understand the issues more quickly. A brief question and answer session would follow.

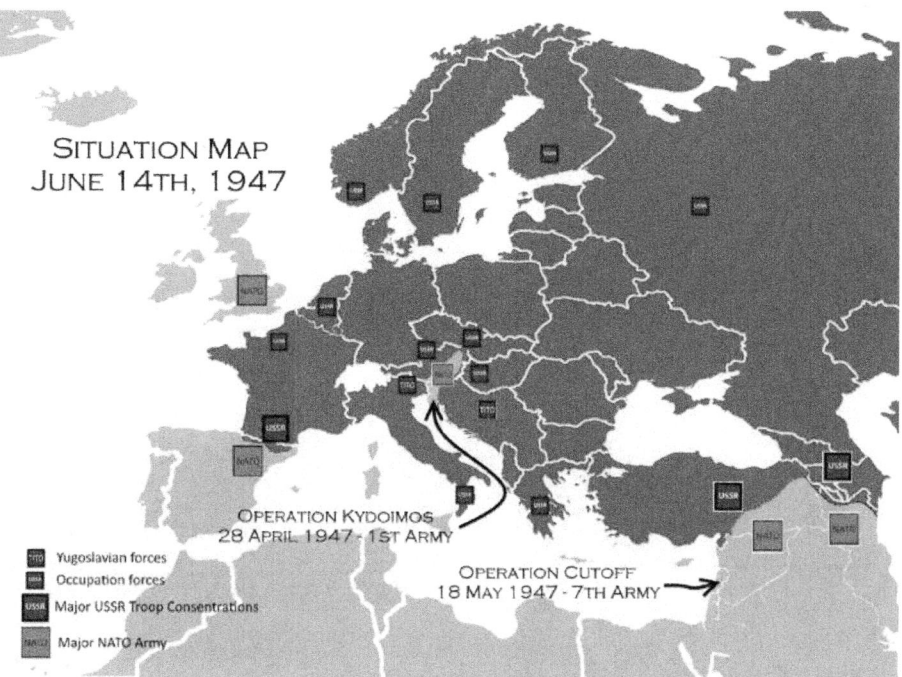

The real challenge would begin when Marshall would meet with the President alone. Today George would review the detailed strategies that the JCS believed was their best bet to end the war before winter.

He opened his locked drawer and withdrew a file prepared by the newly formed CIA. Top Secret was stamped all over it. He loved this report and hoped its contents and the conclusions were correct.

According to the authors of the paper over a million former Soviet citizens had turned against the malevolent Stalin during World War Two. One report said the number was closer to two million. 1.4 million proletarians actively joined the Wehrmacht as Hiwis, short for the German term Hilfswilliger (willing to help).[37]

The Hiwis hated the aberration of communism that was practiced by Stalin so much that they were willing to kill former countrymen who stood in their way. Their aim was to crush Stalinism no matter the cost. The Hiwis were placed in their own units, wore German uniforms, used German weapons and even waved a version of the swastika decorated

---

[37] - SS Hitler's Foreign Divisions: Foreign Volunteers in the Waffen-SS 1940–45 by Chris Bishop

flag.

Figure 38 - Cossacks in the Wehrmacht under the Swastika flag

The CIA paper estimated that fully 20% of the German forces invading the Soviet Union in 1942 were former soviets. If Hitler had played his cards right millions more Ukrainians would have taken up arms against the Stalinist forces.

When the Wehrmacht invaded the USSR during World War Two's Operation Barbarossa, whole towns and villages in the Ukraine greeted the German forces as liberators. The locals acceptance also help explain the German's rapid advance across the Ukraine.

In the end Nazi distain and loathing of the Slavic people in general came to the fore. Despite being treated like barbarians by the Germans, the Ukrainians, Cossacks, Belarusians, Armenians, Azerbaijanis and Georgians still joined the Nazis by the tens of thousands.[38]

According to the experts, Stalin's greatest fear was his own people turning on him. If the behavior of other modern dictators were any indication, Stalin would not give up power until the bitter end. What

---

[38] - Alleged Nazi Collaborators in the United States after World War II by Christoph Schiessl

better way to end this war quickly then to have Stalin's head impaled on a local pitchfork?

The CIA believed that many former Soviets would join NATO's crusade under the right conditions. First they had to be shown that there was hope. Next they had to be given a chance for redemption. Then they needed to be properly armed. Finally, they had to be assured they were not alone in their fight.

The opportunity to save American lives by unleashing these committed anti-Stalinist forces was further reason for Marshall to love this report. The implications were astonishing.

If a million or more former Soviets could be convinced to join Hitler in his struggle against Stalin, imagine how many would join NATO if given the chance? How many potential assassins would emerge? How many lovers of freedom and victims of Stalin's rule would join armies bent on revenge?

In 1942, the Nazis had promised many life and most importantly, revenge. In the end, over a million had rebelled. In 1947, NATO was in the position to fulfill these promises as well and add liberty into the mix.

One Less Nikita

The old woman slowly made her way down the street. She was like a salmon swimming upstream. She ambled along like she didn't have a care in the world. The other pedestrians avoided her and let her pass then continued on their way, hustling off to live the rest of their lives.

The babushka seemed totally oblivious to the hustle and bustle threatening to engulf her. She just continued walking towards her final destination. She had been squatting in an abandoned apartment and was well known in the neighborhood. No one knew or cared where she went, what she did, or if she lived or died. She was just another faceless survivor of Stalin's empire.

If someone look very closely for a long period of time they would have noticed that she was very aware of her surroundings. Her eyes are always moving, her ears were always listening and her hands periodically brushed something in her pocket. That something was a small Beretta 1915 pistol.

She was not the benign babushka that her outward appearance would have you believe. She was in fact the deadly sniper Marie Ljalková-

Lastovecká and she was being coerced into serving the machinations of Lavrenti Beria.

She was not on her way back to her apartment. She was on our way to an appointment with a well-oiled and expertly zeroed in Mosin Nagant 91/30 Sniper Rifle. Nikita Khrushchev was about to make a rare public appearance and she was going to save her daughter by shooting him in the head.

Kazimir Volkov was looking forward to the state dinner later on that evening. He was Nikita Khrushchev's primary double ganger. His appearance at the ribbon cutting ceremony was the price he had to pay for a sumptuous meal. He was told that the theme of the dinner was the sea and all it provided. Since this was a ceremony for the new aquarium it was decided that the expense was appropriate even as widespread famine was occurring just outside of Moscow.

The fact that all the fish for the aquarium had been intercepted and eaten by the villagers of Voytolovo didn't seem to matter. It didn't seem to matter that everyone in the village was just as dead at the hands of the NKVD. The celebration and ribbon cutting ceremony would continue with or without the fish or the village of Voytolvo.

Volokov was waving and smiling at the crowd. The fact that he was thinking of the caviar and poached salmon he was going to eat later was not evident. The crowd saw a diminutive Nikita Kruschev celebrating with them and Marie Ljalková-Lastovecká saw a reticle bracketing his scope enhanced head.

She took a breath and took the shot.

Kazimir Volkov died instantly with the top of his head no longer attached. No memories flashing by, no long slow walk towards a bright light….he just died. Pandemonium reined and the invisible babushka disappeared into the panicked crowd. If you were very observant you could tell she was moving with more purpose than her appearance would warrant. Otherwise she was once again invisible.

As Marie was walking she couldn't help thinking that all of her other kills had been the enemy of the Soviet Union.

This shot was different, this time it was murder. She believed there was one less member of Stalin's inner circle. It didn't matter if it was good or bad. All she knew was that it was either Khrushchev or her daughter, so there was one less Nikita in the world, or so she thought.

One More Nikita

Beria was getting reports that Khrushchev was still alive. He was sure that Marie Ljalková-Lastovecká believed she killed Nikita. To make sure he had abused her daughter as she watched and screamed. Then he raped her and for good measure tortured her as well. Yes... he was sure she had hit the target, but was the target the right one.

Both Stalin and Khrushchev had been known to use look-a-likes, stand-ins or doppelgangers to fool would be assassins. He called them targets. Perhaps Maria had killed one of Nikita's surrogates.

A couple of thousand people had seen what looked like Nikita Khrushchev's head explode yet there was nothing official or a funeral. He would have at least have concocted a story about his being wounded and making a full recovery and then have the real Nikita show up with a fake sling or some such ruse.

He was noticing that the Kremlin was getting less and less crafty in their propaganda efforts. He guessed that Stalin's mind was going fast and he wasn't there to pick up on the other's failures as he had done in years past.

He was a master of manipulating and terrorizing anyone who was unlucky enough to draw his ire. This included Beria himself. Stalin was the only man who could frighten him with just a look.

The ability to terrorize was innate and instinctual. Anyone else would say Beria was pure evil. Lavrenti would say that he was a genius pure and simple. By that definition than Stalin was a genius as well.

Once he was sure Nikita was finished or incapacitated and Stalin was deceased, he himself would rise from the dead to take command. Without Stalin to answer to he would easily be able to manipulate the countries leadership and through them the masses.

A peace proposal would be offered from a position of strength which meant that the timing had to be exquisite. He had the utmost confidence in his abilities for how else had he survived all these years? Years of raping other men's wives and daughters with no retaliation. Decades of torturing his enemies with impunity.

A times he would be made to release them before he was done and yet he was still alive. No ... he was just very good at what he did. The strengths and skills he had used to rise to power would keep him from harm once more.

He was sure Nikita was still alive and that would spoil all his plans. The situation had to be dealt with and soon for the rebellions were stating to take their toll. NATO was using the anger of the proletariat to do what Germany had not been able to do by force in The People's War.

His plan made sure Stalin's death was imminent and inevitable.

A Fleet's Demise

The Battle of the Baltic was short and for the NATO forces, sweet. What was left of the Soviet Baltic Fleet bravely weighed anchor and within hours was attacked by 16-inch shells from 19.4 miles away.

The Soviet Naval Commander of the 8th or Baltic Fleet, Vladimir Filippovich Tributs, had a workable plan. His plan had the possibility of getting at least half his fleet within torpedo range of the enemy.

The VVS and the Morskaya Aviatsiya (Naval Aviation) were doing a worthy job of keeping the NATO planes at bay. Only three Soviet destroyers had been sunk by the NATO air attacks so far.

Tributs had no hope of out gunning the NATO fleet but hopefully his torpedoes could cause enough damage to make the Amerikosi think twice about further mischief. Tributs could at least make them pay for the potential destruction of his fleet.

Four additional battleships had been added to augment NATO's TF 125's original complement of three once Copenhagen had been secured. The situation now unfolding had been anticipated by Admiral Spruance. His request for the four additional battle wagons had been promptly granted. Now, the battleships of the NATO taskforce were waiting for orders to fire.

Admiral Tributs knew that one way or the other his fleet was doomed either to air attack or long-range bombardment. The end result was the same. However going down fighting at least meant a heroic death. Shakespeare was translated into Russian and many were familiar with the proverb "A coward dies a thousand times before his death, but the valiant taste of death but once. It seems to me most strange that men should fear, seeing that death, a necessary end, will come when it will come."

A third alternative was to keep the fleet in port facing a NATO blockade.

Like so many other grand fleets throughout history it would eventually be destroyed having never firing a shot.

The Fleet's 25 ships were heavily manned with all volunteers. 2,489 men to be exact. Most of the ships in Tribut's fleet were small coastal vessels and carried a torpedo or two. The Cruiser Kirov was the only Soviet capital ship of consequence hence she would be the first to die.

The range of her 7.1-inch (180-mm) guns was 41,000 yards. The range of the Iowa class 16-inch guns on the USN battleships was about the same. The Kirov's 7.1 inch shells weighed in at 215 lbs while The Iowa's 16-inch shells weighed 2700 lbs. The outcome was inevitable with the Iowa's outgunning the Kirov by a factor of ten to one.

Just before the Kirov was in range 12 massive eruptions of water straddled her from NATO gunfire. The turbulence tossed the Kirov causing her shells to go wide to the north of the USS Wisconsin. The next three shells from the trailing USS Iowa found their mark. The Kirov staggered from 1 near miss and two direct hits. The near miss stove in her sixth bow plate on the port side. The first direct hit left a gaping hole where her aft turret had been. The shell plunged right through from deck to bottom. The second hit took off her aft funnel along with all three of her 100-mm anti-aircraft guns on the starboard side and 32 crew men.

Ironically the Kirov's second set of three 7.1-inch shells hit the cruiser USS Augusta CA 31 and penetrated causing minimal damage due to defective fuses. Three more hits from the USS Iowa and the Kirov was listing badly and sinking fast.

The majority of the other Soviet ships were sunk before they could come within their effective torpedo range. All in all the battle was like target practice for the larger NATO ships. Yet over 789 Soviet sailors met their death defending their nation's honor.

Figure 39 - Soviet Cruiser Kirov 1945

Figure 40 - Last known Picture of the Kirov - General Quarters after sighting the NATO Fleet

Figure 41- USS Wisconsin fires on the Kirov - Battle of the Baltic

Chapter Eight: Rebellion

Figure 42 - Hungarians Revolt

468

Ihor Chornovil Ruslan was a Private in the US Army attached to Combat Command B assigned to the 65th Infantry Division. The Division had been in the Gdnask area for three weeks. He was on patrol when he became separated from his squad.

Suddenly there was a Russian soldier walking towards him with his hands up in the air. Ihor told him to stop in Russian and a heated discussion ensued. The end result was Ihor took the surrender of over 450 Soviet soldiers.

Ihor had no idea of what to do with his 468 enemy prisoners. They were wearing stolen Soviet uniforms in an effort to disguise their true identities. Ruslan was trying to find his Sergeant.

Whenever he got close to NATO's lines, someone would see the Soviet uniforms and shoot at the group. Not that Ihor could blame his unit. He would probably have done the same thing. Here he was trying to bring these POWs to someone in charge and he was getting shot at by his own guys as a reward.

The really sad part was that three of the voluntary captives had gotten shot and two had died. Being shot at and the casualties were not good for moral. Luckily Ihor's grandfather was Ukrainian and had taught the Private to speak passable Russian.

The fact that he could talk to and understand his detainees was a tremendous help. He had no doubt that if he had been unable to communicate he would be dead by now. The situation was absurd to say the least.

The 468 soldiers were what remained of an original force of about 6,000 Ukrainian fighters. To a man they hated the dictator who murdered millions including their families, more than invading foreigners. First had been the Germans and now it was the Americans.

According to the leader of Ihor's prisoners, in 1941 the Ukrainians joined the Germans against Stalin. After the war it had taken 18 months for these anti-Soviet fighters to reach their homeland.[39] In July, 1947 the remaining 1458 Ukrainians were stopped at the border by a contingent

---

[39] - Operation Keelhaul: the story of forced repatriation from 1944 to the present by Julius Epstein

of 30 NKVD personnel and a hundred or so very scared looking Commissars. The former anti-Stalinist [40] fighters were ordered to return to the front and attack the Amerikosi. The Colonel in command of the intercepting group implied that the men were expected to die in the attempt.

One of the prisoners suddenly shouted, "TO HELL WITH THAT." a general melee broke out between Stalin's minions and the fighters. The surviving Ukrainians were unarmed. Hundreds were shot before they could get their hands on the NKVD stooges and Commissars who were trying to prevent them from going home.

After 5 years of intense fighting thousands of miles from his home, Vladim succumbed to a blow to the head. He died within blocks of his family after having been to Africa and back. Many anti-Stalinist fighters died that day.

Their deaths were not in vain. Eventually the former Hiwis [41] overwhelmed Stalin's men and took dozens of them prisoner after killing the majority. The last 923 Ukrainians knew their situation was untenable. To a man they decided to surrender to the Americans that had landed in Gdansk.

After all, what was a mere 400 odd miles traveling through their sworn enemy's territory and being hunted constantly compare to what they had already been through? And so they started their journey to Gdansk. 468 of them completed the trip eventually surrendering to Private Ihor, 468 half-naked men who hadn't eaten in days.

After 18 hours of trying, Private Ihor was finally able to sneak close enough to a sleepy guard who he recognized from his unit. He convinced the man to get the Corporal, who got the Sergeant, who got the lieutenant, who got the… it took a colonel to make the decision and accept the prisoners' surrender.

The 468 had their first hot meal in months. One ate so fast that he choked to death and now there were 467.

Insurgent Army

A specialized unit in resistance fighting was dispatched from NATO HQ. They spent 14 days interviewing and classifying Ihor Chornovil Ruslan's

---

[40] - Soviet Opposition to Stalin: A Case Study in World War II by George Fischer
[41] - The Vlasov movement of World War II: an appraisal by Robert Bentley Burton

467 POWs. 147 were chosen to continue with the fight against Stalinism. Their assignment was to once again infiltrate behind the Stalinist's lines were they were to recruit, train and lead Freedom Fighters in an insurgency campaign aimed at disrupting the iron grip Stalin had on his countrymen.

All the soldiers were presented and then given proof that Stalin had ordered the death of millions of Ukrainians in three different purges over a 10-year period. Many of the 147 knew or had firsthand experience watching in horror as fellow villagers and relatives were lined up and shot. The murders were for no apparent reason other than the victims were in the wrong place at the wrong time.

How can millions be killed by a leader who is clearly insane? How was he able to stay in power? Fear is the answer. The 147 were no longer afraid of death and had nothing left to lose.

The 147 were to gather additional fighters using a plan designed by a former conman. The plan was an iteration of the classic Pyramid Scheme. One man recruited five who in turn recruited another five, etc., 5 x 5 x 5 x 5. In six generations, you end up with 78,000 recruits. If only 50 out of the 147 were successful, you still had close to 4 million Freedom Fighters.

Freedom movements gain momentum when potential members see help is on the way. The NATO landings in Trieste, the Baltic and now the Black Sea brought hope to the hopeless.

The Scandinavian countries, France, Poland, Italy, Greece, Ukraine and Yugoslavia had substantial resistance operations during World War Two. The concept was not new. In this war many who enlisted were willing and able to take leadership roles. The final elements needed were a catalyst and a supply of arms. NATO provided both.

Substantial numbers of arms caches started to be dropped to resistance units throughout the former Soviet Empire. NATO was using the newly built and acquired air fields located in the captured territories. DC3 Dakotas took off to rendezvous points throughout Eurasia.

At times, these flights were heavily escorted. At other times, they were flown clandestinely. The VVS was far too busy to commit significant resources in stopping these flights. This decision could prove to be a fatal mistake by Novikov.

These flights were sowing the seeds of freedom throughout the rotting corps of Stalin's former dominion. These seeds of freedom were far deadlier to the Soviet body politic than any invading army.

Stalin was well aware of the danger of revolt. His greatest fear was internal resistance. It was, after all, the rebellion against the Czar that brought him to power. Ruthlessly destroying any active or imagined opposition was how he remained in power.

So why didn't he act?

The Toad

The Toad had no idea of what all these men were doing here. She was just trying to hide and not get stepped on. She almost made it when one of the humans picked her up and she did the only thing nature had taught her to do…she pissed on him. The man didn't like that and threw her quite a distance.

Luckily, she landed in a big puddle of water. She hid for a while and then noticed a pile of soft sand nearby. She carefully hopped over to the pile and dug herself in and waited. The sun had heated up the sand nicely and she was very comfortable.

Something landed right near her hiding place. It was big and breathing hard. Now if toads did experience fright she would have, but they don't. She just hunkered down and waited.

The thing that was lying near her was a soldier named Yeorgi and he was in a world of trouble. He had no nice pile of sand to hide in. Within seconds she forgot about the thing.

Her instincts told her to wait until it got cooler to venture out. A toad moving around on a hot beach does not last long and their genes would not be passed on as well. Which meant that most toads who's instincts told them to jump around in the bright sunlight were dead and probably never got the chance to mate.

In evolutionary terms this behavior was eliminated pretty quickly.

The Beach Chair

It was the 25th of July and Yeorgi couldn't believe his eyes. Who could have a fleet this big and what were they doing here in Novorossiysk?

With the naked eye, he could just see the massive ships. Almost simultaneously a cloud of airplanes formed over the town and beach.

Yeorgi had asked for and gotten leave after his 54th sniper kill. He had now shot seven Americans to add to his score of 47 Spaniards. He was no longer proud of either number and was tired of the killing.

Yeorgi used his time off to make his way to the beautiful beach in Novorossiysk on the Black Sea. Although the town itself had been devastated by the Germans, the beach had cleaned in the year-long hiatus from combat. His Grandparents had brought him here as a child and his memories of those visits had drawn him back.

Just as he was thinking he should leave the beach. Large shells started to land inland on the few Soviet defensive sites near the harbor. The explosions were enormous. Bigger than anything Yeorgi saw in his six months on the Pyrenees Line in Spain. He had heard of the power of the Amerikosi's ships and now he knew to whom the fleet belonged.

How could they have gotten into the Black Sea? As he finished his thought, he was suddenly launched 30 feet into the air. He landed in the water and was remarkably unhurt. His ears were ringing and everything ached but nothing was broken. The exception possibly being his ear drums.

By his count he stayed in the water for a few hours. Even the warm waters of Novorossiysk eventually made him shiver. The shelling from the fleet continued the entire time with planes dropping bombs adding to the mix. There were few Soviet military targets left by this time. There was a slight lull in the bombardment as if a crescendo had been reached in some massive symphony of destruction.

He decided to make for shore. Just as he was dragging himself out of the water, one of the few remaining Soviet emplacements foolishly revealed itself. Yeorgi was wondering why the idiots would start shooting now, when he heard engine noises behind him. As he was running he glanced over his shoulders and to his amazement, he saw dozens of landing craft making towards shore.

The crew of the small cannon were doing their duty and shooting at the boats full of soldiers. A close-in US destroyer practically took Yeorgi's head off with a volley of 5-inch shells that silenced the brave little cannon almost immediately. Then, as if adding insult to injury a plane dropped a large bomb right on top of where the gun had been.

He jumped behind the first cover he could find even though it was a half-destroyed beach chair. At least it covered him from view. As he peaked through the slats of the shattered seat, he witnessed something few have seen and lived to tell about.

Hundreds of heavily laden US Marines were jumping out of the landing craft, wading, and running ashore. Yeorgi buried himself in the sand like a crab and held still. Within minutes he heard one of the foreigners yelling very close by. Next, he felt a body land on the sand within a meter of his hiding place.

The man proceeded to crawl right over him got up and started running towards the nearest building. He heard very few shots in opposition and guessed that his comrades had beaten a hasty retreat or were dead.

He remained behind his beach chair under his shallow covering of sand and began to wait. He waited so long that he fell asleep. He could not believe he had slept. What woke him up was something squirming underneath the sand below his left hand.

He slowly moved his hand and within seconds the head of a toad appeared. She or he Yeorgi couldn't tell, looked around and then headed out for the nearest piece of cover.

It was dark, but all around him American soldiers were moving inland along with trucks, armored cars and tanks. The amount of supplies on the beach was staggering. From just what he could see he calculated a whole army could live for a week.

So, there he was dressed only in shorts standing in awe when an American soldier came right up to him and told him in Russian to get off the beach and go home. He must have looked like some ordinary tourist who got caught in the wrong place. He thanked the man and took his advice.

He blended in with the crowds of civilians and started going north. He was headed to his grandparents' home, the Desmans and his eventual death. [42]

Yeorgi would once again hear the cry of the Desman as he was breathing his last. He would hug his grandmother one more time and shake his grandfather's hand as he went off to do his duty. Every step he took brought him closer to his fate. Every step he took brought the final cry of the Desman closer. He had 3 more weeks to live.

---

[42] - World War Three – Book Two – The Red Sky - The Second Battle of Britain - Desmans

When Spoons Attack
1 August 1947

William White injured his finger. Much too often when he used his right index finger to type the letters h, j, m ,n, o, p, u and y he made a mistake. William White did not make mistakes when typing. He was the fastest and most accurate typist by far in the CIA stable of typists. Now he was going to lose that distinction to Mary Hart of all people. He loathed Mary. She was one of those prissy, know it all types.

He hurt his finger playing cards. He and his brother and two cousins were playing the card game Spoons. His cousin Marvin slammed down four aces and everyone grabbed for a spoon. William's lunge for the closest spoon was blocked by his brother's wrist and more importantly, his watch. It was a big Timex and William hit it square with his finger, the collision hurt like a son of a gun.

His finger had swollen to twice its normal size and half of it turned purple. The next day his pointer just would not bend properly. Of all days for this to happen, this was the worst! It was the end of the month report and he was expected to perform miracles on the keyboard. He was so frustrated that he was on the verge of walking out. Which probably would have gotten him shot for desertion in his nation's time of need.

He bravely soldiered on, but he could feel Mary watching his every stroke. William started typing …

24 July 1947

Operation Backdoor was an astounding success at this juncture. The Turkish Straits are in NATO's hands and a 40-mile corridor on either side is in place. The Turks are on the verge of rebellion and an estimated 450,000 Soviet troops are trapped in Turkey.

As usual, William's mind paraphrased what he was typing…

Mathew Ridgeway and his 8th Army would drive like hell for the Caspian Sea. The army would skirt the Caucasian Mountains and trap Zhukov and his command titled the Transcaucasian Front. The soviets would be caught between the 8th Army and the forces commanded by Griswold to the south. Zhukov was rumored to have the best units in the Red Army. Georgy was preparing to attack Griswold and the US 15th Army from his position on the Lessor Caucasus.

Operation Backdoor would put a stop to Zhukov's attack. If everything went according to plan another 670,000 of the Red Army's finest would be cut off from Moscow and their supply lines.

Operation Triple Cross

NATO captured Gdansk and is driving south. Walker and the 1st Army broke out of Vienna. Currently Walker's command is fighting their way north. The goal is to meet up with Truscott and the 5th Army cutting Europe in two along the Vistula River from Gdansk to Bielsko-Biala.

Walker coming from the South would complete what was now being called the European Line. Major Commie forces along the Pyrenees Line and occupying France, Germany, Poland and Italy would be left hanging.

US Army G2 estimated that 2.5 million Reds would be caught in the trap. These soldiers would be desperate, hungry and out of fuel thousands of miles from home. The major concern was that they might turn on the civilian population for revenge and looting. Not that there was much left in Germany to loot.

The key was getting the Reds to surrender peacefully by offering them food, freedom and a one-way ticket back home. All they had to do was fight for their country against Stalinism.

Attack on Pyrenees Line

Within weeks, General Wade Halslip on the Pyrenees Line would join the British Expeditionary Force and its Western European allies. Together the combined armies would attack Marshall Konstantin Rokossovsky and his beleaguered Soviet forces on the border of France and Spain. Months ago, the Reds had been on the offensive. Now the tables had turned and NATO was in the driver's seat.

30 divisions of NATO troops consisting of mainly British units of the Second Army with attached Spanish Corps, Canadian and Regiments of Western European exiles led by Montgomery were set to attack on 4 August 1947. Hum from what he had heard Montgomery was not that good on the attack… politics he supposed. Heavy use of helicopters for what is called "vertical envelopment" are to be used. Something to do with those helicopters again.

Ah…another map…

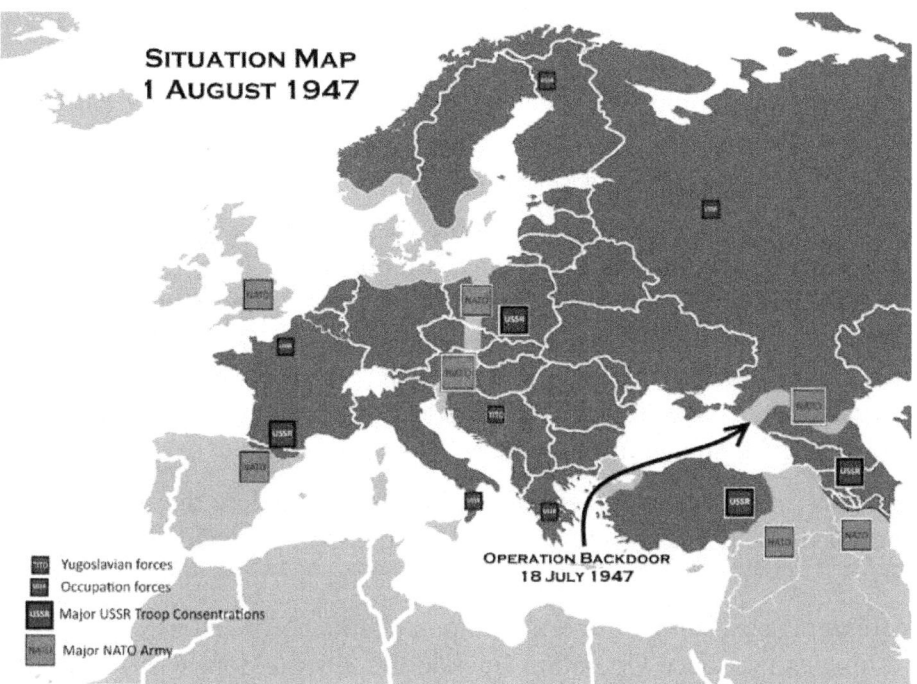

A concerted effort to coordinate with the resurgent French Resistance and Marquis has borne fruit. Over a half a million Frenchman resisted the Germans in World War Two. Many were committed communists who now were part of the puppet government in Paris. A whole new group of freedom fighters would have to be recruited.

At first, French resistance fighters were slow to join the movement as they were reluctant to leave their families again. But a series of atrocities committed by the French Reds and Soviet second line army units suddenly spurred an enormous wave of volunteers. Quite the opposite effect from what the communists intended he was sure.

Research and Development

Let's see if that Dr. Skinner and his group are staying one step ahead of the Reds in the battle of technology. The group's ideas of heated balloons over the ships are working for now. According to his report, Skinner feels it's only a matter of time before the Soviets guess right and NATO ships start to take some serious casualties.

Damn he goes on to say that a few dozen hits by those bird guided missiles and the Navy will probably "reassess" its mission.

His mind wandered as he recalled how the US Navy pulled the plug on the Marines at Guadalcanal when they took some heavy losses. Admiral Fletcher was blamed for what the Marines called the 'Navy Bugout'. Despite winning the first three carrier battles in history and a fourth at Guadalcanal Fletcher was always tainted by his decision to leave the Marines stranded.

He continued to paraphrase Skinner's report in his head. It just goes to make the point that the US Navy will 'Bugout' rather than take heavy losses and live to fight another day. In this case, a Bugout would mean the abandonment of the US Army in Vienna, the Pyrenees, Poland and Crimea. Basically, the war would be lost with hundreds of thousands of US soldiers stranded in Eurasia.

Skinner's felt that it was essential to win the war before the situation got out of hand. It was a race against the clock with the odds favoring the Reds.

Hummm, new subject, the ubiquitous challenge of oil. US Army G2 estimates that once Operation Backdoor shuts the door (heh) on Baku that Moscow will be on its last reserves. Units in the Pyrenees will be immobile along with the Red Fronts facing Walker and Operation Triple Cross. Further, the NATO Taskforce in the Black Sea will effectively stop anything from moving on the water and within 200 miles inland. This interdiction should limit the Red's crude oil transportation capabilities by 80%.

The loss of access to fuel should be almost instantaneous with the vast majority of USSR units forced to defend in place. Millions of Red soldiers will be left stranded with no hope of rectifying the situation.

Stavka's Plans

G2 has learned that the Stavka has amassed a strategic fuel reserve near Moscow. The question is where will it be used? Best estimate is that an all-out effort will be mounted to break out Zhukov and to open the supply route from Baku and adjacent areas. Zhukov does have a large enough supply of fuel that he was going to use for an offensive aimed at Griswold and the US 15th Army in the south.

Whoa all this information is getting too much for my limited abilities to keep up with. Plus the pain emanating from my right pointer finger is really wearing me down.

He was sure that the experience of being attacked by a spoon is something he would never forget.

Bottom line is that Zhukov will get the last shot at saving Stalin's ass.

By Fiat

He peered cautiously around the corner. He was within stone's throw of the Transcaucasia Front's Headquarters. His target, Marshall Zhukov, was less than a block away. Mario Fiat had to figure out a way to communicate with Zhukov. Mario was going to make Zhukov an offer he couldn't turn down, an offer that would save tens of thousands of Soviet lives.

But first, he had to make contact. Zhukov's best friend had been captured near Sevastopol. Having custody of this valued friend was Fiat's leverage. Mario hoped that their friendship was such that Zhukov would be compelled to meet with him. Gaining access to the Marshall was the key to making his plan even remotely feasible.

Zhukov's friend was the blind genius Konstantine. Until Mario met the man, he did not believe that the fellow existed. Konstantine was in fact the mythical advisor that Zhukov and Stalin trusted completely.

Fiat spent days talking with the myth. Both men enjoyed the mental exercise and challenge that they presented to the other. Neither man felt intimidated. Both felt as though they had known one another their entire lives. Yet they had grown up in totally different worlds.

Konstantine's was a world of darkness. He was teased and bullied in the small village where he was born. Blind from birth yet of towering intellect he soon devised ways to not only survive but to expertly manipulate and control his would-be tormentors.

The bullies always seemed to get into arguments among themselves when they attempted to harass Konstantine. Somehow, the situation would invariably turn in the blind boy's favor. Soon the bullies stopped trying and started to seek his advice and counseling.

To his mother, it was astonishing to see her blind son leading his bigger and older converts in whatever direction he chose. Whether the outcome for the boys was good or bad, it didn't matter. It was a case of the blind leading the sighted.

Gradually, Konstantine's reputation caught the attention of higher ups in the Soviet military. Subsequently he was enlisted as an intelligence agent during the "People's War."

His brilliant observations and the ease in which he could seemingly read the minds of his enemies soon brought him to the attention of Marshall Zhukov and eventually Stalin himself.

Mario Fiat on the other hand, was raised with a silver spoon in his mouth. As the son of a wealthy lumber baron in Chippewa Falls, Wisconsin he and his family enjoyed the finest imports available.

When he expressed an interest in learning to play the organ, his mother installed a full pipe organ in the living room. The project required the removal of the second story of the mansion. The pipes towered over the Vestibule and Main Hall with the Grand Staircase intertwined.

It was quite a sight and Mario didn't think anything of it when he was six. Just how privileged he was started to sink in when he was eight and played with the Head Groomsman's son. He soon learned that everything he took for granted was anything but ordinary.

The fact that such a diverse a group could coalesce around a blind theorist was rather exceptional. On one hand, was a former bon vivant turned master spy and on the other a psychopathic mass murderer, with one of the greatest military minds in between. All fast friends with Konstantine.

Mario was going to use their complex relationship to convince Zhukov to defect. Hopefully taking as many of his men with him as he could. Fiat had proof positive that if Zhukov survived the coming battle, Stalin would have him killed rather than face him as a rival.

While debating with Fiat, Konstantine eventually defected on his own volition. If Zhukov's most trusted friend could see the error of his ways than so could the Marshall. Logic dictated Konstantine's apostasy and rejection of the Communist cause. Mario would bet his life that the combination of Stalin's growing insanity, Konstantine's renunciation and Zhukov's own dire situation will be enough to persuade the Marshall to join in the anti-Stalinist crusade.

NATO was not waging war on the Slavic peoples of the world but on Stalinism and all it stood for. Millions of former Soviets came to the same conclusion. Insurgents were joining the rebellion at the rate of ten thousand a day and growing.

Getting the Marshall to turn and bring his men with him would save tens of thousands of lives. Zhukov's situation was now totally hopeless. He had to be convinced of that and Mario was the man to do it.

Konstantine had told him that he would have to overcome the Marshall's long held beliefs by logical fiat. The pun was not lost on Mario.

Power and Compulsion

The NATO landing in Novorossiysk slammed the trap shut on the Armies of the Transcaucasian Front. To their total surprise Zhukov and close to a half a million Soviet military personnel were caught in their high mountain fortress. The Stavka never imagined an amphibious invasion via the Black Sea.

Shortly before he lost contact with Moscow, Zhukov had been contacted by a former aide to Beria. The man claimed that, not only was Lavrenti Beria alive, but he was planning on taking over the government after he killed Stalin and Khrushchev. Zhukov took the information at face value and read on. After all, there was nothing he could do about what was happening in Moscow.

However, the next revelation was life altering for Marshall Giorgi Zhukov. According to the note, Beria was going to sue for peace as soon as he gained power. For public consumption, Beria would extol the armed forces to fight to the end. But in secret, he was planning on betraying the homeland as well as the revolution they had all fought and sacrificed for. The millions of people who died, bringing the glories of Communism to the masses, had been in vain. The former slaves of the Czar would now become the slaves of the Capitalist pigs.

The end result of an Imperialist victory was evident. Everyone had seen propaganda of American children forced to work in coal mines and their poverty before the war. Just months ago America and several western European countries were caught using Germans as slave labor. How can Beria surrender to men like that? How could he betray the revolution?

Zhukov was still reeling from this information when he noticed a small package. It just appeared on his desk chair after he returned from a staff meeting. It was wrapped in brown paper and tied with the kind of twine used to bail hay.

At first, he thought of calling the guard and having him deal with the object. Then something made him pick up the package and examine it.

He couldn't quite place what was so compelling about the parcel. Suddenly his mind jumped to the answer. The package had a familiar odor. It smelled like his close friend and confidant Konstantine!

Throwing caution to the wind he opened the package and neatly displayed in a jewelry box was Konstantine's ring. It could only be his and it could only mean that something had happened to his friend.

A wave of grief overcame him and he almost missed the small note just barely sticking out from the back of the box. He eagerly opened it and read the few lines.

GOGA, KONSTANTINE IS QUITE WELL. HE SENDS YOU HIS GREETINGS. PLEASE GO OUTSIDE THE NORTH ENTRANCE FOR A CIGARETTE AT 19:13 HOURS.

What was going on?!?!? Only Konstantine called him Goga and that was in private. Given the ring and accompanying note Zhukov was filled with grave concern. What to do…what to do?

With his world falling apart around him. He decided to have that cigarette. His pistol would be in his pocket along with his hand. He was prepared to use it. He had killed before and would not hesitate to do so again.

In the end, it was his olfactory nerve which had triggered Zhukov's memories and affected his decision. Memories are powerful, especially in times of stress. The memory of a smell was particularly compelling. Giorgi was led by his nose and driven by fond memories to meet with the man or woman who he thought held Konstantine prisoner.

Little did he know that Konstantine was anything but a captive. In reality, Konstantine had willingly given up his most prized possession in the hopes of convincing his old friend to join him in the quest for self-determination.

He was actively helping the rebellion and the Freedom Force being organized by former White Russians and anti-Stalinism groups.

Konstantine was feeling compelled as well. He was bound by the power of truth and the logical consequences of his beliefs. The blinders of absolutism had been raised by Mario Fiat. A true force of nature had been unleashed as Konstantine began using his formidable powers to actively destroy what Stalin had built.

Zhukov would be one of the first to feel that power.

Chapter Nine: How to Succeed or Try Dying

Figure 43 - One of many funerals in Moscow in 1947

Deadly Dose

She carefully measured out the final dose as directed. She had no remorse about killing Stalin. The monster ordered the murder of her mother based on a false rumor. When she was 12 years old she witnessed the gruesome death of her beloved parent

Reportedly, Stalin never killed anyone personally. He probably didn't have the guts for it. He deserved to die a million times over.

The snake venom she was administering (administering…what a strange word…so benign) was the deadliest known. She had been told by her handler that the poison came from Australia. It was so diluted that it had taken months and many doses to reach this critical juncture. She could have been discovered at any time. The venom was crystalized and hidden in the special salt that was imported for Stalin's personal use. Anyone tasting the mixture would never suspect how deadly it was.

The effect was cumulative. Stalin's kidneys were the first to go. Somehow, he survived. All of his organs would eventually fail. It was apparent from his color that the liver was next. He was turning yellow and his breath had a terrible smell.

Putting the salt on Stalin's food was one of her chief occupations as an assistant to the Head Cook. Her prey was very particular that the seasoning be just the right amount for every food and its portion. She became an expert at determining his mood. Like most paranoid personalities know, any kind of routine can lead to an opportunity for those planning harm. Stalin was definitely not a creature of habit because he understood the dangers that lurked.

One of the rare exceptions was his salt obsession. That addiction would lead to his excruciating death as all his organs shut down one by one. The poison's effects were similar to scurvy in regards to the loss of teeth, shortness of breath, bone pain and neuropathy.

Luckily, no one connected the unusual death from kidney failure of Ivanna the scullery maid to Stalin's own near-death experience. Ivanna's malady had coincided with Stalin's own kidney problems. She must have been taking Stalin's salt and using it for her own purposes.

The assistant cook supposed that someone higher up in the unfolding plot had suppressed information. No one remarked on the fact that two very different members of the household had simultaneously experienced kidney failure. Earlier Stalin had a reprieve from death after receiving a kidney transplant.[43]

Stalin was finally on his deathbed and failing fast. The last time she saw him, he looked as if he were dead already. She yearned to tell the world that it was her, Natlya Kozlov, who had killed the greatest mass murderer of all time.

She made the final arrangements for her escape. All the actions needed were in place except for the initial ride to the farmhouse. She had to make sure Yuri would follow his crotch. Luckily, he was handsome and it was a pleasure to lead him on. She would miss him most of all.

They had agreed that they should wait at least three days after Stalin's death before initiating the plan. Leaving immediately would likely cast suspicion on her. A telegram would come informing Natlya that the aunt who raised her was missing and her uncle wished her home. This news would launch her escape.

That night Stalin breathed his last. Natlya had the pleasure of being in the room. His breathing was labored and he was wincing in pain. His last words were "make it stop." Whether he was answered by God or not is for others to decide.

Natlya was leaning towards the devil, who must have been elated to have this most heinous of souls added to his collection.

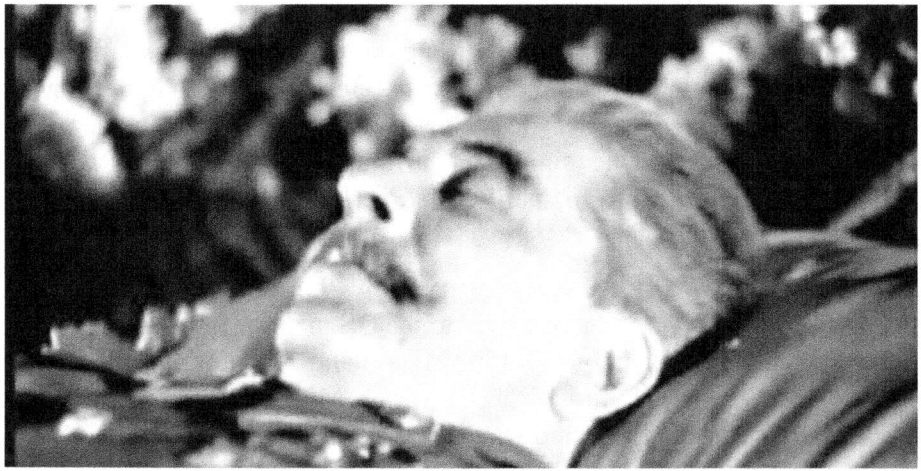

Joseph Jugashvili

---

[43] - The Transplant - World War Three 1946 – Book Four – Page 172

Stalin's given name was Joseph Jugashvili. Stalin was only his pseudonym and was a combination of the Russian words steel and Lenin. Joseph Jugashvili figuratively died in 1912 and Stalin was born at the age of 34. Now both were dead at the age of 68.

The news took a while to be assimilated by most people. Georgy Maximilianovich Malenkov happened to be the first one of the Ruling Circle to learn of Stalin's death. He was paying an obligatory visit to the despot and was present when the doctor informed the staff to prepare the body. Georgy immediately commandeered a phone and called Lazar Kaganovich, who in turn felt obligated to notify the supposedly deceased Khrushchev. Deep in his hiding place Lavrentiy Beria was also advised that Stalin was dead before many others in the Soviet elite received the news.

Life without Stalin was going to be unsettling for many of the Soviet population. He had been in power for over 40 years. He was the Soviet Union. Only other members of the ruling elite understood that Stalin had perverted the ideal of communism into his own personality cult. Now it was time to move on.

Most believed that Khrushchev was dead, with hundreds having witnessed him being shot in the head. Of the five remaining members of the Ruling Circle, Malenkov held the most power. With Nikita's reported assassination, Georgy became the obvious choice for becoming General Secretary of the Soviet Union.

Due to his families ties with Lenin, Malenkov experienced a swifter than average rise within the Communist Party. Georgy had cohabitated with Valeriya Golubtsova for decades. They had three children together. The couple's relationship was significant in that Valeriya's mother was an associate of Lenin. Both his partner's career and that of Malenkov leap frogged over others.

During World War Two Georgy oversaw the production of Soviet aircraft. The USSR was second only to the US in aircraft production with over 138,000 built from 1940-45. [44] His planes eventually cleared the skies over the Soviet Union of Nazi aircraft. Malenkov was in excellent position to rule the USSR and was planning on doing just that.

The official announcement of Stalin's death came on 30 July 1947. Some

---

[44] - Air Power and Warfare - Edited by Colonel Alfred Hurley and Major Robert Ehrhart USAF

wept, some rejoiced and some prayed for the first time in decades. Many ordinary people of the Soviet Union just wanted peace and to be left alone. Those wishes were now a real possibility.

The French were in open revolt with many regional communist officials being hung by local citizens. In the Scandinavian countries, The Resistance was openly fighting their occupiers. Belgium and Denmark were virtually free of Red Army units and taking prisoners by the thousands.

The Red Army in Western Europe was ceasing to exist by attrition. Apart from the half a million men on the Pyrenees Line in Spain, many units were surrendering to the nearest NATO officer. For the most part, the Soviet soldiers were being treated with humanity and respect when they surrendered peacefully.

They were promised a one-way ticket home and food for their journey. Some were talked into joining the Freedom Force. Many took off their uniforms and just started heading east.

Families along the way found it much easier to give the ex-soldiers food, then to have their homes looted. The former Red Army military personnel were required to turn in their guns and arms before they were given safe passage. By the hundreds and then by the thousands they started the long journey home.

Most had no idea if their wives, lovers, children, parents or siblings were still alive. Were their homes still intact? Who was now in command? Would they be shot for leaving their posts?

There were so many questions and no answers they just took one step after the other. Once it is said and done, you can always take one more step...one more step...one more step.

That Bodes Well

Georgy Zhukov was very good at hiding his true feelings from his staff. Inside, his guts were churning as he thought about his upcoming meeting with the unknown spy. The go-between claimed connections to Konstantin. Just speaking to the agent could get Georgy killed even though Stalin was recently dead.

To his relief the briefing on the planned attack was short and to the point. His chief of staff had done a good job. Zhukov answered a few questions from junior staff.

He casually glanced at his watch. It was 19:03 and he indicated that the briefing should end. The colonel quickly summarized the proceedings and the officers started to leave. It was 19:10.

Zhukov told his aide that he was stepping out for a smoke as he often did. Nobody thought twice about his leaving by the back door. It was 19:12 when he lit a cigarette and a man came out of the shadows. The Marshall's hand was on the gun in his pocket and he was watching the man intently.

He could see why the shadowy figure made a good spy. He blended in with his surroundings and looked completely benign.

"Konstantin sends his greetings, Goga."

"Stop calling me that! That name is reserved for my friends."

"Then I shall earn the right."

"What do you want? What is it that Konstantin wishes to be known to me?"

Fiat starts out slow, building a case one logical step at a time. He tells of the atrocities committed by Stalin and the dangers of the 'cult' of Stalin. Stalin's sins include mass murders, creating famine in the countryside, and directing the assassination of real and imagined enemies.

Zhukov is listening, but both men feel time is of the essence. A noise indicates that the door is about to be opened and the Marshall is distracted. When he turns around the spy is gone. The Marshall knows he will see the man again soon.

Meanwhile Georgy has many choices to consider. He thinks to himself, this fellow is persuasive...much like Konstantin. I sense that they have talked long and deeply about the future of Russia. That bodes well.

"Excuse me sir but the officers for your next meeting are waiting." An aide quietly informs the Marshall.

"I will come straight away."

"Thank you, Sir."

The whole-time Zhukov's mind is reeling with the possibilities of a free Russia and what it means for its former republics. How will the Ukraine react to Stalin's death and the choices it brings? Latvia, Georgia, Estonia have all expressed and been punished for acts of independence. Now might be the time to start anew.

Acceptance and Action

Marshall Zhukov was wrestling with the explosive information that the spy Fiat had imparted. In their 10-minute conversation, much of what he suspected had been confirmed.

Zhukov was aware of several mass killings perpetrated by the NKVD. In fact, he was involved in a few by association. For each incident, he had been told that the victims were murderous partisans who had killed women and children. From the information provided by Fiat, he now knew that they were the wives and children of Stalin's political enemies.

He also learned of the systematic starvation of politically unreliable peasants in the countryside. He had seen evidence of this famine but had deluded himself into thinking that the situation was an act of nature. In reality food was deliberately redirected to loyal urban areas. Millions of poor farmers and laborers along with their families had perished.

Zhukov realized that he could no longer feign innocence in these matters. He felt morally obligated to begin righting the many wrongs perpetrated on his countrymen. He now knew and believed, what he previously only fleetingly guessed. He trusted Konstantin implicitly and the information provided through the spy.

It was time to address his own culpability and begin making amends for the excesses of Stalinism. Tonight he would personally approach key officers and provide them with Konstantin's conclusions about Stalinism. He was confident that the first dozen names on his list would see the truth and join him in his crusade to end the aberration labeled the USSR.

He was not enough of a politician to suggest what the alternatives might be. He would leave that job to Konstantin and others more adept at compromise then he.

The awareness that brought him fully into the anti-Stalinist camp, was the saving of lives. Over his career, he had caused the deaths of tens of thousands. Now he had a chance to save tens of thousands. Whatever the consequences, he was ready to take that chance.

Once he made up his mind, the mental wrestling immediately ceased. Zhukov was a man of action once the choice was made and his course was clear. The time for reflection was over, it was time to take action and affect change.

So far, his plan was falling into place. One by one Zhukov located and spoke with the dozen officers whom he believed would support and assist him with his stratagem. He had made it a point to approach the men in a single evening to control security. A few times he had to wake officers as the hour grew late.

10 out of the 12 men were swayed by the promise of ending this deadly war. Every one of the dozen was a general. Some were in command of fronts, corps and some divisions. All were beloved by the troops they led. All could sway the vast majority of the men and their units by appealing to their loyalty and using the truths provided by Konstantin.

Zhukov advised the Generals to neutralize their embedded commissars before initiating the recruitment process. The commissars were obligated to report any deviancy from the party line and were solid Stalinist's that could not be trusted.

Then he cautioned The Dozen to keep their men from talking to other units. The time and date of separation would be 48 hours from now. At that time everyone who wanted to join the cause of freedom would start walking towards the NATO lines with their weapons above their heads.

This offer of acquiescence to the Capitalist forces would coincide with Zhukov's fabricated attack.[45] Devoid of the Marshall's units, the delusional Stalinists would fail in their assault. As these troops fell back the anti-Stalinists would leapfrog them and renunciate their errant beliefs to the Amerikosi.

It was a certainty that there would be attempted retribution. Men who wished to join the forces of freedom would wear face coverings to disguise their identity.

Zhukov was taking every precaution to protect his men's friends and relatives. He did not want anyone to be subjected to retaliation for shifting loyalty, wanting change and a better life.

This mass abandonment of Stalinism would be filmed and used for propaganda purposes.

In less than 72 hours Marshal Zhukov and 300,000 traitors/freedom fighters were resting under the uneasy gaze of the American and British forces that hours ago had been trying to kill them. The Soviet prisoners could see that any mistake or miscommunication would end in their

---

[45] - When Spoons Attack - World War Three - Book Four - The Red Sea

deaths at the hands of their former adversaries.

Fire, Flames and Cremation

What is it about fire? Ruslan could have watched his commander's car burn for hours, the flames dancing out the broken windows, seats ablaze as the fabric burned and of course his commander's body melting away. Finally, only the skeleton of Marshall Rokossovsky remained. The Marshall had been the focus of every waking and sometimes nightmarish moments, still looked vaguely human. Everything else was just fire.

An Amerikosi plane had come out of nowhere and strafed them before he could react. The commander in the back seat was killed on the first pass. Ruslan had opened his door, fallen out and rolled as the car slowed down. He had quickly gotten to his feet and dove behind a pile of rocks. From this position, he had watched the burning car.

Planes circled overhead as if they had not a care in the world. He guessed from the enemy's behavior that the VVS was not a concern.

Overtime Ruslan had developed the habit of glancing at reports when he was sitting in his superior's office waiting to drive him somewhere. He had seen enough to know that the Red Army was losing. Rokossovsky's command was trapped between the British and Spanish in the Pyrenees Mountains. Additionally, to the east, the Amerikosi held a strong defensive line running from Gdansk to Trieste.

The cowardly Occupation forces were surrendering all over Western Europe. However, the Marshall had been holding the line here in Spain. On his death, his incompetent second in command was put in charge. To Ruslan, this change in command would surely lead to a major defeat leaving him far from home.

So far, the moral of the Red Army's Trans-Pyrenees front was good. He and others from HQ had been sent to spy on the men in the frontlines. They were told to ask leading questions that seemed to point towards giving up. Ruslan had almost been shot when a squad he was infiltrating reported him to their Leader. The man showed up, pointed a gun at Ruslan's head and gave him five minute's lead time to run away as fast as he could…which he did.

His fellow spies also reported that moral on the front was strong. Because the fighting had been so up close and personal, most of the soldiers they spoke with could not conceive of giving up and surrendering. Many men claimed they would fight the British and Spanish foes at their front to the death.

Ruslan believe them. He had been involved several hand to hand combat situations. Fighting in the mountains was a lot like combat in a large city. You fought over and over the same piece of high ground. Often, in both the city and mountains, you could not see your enemy until you stumbled upon each other. Thus, the numerous close combat encounters.

You would not think that fighting in the mountains would be so visually impaired. The deep valleys and rocky outcroppings combined with surprisingly high grass in the summer, greatly reduced the line of sight. It seemed that even if you knew where the enemy was you still came upon additional threats unexpectedly in the most benign of locations. These small meeting engagements would quickly escalate into major battles as units from both sides tried to support their comrades and friends.

Marshall Rokossovsky had been confident that the Limeys were about to start something. There was all sorts of activity being reported on the enemy's side of the lines. The Spanish were stirring as well. There probably would be an attack following the recent landings in the Black Sea and Baltic.

Rusland had no time to dwell on the latest news and gossip. He needed to get back to headquarters and report on the Marshall's disastrous death. It was difficult to tear himself away from the fascinating sight of the fire and what it was consuming. Besides, the scene was attracting enemy planes like moths to a flame.

Fire is universally fascinating to humans. We love to start them and then hurry to put them out. The one thing humans can't do is to ignore the fire no matter how horrific the scene.

Bleeding
With his new face, Beria could walk freely throughout Moscow. Today he is carrying one of his favorite knives. Nothing fancy, just a Finka.[46] that he has used many times. The execution of Nikita should be routine so nothing fancy was called for.

He was making his way towards the Kremlin and what he hoped was a

---

[46] - Dictionary of Russian Slang and Colloquial Expressions by Vladimir Shlyakhov, Eve Adler

short encounter. His plan was to take Nikita by surprise.

Beria was confident that Khrushchev knew about the hidden door into his office. He reasoned that Nikita would never expect someone else using it to rush in and attack.

The assault would be so unexpected that Lavrenti anticipated an easy kill. But first, Beria had to enter the Kremlin without causing suspicion to reach the hidden tunnels. The door to the tunnels was through Lenin's Tomb and had been placed there at Stalin's order during the last renovation. The Tomb was not busy today. There were not many visitors with the war now so close to Moscow.

Beria lit a harmless smoke bomb as a distraction and while everyone was dealing with that he slipped into the passageway. The path led to two offices inside the President's Residency, Stalin's and Khrushchev's. He made his way to the junction and turned left to enter Nikita's office.

He opened the heavy door just a crack to listen and heard someone moving around and talking on the phone. Good! He thought, He's alone.

Everything went according to plan. He opened the door silently, swiftly walked up behind Nikita and slit his throat. Only it wasn't Khrushchev. Even before the body drops he knows that it is once again a look-alike.

Before he could even think, Nikita entered the office and Beria almost puts an end to the fight before it starts. He is as shocked as Khrushchev and botches the initial attack. The two diminutive fighters circle each other in the large room. Neither man says a word for none is needed. Stalin is dead and to the victor belong the spoils.

From somewhere in his suit coat Khrushchev pulls out his own knife. The two men start to feign attack. Both are surprisingly experienced. Beria, an expert at torture, is taking small pieces of Nikita off. Nikita, bleeding from a half a dozen small wounds is a patient brawler waiting for his opening.

When the opening comes, Khrushchev lunges with his knife for Beria's throat with his right hand. His left hand is the real weapon and he grabs Beria by the balls in a vice like grip knowing he will take at least one knife strike from Beria's expert hands.

As Beria's brain is taking in the experience of the pain in his crotch, Nikita diverts his knife and plunges it into Beria's groin. With all his might he rips it upward until it strikes Beria's sternum.

Beria gets in a feeble strike to Nikita's neck just missing the left juggler as the thought of imminent pain interrupts his attack. Lavrenti staggers backward as his intestines slide out. He trips over his own colon and sits down in the gore spilling out from his body. He tries to put his guts back in and hold them in place.

Khrushchev gets up from where he had landed after getting sliced in the neck. He calmly staunches the flow of blood by putting pressure on the bleeding wound with his handkerchief. He warily walks behind the barely comprehending Beria and slices his neck from ear to ear.

Lavrentia's carotid artery did not bleed profusely as Khrushchev would have imagined. He wondered if the lack of blood was due to the administered disembowelment. Nikita half expected the devil himself to flee Beria's body. He died like any other man with his throat cut, gurgling and gagging on his own blood. One last coughing spurt and the devil incarnate finally was dead.

Belatedly, Khrushchev's aide knocks on the door and looks in to see what all the commotion is about. Upon seeing Beria lying in his own blood and guts, his boss' bleeding wounds, he turns his back and vomits in the reception area. He then shrieks for security.

Nikita Khrushchev makes a note to replace the aide. Then he sits down to plan how to end the war on terms that would be favorable to the Soviets. Now that Beria is dead he can resurrect himself. Then he will take command as soon as he dispenses with Malenkov[47].

As he was being treated for his many stab and slice wounds, Nikita was considering how best to contact the traitor Zhukov about initiating negotiations with the Americans.

One of the security guards slipped and falls in Beria's pile of remains. Khrushchev is immediately brought back to how close he had come to being assassinated. For a brief second, he thinks about his double. He probably never stood a chance. By all rights it should have been him, the real Nikita, slumped over his desk with his throat cut.

His mind drifted back to Beria's attack. Their knife fight had determined the fate of millions. The bloody melee was between two small men in stature but towering in ambition. And, he had triumphed. But what had he won in the end?

---

[47] - Comrades!: A History of World Communism by Robert Service

Khrushchev believed that the peoples of the Soviet Union were masters at survival and would adapt. He would lead them into a new era. Now, if he could only stop bleeding.

Chapter Ten: Means to the End

Figure 44 - Tanks as far as the eye can see

Debating Unconditional Surrender

"I tell you that it was the biggest mistake of the war!"

"You're full of shit, Morgan!"

"When FDR called for the unconditional surrender of both the Japs and the Krauts it guaranteed a life and death struggle to the absolute end. Hitler and Tojo both knew they'd be hung so they fought until the very end, destroying and taking as many lives as they could."

"On the upside, the pronouncement gave our troops and the folks back home something to fight for..."

"You could have done that a dozen different ways. Why I'll bet..."

Wall Doxey, the 19th Sergeant at Arms of the United States Senate, comes storming around the corner and bellows.

"SHUT THE FUCK UP YOU IDIOTS! Who in the hell do you think you two are! No one wants to hear what a couple of Pages has to think or say, much less when important matters are being discussed in closed session.

Both of you are in deep shit. Now clear out of here pronto and report to your supervisor in 10 minutes."

"Yyyyeeessss Sir!"

As the two pages scramble to beat each other from Doxey's glare, Wall turns and slightly opens the door to the Senate Chambers. He used to be a Senator until he was beaten by that shit Eastland. As he squeezes through the open door, the afore mentioned Senator Eastland is pontificating on why we should demand unconditional surrender from the Russians.

Once again, James Francis 'Jimmy' Byrnes was at the center of an unconditional surrender debate. First the Japs and now it is the Ruskies. Jimmy believed in the virtues of such a surrender even as others was contemplating something else entirely. They were of the opinion that both Germany and Japan became more fanatical when FDR insisted on unconditional surrender. Many thousands died because of this.

It was sheer madness or hubris to think that the exhausted Western Powers could, would or should occupy the former Soviet Union. The USSR land mass was over 60 times as big as Germany's with a population twice as large who spoke 120 different languages.

However, the NATO Alliance would insist that the each of the former republics be freed from the Union and allow to be self-governing. The focus of America's efforts would be the republics that border Western Europe and Turkey, specifically Ukraine, Belarus, Moldova, Georgia, Estonia, Latvia, Azerbaijan and Armenia.

The attempt to rid the republics of their local communist leaders would have a similar outcome to the denazification debacle in Germany. The effort had been an attempt to remove former Nazis from leadership and positions of influence. Some of the initial proponents of the German program wanted ex-Nazis restricted to only manual labor in an attempt to manipulate German society again.

Hundreds of thousands of records were captured that identified who was and who was not a member of the Nazi Party. The US pursued denazification in a zealous but bureaucratic fashion. All Germans were required to fill out a questionnaire.

Eisenhower initially estimated that the denazification process would take 50 years.

A nearly complete list of Nazi Party memberships was turned over to the Allies (by a German anti-Nazi who had rescued the files from destruction in April 1945 as American troops advanced on Munich) [48]. The list made it possible to identify the 1.5 million Germans who had joined before Hitler came to power. They were deemed to be hard-core Nazis.

Finding a comparable list of communist party members was considered highly doubtful once this war was won. By 1945, the membership of the communist party in Russia alone was in the millions. How many of them joined for expediency is a matter of debate.

Any public talk of punishing members of the Soviet Communist Party would probably lead to even more fanatical fighting. It was estimated that over half of the current anti-Stalinist units fighting for the Freedom Force were former communists.

Ridding all communists from leadership roles in the old USSR was seen as a hopeless tilt at windmills. However, Senator Joe McCarthy made this idea one of his main talking points. So far, the majority of Americans did not support his vision. He was a lonely ideologue shouting into the

---

[48] - Taylor, Frederick (2011). Exorcising Hitler: The Occupation and Denazification of Germany. Bloomsbury Publishing

wind.

For many the quest to de-communisticate the Soviet Union would be put on a back burner along with any demand for unconditional surrender.

Armies Meet

General Walker and Truscott shook hands on the bridge over the Stradomka River in Czestochowa, Poland. Their respective armies had both fought their way to the rendezvous point. Walker and the 1st Army had come from Vienna via Trieste. General Truscott, and the 5th Army had come from Gdansk and Warsaw to the North. Now they had met cutting the supply lines of the Soviet occupation forces in Western Europe and the Trans-Pyrenees Front.

Truscott and the 5th Army had come close to running out of some weapons and ammo along the way. The shortage was not caused by combat but by supplying the endless number of Anti-Stalinist groups that had emerged from seemingly every hiding place along the way.

These rebel units were hell bent on burying the USSR and replacing it with a democracy. Not all held the same vision of what a Russian "Democracy" would look like, but all agreed that Stalinism was going to end.

It's a chore to fight your way through battle hardened troops. Especially when you a supplied through a partially damaged port, while at the same time suppling half a million men with small arms. Truscott had done it. Walker had read the reports and was very congratulatory of what the General had accomplished.

Walker's task was no walk in the park as well. His route to the meeting of the two armies was much more constricted using canyons and rivers at times. The roads were secondary at best and his initial supply head was the Port of Trieste which was not in the best of shape. In addition, he had an active opponent as well. The Red armies that were trying to contain him in Vienna put up a stiff fight along much of his advance.

Any and all Soviet caught between their mutual defensive lines and the border of Spain and France were cutoff. They were cutoff from supplies and the Stavka. The continuous line formed by the NATO Armies north to south across the European landmass was designed to withstand numerous attacks from both the west and east.

The entire operation was the granddaddy of all pincher movements. It encompassed almost ten times the area as the Battle of Kiev and was the first time this ancient maneuver had been carried out on a continent-wide campaign.

The Meeting at Czestochowa was conceived by General Douglas McArthur, made possible by the organizational skills of General Dwight Eisenhower and brilliantly executed by Generals Walker and Truscott. It dwarfed any other single military operation in sheer audacity and scale.

The meeting of these two armies had sealed the fate of millions of enemy soldiers and tens of millions of civilians.

Off camera Truscott and Walker toasted their historic meeting with whiskey…Johnny Walker of course.

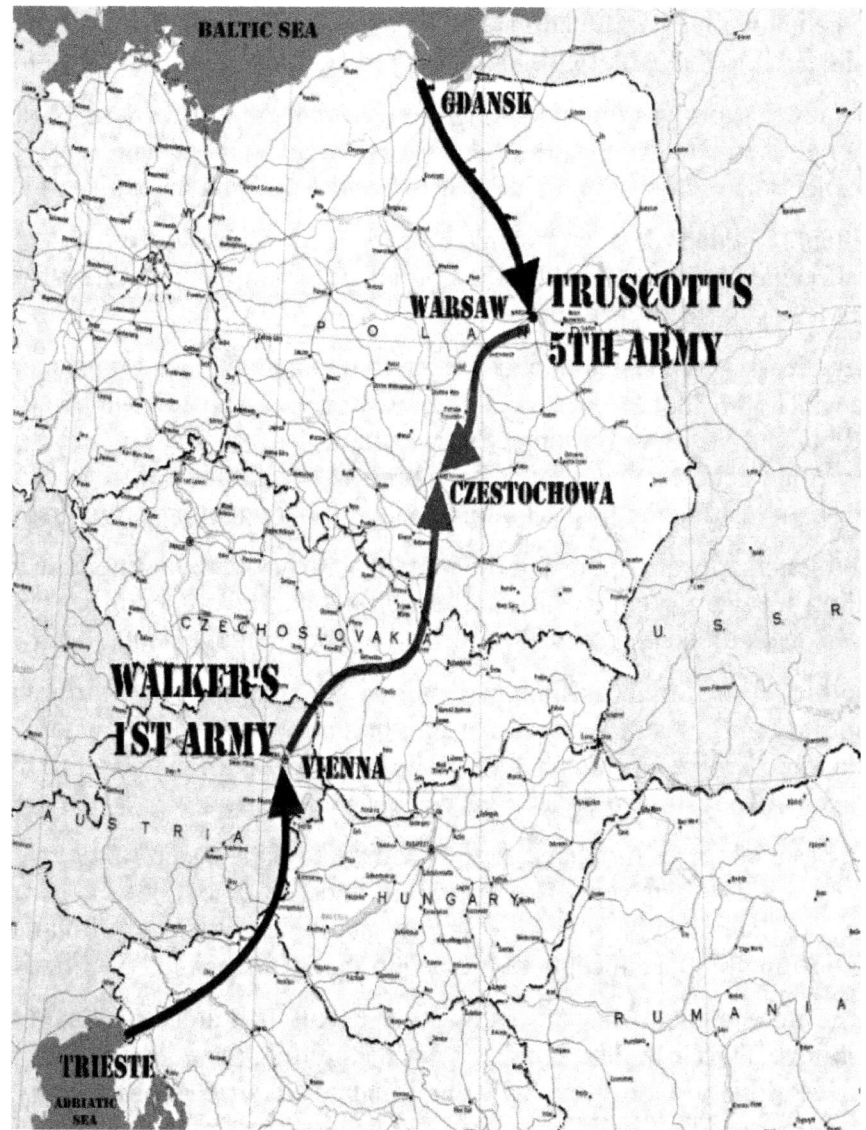

New Tanks, New Tactics

Martin Williams maneuvered his well-traveled M-50 Patton tank into a hull down position. He depressed the 90-mm canon muzzle and waited. He did not have to wait long. He heard the enemy before he saw them. You could tell by the sounds of the engines that the enemy's tanks were heavies. It was probably a squad of IS-3s.

Williams was a veteran tank commander. He had extensive experience with the M-26 Pershing in combat. The M-26 was now being replaced by the innovative M-50 Patton. The Pershing was a good tank when you could get it to the battlefield. In a static position, it was a formidable foe.

The new Patton was mobile enough to negotiate all normal tank terrain as a light tank yet had the armor and firepower of a heavy tank. It was an excellent machine that combined British and American ingenuity.

Williams' squad of Patton tanks was joined by a squad of M-38 Wolfhound armored cars with the upgraded 75 mm gun and turret from the M-24 Chaffee light tank.[49]

These "cars" were fast and lethal but couldn't tolerate much punishment, if any. The M-38s were designed to quickly get into an ambush position and be ready to fire. The objective was to destroy enemy armor before they could get off a shot. In this engagement, Wolfhounds were to shoot and scoot leaving the heavy Pattons to slug it out with any survivors.

Scott Peterson was supporting the Pattons with a squad of armored cars. Martin felt very secure with Scott on his flank. He was confident that Peterson would keep him well informed of enemy movements.

The history of Soviet military operations is convoluted and torturous. Repeated purges and betrayals drove the architects and innovators of groundbreaking concepts from the halls of power. The key to victory lay moldering in restricted collections of books and papers.

The basic concepts of what was to become known as Deep Battle, were developed 20 years ago. The execution and tactics of the Red Army changed dramatically in 1944 as they began the employment of massed armor. Finally, the concepts developed in the 1930s would be realized.

Large amounts of artillery fire now preceded all their attacks. The initial shelling was followed by hundreds of tanks hitting the enemy's lines all at once along a wide front. Next the infantry advanced in long-drawn-out wedges. The combined arms of artillery, armor, air power and infantry became known as the Deep Battle tactic.

---

[49] - The World's Greatest Tanks: An Illustrated History by Michael E. Haskew

Figure 45 - Soviet Troops Using Tank Desant

The Soviet armored thrusts were very deep and almost always in a straight line. The infantry advanced until dark and then dug in. Massive amounts of reinforcements arrived during the night. [50]

In 1945, the Soviet infantry would travel by riding on tanks as they advanced. The ground pounders would then dismount and dig in. In the latter parts of the last war and in World War Three, the thrusts went far behind enemy lines. The troops often lost contact with their main force and waited until relieved.

Against the Germans Deep Battle was extremely effective due to the lack of German reserves in their war against Stalin's best from 1944 to 1945. The American's of 1946 and 47, did not suffer the same constraints.

All along the line the US had reinforcements. By interrogating and listening to their former German enemies, the Americans were ready to respond to Red Army breakthroughs with counter attacks.

In contrast the Soviet generals on the ground were fighting this war like the last one, using concepts developed in the 1930s and demonstratively perfected in 1944.

---

[50] - *The Soviet Conduct of Tactical Maneuver: Spearhead of the Offensive* by David M. Glantz

Assuming your new enemy would ignore history and disregard the lessons learned by others, always leads to unintended consequences.

What's New is Old
"Spread out! Move in a V formation."

The squad of Soviet tanks maneuvered into positon with practiced ease. These tankers were veterans of over a dozen major tank battles in this war and the last.

Anatoly loved his radio. For most of World War Two his company had used flags to communicate. Now they had proper wireless equipment making life much easier.

Morozov was commanding a squad of T-54 Soviet tanks. The upcoming attack would be his first encounter with trained and possibly veteran American troops. His previous experience was with the US Occupation troops in Germany and against the Spanish in the Pyrenees. Both opponents lacked training and were easily defeated.

Anatoly had a bad feeling about the terrain ahead. "Timur take C and go left. Let your infantry cover and scout ahead...I know Timur I'm just making sure... Timur... Timur stop talking...shut the fuck up and listen. That's an order.", Anatoly growled into the mic. Maybe he didn't like the radio after all.

"Now move your ass!

Grigori take B and move right. Cover each other and use your assigned infantry. I'm going to call in smoke. Wait for my orders to advance."

Anatoly calls in the request for smoke and waits. The radio squawks and informs him that the smoke screen is incoming.

"Remember the Amerikosi can see heat signatures just like us. The smoke is a distraction not a solution. On my mark... let the makhra[51] move out and take the lead"

The Red Army squad leader was being very cautious despite orders to attack quickly. His caution saved 3 of his six tanks. The other three fell to the guns of two US Patton M-50 tanks and one M-38 Wolfhound.

The Americans, anticipating Soviet Deep Battle tactics, had weathered the initial barrage in their heavy tanks while the armored cars withdrew

---

[51] - Russian military slang for infantry

to the rear. As soon as the shelling stopped the Wolfhounds quickly repositioned themselves on the flanks of Martin Williams' Patton tanks and waited.

Morozov had ordered his tanks forward 3 minutes too late. If he had left earlier he would have caught the vulnerable armored cars in transit. However, he didn't. By delaying he drove right into the well positioned combination of 90 mm and 75 mm guns. The new NATO armor-piercing capped ballistic cap round made short work of even the T-54's thick armor. The first two Soviet tanks that were destroyed never knew what hit them. The third had a terror filled 5 seconds trying to back out of danger before he turned into a flaming pile of metal.

Anatoly's tank did manage to get one shot off before he escaped. The 100 mm APHE round buried itself into the dirt wall in front of Williams' tank and harmlessly spent its kinetic energy.

U.S. 75 mm Anti-Tank Round

All down the line the Soviet armor was taking heavy losses. A large number of the Red Army's remaining experienced veteran tankers died that first day.

Three great holes were made in the American lines as the Reds tried desperately to link up with their comrades to the east. Shortly after the breakthroughs the lead Soviet columns were cutoff and isolated. Their follow-up reinforcements were decimated as the gaps were quickly closed by the Amerikosi.

The Soviet Deep Battle had met its match in the mobile forces and well-placed support units of General "Johnny" Walker and General Lucian Truscott near the outskirts of Torun, Lodz and Czestochowa, Poland.

The old tactics that had worked a year earlier were now being thwarted by the combined arms and large reserves of the NATO forces. The Soviet Deep Battle that won World War Two in 1944-45 was now losing World War Three in 1947.

Resurrectio - Dux

With Beria and Stalin dead it was time for Nikita Khrushchev to make his play for power. He had been preparing for this moment for the last six years. Finally, it was time.

First, he walked in and surprised the Stavka leadership. Having the support of the military was critical. He quickly won them over due to his service as a commissar in the battles of Kharkov and Stalingrad. He inflated his involvement when he spoke of his record. However, the fact remained that he and he alone among the Ruling Circle had seen combat. His field experience proved significant in gaining the Stavka's trust.

Georgy Malenkov was shocked when Khrushchev suddenly burst into his office accompanied by several Stavka officers. At that point, Georgy knew that he had lost his chance at leading the Soviet Union. Fighting for his life was his new priority.

Looking back on the situation years later, Malenkov concluded that Khrushchev behaved quite magnanimously towards him and his family. Stalin would have turned him over to Beria.

Georgy Malenkov was astonished to hear that Beria had still been breathing as of yesterday. He had been under the impression that Nikita and Lavrenti were dead. Instead both had been alive with Beria pulling strings from behind the scenes until killed by Nikita. Georgy's ignorance of the true situation explained his fall from power.

By now, many in the Kremlin witnessed Khrushchev going from office to office proclaiming his authority. Soon the people on the street learned of the resurrection of Khrushchev and his assumption of command.

In the following week, Nikita gathered more and more support. His influence grew even as his territory shrunk and his armies became trapped and isolated. Revolts were increasing throughout the Soviet Union and conquered lands. Fewer resources were available to deal with the insurgencies. The Soviet Union was rapidly running out of options.

More than once Nikita wondered if becoming the leader of the Soviet Union was in his best interest. As usual his ego overcame all objections his logic could raise and he soldiered on. He did have to make peace soon, or he would be talking to the Amerikosi on the porch of the Kremlin.

Khrushchev remained confident that if anyone could negotiate a just peace it was he. After all, not many people outside of fairy tales and the Bible rise from the dead.

Ursus Arctos Beringianus

The Soviet Union still had a few functioning spies within the US and UK governments. Some reported on the debate calling for unconditional surrender. Khrushchev knew he had to prepare his opening proposal before NATO imposed its harshest possible sentence on the Soviet people.

If NATO's only choice was full surrender it would be almost impossible for them to retract their demand. The USSR could only respond with a fight to the end. Nikita's spies were keeping him informed of the various discussions going on in the West. Unfortunately, their communiques were over a week out of date.

Khrushchev and his cabal still had to neutralize a dozen Politburo members before proceeding. He needed to further consolidate power to effectively negotiate with NATO. Meanwhile his remaining generals and Stavka members were advising him that the NATO forces appeared to be stalling in an attempt to give the Soviet Union more time to formulate an acceptable plan.

The NATO armies were only advancing a couple of kilometers a day. Nikita finally began to believe that a signal was truly being sent. He decided to heed that message and the implied alternative it conveyed of something other than absolute capitulation.

The easiest and fastest way to accomplish what he needed was to simply kill his opponents. He picked up the phone and ordered his new director of the NKVD to come to his office within the hour.

He decided not to emulate Stalin and rule by fear alone. One by one he had the opposition come into his office and pledge fidelity in front of witnesses. Nikita knew that a few were just saying the words but that would do for the moment. Once he had a dozen of his former enemies groveling at his feet he extended olive branches, positions of esteem and potential wealth.

The largely ceremonial offices did not wield great power. The newly created posts were seen by all as the bribes they were. These appointments were a chance to retire in comfort instead of being tortured to death. The men took the proffered life raft but one. The man defied Khrushchev's legitimacy and eventually paid with his life.

Nikita felt that things were going too well. In his soul Khrushchev was a superstitious man. His experience had shown that too much good luck was always balanced by misfortune.

True to his fears three hours later he was informed that the US House of Representatives had just voted to urge the President to demand unconditional surrender. Khrushchev knew that this was the branch of the US government that was closest aligned with the feelings of the masses. He also knew that the President and Senate could see reason and refuse to acquiesce and in essence defy the will of the common man.

He needed to communicate with the US leadership. He had to convince them that the peoples of Russia would fight to the end rather than be humiliated. Yes, all the other republics would run to hide behind the skirts of NATO but true Russians would never relent and it would be a blood bath for both sides.

Quickly he called on his chief of staff to organize a large gathering of the faithful. He would give them a rousing speech that would, in truth, be aimed at Harry S. Truman, the Senate leadership and congressman who could be swayed to change their votes.

Khrushchev would evoke memories of Leningrad and Stalingrad as proof of the resolve of true Rus' [52]. Rus' was the historic name for the original Russians. He would draw on that primeval image to inspire the proletariat.

The vivid image he had to convey was you never back a bear into a corner, for a trapped animal has nothing to lose.

---

[52] - The Origin of Rus'. by Omeljan Pritsak

Someday, Neither Them nor Us

Ike and Marshall are deep in conversation when there is a knock on the office door and Ike's longtime aide peeks in.

"This better be good Miss Summersby." Ike muttered.

"Excuse me for interrupting Sir. G2 just reported that Stalin is dead!"

Marshall gets up and stands behind his chair looking at Kay Summerysby with somewhat of a blank look on his face. Ike is immediately animated.

"Thank you Captain."

"You're welcome Sir."

She leaves the room and General George Marshall begins to run all the possible implications through his mind.

"Well that changes the whole ballgame." says Ike to no-one in particular.

Marshall replies, "We just went from football to baseball, from brute force to out-thinking our opposition."

"Yes this will increase our options depending on who takes over. I believe it will be that Malenkov fellow since the little bald one is presumed dead."

"Which one is Malenkov?"

"He's the heavier set one. Looks weak but supposedly is one tough son of a bitch. Led the purge before the war killing off most of the Soviet-trained general staff weeks before the German's attacked. He opened up many opportunities for guys like Zhukov and Konev."

"You like that Zhukov fellow don't you?"

"We actually had a good time when we met. He seems to be honest and a good leader. I'm glad he's now on our side. He brings a lot of credibility for the Freedom Force. Our recruitment has doubled since he surrendered.

I don't speak Russian but even I heard the passion in his voice. I happened to witness an impromptu speech he made to a small group of former Reds. The men were on the fence about fighting again. Really seemed to stir them up and all joined on the spot."

"Why did he... change sides, Ike?"

"From the reports, George, one of our spies opened up communications between Konstantin and him. They are good friends and the rest is history. Zhukov brought over 300,000 of his men when he made his move. Some call him a traitor. I'd call him pragmatic and logical. Why fight and die for a man, like Stalin, who will kill you as soon as he no longer needs you?"

"He does seem to be a standup guy. I wonder who he will back as the next leader?"

Ike looks pensive for a second. "It won't be Malenkov, he was too close to Stalin and thinks the same way. I suspect that the Freedom Force will actually see some combat. That's a shame. Can you conceive of fighting your friends and neighbors? It's like the Civil War but with tanks, machine guns and airplanes."

"These Russians are tough. Imagine living under the Czar, going through a bloody revolution and then having the Nazis rape and pillage your country. Then we come along and kick their ass. Think of having Sherman marching through your hometown every so often for 30 years.

One day the authorities are your friends and saviors, and the next day they are your enemy.

"Rather them than us, Ike."

"I'd like to think that someday it will be neither them, nor us."

The Offer

Nikita Khrushchev took complete power over what remained of the Soviet Union at 13:09 on 6 September 1947. His first act was to initiate negotiations with the leadership of the NATO Armies slowly advancing towards Moscow.

Khrushchev's situation was dire. The Stavka had lost contact with the entire Trans-Pyrenees Front and the Soviet forces between the infamous city of Stalingrad and NATO existed only on paper. However, a stout defense was occurring against the NATO forces in the Ukraine.

General Eisenhower received an un-coded message from Nikita Khrushchev proposing a cease fire and conditions under which the Red Army would end the struggle.

The former Soviet Marshall Zhukov was the new commander of the Freedom Forces who now numbered 10 divisions of tough, determined and ex-communists. It was necessary and prudent to include him in any negotiation.

The terms were rather simple much like Khrushchev himself.

1. A general ceasefire would commence on an agreed-upon day and hour.
2. All Red Army forces would lay down their arms and withdraw from contact with NATO forces.
3. All Red Army units would immediately pull back until they were within the borders of the pre-World War Two USSR.
4. The military forces of the former USSR would be demobilized within 30 days of returning to Soviet territory.
5. NATO would supply the resources necessary to supplement the nutritional needs of the former citizens of the USSR for one year.
6. Zhukov spent a good minute reading the translated message. Churchill, Truman and the Joint Chiefs of staff of the US and UK had discussed the proposed surrender hours before. All knew that Zhukov and NATO had to be of the same mindset in their reply.
7. Eisenhower and Zhukov had discussed the terms they deemed necessary to avoid more bloodshed weeks ago. The NATO

leadership wanted to make sure that there was agreement by all parties before responding.

Zhukov answered through an interpreter. His voice starting out in a low rumble as was his habit and growing in volume and intensity.

"I'm afraid this does not go far enough in freeing the peoples of the former Soviet Union. We need to demand a change in the very governmental system and the "retirement" of the current leadership with free elections. In addition, my comrades…err fellow Freedom Fighters would demand a new constitution be developed under the guidance of NATO and a new construct of government be developed to serve the decimated peoples of the former USSR.

As we all know the men and women who make up the bulk of the Freedom Forces are not, in fact, Russian but come from the regions that border the West. These Regions want autonomy. Armenia, Azerbaijan, Belarus, Estonia, Georgia, Latvia, Moldova and Ukraine have all demanded sovereignty as do the newly liberated countries of Poland, Czechoslovakia, Hungry, Austria, Romania, Bulgaria and Albania."

Zhukov finished and Eisenhower spoke for the NATO leadership.

"The collective leadership of NATO agrees with your assessment Marshall Zhukov. Our demands will include a change in leadership, a regime change, a new constitution and the liberation of the regions and nations."

As the NATO leadership is drafting a response, a door is closing in the US Senate. By a 45 to 52 margin with 3 abstentions, the Senate has urged the President to demand the unconditional surrender of the Soviet Union. The preverbal ball is now in the court of Harry S. Truman, President of the United States of America.

Three Stories

Simultaneously three history making events are taking place. In Moscow Nikita Khrushchev is within minutes of giving a speech in front of a huge crowd of coerced residents from the neighborhoods surrounding the Kremlin and Red Square. The NKVD and Kremlin Guard had roused everyone who could walk and forced them to form a huge crowd.

At that exact moment, NATO's leadership is finishing up a response to a cease fire proposal from Nikita Khrushchev. They were collectively pouring over the final draft of their response. This document would then be sent to the leaders of the free world and the wait began for the military arm of NATO.

In Washington D.C. a very tired Harry Truman was listening to a very heated debate between two of his top advisors. One was James Byrnes, who had strongly advised Truman to use the atomic bomb on Japan for the expressed purpose of intimidating the Soviets.

The other, equally verbose, individual in the room was speaking out against the concept of unconditional surrender. This was a debate of titans and quite frankly, Truman was somewhat entertained. The other in the room was Winston Churchill.

The discussion went back and forth with each citing fact and figure, then switching tactics and appealing on a more basic human level, Byrnes for revenge and Churchill for a quicker end to the killing. Truman admired their enthusiasm and debating techniques. Churchill had one quip that almost made Byrnes smile.

"When I am abroad I always make it a rule never to criticize or attack the Government of my country. I make up for lost time when I am at home."

True, this was a recycled joke but still entertaining when delivered by Churchill.

In truth, Truman had already made up his mind and was placating his various audiences. After demanding completed subjugation from the Axis powers, how could the USA not demand the same from its former ally. An ally who had brutally stabbed them in the back?

He would announce his decision as soon as he spent a reasonable amount of time pretending to weigh the various points of contention, Truman would then announce to the world that the United States would ask no less than the Unconditional Surrender of the Union of Socialist Soviet Republics.

At 15:06 Greenwich Meantime, it was 10:06 in Washington D.C. and Harry S. Truman was announcing his decision. In London, an agent of NATO was clandestinely talking with a Soviet contact. They were discussing the possible ramifications of a demand for total surrender. Another agent, who was listening to the live broadcast of Khrushchev's speech, was desperately trying to get his colleagues attention.

In Moscow it was 18:06 and the self-appointed General Secretary of the Central Committee of the Communist Party of the Soviet Union, Nikita

Khrushchev had just ended his speech with a flourish. He made the central theme of his discourse a warning to the West about the danger of dictating its demands on the Rus' and expecting anything but a fight to the death.

67 minutes later, Truman read the transcript of Khrushchev's warning. Almost simultaneously NATO had learned of Truman's decision, Truman learned of NATO's clandestine negotiations and Nikita Khrushchev learned of Truman's demand for Unconditional Surrender.

It was a classic case of the right hand not knowing what the left hand was doing. In this instance, the stakes were high. The consequences were on the order of over an additional million lives lost.

Khrushchev's blood was up and his famous temper washed over the roomful of staff. One very brave aide reminded the Chairman of the deteriorating state of the Red Army. What he received for his act of bravery was completely unexpected.

The little bald man with the gapped tooth smile, calmly walked over to the aide, swiftly drew the knife he had killed Beria with and stabbed the aide in the hand. As everyone else in the room recoiled in horror, Nikita was an island of calm.

He had decided to die for the motherland and would order all true Rus' to do the same. The mandate of Truman was unacceptable and would be answered in blood.

An honorable peace was only minutes away and now it would be an eternity for thousands.

Winning and Influence

The Soviet supply column was headed back to Moscow. It was carrying the wounded and the dead. The men who were alive and driving or riding, were not looking forward to unloading their cargo. The dead stank and the wounded frantically screamed in pain when transferring them on stretchers.

Gleb was a partisan leader in western Ukraine. From his spies in the Red Army brigade headquarters, he knew about the convoy and what it carried. He was not interested in the cargo but in the trucks. He was tired of walking everywhere. He looked forward to travel in relative comfort.

The Amerikosi would be here soon and he would like to greet them with his own convoy of fighters aboard the trucks.

The attack and capturing of the vehicles would certainly earn him high praise the capitalists. Since the Stalinists lacked an air force there would be little risk of danger from the air.

He had already decided to leave the wounded in the care of their drivers. He would send word back to the Stalinists that their men were stranded by the roadside because Gleb and his partisans had taken the trucks.

Informing the enemy about the location of their wounded and dead was the humane thing to do. Above all, he wanted to look good for the Amerikosi. He had heard it was important to make a good first impression with the capitalists. One of his fighters had brought him a book written by a man called Dale Carnegie entitled, How To Win Friends and Influence People.[53]

It was written in Russian! How it escaped the censors he will never learn. He read the entire book twice and was practicing so he could excel in the new Russia.

He had memorized and was now practicing the five principles…

Build greater self-confidence

Strengthen people skills

Enhance communication skills

Develop leadership skills

Improve attitude and reduce stress

He could tell that his men thought he was going insane. He kept repeating the same phrases in response to his men's concerns. He supposed they must have seemed like nonsense to somebody who had not studied the five principles of Dale Carnegie.

No matter, he would be prepared to meet and greet the Amerikosi on their terms. He would recite the five principles in English to any NATO soldier he met. He felt confident that his of knowledge of Dale Carnegie's edicts were sure to win him high praise and advancement in the capitalist world.

It made sense that you could not fail in life once you knew how to win

---

[53] - Self-help Messiah: Dale Carnegie and Success in Modern America by Steven Watts

friends and influence people. Much of what Carnegie wrote about must be the backbone of a free society. Carnegie's reasoning was simple and any system that could compete and apparently defeat communism had to be the greatest force in the universe.

Since Carnegie was the leader of the free world his word must be godlike. The impact of his writings and speeches must be similar to the now dead Stalin. How else could you defeat the logic of Karl Marx and the teachings of Lenin.

He was certain that this Carnegie fellow was the key to not only surviving in a capitalist society but also thriving in one. Now he was prepared for whatever changes occurred.

While Gleb had been using his new techniques on his men, he found that they were too ignorant and stupid to understand. He would have to wait for the men from the west to appear in order to win the Amerikosi's friendship. Then, he could influence them into giving him money, preferably gold.

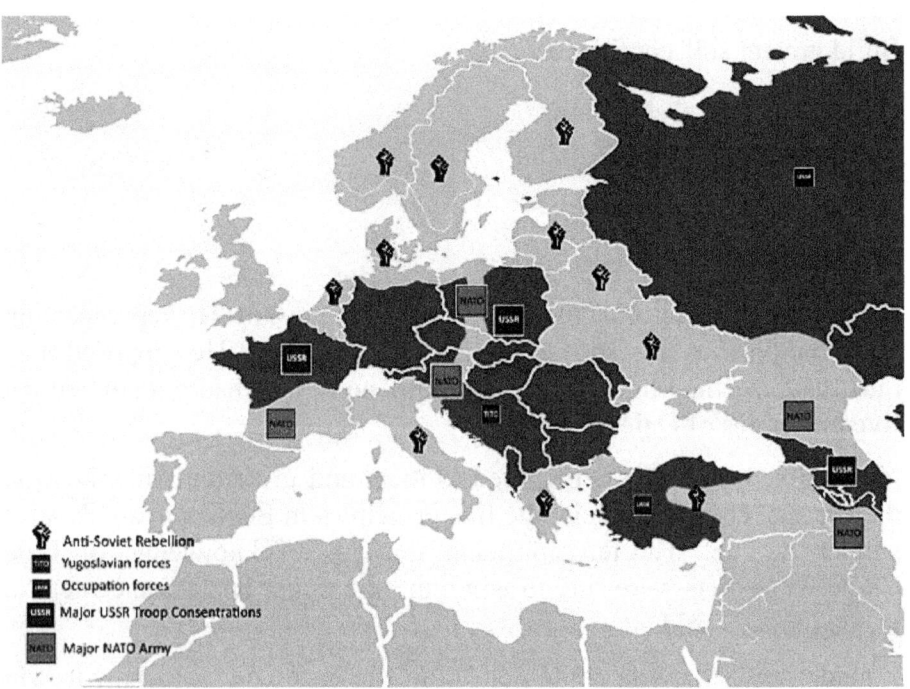

Figure 46 – Anti-Soviet Partisan Movements, October 1947

A Pain in the Ass

Joe Stein was hurting. His hospital bed was hard and uncomfortable. He had been shot in the ass during a firefight in Bielsa, Spain.

Stein was assigned to the 42nd "Rainbow" Division. HIs Division was scheduled to assault the Reds on Wednesday. The day before the attack he was on a routine patrol when the squad was surprised by the enemy and overwhelmed. Joe was shot as he was "advancing" away from the area. Three others were killed and two wounded.

Joe was able to fire a couple of shots and was sure he hit at least two of the bastards. The unit was fortuitously rescued by some guys from C Squad before the whole unit was lost. His Lieutenant had been advised that the Reds were falling apart fast and the patrol should not run into much, if any, opposition.

It turned out that at least one pack of Reds still had some fight left in them and B squad was unlucky enough to run into them. Due to the misinformation given his Lieutenant by G2, three good men died.

Joe was upset by more than just the pain in his ass. The guys killed were his buddies and he had fought alongside them over the last three months. Those clowns in G2 should be forced to go on patrol for once. Clearly, Brigade G2 was not on top of the situation and the whole US Tenth Army was in for one hell of a fight.

Joe had a friend in G2 who had been leaking to him all kinds of secret stuff he shouldn't have. Joe wasn't going to tell him to stop and just kept listening.

His buddy revealed that the Reds had attacked in force and swarmed over hill 324. The hill was a critical strategic prize and would have been a major loss to the US 10th Army. Such a loss would have delayed the planned NATO offensive by a good week or more.

Yet the Reds did not use their victory for military gain. They apparently were just interested in the large cache of foodstuffs behind the Division Kitchen. They cleaned the place out and then humped back to their original lines with each commie carrying as much food as he could.

The doctors examining the dead Soviets remarked at how malnourished they were. G2 thinks that these Reds that refuse to surrender are, in fact, starving to death.

General Haislip was contemplating leaving them be. The Tenth Army would wait for them to surrender or become so weak that they couldn't defend themselves. The thinking was why waste more NATO lives when the bastards were within weeks of capitulation (Joe thought that it meant giving up but wasn't sure).

Joe's friend was telling him how Monty would have none of it. The General wanted to attack as planned, then lead the charge into France personally liberating Paris. Monty was such an ass hole. Imagine getting us killed so he could be the center of attention and go down in the history books.

Joe guessed you had to be pretty self-centered and a megalomaniac to make it all the way to four-star general or Field Marshall as the Brits called them.

Come to think of it, it would be anti-climactic to watch the poor bastards starve. No glory in that for either side. Joe wanted glory as much as Monty did, a lasting legacy and all that.

Instead, he was in the hospital, far from any opportunity to win any metals. To make it all worse he got shot in the ass. He had to get back into combat to fulfill his ambition of being a decorated war hero and then running for political office. Definitely getting shot in the butt was not the way forward in realizing his ambitions.

Looks like the Brits and Montgomery were going to get their wish. Everyone was running around the hospital and gossiping about all the casualties that were going to start coming in tomorrow.

Damn it, he was going to miss the action. Well, sure as spit he was going to get his picture with his rifle looking for Reds in front of that Eiffel Tower thing. He'd need that image to show the folks back home. He planned to use the photo in his campaign for political office.

He started to daydream about being the Mayor or even County Supervisor. Sitting behind a big desk and ordering people around...

Just Dropping In, D-7 and Counting
"I didn't think the old man had it in him."

"I know it's shocking and that's why it just might work. No one would have expected Monty to pull off such a radical tactic, especially since the debacle of Market Garden."[54]

"Yes truly a bridge too far."

The two-staff officer's gossiping is drowned out by yet another flight of helicopters being deployed just behind The Pyrenees Line in Spain.

"Already the boys have got a nickname for the helicopter...Choppers."

"What was that again?"

"Choppers."

"Humm...good name."

"So what is the plan on how to use these things?"

"The theory is that instead of being all spread out like a parachute drop, these choppers can fly together and land in the same area. You know ...concentration of force at the point of attack.

So far, the 'eggbeaters' have worked out pretty well. That whiner Jones keeps saying that the element of surprise and the uniqueness has made the chopper operations so successful. Jones could be right, but as long as the actions work we'll keep using them."

"How are they doing in this high mountain altitude?"

"They have to stay low and run up the valleys. No going over the top for these guys. The choppers just aren't powerful enough to gain the altitude needed in this thin air."

"I personally think the Reds are ready to break. They haven't had supplies in 3 weeks and you can tell that their volume of fire has slackened."

"How long have they been in these mountains any way. We just got here three months ago and I'm already going bonkers from the lack of air and good food. Shit, I'd surrender in a flash if I were in their shoes."

"Really? You think that you would be willing to give up and go into a POW camp 3,000 miles from your wife and kids just because of crappy food?!?!"

"Well, I guess if you put it that way...maybe not. But I'd still be tempted."

Once again all practical conversation is drowned out by the incredible

---

[54] - A Magnificent Disaster: The Failure of Market Garden, the Arnhem Operation September 1944 by David Bennett

noise the helicopters generate. The two men will just have to wait until the machines are gone or the pilots turn off the engines.

Finally, they get a chance to continue their discussion.

"I wonder how long the novelty of those things is going to last? They look pretty vulnerable to me. Why I could easily pick off the pilot while they're hovering. It would be an easy shot for any boy from Kentucky."

"You from Kentuck? Where abouts? I'm from over by Mingo County way…"

Cousins

The date was 3 October 1947. After maneuvering and marching 1,450 miles The Freedom Force Army led by Zhukov, finally confronts the remnants of the Red Army of the USSR led by Nikita Khrushchev. The Slavic Freedom Force consists of units from Russia, Ukraine, Moldova, Georgia, Azerbaijan, Belarus, Latvia, Estonia, Poland, Hungry, Romania, Bulgaria, Czechoslovakia, and Lithuania. Already the Freedom army was self-organizing into units based on nationality.

The Red Army overwhelmingly Russian or Rus' plus a host of committed communists. These communists still haven't realized that the USSR was never an experiment in Communism, but a good old-fashioned oligarchy led by a ruthless dictator.

Today's fight would truly be a clash between cousins and possibly brothers, sisters, fathers and mothers, much like America's Civil War or the Revolutionary War with the British. The scale will dwarf the original battle of Kursk, which was the largest tank battle in history.

In the 1943 battle between the Red Army and the Wehrmacht over Wehrmacht, tanks and armor vehicles were involved. In that titanic struggle the Soviets lost five vehicles for every German machine destroyed yet the Red still were considered the victors. At the end of the confrontation controlled the battlefield and were able many nearly demolished vehicles. Some were repaired and returned to the field several times following major damage.

For the Soviets, the battle of Kursk was the true turning point in World War Two. After Kursk the Germans never regained the initiative. The Soviets dictated where and when the battles would be fought from 1944 on and were constantly advancing towards Berlin.

The Freedom Forces continued to control when and where to engage the enemy. Ever since Zhukov had taken command, the ex-communist fighters were steadily advancing on Moscow. NATO was supplying air support and equipment with the Freedom Fighters providing the boots on the ground, backed up by blood and guts.

The eastern Republics were more reluctant to attack their former tormentors. Proximity and familiarity made it difficult to demonize friends and neighbors. A good percentage of the citizens in these adjoining lands were of Russian origin.

Kazakhstan, Kyrgyzstan, Uzbekistan, Tajikistan, Turkmenistan started to settle their own feuds and old scores. Stalin had encouraged animosities as he pitted peoples and countries against one another. Zhukov was probably the only military leader who could keep this diverse group focused and sustain their momentum.

The armored forces supporting the Freedom Fighters were a mixed lot consisting of American Shermans, Stuarts, a few Pershings and the new Pattons. The Brits contributed to the mixture with their Centurions, Cruisers, Churchills and Valentines. Even a couple of hundred German Tigers, Panthers and Panzer IV were being thrown in.

The Reds responded with the venerable T-34-85, T-44, and the T-54 in large numbers.

The upcoming conflict would be a struggle of main battle tanks. The infantry and artillery would have a negligible impact due to the fluid nature of the encounters.

The air forces of both sides were not in a position to intervene in any concerted effort. The Freedom Forces and the Stalinists had armored piercing rounds that could easily kill any tank on the battlefield from 1000 yards. Under these conditions, it was tactically expedient to be hull down waiting for the enemy to advance. Unfortunately for the tankers on both sides, neither Khrushchev nor Zhukov wanted to be on the defensive.

Flanking maneuvers followed counter attacks, which followed head on rushes on a six-hundred-kilometer front. Breakthroughs would be summarily cut off and destroyed.

The Battle of The Sosna
The titanic battle of metal beasts was given a name by each side. The

Loyalists Reds or Stalinists named their defeat after the small city of Livny. The Freedom Forces chose the neighboring town south of the Sosna River. History has now named it "The Battle of The Sosna".

To the victors belonged the spoils. There were many perfectly good but disabled tanks that the Freedom Force could repair. The process was fairly easy. The Cleaners (for lack of a better term) entered the vehicle first. The inside of a breached tank is a biological mess. If all was safe, they commenced to clean up any remnants of the crew left behind, brains, hands, toes, etc. You get the idea I'm sure.

Next the mechanics checked out the engine. If they could get it running, they drove it to a recovery area. Occasionally a piece of human debris would roll or vibrate out of some hiding place that the Cleaners missed but for the most part, the journey was uneventful.

After the Mechanics were done the Armorers took over and replace or repaired all the guns, external mortars, and grenade or smoke launchers. They also fixed the pieces of armor that had been damaged, compromised or had a hole melted in it by a HEAT round.

Once the tank was lethal again the Electricians went to work on the radios, control panels, hookups for the heating and cooling systems, etc. Any time after the tank could move and shoot the new crew would show up and assist in the renovation. The men would crawl all over the vehicle, whistling and shouting exclamations to each other in awe of the damage that killed the previous crew.

Then it was back to the front as the crew tried their hardest not to become hamburger and to make the other guy into the same.

A general rule was that 50 percent of the vehicles could be restored on a division level. Another 25 percent would have to be sent back to levels above the division maintenance shop and or even the factory. The remaining 25 percent was either destroyed or had burned up and were scrapped.

As you can see occupying the battlefield was a major goal. Fully 75% of the tanks previously inert found new life. These tanks could once again win new territory and terrorize the enemy.

Following the largest tank battle in history the defeated Stalinists retreated towards Moscow. Zhukov's Freedom Fighters were always close on their heels with the NATO forces bringing up the rear and keeping Zhukov in supply.

The prevailing attitude of the Western soldier was let the Stalinists retreat. We'll surround them in Moscow and starve them out. There was no need for house-to-house fighting and mass casualties. What was another few months of siege duty compare to death far from home? A Captain was overheard commenting, "It is 5,327 miles from Moscow to Rolla, Missouri, for example."

The vast majority of anti-Stalinists and people from former enslaved republics of the USSR wanted none of it. They wanted to finish off the architects of the most brutal regime in history. The Freedom Fighters wanted to make the monsters who had killed, tortured and maimed their loved ones, suffer.

The perpetrators of Stalinism would not go unpunished.

Outside Man

On a tactical level the best cover for a tank on a large open battlefield was another destroyed tank. The optimum way to gain an advantage was to have someone outside of your vehicle with field glasses and a good pair of ears, informing you of targets of opportunity and possible ambushes. Unfortunately, these brave souls that were outside the protective armored cocoon, were prime targets for the hungry machine gunners that all main battle tanks had.

One lucky man was Vova Klimenko. He lasted the whole three-day battle against the Stalinists, while outside the hulls of his compatriots. He assisted his fellow tankers by being their eyes and ears.

Being inside a metal box that has a very noisy diesel engine strapped to it is not conducive to situational awareness. You can't use any of your senses very well even when the engine is idling. Hearing is out of the question and sight is very limited when the tank is buttoned up. Tanks never, ever sneak up on anything else but another tank. Anybody with halfway decent hearing can literally hear a tank coming from a mile away.

Vova was constantly being shelled and shot at by machine gunners yet managed to seek revenge on anyone who dared attempting to end his life. He is credited with assisting in 54 kills by various tanks in D squad- Third Company - 1st Regiment - of the Tenth Ukrainian Volunteer Division. Corporal Klimenko directly assisted his division commander on one occasion.

The General was visiting the front lines in his command tank. Vova Klimenko heard a long wolf T-54 engine idling somewhere nearby and informed the General after locating the enemy. The General decided to contribute directly to the war effort, went out, and did an exemplary job of ambushing the hidden tank.

After that encounter, Klmenko had a standing invitation to join the Division staff. He declined the position and continued to defy the odds throughout the war against Stalinism.

Two of the tanks he was instrumental in destroying were crewed by his own distant cousins. Vova never knew this and it wouldn't have made any difference. He would have done almost anything and killed almost anyone to rid the Ukraine of the dreaded Rus' and Stalinism, including his cousins three times removed.

Vova survived the war had six children and died in a car accident on his 78 birthday.

Figure 47 - Vova Klimenko using the outside intercom. All the uniforms and small arms were supplied by the US Army.

Deaf, Smart and Blind

As usual, the noise was deafening and lieutenant Egorov couldn't hear a thing. That part hadn't changed by the introduction of the newer tanks. The T-54 was little better than the T-34 decibel level wise. When the tank commander had to close his hatch his ability to see and his lane of observation was cut by 60%. With the clang of a hatch, one of the oldest tool's nature had given man stopped.

He had to rely on looking through view ports and his periscope. Many a fighter pilot and common soldier's life was saved by catching something moving using his peripheral vision. The use of this elemental of all abilities of the Mark One Eyeball was all but eliminated in a buttoned-up tank.

An individual's situation awareness was markedly reduced as one's sight lane was drastically reduced. A Squad Leader's effectiveness was greatly hampered when inside the tank. He had to take it on faith that his tank commanders were following their training and orders.

In this, the largest tank battle in history, there was no hope of sitting back and observing your opponent from afar, devising a plan and watching with pride as your men carried it out. There were so many tanks in such a relatively small area that you very often became aware of your next opponent in single combat, at a distance of 100 meters or less.

All the tanks in this battle could kill any other tank with one shot at 100 meters. With the new armor piercing rounds fired by both sides even the venerable Sherman or T-34 could easily take out the newest model Patton or T-54.

The combatant's equipment was a collection of many nations and tank models. NATO was reluctant to give Zhukov's units many of the new M-50 Patton. Eisenhower was not confident about the outcome of the battle and didn't want to face reconditioned Pattons in the future. What Ike wanted…Ike got.

The bulk of the Freedom Force was the ubiquitous M-4 Sherman 76 using armor-piercing capped ballistic capped or APCBC round almost exclusively. This round could penetrate up to 2.5 times its caliber at 100 meters. Thus, a 76-mm round could kill a tank with up to 190 mm of armor. The only tank in the world that could withstand this round at 100 meters was the Soviet IS-3.

The British did see fit to supply the FF with earlier versions of the

Centurion. Armed with a 17 lber, (76mm) main gun, it too could defeat any tank but the S-3. The remainder of the tanks were T-34 85s with the 85-mm gun, which using the APCBC round could destroy an IS-3 at 100 meters at any angle.

The real tank killer would end up being the fighter bomber using a combination of napalm, rockets and conventional bombs. At the insistence of the former armorers and VVS pilots thousands of PTAB bomblets were adapted for US fighter-bombers and used as well.

The PTAB was by far the most potent tank killer of the battle. The Stalinist forces failed to learn the lessons of the German panzers and maneuvered in columns and tightly packed groups. This earned them the final designation, of casualty. One flight of four P-38 Lightnings destroyed 10 Stalinist tanks in one pass.

The two opposing forces were of roughly equal size with Zhukov's men being better trained. 2354 main battle tanks of the FF faced off against 2689 of the Stalinist Force.

The night before the battle the FF that friendly fire would be a bigger threat than lack of camouflage and elected to paint Invasion stripes on all of their armored vehicles similar to what the Allies did to their planes flying over Normandy on D-Day.

Three big and bold bright yellow stripes adorned every FF tank to help everyone quickly identify to which army the vehicle belonged. It was hoped that painting the stripes within hours of the commencement of hostilities would forgo any skullduggery by the enemy using copycat stripes. The enemy would have a hard time finding yellow paint in large quantities and distributing it in a few hours' notice.

Figure 48- M4-Sherman 76 with Sosna stripes

The Battle for Moscow 1947

I'm not going to bore you with specific details concerning the battle for Moscow. The battle has been written about extensively in other venues with more than 50 books being dedicated to the subject. I'll give you a brief overview and let it go at that.

Both Napoleon and Hitler attacked Moscow in the early fall. They were defeated by a combination of "General Winter," moral and lack of supplies.

Once again, a large army is threatening Moscow in the early fall. This army is different. It is well supplied, consisted of numerous former denizens of the city and most have lived through many a Russian winter.

Commanding the attacking force is Marshall Zhukov, the hero of Leningrad, Stalingrad and Kursk. He was possibly the most battle tested leader in modern warfare. Opposing him was Nikita Khrushchev, a former commissar who Zhukov had just defeated at the Battle of The Sosna.

Zhukov's Freedom Force had close to three times as many men as Khrushchev's Stalinists. Almost every Stalinist, still alive, had migrated to Moscow hoping against hope that Khrushchev could win and save their lives. Every other option was taken away from them. Gathering in Moscow was their only chance at survival and left without options made them, especially dangerous.

Many were not soldiers, but many had killed before. Some were experts at torturing helpless women, men and children. Few fought an enemy hand to hand. They would have to learn fast or die.

Zhukov did not mount the usual massive artillery barrage. In his experience when fighting in the city, shelling an area on an immense scale, did little but create rubble which the enemy used as cover.

He did unleash his ground attack IL10 Sturmoviks behind enemy lines with particular emphasis on heavily defended areas in the enemy's rear. The Stalinists were without an air force, but they did have a supply of the proximity fuse. The altitudes flown on ground attack missions were low. Consequently, the VT fuse was not of much use. A good old-fashioned Bofers was more of a threat.

As each building was cleared Zhukov's men took their revenge on any prisoners or wounded. The Stalinists were given no quarter and retaliated in kind. They were fighting for their lives and it is amazing how valuable life is to a murder of women and children. They probably fear the afterlife more than most because of their sins.

They fought tenaciously as only Russians can, taking as many other souls with them as they could when they died. The one thing they didn't do was to sacrifice themselves for their fellow fighters and that is probably why they lost. Unlike the fighters in Leningrad or Stalingrad there was no altruistic behavior and no martyrs. The Stalinist fighters usually ended up dying alone after abandoning their fellows to live another ten minutes.

To someone who believes he's damned, ten minutes is worth any betrayal or the sacrifice of others.

The ease with which the lives of others were forfeited led to a deep mistrust of your fellows. Not only did you have to watch for the enemy in front but for betrayal from behind.

Building by building and block by city block, the Stalinists were eliminated or found places to hide abandoning their fellows. As the Freedom Fighters worked as teams, the Stalinists died alone.

Khrushchev died rather early in the fight. He stepped on a Bouncing Betty or German S-mine. The S-mine was introduced in 1935 and became one of the most successful mines of modern times. Instead of just exploding when triggered it was propelled 3 feet in the air and then detonated showering a much greater area with lethal shrapnel.

Nikita was almost severed at the waist and took 15 minutes to die.

Both sides refrained from using high explosives in the fight for the Kremlin. As if by tacit agreement, only small arms were used thus preserving the few items of value still on the grounds. The casualty rate on both sides was enormous as the Kremlin was claimed by both sides as a symbol of what they believed was the truth.

Pistols and knives replaced grenades and C4 explosives. Men were killed one at a time in hand to hand fighting. The battle was reminiscent of the knights of old with an entrenching tool being more useful as a weapon than a 150 mm howitzer or P-47 Jug.

The fact was that the Freedom Force had more men. That made the difference in the end. They could send in more men than the Stalinists could kill and those surplus men killed every loyal Soviet one by one. Daily, for over a week, more men died by blunt force trauma than at the Battle of the Little Big Horn.

By 23 October the Kremlin was firmly in Zhukov's territory. His men searched in vain for records documenting the fate of millions, millions of family members, lovers and friends.

The Stalinists used their time wisely while delaying the capture of the Kremlin. Untold tons of paper and even microfilm were all destroyed trying to hide the truth from those seeking righteous vengeance.

The Battle for Berlin lasted 18 days. The Battle of Moscow, 1947 lasted 33 days. The final bastion of the Loyalists fell after taking direct fire from 24 Bofers and 88 mm guns shooting at 100 meters. The 88s would make a hole in the wall and the Bofers would pour 40 mm HE into it. Not much can survive that kind of assault and few did.

Of the 210,000 Stalinists who streamed into Moscow, only 1890 survived. Enough killing had occurred and the survivors were treated quite well considering some of their alleged crimes. Most didn't stand trial although trial, deserved it.

Scores of the 1890 survivors were wounded, most horribly so with missing pieces of their anatomy or terrible burns caused by in close use of flame throwers or napalm delivered by various means.

Misplaced pity kept them alive. A number did of them did not want to live and took their own lives after they could not stand the pain any longer. The hospital was set up and staffed by NATO troops and had over 10,000 patients at one point. Luckily, this was anticipated and enough supplies were brought in ahead of time.

Now what? Many were saying and thinking. Most had only known Stalin as their leader. Good or bad sometimes familiarity is better than change. The emotions caused by stress can be destructive or invigorating. Invariably, "The good old days" are talked about with nostalgia and the millions of dead are temporarily forgotten.

Andrei Who?

General George Marshall is walking about his office reading from a file to him by the Colonel, who managing the Soviet Desk. George's audience of one appears totally uninterested. Perhaps his subordinate has other things on his mind other than listening to a boring biography of a fairly boring man being read very badly by another very boring man. Eisenhower is approaching the end of his very long stint as Allied and NATO Supreme Commander.

Marshall drones on…

"Andrei Gromyko leaves rural life behind and enters the world of academia in the 1930s. The great Stalin instigated purge of 1938, opened up many positions in the diplomatic corps. In late 1939, Stalin meets Gromyko and states'. The Soviet Union should maintain reasonable relations with such a powerful country like the United States, especially in light of the growing fascist threat."

Andrei was to go to America and become the second-in-command at the Soviet embassy in New York City.

By a circuitous route that involved traveling through Romania, Bulgaria, Yugoslavia and Italy, he boarded a ship for America. The working-class neighborhoods of New York strengthen his strong negative feelings of the inhumanity of capitalism.

In 1943, Andrei became the ambassador to the United States. In April of 1946, he left for returned to the USSR for a "vacation."

Shortly after World War Three started Gromyko and his entire family left Leningrad. They emigrated to Canada via Finland just ahead of the Soviet airborne assault on Finland, Sweden and Norway.

Andrei found himself in high demand and chose a prestigious position at

McGill University in Montreal. He regularly gave lectures and speeches on the evils of Stalinism and the failures of both communism and capitalism, preferring what he called "democratic socialism."

He was watched with great interest by the CIA as he in turn watched with great interest the destruction of the Soviet Union.

In November of 1947 he volunteered to work with the International Red Cross on refugee resettlement. His particular focus being the Ukraine."

Finally, Ike can stand it no more and blurts out.

"Why do we care about this man?"

"Well Ike he may just be the next leader of Russia."

"Why in the world would we let a former commie insider lead our sworn enemy?"

"He got out early and renounced communism and particularly Stalin when the Red Tide was sweeping Western Europe. The Reds were poised to win the whole kit and caboodle when he made his move putting his and his family's lives in danger. He was within hours of being trapped in Norway by Soviet Paratroops.

He's not some Johnny come lately Freedom Fighter that switched sides when the USSR started to lose."

"You really don't like Zhukov do you?"

"Ike, my personal feelings are irrelevant. We can't have a military man take over Russia. This Gromyko guy has never fired a gun and has been a diplomat all his life. He spent years here in the states and understands us…"

"Well that's more than I can say."

"You know what I mean."

"Who else knows this guy and is backing him?"

"Truman, Stenson, Souers, Patterson, Harriman…"

"Okay, I get the idea. Why does everyone know this guy?"

"He flitted around New York for three years. He was always saying 'neyt' but still most respected him. You don't exactly hobnob it in diplomatic circles, Ike."

"Neither do you George."

"And that's why I'm reading this report."

"Point taken. Continue on please, I will stay awake."

"Hopefully I can as well."

Another Time Another Place

"Andrei Gromyko was to go to America and becomes the second-in-command at the Soviet embassy in New York City."

Zhukov interrupts the reader. "Excuse me for interrupting my friend Konstantin…but why have you evacuated my office of all personnel and are now reading me this biography of Gromyko?"

The blind monk-like figure of Konstantin seemed to peer right through Zhukov's flesh and bones and into his soul. The man didn't speak for close to a minute. Zhukov was used to such behavior from his friend and confidant.

Finally, his mentor spoke using Zhukov's code name. "Goga, you have expressed many times your belief that a mind trained in the military arts should never lead a nation-state in time of peace. Is that belief still in your heart?"

"Why yes…yes of course but why would you ask such a thing?"

"Many have put forth your name as the next leader of the Rus'. I have repeatedly told them of your conviction against such a scheme. Even Eisenhower himself has suggested you.

As much as I know you would do your duty, you would have to forsake one of your most earnestly held principles to do so. You would not be a happy man. I fear the compromises needed would frustrate you beyond your endurance.

You have sacrificed many things to free the Rus'. First, you defeated the Hitlerites, Then you led the Freedom Force against the Monster Stalin once you knew his true crimes against life itself. Stalin took all he could from you at one time. You defied him and then he asked you to save him. Stalin did this after ordering Beria to cause you as much pain as possible.

You maintained the belief that your actions were saving the most lives. In the end, you saw Stalin and his henchmen for what they truly were. The blinders of lies were lifted. Once you saw the truth you made the decision to end his tyranny.

Stalin held your family members hostage and eventually murdering each and every one. Any person he could seize, who called you friend, was summarily executed. There was an attempt upon my life as well.

You have been tortured, starved, physically attackedattached and mentally abused. You deserve to build in peace. You do not deserve to suffer the indignities of politics.

You have become a master of war and chaos but only as a means to end oppression. However, now is another time and another place. Your destiny is to enjoy what life has to offer. Negotiating and rebuilding Russia are tasks reserved for men like Gromyko.

Trained to Kill

Marie taught her niece to shoot. Not only to shoot, but to find the perfect place to shoot from. She taught her niece Oksana to kill men. Before Marie had left for the last time she had given Oksana the tools as well. It was not so much the rifle at it was the scope. The Zeiss Zielsechs 6x or ZF42 was one of the finest scopes ever produced. The visual path was filled with inert gas to prevent fogging p due to temp and humidity changes also, the best German optical glass was used for optimum clarity.

Aunt Marie was none other than the famous sniper Marie Ljalková-Lastovecká

With the ZF42 scope and almost any common sniper rifle, Oksana was an even better shot than her aunt. She could hit a small coin at 1,000 meters.

The real question was, could she hit a man at any range. Did she have the killer instinct?

Before she disappeared, Aunt Marie had spoken extensively to Oksana regarding the need to defeat Stalinism and all it incurred. Marie was very active in a Freedom Cell that met regularly. She took Oksana to a meeting and Oksana was enthralled by what she heard. Then her aunt was gone.

Her skill with a rifle remained a secret between Oksana, her aunt Marie and the leader of the cell who's code name was Ivan. It was as if Marie and the cause of freedom had a use for her niece in the future. A use that required anonymity as an expert marksman.

Three weeks ago, Ivan contacted her and gave Oksana an assignment. The task involved her singular talent that had been nurtured by Aunt Marie.

Developing and employing this special skill must be my purpose in life, Oksana thought as she quickly peeked through her unmounted scope at the assigned target. Only about a fifty-mm square area of his head was visible and remained rock steady over long periods of time.

The occasion was the victory parade for the victorious Freedom Forces in what was formerly Red Square now re-named Freedom Square. Every manner of prominent world leaders was going to be present, including her intended quarry.

The peace accords were going to be signed and the UN along with most nations would once again recognize Russia. No Republic, no Union, no Communism as well, just the Nation of Russia. It was a day of joy for most but terror for others.

If her target remained alive, he was going to spread terror world-wide. The kind of men who would fill the void left by those assassinated today was frightening. First, they would use the public killings as an excuse to eliminate their rivals. Then they would manipulate and persecute specific ethnic groups much like Hitler did using the "false flag" of the Reichstag Fire. [55]

Oksana believed that counterfeit acts of terrorism were often used to aid those seeking despotic power. Not only were the acts themselves heinous the following calls for revenge and "justice" led to changes in power.

Her mother, father, cousin and aunt had been killed and tortured by men like her planned victims, men who hid their true identities and proclivities from others.

Far below the huge crowd started to stir as guards and security men filled the stage. Then Andrei Gromyko came within full view. She quickly mounted the scope to her Nagant rifle, all the time cursing herself for not doing so earlier.

She acquired her target and fired for she could see that her mark was about to pull the trigger himself. Blood spattered the wall opposite the small opening she fired through.

---

[55] - Burning the Reichstag: An Investigation Into the Third Reich's Enduring Mystery by Benjamin Carter Hett

She experienced no hesitation. The opening simply became another object to hit. She forgot the man behind the hole and just pulled the trigger. She didn't' have to see the results of her shot. No nightmares for her.

She calmly put on her disguise as a cleaning woman. Oksana wiped the gun down to remove any evidence and picked up the mop and bucket. Making her way down the stair well she suddenly heard footsteps violently coming up with a vengeance in every tread.

Next, Oksana entered the nearest floor walking to the middle room. Once in the closest office she began mopping the floor.

She was almost annoyed when it took a full ten minutes for one of the police to find her. After a few questions and a rough examination of her body, he was joined by another who was higher up on the seniority list. As was often the case, he turned out to be of lesser intellect than his junior. The supervisor let her go after only a few questions!

He looked at her papers, took a few notes then sent her packing escorted by the first man. The fake name and address would do him no good, so who cared? If need be she would escape her escort with a swift kick to his groin, discard her disguise, pick up her stash of genuine papers and be on her way.

Luckily for the man's balls, he let her go as soon as they were down stairs muttering something about not wasting his time.

Oksana did it! She killed the most dangerous man still alive from the Stalinist era. A man who her aunt knew would be against freedom and would do all he could to bring terror and another demon like Stalin into being.

Now he and his evil plot were done.

Viktor Nikolayevich Leonov

Leonov was the leader and veteran of close to a hundred commando raids during the last war against German and Finish targets. He was the Soviet equivalent to the German Otto Skorzeny, who liberated Mussolini from his mountain prison.

Leonov led raids that destroyed military installations, killed hundreds of Germans and Finns, captured dozens of prisoners and released hundreds more from POW camps.

Some of his more well-known raids include…

28 July, 1941

Cape Pikshuyev Raid

Viktor Leonov and his men raided this German strong point. When a German company came to the fort's rescue, the Germans were ambushed by Leonov's 181st Special Reconnaissance Detachment and fled from the battlefield leaving over 40 dead Nazis.

October 1944

Cape Krestovy Raid

Leonov initiated the operation by directing his company in a secret landing further along the coast. The force then undertook a two-day cross-country march to Cape Krestovy.

Leonov and his troops attacked the heavily defended German coastal artillery emplacement. Their 15 cm German guns covered the entrance to strategically vital Petsamo Bay on the Kola Peninsula.

There the Soviets captured a battery of 8.8 cm dual purpose guns using them to repel a counterattack and shell the main gun position. These actions forced the Germans into destroying the coastal guns to prevent them from falling into Soviet hands. Leonov was awarded Hero of the Soviet Union after this raid.

Leonov was a living legend and twice hero of the Soviet Union receiving one of the medals from Stalin himself.

His current mission was the one he considered his most important assignment. The undertaking was designed to save the Soviet Union and communism from obliteration. By sheer will, guile and bravado, he escaped the siege of Moscow. He had made his way out of the city as the army of traitors closed in on the last bastion of the true believers and followers of Lenin and Marx.

Leonov vowed that the deaths of his compatriots would not have been in vain. All he had worked for and killed for could not be relegated to a footnote in history. He had to make the capitalists understand that they could never kill the dream of a worker's paradise.

Regrets and Retaliation

Former Soviet Navy Commando, Viktor Leonov, searched in vain for weeks for anyone who could assist him in his quest for revenge and salvation. He had the germ of an idea of how to fulfill his destiny but needed information and some help. All of his comrades in arms were dead. Many a night he wished that he could join them in one more glorious fight.

Leonov was a true Stalinist. He never questioned his orders or his leader's motives.

He started to go to his dead comrade's relatives. However, none would listen to his story for long before turning him away. To family's credit, no one reported him to the authorities. He was desperate and running out of places to hide. His face was well-known and a number of times he had heard his name whispered.

Then by chance he met a young woman named Oksana, who happened to be the niece of a gunnery instructor. Her aunt tried to teach him the art of sniping. Leonov was not interested in target practice disguised as killing. If he was going to kill he wanted to see the light fade from the eyes of his prey. He felt that was the only way to honor those who he killed and doing so helped him to sleep at night.

The gunnery instructor happened to be a woman who he heard had fallen to the cruel hands of Beria. He also heard that her daughter Sonia was killed right before her eyes. He hoped that Beria died a very painful and cruel death for all his crimes.

He had relations with the gunner instructor Marie. He called it relations but if he was really honest, it was rape. She had led him on and he had only followed. At least, that was his logic.

When the young woman mentioned her aunt and how she was a very good sniper. he immediately became suspicious. Could her aunt have told her about him before she died? Is she out for revenge? But for what he thought? All we had was sex, sure it was kind of rough and she didn't seem to enjoy it but that was the way of women. They teased you then led you on and cried rape when the act is done.

He was running out of options on how to carry out his plan. When the girl mentioned that she was a cleaning woman in a building overlooking Red Square he was very intrigued. On this very day, the new government of traitors had announced that there was going to be a Victory Parade in

Red Square. All manner of world leaders and the new Russian government would be present. The event was scheduled for one week from today.

He didn't jump at the chance she unwittingly offered. Keeping calm he continued with the conversation. Oksana finally had to take her leave and he asked if he could see her again. She agreed and they set a date and time. If she hadn't consented, he would have followed her home and gotten the information he needed by force. Desperate times lead to desperate measures.

He followed her home anyway just in case she didn't show up tomorrow.

The next day they met. Eventually, he got around to asking her about her job and she shared the information he needed. They talked at length about her aunt, the great sniper Marie Ljalková-Lastovecká.

Apparently, Oskana had no idea what had happened to Marie and how or if she died. Leonov decided not to tell her what had happened to her aunt and niece. Why burden this young mind with tales of horror and give her nightmares? Ignorance is sometimes a blessing.

They met two more times with Leonov gaining more intelligence each time, seemingly without creating suspicion. As soon as he had enough details, any further contact with Oksana would endanger his dream of revenge.

He seriously contemplated "having relations" with her but decided that doing so twice in the same family was bad luck. She had been nice to him so in his mind she wanted to have sex with him.

He was a little bit unnerved that the only person he had confided in about his ultimate plan was her Aunt Marie. Marie had expressed her wish for a more inclusive government and he had gone on about the strengths of the current system. As the vodka flowed he described his scheme should capitalism ever begin to take hold in the USSR.

It was a simple concept and was one of the reasons he was in sniper school. If the USSR collapsed and was in danger of falling into the capitalist cesspool, he would spend the remainder of his life assassinating the leaders of this monstrous system. If nothing else his actions would bring a change in leadership. The current bunch of capitalist lackeys and war criminals were particularly heinous. Hopefully, their deaths would lead to other forms of government.

He now had his chance with the "Victory Parade" only days away. Leonov would have plenty of targets. With the knowledge gained from Oksana he had a place to shoot from. It was a place she described as her retreat during breaks from work. It was concealed and isolated yet gave a good view of a large portion of Red Square.

Oksana also mentioned that she had listened to many a speech from her place of solitude and could see quite clearly the usual spot that the speaker's podium was placed.

It was such a perfect setup that alarm bells of all kinds rang in his mind. Normally, he would have passed up on such a too good to be true situation. However, he was at the end of his resources and had to act, or he would fail in his last mission. For Viktor Nikolayevich Leonov the only acceptable outcome was completing his pledge.

A week later, Gromyko's head was squarely in the cross hairs of his sniper scope. He had just exhaled and his finger was starting to tighten on the trigger. He had his finger lightly on the trigger as he had been taught by Marie.

Then his life ended. There was no drama, no pain. He just ceased to exist in this world. The leader who put himself in extreme danger for over a hundred small skirmishes and raids was dead.

Leonov's head was almost split in half by the bullet from Oksana's rifle. The round hit him in the left temple. He died instantaneously.

If he could have, Leonov would have complimented the shooter on such an excellent shot.

The authorities who discovered his body could not identify him due to the damage. They did identify the kind of rifle the bullet came from but never did find the gun.

Figure 49 - Viktor Nikolayevich Leonov

Credit Where Credit is Due

Stanislav rounded the corner and spotted the little river of blood coming from behind an air return duct. He was too young to have been in combat and had only seen one dead man, that being his father.

He was a book worm and enjoyed research and lab work. He was drafted for this assignment because of the need for manpower. Much of the former Moscow police force was dead because they were Stalinists. They needed everyone who could walk to search for the location of where the mystery shot had originated.

Last, he heard they had not found the spent bullet. This was odd. It should have been found by now with the number of men looking for clues. He had lobbied to be assigned to the exterior investigation. Instead here he was in dark buildings hunting for who knows what or whom.

Many of the combat veterans knew the sound of a Nagan sniper rifle. Just one shot was heard, but that was enough to have everyone diving for cover except for Gromyko and Stanislav. They looked at each other with neither comprehending what had just happened.

The irony was that Gromyko was probably the intended target. His appointment as the new leader of Russia was announced two days ago and this parade was his first official outing. The NATO and the Freedom Force leaders still had not agreed on what form of government to adopt. So, Gromyko did not have an authorized formal title.

Teams of men were directed to clear various buildings. His building was one of the largest. Stanislav reasoned that the roof would be the most logical location for a sniper. Now he regretted his reasoning.

Looking at the blood, he just wanted to ignore the whole thing. What would happen if he simply walked away and let someone else find the body?

He would probably get yelled at and punished for not properly doing his job and maybe even docked a day's pay. On the other hand, he wouldn't have the nightmares he was imagining would come from seeing what was around that duct.

Stanislav had decided to walk away when the voice of his immediate supervisor asked him what he was looking at?

He had to tell him for he was sure to get caught lying.

"I think there is something over there."

"Have you not gone to see?"

"Not yet Supervisor."

"And why not? You are lucky that you are good at other things Stanislav otherwise, you would be disciplined.

Now go over there and tell me what you see."

"I saw a pool of blood, Supervisor…"

"WHAT! Get out of the way Stanislav."

The Supervisor took all the credit and that was fine with Stanislav.

Two weeks went by before the body was identified. They finally ascertained from fingerprints that the corps was that of Viktor Nikolayevich Leonov. Many were surprised that the twice Hero of the Soviet Union was still alive.

Gromyko and the new leadership decided not to acknowledge the shooter's identity. There were too many questions still unanswered.

Leonov's death by sniper caused much consternation among the leadership of the new nation. How was it that he was still alive? Who shot him and why? What was he doing with a sniper rifle on that roof? The possibilities are endless.

The head of the Moscow police held a big meeting and told everyone to basically shut the fuck up about this event. The official story was an accidental discharge of a rifle dropped by a child in one of the nearby apartments. The father was a soldier who lost both legs. He was dead drunk when he was supposed to be watching his three-year-old son.

Stanislav stopped listening after a while knowing the story was not the truth. He never did learn the identity of the dead man. He was oblivious to war heroes anyway. It seemed everyone who came back had some kind of medal for heroism.

If he really examined his motives, the end conclusion was jealousy. But of course, he didn't examine his motives. Few people do. Instead, they come up with justifications then go on with their lives.

101 WPM

William White had been told that this was the last report he would work on for the CIA. The war was over and the agency was cutting back on its workforce. With communism defeated, there was no enemy that justified a large office pool. All throughout the agency layoffs were occurring and many an underling were losing his or her job.

He was somewhat flattered. White was to type the final report to the President on World War Three. The report was going to be a grand summary. The typing would take him and six other typists two weeks to finish. Then he would receive two weeks separation pay and that would be it. His career in the CIA was over only six months after it started.

He was assured that his references would be most impressive and that he should be able to land a job with either the government or a large corporation. Either was fine with him.

As usual, his mind wandered, and he paraphrased what he was typing in his head.

Huh, from the reports and investigations just completed, it seems that the war actually started on 15 December 1945 when an assassin shot out the front tires of a bus in Nevada. The bus was carrying teams of engineers who were responsible or assembling Atomic bombs. The production of our A-bombs was stopped cold with their deaths.

The incident was deemed an accident until recently when records of the war started showing up. Most of the documents were being mailed from Europe and were of a highly sensitive nature.

Well, I'll be damned.

Holy shit!

A Soviet spy had infiltrated the Manhattan Project and had somehow become the Health Safety Officer. From what the FBI could piece together the fellow got a hold of some pretty nasty stuff…Polonium. Then he managed to spread the deadly powder to hundreds…no thousands of nuclear workers, engineers and scientists many of whom later died from radioactive poisoning.

I was wondering why we just didn't bomb the Commies with our A-bombs. Now I know. Man the things they don't tell the general public. Says here they have no idea where this George Koval aka Delmar disappeared to.

Great the guy kills a couple of thousand people and they don't know where he is?! I would have thought that J. Edgar Hoover would have lost his job over that kind of screw up.

The Joint Chiefs fall back to a series of plans titled Pincher. The overarching plan basically calls for retreating to the Pyrenees Mountains and hanging on for dear life against the Red's attack.

Two hours later.

 Skinner, I remember that name. Huh this report credits him with saving NATO's ass. He and some kid name Jim Crenshaw figured out a way to defeat the Soviets magic missiles. Well good for him.

Time for a break

Break Time
William gets up and makes a point of walking past Mary Hart's desk. He just happens to glance at what she is working on.

Ha, she got stuck typing cargo manifests! While I got the final report for the war and she gets manifests. Well ain't that something.

William is feeling terrific is uncharacteristically humming as he pours himself a cup of joe. Ruth Ann comes in and comments on his good mood. Which puts him in even better spirits.

He saunters back to his desk. As he nears Mary, he hears her swear beneath her breath. Before she realizes that William is watching she reaches for her eraser. She notices him and very pointedly puts the eraser back and continues typing.

White can hardly contain himself as he sits down and turns the page. She had made a mistake and tried to hide it from him.

Let's see, where was I? Chuckling to himself, he thinks I can't believe she just did that. All right enough of that.

Let's see what's next? Since the A-bombs are now a bust with most of the scientist's dead, the Joint Chiefs of Staff need a new plan.

Their decision is to dust off a proposed plan previously developed by General MacArthur at the beginning of the war. MacArthur's concept revolved around a series of invasions. Each subsequent action was designed to escalate the stakes with increasingly daring tactics. Each attack was meant to inflict the maximum amount of troops cut off from

Moscow. The ultimate goal was to lure the Reds further and further away from Moscow and isolate them from all support.

Oh, yeah, I remember that report. Something about bombing the Reds from Turkey. NATO's air raids forced the Soviets to invade Turkey and then Egypt in an effort stop the attacks.

The US landed the 1st Army in Italy on the border of Yugoslavia and they go north to Vienna. The Reds don't play along and just kind of sit there still going for Egypt. Next, we land in Lebanon and cut off the Red armies attacking the Brits in the Suez.

The combined NATO operations forced the left-over commies to retreat to the Caucasus Mountains to the north and dig in thinking they're pretty safe. Next we break into the Baltic taking Copenhagen and landing in Poland. Let's see who's the general? Oh yeah Truscott and the 10th Army.

Truscott's army heads south and the 1st Army under General Walker heads north and they meet in Poland cutting the continent in two and trapping over a million Soviet troops in France and Germany.

Wow! The things you learn from these reports. I suppose it was in the news, but I never realized how it all fit together.

Mary

Mary Hart finishes up the manifests and reaches for the next paper in what seems like an endless pile. But the task will be finished soon. The war is over and so is her job.

She begins to type.

"The Soviets attempt to break the Eurasian Line, as it is now called, and are defeated with significant losses. At the same time, a series of NATO invasions called Backdoor commences with the forcing of the Turkish Straights. The final amphibious assault in the sequence of invasions enters the Black Sea and lands behind the Red Army. Dug-in along the Caucasus Mountain Range hundreds of thousands of Soviet units are trapped, including the famous Marshall Zhukov."

Ten minutes and a thousand words later.

"Throughout this time-period rebels are coming out of hiding. Partisans from occupied France, Germany and most important of all, the former republics of the USSR are establishing resistance units.

On 23 August 1947, Stalin dies by poisoning. Lavrenti Beria is suspected of the assassination. One man stands between Beria and becoming dictator. That man is Nikita Khrushchev. Khrushchev was thought to be dead, killed by an assassin's bullet months before. The reports were erroneous.

"An agent with the CIA, Colonel Mario Fiat, proposed a plan to convince Marshall Zhukov to defect. Fiat spent the last three months in intense philosophical deliberations with a mystery man named Konstantin.

Konstantin had willingly surrendered to British troops a few weeks before. He was a known associate and friend of Marshall Zhukov and was rumored to be an advisor to Stalin.

Colonel Fiat was able to convince Konstantin of the evils of Stalinism. Fiat reported that labeling the Soviet version of communism, "Stalinism," is an excellent tactic to employ in any defection scenario. Konstantin is recruited to lead an effort to change the hearts and minds of the Soviet citizens.

His first assignment is to aid Mario Fiat in the defection attempt directed at Marshal Zhukov. The attempt is successful (see addendum S4).

On 27 August 1947 Marshal Zhukov leads 300,000 men in a mass defection and all renounce Stalinism.

According to British Intelligence, Beria tries once more to personally kill Khrushchev but dies in the attempt. Khrushchev seemingly rises from the dead and appears in public on 5 September 1947 announcing his assumption of leadership.

Negotiations begin that focus on the surrender of the Soviet Union. Weeks later, the talks stall with NATO announcing its "Unconditional Surrender" policy which the Soviet Union summarily rejects.

'Huh... nice.

So let me get this straight in my mind.

According to a whole shitload of secret Soviet documents and leaked reports Stalin was poisoned by Beria, Beria was kidnapped by Khrushchev but escaped. Beria then instigated a plan where he kidnapped high-ranking officials' kids and forced the parents to do his bidding.

Some parents were coerced into assassinating Molotov and other politburo members by strapping a bomb to themselves and then committing suicide while hugging their victims.

Now that's not normal.

Khrushchev's assassin screws up and later a stand-in is shot while giving a speech and everyone thinks that Nikita is dead…but he's not!

Holy mackerel this is some story.

This is juicy stuff!

No Words
William continues typing and thinking.

All this insider super-secret information is coming from a former official who kept meticulous records. Somehow, he was able to preserve them during the chaos of battle. In several instances, the files include photos, recordings and even film. The depth and breadth of the material is astounding as well as a bit disconcerting.

Some of the images and audio come from meetings with the Joint Chiefs of Staff, the President, Prime Minister, NATO leaders, etc. Meetings that no one, much less a Soviet spy, should have been able to attend and record.

We know the information is factual. When confronted by the evidence provided, dozens of the surviving participants in the meetings confess to fabrications. All are visibly shaken after being challenged with the truth, including members of the current administration and US military.

Whoever this man or woman is, they have opened up a real can of truth. The revelations really stink for some and for others, it has vindicated their version of history.

Identifying the individual and where the treasure troves of materials are hidden is becoming a major obsession for a number of agencies and staff.

Well shit I know who it is! It's that fellow that Skinner was matching wits with that disappeared about six months ago…it's got to be him!…

William White almost said this aloud. He catches himself in time and looks around to see if anyone is noticing. And there is Mary Hart staring right at him. He tries to disappear behind his typewriter, but she gets up and comes over to his desk.

"You know don't you?!"

She says as she tries to look at his papers.

"Hey, stop that. Know, know what?'

"Ssssh, we can't talk here. Meet me in the mimeograph room in five minutes."

"Why should I?"

"You will if you know what's good for you." She says sternly.

She turns and stalks off. William notices something odd in her walk.

Exactly six minutes later, he gets up and heads in the direction of the mimeograph room. He looks around to see if anyone is watching. He reaches the door and turns the knob. The lights are off and he whispers…

"Mary, where are you? Listen I don't know what you think I know but…"

Mary almost slams her body against him and proceeds to kiss him with a passion he never knew existed. He returns the embrace with urgency and nature takes its course.

Forgotten are films, spies, recordings and secrets.

Sergo Arises

"I was buried alive…a nightmare come true. Apparently, a living nightmare; I think, therefore I'm alive; a Descartian paradox. I was cold, it was dark and I was feeling nothing. For the moment feeling nothing was good. No explosions or shouting and no danger. Yes, most of the time now nothing was life. I was alive because of nothing, yet would also die because of nothing. Eventually nothing means a lack of food, water and even air.

I could feel panic starting to spread throughout my body. It was another sign that I was still alive, wasn't it? Is this what death is, blackness, silence, nothing? No, they had not killed me yet. God knows they've tried.

Was it possible that it was over? I think not. So many times before I thought the end was near and so many times, it wasn't.

My life, up to now, has caused millions of people to have nothing, to lose everything. I suspect that they would have died of nothing anyway if I had not existed, just not so soon or as quickly.

I blink and can't tell if my eyes are open or not. Somehow the air was still good. Someone had designed that well. I could still feel the cold wall at my back...another good sign.

The ambient temperature at this depth was a constant fifty-eight degrees. Without any variations, and with no outside power or inside heat, it stayed at fifty-eight degrees. Dead silence, dead cold, even my sense of smell had shut down. I suppose it stank, or at the very least smelled like my last meal. I was out of water, so one way or another, I had to rise from the dead and survey my surroundings soon."[57]

Beating the Odds Yet Again

For days, there were almost continuous explosions above his bunker. Now more than a week passed without a sound.

Sergo's radio could receive almost any band. However, there was a significant problem with reception. He had embedded several antennas in the factory walls, but only one out of a dozen was working.

In the end, it was good old-fashioned AM band radio that told him what he needed to know. The victors wasted no time in getting the radio system back up and running. It was probably the best way to communicate to the masses.

The war was over and Stalin was dead. Khrushchev had presumed the post of "dictator in crime" for a total of 63 days. Ultimately, he was killed in the fighting around Moscow.

It took another month to round up all the Stalinists and end the fighting completely. The cessation of hostilities was Sergo's cue to escape his self-chosen solitary confinement.

Given all the explosions from heavy ordinance, he was sure the factory was rubble. It was time to see if his shaped charges could extradite him from a situation that was rapidly becoming hell.

He ran out of water a few days ago. One of the explosions cracked his cistern. Unbeknownst to him he lost almost a year's supply of water in a week. Ah, the best laid plans of mice and men.

---

[57] - World War Three 1946 – The Red Tide - Stalin Strikes First – Prologue by Harry Kellogg III

The first charge in his series of detonations was the most critical. The device was like a large cannon. The strongest sewer pipe available had been sent before the war all the way from Germany in thirty-foot lengths. Each segment will be acting like the barrel of a very big gun.

Sergo was confident that if the whole building collapsed he was still be able to escape. The rubble should put up as much resistance as a pile of cardboard in front of a high-powered rifle.

He knew that there would be great interest in even the rubble of his former creation. The facility was the biggest in the world and the most advanced in the production of aerospace weapon systems. He presumed that no one in the West knew about the huge facility that was just outside Moscow.

Once they discovered the site, he was sure the capitalist pigs would be crawling all over his once beautiful facility.

The blast would surely be noticed unless he timed it correctly. He imagined blowing his hole to freedom only to walk right into the hands of the enemy and returned to a prison cell.

He contacted Georgie using their hardwired Morse Code Keyer He sent the code and received the proper response. He was glad to know that Georgie was alive and would help him negotiate the alien world he was about to enter.

Their agreed-upon plan was to start blowing holes in the earth at 03:25 the next morning. That was about 12 hours from now. He had broken protocol and asked Georgie to bring some water with him. He had had nothing to drink for over 24 hours now.

Wham! and Double Wham!
He was lucky to have a job. Sure, the job was not what he was trained to do. There were no demands on his brain or use of his extensive education in any manner, shape or form. At least, he could eat. That was a lot more than most in Moscow could do these days.

The war was over, and he would miss working in the now ruined factory he was guarding. He used to design machines that produced wondrous things here. But his luck had changed; he thought as he counted the money for the sixth time.

There was a year's salary here. What would he do with it? That giant guy had told him that if he kept quiet and did his job, he would get another vast sum of money in one year's time. But if he told anyone what he saw, the guy would kill him, his family and all his friends.

Former engineer Vitaly Delov was now the watchman at the Sovetskiy nomer odin zavod or Soviet Factory Number One site. Despite the destruction of most of the complex, some valuable machines and tools remained untouched. The facility was gradually being rebuilt. He was a member of the night security detail.

Six hours ago, he was watching the metal rusting on a huge milling machine when the ground beneath his feet shook. He quickly stood up and another deep underground rumble occurred slamming him to his knees. Then the ground exploded not 50 meters in front of him sending debris 500 meters to the north. Luckily, he was to the south.

He just sat there staring and wondering what to do when the biggest man he had ever seen came around a destroyed wall from the direction of the explosion. Vitaly thought that he must have come from the hole caused by the eruption.

The guy walked right up to him, picked him up with one hand until he was suspended in the air and choking from the constriction of his clothes around his neck. He was beyond scared and just looked in horror as the hulk drew back his other hand and made a fist. He was sure he was going to die.

Suddenly a little guy showed up out of nowhere and got the big guy's attention. He told him nicely but firmly to put Vitaly down. Turns out the big man's name was Georgie.

We'll let Vitaly tell the rest of the story.

"Without hesitation, Georgie dropped me and knocked the wind out of my lungs. I remember hearing stories about Georgie. I bet they were all true.

When I recovered, the little man had just finished drinking some water. He then told the big guy that those days were over and we didn't hurt people anymore. That we had to behave differently. The big guy just kind of looked down and indicated that he understood.

Georgie's boss gave me this handful of new Russian rubles and told me to keep quiet or … then the big guy took over and made threats and the offer of a reward next year.

What could I do but agree? They walked away disappearing into the debris. Next, I heard two more explosions that must have sealed the nearest hole and probably another that I didn't know about and didn't want to know about. One secret hole was enough.

A New Day a New Life
Russians Elect New Government

January 18, 1948

Associated Press

Reporting from Moscow

By Robert T. Sloan

By the time you read this article it will be the start of a new day in Russia. Gone is the Union of Soviet Socialist Republics. Gone is the human-made aberration known as Communism.

And God willing, soon we shall be rid of all dictators as the world's people see the shining star that is America and long for our freedoms.

Someone behind Bob is looking over his shoulder as he types.

"Let me see that."

Robert's roommate and boss rips the paper from the typewriter.

"Hey!"

"How can you write this drivel Bob?"

"Come on Joe it's what the editor wants because it's what the public expects."

"All right I understand, but let's talk about the story for a minute. How's about you kind of lay it out for me? I'm leaving tomorrow and you ain't going to have me around to steer you straight anymore. It's not like you can pick up the phone and call me from here."

"What do you mean? What do you want me to do?"

"Paraphrase what you're going to say so maybe I can help you out."

"Well OK. It is my first major story from overseas and I could use some pointers."

"Good, so go ahead."

"Let's see, well I was going to start with the elections. You know how Ike and the military appointed Gromyko. Who then named his cabinet after which they held elections for the district leaders quick like."

"Good start."

"Then I was going to use some quotes like Gromyko's "This is only the first of many free elections. I want to thank the American people for assisting us in throwing off the yoke of a ruthless dictator…" You know the one he made at the ceremony where they got that sniper."

"Jeez don't mention that! We're not supposed to know about that fiasco."

"Nah, don't worry, I'm not stupid. So where was I, so then I was going to wrap up the last couple of battles here in Moscow. Next I would mention how the Stalinists fought to the last taking many a good Freedom Fighter with them to the grave. Then I was going to get into how that Zhukov fellow was almost forced into office by those riots. Then he gave that speech and endorsed Gromyko."

"All-good good stuff but how are you going to wrap this up?"

"You know with the usual about how we came we saw, and we conquered. Nothing now stands in the way of the freedom-loving people of the world. Now that the commies have been defeated all the countries on earth can follow America's shooting star.

"Yeah, I wonder how that is going to play out?"

"What do you mean?"

"We have no enemies to speak of. What are guys like McCarthy going to do without the commies to bash around anymore?"

"Don't worry, guys like him always gin stuff up."

"That's exactly what I'm worried about. You're Jewish, right?"

"Yeah, what of it?"

"Nothing, I was raised a Muslim."

"Well what do you know."

"My point being are they going to start coming after us now that the big Red bogey man is dead?"

"Why would they do that and who is they?"

"You know the bullies of this world. The guys like McCarthy and his henchman Cohen. The ones who only feel good when they're shitting on people.

Well enough of that. You have a deadline to make, don't you?"

"Shit yeah!"

Epilogue

Stalin is dead. Communism is eradicated. America stands alone astride a world that has been knocked out. Millions have died and millions are homeless in a Eurasia that has been decimated by three world wars, in 30 years. Each war has slaughtered a generation of young men. A crippled France and England kneel by our side while a prostrate and helpless Germany, Japan, Italy and Russia lay at our feet.

The incomprehensible China has defeated its Red Menace and now faces a monumental rebuilding process.

The American people have had enough. Isolationism is rearing its ugly head. Demagogues are arising from the ashes of the old political parties. Men with no soul are exploiting the chaos. Tens of millions of returning service men are all looking for jobs, an education and a better life after seeing hell and surviving.

Without good-paying jobs, there is no income. With no income, there is no demand. With no demand, there are no good-paying jobs. Without all three, you have a looming depression.

Men like the Dulles brothers, Morgenthau, McCarthy and Bernstein have held sway. The infamous Directive JCS 1067 was still being enforced in Germany[58]. Its main tenant is"...take no steps looking toward the economic rehabilitation of Germany [or] designed to maintain or strengthen the German economy." The goal was to make Germany one big farm with no heavy industry.

Stalin attempted to rid the world of capitalism. Instead, the world purged

---

[58] - The Morgenthau Plan: Soviet Influence on American Postwar Policy by John Dietrich

itself of Stalin and his version of Communism.

America now has no rival. The historian Francis Fukuyama wrote a provocative book entitled "The End of History." The premise is not that history or mankind is terminal.

"The End of History instead proposes a state in which human life continues indefinitely into the future without any further major changes in society, system of governance, or economics."

Without an alternative to Capitalism could this now be our future after World War Three? Without a rival or alternative, will history indeed end with the consumer based American version of Capitalism triumphing in a winner take all world?

Of course, you know the answers. By the time this book reaches print you have lived that future. You have the advantage of hindsight.

As I write Joseph McCarthy is on track to run for President of the United States. With the death of Communism, he has focused his impassioned prejudices towards halting immigration, assaulting the civil rights of minorities and women.

He is preaching isolationism once again at a time when Eurasia needs us the most. Europe and the Slavic world are literally dying before our eyes.

Many of our ancestors came from the very cultures, towns and villages that some are proposing we allow to vanish from the face of the earth. They offer this heinous act of negligence even though we possess the means, in abundance, to save the foundation or our traditions, heritage and legacy.

Former General George Marshall has an alternative. He is quoted as saying:

"Our policy must be directed not against any country or doctrine but against hunger, poverty, desperation, and chaos. Its purpose should be the revival of a working economy in the world so as to permit the emergence of political and social conditions in which free institutions can exist."

Marshall proposes reaching down and pulling the world up to our level. His solution will be very costly to us. I would argue that the cost will be exclusively in material things.

McCarthy's attack on our values will cost us our soul.

Only time will tell which path we choose. We will be recording the choices made and will present them in the years to come.

One of The Ends

The Future

We hope you have enjoyed this trip down an alternate path. With the years to come, we have many more to present such as…

What would a world look like with one super power, who had no rival? A world that did not know the cold war and communism was eradicated after World War Three.

What if Stalin had started and won World War Three? We will explore a future where all the riches of Eurasia are controlled by a madman.

What if, at a critical juncture in history, a demagogue became President of the United States. Would the world survive an unrivaled super power led by a person such as Tail Gunner Joe McCarthy?

We intend to explore these alternatives and many others in future offerings.

World War Three 1946 Facebook page

https://www.facebook.com/WorldWarThree1946/

Coming Soon

Timeline for World War Three 1946
Book One - The Red Tide - Stalin Strikes First

May 2nd, 1895 - Sergo Peshkova is born

Aug 3rd, 1943 - Sergo attends a party where he meets Stalin and their unusual relationship begins

Aug 13th, 1943 - Sergo becomes an advisor to Joseph Stalin specializing in aerospace

Nov 24th, 1943 - Sergo is given full control of Soviet aerospace research and development.

Jan 4th, 1944 - Research on the German Wasserfal Ground to Air missile and the X4 air to air missile becomes a top priority under Sergo's leadership using stolen materials from Peenemunde

Aug 1944 - Three USAAF Superfortress B-29 bombers fall into the possession of the USSR

Dec, 18, 1945 - 17 of the 22 members of an elite atomic bomb assembly team are killed in a series of seemingly accidental events during the holidays. 15 die in a bus crash. These deaths delay the American Atomic Weapons program for 6 months

May 1st, 1946 - May Day Parade in Berlin and Moscow

May 2nd, 1946 - World War Three begins with a surprise attack by the Red Army consisting of 60 divisions and over 7,000 combat aircraft.

May 11th - NATO is formed.

May 13th, 1946 - The surprise attack is a complete success with 13 out of 22 US, British and French divisions overrun.

July 3rd, 1946 - Denmark surrenders to the forces of the USSR.

July 13th, 1946 - France surrenders to the USSR.

July 13th, 1946 - The Soviet Agent known as Delmar (George Koval) assassinates hundreds of American nuclear scientists using the world's most deadly substance, Polonium, at conferences in Oak Ridge, TN and DaOH. This cripples the US nuclear program for another 12 months and possibly forever.

July 27th, 1946 - USAAF attempt to drop an atomic bomb on Leningrad. The NKVD and its stable of spies is instrumental in warning the Soviet

Red Air Force VVS. With a combination of the new Wasserfal Ground to Air guided Missile and hundreds of fighters the raid is decimated and an atomic bomb is lost in the Baltic Sea.

July 28th, 1946 - The Red Army is stopped temporarily on the Pyrenees Line by a combination of US and Spanish divisions using the rugged terrain of this mountain range located on the border of France and Spain.

Aug 2nd, 1946 - Italy is abandoned by the NATO Allies and all forces are pulled back to Sardinia.

Aug, 15th, 1946 - The Soviet VVS demonstrates its newest aircraft by flying at great heights over the entire British Isles in an attempt to intimidate the British people. This demonstration proves that the entire British Isles can be attack from the air unlike the First Battle of Britain where the Luftwaffe was severely limited in range.

August 17th, 1946 - The Strategic Air Command is formed with Curtis LeMay named as commander.

August 20th, 1946 - The Soviet VVS continues a massive buildup of the Red Air Force on the Channel coast. It appears that a Second Battle of Britain is about to be fought.

Timeline for Book Two

Once again a few brave men would be asked to do the impossible over the skies of Great Britain. This time the enemy was not lead by a buffoon in the form of Herman Goring. The Red Air Force VVS was led by a master of strategy in the form of one Alexander Alexandrovich Novikov, the man who ruled the skies over Mother Russia, Manchuria, East Germany and now most of Europe.

Sept. 1946 - Throughout the month of September the Soviet VVS feints and simulated massive air attacks on the Isles of Great Britain.

Sept. 1st - The US Strategic Air Command or SAC, is created with Curtis LeMay named Commander.

Sept. 15th, 1946 - From two different direction massive air raids consisting of 2056 Tu2s, Lag 7s, Yak 9DDs approach the southern and northeast coast of the British Isles. The RAF is unsure of the Soviet targets. The targets are the "bone yards" and maintenance facilities of the British. The unexpected choice of targets and the effectiveness of the raids leave the RAF with very few serviceable fighter aircraft and few repair facilities.

Sept. 14th, 1946 - Scandinavia falls to a massive airborne assault.

Sept. 25th – The Second Battle of Britain begins. The VVS suffers from none of the constraints that the Luftwaffe encountered.

Using external drop tanks, the VVS planes have the range to hit every target in the British Isles.

1. They outnumber the RAF by five to one.
2. The RAF has very few replacement aircraft.
3. The Soviet spy network is in full play. There is no lack of intelligence on the exact location of targets and the effects of their previous raids on those targets.
4. The Soviets have used captured US jammers to spoof the vaunted "proximity or VT fuse". During the first critical raids the RAF airbases are virtually defenseless.

The effects are almost immediate with the RAF on the losing end of the battle.

Within weeks the VVS is roaming freely over the British Isles and ravaging the transportation systems and storage depots of the RAF. Britain is virtually defenseless from air attack.

Sept. 30th, 1946 - The Soviets publish, in Pravda, an article and picture of what appears to be an intact atomic bomb from the Leningrad raid. The crew and the Silverplate B-29 appear to be in the background. The inference is that the crew and bomb have defected to the Communist cause.

Oct. 2nd - Four atomic bombs are dropped on the oil production facilities of the USSR. The B-29s were based in Egypt with their fighter escorts flying from bases in Turkey. These four bombs are the last of the atomic bombs in existence.

Oct. 18th, 1946 – William Perl, Joel Barr and Alfred Sarant have all defected to the USSR and bring with them unimaginable intelligence on American and British weapons systems.

Oct. 22nd, 1946 – The fast response by the VVS and the addition of the Stalin's Fire SAMs start to deplete the B-29s of SAC.

The Soviets attention is diverted, and the Second Battle of Britain and the Battle for Iberia are severely curtailed. Stalin and the Stavka prepare for an invasion of Turkey, Iraq, the oil fields of Kuwait and the Levant. Their ultimate goal is to capture Egypt and Gibraltar.

Synopsis – Book 3 – The Red White & Blue – A Giant Re-Awakes

Stalin and the Stavka are forced to invade Turkey to reach Egypt. The Cairo area is rife with US airbases which are raiding the Baku Oil Field region.

On 25 November, 1946 the Red Army crosses the Turkish border in force. Within hours, both Turkish fronts collapse, as the Soviets use amphibious and paratroop units to by-pass the static defenses. Specialized units of the US and NATO armies are dispatched to advise the Turkish defenders and are caught up in the Stavka's Deep Battle tactics.

The Soviets brush aside the Turkish defenders and close in on the Levant. Baghdad, Beirut and Jerusalem fall in turn. The Soviet forces are being led by Marshal Zhukov. The Soviets are poised to force the Suez Canal defended under the leadership of Sir Montgomery and the British 8th Army.

The Giant of America has been re-awakened and a series of daring strategic attacks are planned.

The Soviet Navy wrestles control of the Stalin's Fire Missile from Sergo and develops a guided anti-ship missile. Three unlikely American heroes discover the secret of the Soviet guidance system and assist the US Navy in "spoofing" the first generation of Soviet Anti-ship missiles.

The initial, of four, well timed invasions takes place as US General Bull Dog Walker and the US First Army land in Trieste, Italy. They swiftly move inland to capture Vienna.

The date is 25 May, 1947 and it has been a long cold winter in Europe. NATO makes the first move in what they hope is the final end game between communism and capitalism.

INDEX

10th Army, 176
15th Army, 143, 146, 193, 196
15th Division, 19, 20
1st Army, 176, 193
29th Division, 70
5th Army, 176, 193
6th Fleet, 37, 38
7th Armored Division, 37
8th Army, 193
AA missile, 38
Admiral King, 38
America's Ace of Aces, 27
anti Stalinist, 180
anti-Stalinist, 187, 188
APCBC, 240
Armenians, 179
Azerbaijanis, 179
Babushka, 25, 34, 55, 128, 155, 173
Babushka Mini-subs, 25
Backdoor, 164, 168, 175, 176, 193, 195
Baghdad, 44, 70, 83, 84, 85, 91
Baku, 88, 90, 91, 118, 142, 195, 196
Baltic, 114, 122, 133, 134, 143, 146, 151, 152, 153, 154, 155, 274
Baltic Fleet, 154, 155, 161, 165, 182
Baltic Sea, 114, 122, 133, 134, 146, 151, 274
Beirut, 44, 63, 65, 69, 80, 81, 85, 91, 92, 105, 110, 120, 122, 143
Belarusians, 179
Beria, 22, 48, 49, 50, 51, 62, 66, 67, 68, 69, 85, 89, 101, 102, 103, 135, 136, 137, 138, 139, 164, 181, 198, 204, 210, 211, 212
Bielsko-Biala, 193
Big Belt, 152
Big Ben, 154
Bill Weisband, 42
Black Sea, 87, 90, 109, 118, 119, 143, 146, 167, 168, 176, 189, 195
BOPA, 132, 133
Bornholm, 171
Bougainville, 43
Brooks, 143
Budyonny, 140
Bull Dog Walker, 16, 17, See General Walker
Carl Vinson, 154
Caucasus, 83, 87, 88, 89, 90, 97, 117, 122, 138, 139, 140, 142, 143
Causeway Construction Unit, 153
CIA, 119, 120, 178, 179, 192
Columba Livia
   Pigeon, 34
Communist Party of the United States of America, 177
Construction Battalions, 26
Copenhagen, 146, 148, 149, 150, 151, 152, 153, 154, 161, 169, 176, 183
Cossacks, 98, 179
Cruiser Kirov, 183
Dale Carnegie, 230
Danish, 114, 132, 133, 134, 150, 151, 159
DC3, 189
D-day, 19, 20, 146, 148

World War Three 1946 – Book Four – The Red Sea

D-Day, 16, 24, 138

Deep Battle, 6, 220

Dr. Skinner, 35, 127

DUKW, 17, 18

Eisenhower, 36, 37, 38, 122, 169, 175

Essex, 117, 154

Eurasia, 90, 150, 189, 195

F-80, 20, 139

Fargo, 33, 39, 139

Feather, 39, 139

First US Army, 25

Freedom Fighters, 188, 189, 227, 235, 237, 243

French Foreign Legion, 17

French Resistance, 148, 194

G2, 65, 142, 145, 149, 193, 195, 196

Gdansk, 146, 148, 155, 173, 176, 188, 193

Gdansk/Gdynia, 146, 148, 173

Gdynia, 157, 176

General McArthur, 27

General Walker, 16, 23

Georgians, 179

Gerhardt, 70

Gerow, 44, 45, 69, 70, 120, 141, 143

Golubtsova, 204

Graz, 22

Great Belt, 133, 151

Great Lakes, 176

Griswold, 43, 44, 120, 122, 143, 193, 196

Guadalcanal, 195

Hailslip, 176

Hallett D. Edson, 19

Halsey, 37, 38, 154

Halslip, 194

HEAT round, 236

helicopter, 115, 117, 122, 124, 146, 149, 150

helicopters, 115, 116, 123, 124, 147, 149, 150, 151, 156, 157, 160, 167, 194

Hilfswilliger, 178

Hitler, 16, 94, 108, 132, 148, 151, 152, 178, 179, 180, 214, 215, 242

Hiwis, 178, 188, See Hillfswilliger

HUP1-H25, 150

Ike, 36, 37, 38, 44, 64, 141, 143

Indiana, 24

Iowa, 24

Iowa class, 183

IS-3, 78, 240

JCS, 178

Jeep Carrier, 174

Jugashvili, 203

Kaganovich, 204

Kastellet, 149

Kazimir Volkov, 180, 181

Kharkov, 42

Khrushchev, 69, 101, 102, 135, 136, 137, 138, 181, 198, 204, 210, 211, 212, 222, 223, 224, 226, 228, 229, 234, 236, 242, 243

Kirov, 183, 184

Klimov, 139

Konev, 49, 50, 61, 62, 63, 64, 65, 66, 69, 70, 71, 91, 94, 104, 225

Kremlin, 42

Kursk, 140, 235, 242

Kuznetsov, 33, 34, 53, 54, 55, 56, 85, 86, 87, 102, 103

Kydoimos, 19, 23, 28, 32

Lavrenti Beria, 51, 180

Leningrad, 90, 106, 165, 166, 224, 242, 243, 245, 273, 275

Lessor Caucasus, 142

Levant, 7, 49, 59, 62, 64, 66, 70, 87, 105, 106, 118, 276

Lucky Seventh, 20

M-26 Pershing, 78

M-38 Wolfhound, 220

M38A3 Wolfhound, 24

M-50, 77, 78, 79, 217, 218, 240

Malenkov, 69, 102, 204, 212

Marie Ljalková-Lastovecká, 136, 137, 180, 181

Marquis, 194

Marshal, 61, 65, 66, 67, 71

Marshall, 36, 37, 42, 44, 45, 47, 48, 49, 50, 64, 67, 68, 69, 70, 139, 140, 175, 176, 177, 178, 180

Marshall Bagramyan, 42

Massachusetts, 24

McCarthy, 177

McNarney, 28

Mediterranean, 6, 8, 44, 64, 121

Middleton, 16, 20, 24, 122, 143

Mig 9, 139

Mig-9 Fargo

Mig-9 Fargos, 33
Mig-9 Fargos, 32

Mitscher, 154

Monte Cassino, 142

Montgomery, 44, 63, 138

Moscow, 17, 51, 68, 85, 91, 101, 105, 136, 140, 146, 150, 165, 181, 193, 195, 196, 198, 210, 226, 228, 229, 235, 237, 242, 244, 250, 273

Mosin Nagant 91/30 Sniper Rifle, 180

Mount Judi, 141, 142

Mulberries, 25

Mulberry, 25

napalm, 39, 240, 244

NATO, 6, 7, 22, 25, 28, 29, 30, 32, 38, 42, 43, 44, 45, 47, 50, 62, 64, 65, 66, 69, 70, 76, 77, 83, 87, 88, 90, 91, 93, 94, 111, 114, 121, 123, 127, 128, 132, 133, 134, 139, 140, 150, 151, 153, 161, 167, 168, 169, 170, 176, 179, 180, 182, 183, 184, 187, 188, 189, 193, 194, 195, 273, 274

Nazi, 49, 119, 132, 179

New Georgia, 43

New Jersey, 24

Nikita Kruschev, 180, 181

Nimitz, 23, 24, 25, 26, 28, 122

NKVD, 42, 53, 68, 107, 161, 181, 187, 188, 273

Noah's Ark, 141

Novikov, 66, 91, 189, 275

one time pad, 42

Operation Bagration, 140

Operation Barbarossa, 88, 179

Oresund, 114, 133, 151

P-80, 27, 32, 33, 40

Patton M-50, 220

Pattons, 218, 235, 240

Peleliu, 117, 150

Peshkova, 6, 35, 56, 57, 135, 137, 273

Philippines, 27, 43

pigeon, 36, 56, 129

pigeons, 34, 35, 36, 128, 129, 168, 169, 170

Place of Descent, 141

Project Pigeon, 35

PTAB, 241

Pyramid Scheme, 189

Pyrenees Line, 36, 37, 62, 140, 176, 193, 194, 274

Pyrenees Mountains, 6, 62, 209, 257

Richard Bong, 27

Ridgeway, 193

Ridgway, 44

Rokossovsky, 140, 194

SAM, 38

Seabees, 26, 27

Sergo

Sergo's, 6, 33, 35, 36, 51, 52, 53, 54, 55, 56, 57, 77, 85, 86, 87, 135, 137, 273

Seventh Army, 44

Shakespeare, 61, 183

Sherman, 226, 240

Shooting Star, 20, 33, 40, 114, 139

Sicily, 16

SIGINT, 42

Simpson, 143

Sinai, 62

Skinner, 35, 86, 121, 126, 127, 128, 129, 168, 169, 170, 195

Sosna, 236, 242

Spruance, 42, 154, 155, 173, 183

Stalin, 6, 7, 16, 17, 22, 26, 33, 34, 35, 38, 47, 49, 50, 51, 53, 54, 55, 56, 66, 67, 68, 69, 78, 83, 85, 86, 87, 94, 101, 102, 106, 107, 108, 126, 129, 135, 136, 137, 138, 140, 148, 151, 161, 177, 178, 179, 180, 181, 187, 188, 189, 196, 273, 276

Stalin's Fire, 38

Stalin's Fire Missile, 33, 34, 35, 126

Stalingrad, 136, 140, 222, 224, 226, 242, 243

Stalinism, 53, 92, 178, 188, 194

Stavka, 7, 22, 25, 33, 37, 42, 43, 47, 50, 56, 66, 67, 87, 88, 90, 118, 139, 140, 150, 175, 176, 196, 198, 222, 223, 226, 276

Stukas, 20

Suez Canal, 7, 44, 47, 51, 61, 62, 63, 65, 66, 83

T-34, 22

T-34-85, 236

T-44, 78, 236

T-54, 40, 77, 220, 221, 236, 238, 240

Tail Gunner Joe, 177

Task Force 125, 151, 153

Task Force 38, 151, 154

Tito, 20, 22, 28, 29, 30, 31, 49

Tito's, 20, 28, 49

Transcaucasian Front, 140

Tributs, 182, 183

Trieste, 16, 23, 24, 25, 27, 28, 29, 37, 38, 47, 49, 50, 66, 70, 105, 120, 121

Triple Cross, 122, 123, 134, 154, 157, 175, 193, 195

Truman, 176, 177

Truscott, 123, 146, 148, 176, 193, 216, 217

Tu-2 Bat, 32, 33

TU-2 Bats, 32

Tulagi, 152, 171, 173

Turkish Straits, 133, 140, 164, 166, 167, 168, 193

U.S.S. Tulagi, 151

Ukrainians, 179, 187, 188

USAAF, 20, 22, 25, 27, 32, 33, 115, 273

USS Augusta, 184

USS Franklin, 23, 153

USS Franklin D. Roosevelt, 23

USS Iowa, 166, 183, 184

USS Solar, 154

USS Wisconsin, 24, 42, 134, 152, 183

V Corps, 69, 70, 120, 141

V2 rocket, 34

Venona

   Venona Papers, 42

Venona Papers, 42

Vienna, 20, 21, 22, 24, 25, 27, 29, 37, 38, 40, 47, 66, 70, 118, 121, 143, 146, 176, 193, 195

VII Corps, 24

VIII Corps, 16, 20, 21, 23, 27, 38, 121

Vistula River, 193

voice-pipe, 155

Voytolovo, 181

VT fuse, 70, 242, 275

VVS, 7, 20, 32, 40, 123, 139, 154, 182, 189, 209, 241, 273, 274, 275, 276

Wake Is Island, and, 27

Walker, 16, 20, 23, 24, 25, 26, 28, 122, 143, 146, 147, 148, 176, 193, 195, 216, 217, 221, 259

War of 1812, 176

Washington, 24

Wasserfal, 36, 273

World War Two, 20, 43, 44, 62, 70, 78, 79, 91, 94, 101, 120, 121, 132, 138, 140, 142, 152, 157, 159, 166, 174, 178, 179, 189, 194

X4, 38

Yugoslavian, 19, 20, 22, 24, 27, 30

Zhukov, 45, 47, 49, 50, 51, 61, 64, 65, 66, 67, 68, 69, 89, 90, 91, 110, 139, 140, 168, 193, 196, 197, 198, 199, 200, 205, 206, 207, 208, 212, 225, 226, 227, 235, 236, 237, 240, 241, 242, 243, 246

Printed in Dunstable, United Kingdom